MW00916237

A Gathering of Dust

A Novel Out of Africa

Samantha Ford

Dedicated to the memory of John Gordon Davis

By Createspace
All Rights Reserved.
Copyright © 2018 Samantha Ford
(ISBN: 978-1724610911)

No part of this book may be reproduced or transmitted in any form or by any means, graphic, electronic, or mechanical, including photocopying, recording, taping or by any information storage or retrieval system, without the permission in writing from the copyright holder.

The right of Samantha Ford to be identified as the author of this work has been asserted in accordance with the Copyright, Designs and Patents Act 1988 sections 77 and 78.

This is a work of fiction. The characters and their actions are entirely fictitious. Any resemblance to persons living or dead is entirely coincidental.

******

Acknowledgements

My first and most special mention is for John Gordon Davis, my inspiration, and one of the best authors ever to come out of Southern Africa. Meeting John in Spain, before he died, and participating in his last writing course there, shall remain one of the highlights of my life. I like to think of John wandering around his beloved Africa again, invisible to the eye. His ashes are scattered in the Kruger National Park.

John A Byrne, Director of Research and Development, Galana Wildlife Conservancy, Kenya, for his expertise and advice on DNA.

Derek Wilson MBE. Chevalier dans L'Ordre National du Mérite. For his support and encouragement, and being brave enough to be the first person to read the final manuscript and give me such positive feedback. Thank you Derek.

To my sister, Jacky, who tried not to roll her eyes when I asked her to read the story over and over again as I made changes, then more changes and more.

To Monty Jones who always made sure my glass was never empty as I slaved over the editing process, in all weathers, on the deck of the restaurant in Plettenberg Bay. His knowledge of the San people, their ways, and their history, was invaluable. Monty is a direct descendent of the Royal House of the Griqua people.

To Mark Baldwin for the superb front covers of all three of my books. baldwin@mweb.co.za. His extraordinary talent shines through and captures the absolute essence of each story.

To Royal Malewane, a sumptuous safari camp in South Africa where I enjoyed a "bedouin" styled bush dinner which I have used as a scene in A Gathering of Dust. www.royalmalewane.com

And, to all the lovely people who bought my books and posted wonderful reviews on Amazon.co.uk. I thank you all. To be compared with John Gordon Davis and Wilbur Smith is beyond my wildest dreams.

A beautiful mistress. Relentless, ruthless, unforgiving. A lover you can never have or own…a lover who will take everything from you. Your heart, your thoughts, your mind and your soul.

When it's all over, and you leave her, she will stay with you; tormenting you with the memories of what you can never have again, no matter how you try to forget and replace.

For the rest of your life you will want her, remember her, compare her, weep for her – but never regret her.

The glimpse of something on television – the haunting cry of a fish eagle, the sound of Africans singing, in perfect harmony, with no music other than their own clear voices. The earth- shaking thundering of the gum boot dance, the reverberating beat of Zulu drums, will bring you to your knees with longing for the love, and place, you have left.

The sound of her, the scent of her. The one thing you want more than anything in your life, to have again.

You gave her everything, wanting to possess her. She promised you nothing, gave you nothing, only her breath-taking beauty.

When you left, she had already forgotten you, for you were just one of many dazzled by her.

She broke your heart with her beauty. And with her pain. She is unforgettable.

She is called Africa

Chapter One

The *click click* of the wheel of the chair was the only sound coming through the dense veil of mist and the muffled pounding of the surf.

The old car, one door half open, stood in silence. The rain pooled on the footwell where the driver's feet had been.

The elderly African, Jakub, leaned his bicycle against the abandoned car and walked to the verge of the cliff, then looked up at the swollen clouds. He squinted and let his eyes wander back to the rocks below.

He walked around the chair, stilling the wheel with his muddy boot, then went to the car and peered inside.

Not touching anything, Jakub hunkered down next to it waiting for the sun to burn away the cold mist.

He had been fishing these waters since childhood, they were as familiar as the knotted veins on his hands. Like a beautiful woman with a treacherous heart, he knew how dangerous the waters could be, with the currents and rip tides. The fishing was good, for a man with courage. But not for one with fear of sharks.

Jakub reached inside his pocket for his pipe, tobacco and matches. He tamped down the tobacco and sucked until puffs of smoke took hold. The person who had fallen off the cliff would not be there anymore.

The South African sun rose high, burning the mist away. The fisherman put his pipe away and went back to the edge of the cliff. The jagged black rocks rose up, big and strong; now he could see below.

Jakub narrowed his eyes – nothing.

From his pocket he pulled out a pair of thin plastic gloves, rolling them over his hands. Righting the wheelchair, he pushed it towards the cliff edge and tipped it over, hearing it bounce and scrape against the rocks, the sounds fading as it made its final journey.

As nimble, and sure footed, as a goat Jakub made his way down through the bushes and around the rocks, searching for any signs of the

1

body. The path was narrow and precipitous, without handrails or holding places, the rocks slippery with seaweed.

He reached the sand below then picked his way along the treacherous shoreline. The wheelchair lay upside down, broken and buckled by the fall, one bent wheel still turning.

With effort the fisherman dragged it through the sand until he reached the edge of the roaring surf. Lifting it up he threw it into the cauldron of boiling water.

Seagulls screamed overhead as Jakub searched for the body from the wheelchair.

He found a black boot wedged between some rocks. He examined it and clicked his tongue. *Eish*, this boot must have cost much money, perhaps he would find the other one. His own boots gaped on his feet, the laces long gone. He sighed, one boot was good only for a man with one leg.

Jakub knew the tide would have taken the body out into its unforgiving depths; then would come the sharks.

Not finding the boot's mate he threw it far out into the sea where it appeared silhouetted against a sheer wall of water before disappearing into the tumbling surf.

Jakub picked his way back up the narrow paths, through the rocks and thorny bushes.

Now he would have to get rid of the car. He shrugged his shoulders. *Eish!* This car was old, it was true, worth much money. But he had been given his instructions.

Jakub reached inside his pocket pulling out the gloves, before moving to the back of the vehicle. The car teetered on the cusp of the cliff and with a final shove from the old man, plunged over the edge.

The task now complete, Jakub mounted his bicycle, wobbling through the drying mud before reaching the dirt path leading back to his village. With a final backward glance, he peddled away.

They wanted his payment money to be put into an account in East London, the nearest big town to this place called the Wild Coast. But what good would this do when he lived so far away from this bank? *Oupa* Pieter was keeping the money for him in his safe for collection when he was needing this money. Jakub cleared his throat and spat into the bush. Enough to keep an old man happy until the end of his days.

The fisherman had picked this remote spot and shown it to the farmer, *Oupa* Pieter, who had agreed it was a good place. Was he not the eyes and ears of *Oupa* Pieter? Was it not so that he, Jakub, knew the mood of the tides like no other? Last night he had waited for them in the dark, so they would find this place.

Jakub had seen the body before it was tossed over the cliff. The man was looking like a San person, with the bones on his cheeks sitting high, his light brown skin and pale eyes staring into no-where, or maybe to his God. But he was tall for a San person.

But what would a dead San person be doing here? Were they not a secret tribe of hunter-gatherers, uncanny trackers, admired by all peoples of Africa? Their strange language, full of clicks, handed down through the generations. He had much respect for these people of the desert, these secret people who heard and knew of things before others, for he was one of them.

Oupa Pieter, was a big Afrikaner and when the body of the man was gone, Jakub had seen *Oupa* shaking his fists at the heavens above, before falling to his knees, squeezing the wet mud in his fingers, howling like a stricken beast.

Then *Oupa* Pieter had lifted his wet face and called out something, almost carried away with the strong wind. *Janine! Hem-er-lee!*

The old fisherman knew of Janine. The daughter who was dead when the big planes hit the buildings in this place called New York. *Oupa* Pieter was crying for her lost spirit. But who was *Hem-er-lee*? Another spirit perhaps. Or was it another place, like this New York?

But why was the dead San person wearing the purple dress? Why was he wearing the black cloth tied many times around his neck, with the big Jesus cross?

Why had *Oupa* Pieter lifted the big rock and broken the face of a man already dead?

Eish! His wife would be angry with him when he got home, there would be no fish for the table this night.

Chapter Two

Emily followed the trail of a speeding rain drop with her finger. Outside the trees battled with the wind. The bloated sky, the colour of cigarette ash. The gutters gurgled with more rain than they could cope with. She looked at her pale reflection in the window. A ghost from another world.

Emily leaned forward and unhooked the window, dangling her hand until it was soaked, then wiped it over her face and neck. She swung her legs around and put her feet out of the window, twirling her ankles, enjoying the coolness, the wetness, on her skin. Her feet, no longer darkened by the African sun, were white and soft now, like a brace of doves, her ankle bracelet faded and dull from lack of light and air, the once blue and grey beads now indistinguishable from each other.

The evening before, she'd stopped at one of the trendy new wine bars for a glass of wine. Determined to bring a touch of Europe to London there were chairs and tables on the pavement, under an irritating flapping canopy. Wrapping her coat around her she'd sat outside, blowing into her cupped hands, she'd watched the crowded buses push their way down the street, the windows steamed up with the warmth of its passengers, and their resigned expressions, drained of colour and bereft of joy, staring straight ahead, dreaming hopeless dreams which would never come true.

Commuters hurried past towards the underground station, umbrellas at the ready. She had tugged her sleeves down over her icy hands and reached for her glass. The wind picked up as she huddled into her coat, pulling the hood up. A car went past, music booming, making her body throb with annoyance.

Her phone rang jolting her back to the present. *Rebecca.*

"You're not going to cancel tomorrow are you Em?"

"No, of course not, why do you ask?"

"Just checking. I know you, cancelling things at the last minute…if you don't pitch, my girl, I'll fire you okay?"

Emily laughed. "I'll be there, I promise."

"What are you up to?"

"I'm washing my face in the rain, Becks."

"Oy, of course you are. Why am I not surprised? We have taps over here you know, those silver things on top of the basin, turn them on and out comes water? See you tomorrow, okay?"

Emily closed the window and her eyes, remembering the rains in Africa.

The sudden stillness, the silence and the strange light, the bleached whiteness of the wings of birds against an indigo sky. In the distance, the ground would shake with booming thunder, as the lightning spat across the sky, the clouds the colour and size of a herd of elephants. The leaves quivering, then still again.

The first bloated drops bouncing off the ground like marbles, then running out into it, dancing with joy. The smell of the parched earth colliding with the wetness, the hiss and wisps of mist as it hit the scorching tarmac.

Sitting on *Oupa* Pieter's veranda in a sagging cane chair, the hammering on the tin roof, drowning out any conversation. Watching it sweep over the polished red stone floor, feeling the spray on her face and feet. The banging of the fly screen door hitting back at the wind. In seconds, pools of water became small rivers snaking across the lawns of the garden.

Then, when the storm was over, the chorus of frogs croaking in discordant harmony, the birds returning as a joyous choir, and the sound of the hollow monotonous drips on the banana leaves. The mists of the rain covering the hills like a widow's veil.

The next morning the endless skies of blue, the heat of the sun, and the puddles glittering briefly, before the ground devoured the last of the moisture.

There was no dancing in the rain here in London. No colour of any kind. Black umbrellas, black raincoats, black and brown boots. Tomorrow the skies wouldn't be the sapphire blue of Africa, she wouldn't feel the prickle of hot sun on her arms, or the warm wind caressing her skin like a lover.

Sometimes the longing to go home would make her stomach somersault, but she couldn't go back. Couldn't face the devastation of what had happened there, the memories often waking her, her eyelashes encrusted with salty residue.

Emily stood up, looking out into the darkness at the street below. Still expecting him to be down there one day, illuminated by the street light - looking up at her, waiting for her.

Unnerved, Emily drew the curtains, put the television on with the sound turned down, and tuned into Classic FM.

Chapter Three

Emily drove through London, glancing at the festive shop windows, imagining the snug rooms where families gathered, no doubt surrounded by mounds of wrapping paper, toys scattered everywhere, the children in their pyjama's squealing with delight.

She pulled up outside the familiar Notting Hill drive, parking alongside Rebecca's battered Range Rover. Stamping the rain off her boots she rang the doorbell. Rebecca swept open the door and hugged her.

"Come on in, it's freezing out there. I'm in the kitchen doing battle with the smallest turkey I could find. Come on in."

Emily inhaled. "Dinner smells delicious, very Christmassy, thanks for inviting me Becks."

Rebecca hugged her again. "Give me your coat, my girl, and grab a glass of champagne."

Emily shrugged off her coat and handed it to her friend, then followed her into the kitchen. Emily warmed her hands on the Aga, feeling the heat seep through her numb fingers.

Rebecca Hawn's auburn hair was coming loose from its clip, small tendrils sticking to her neck from the heat of the kitchen. She pushed her fringe away with the back of her hand, exposing a heart shaped face and deep-brown intelligent eyes, with thirty-eight years of life spiking around them. A small Star of David, on a chain, glinted at the base of her throat.

Over dinner they talked about the past year and their plans for the new one. Rebecca watched Emily as she picked at her food, moving it around the plate, in between taking sips of wine, then Emily placed her knife and fork together and looked up.

"Sorry, don't seem to have much of an appetite at the moment."

"You never have an appetite, unlike me!" Rebecca speared another potato and covered it with gravy before consuming it with relish.

"What was Christmas like in Africa?"

Emily smiled. "Hot as hell! Mom would spend hours in the kitchen preparing the turkey, her dress sticking to her back. Even the kitchen floor was too hot to stand on barefoot."

Rebecca laughed. "Can't imagine that kind of heat. Why didn't you have a salad, or pasta, or something light?"

"My parents were English, so our Christmas was always traditional. After lunch, we'd dive into the pool and spend the rest of the day there, regretting the vast amount of food we'd eaten, promising ourselves that next year we would have a *braai* instead!"

"Braai?"

"You call it a barbecue here, but somehow a back-yard barbecue, with an umbrella over your head, isn't quite the same as a barbecue out in the bush, where you're grateful for the cooling of the evening, and if there's a storm coming it's a prayer answered!"

Rebecca took the last two potatoes from around the crumbling carcass of the turkey.

"So, what did your parents do?"

Emily took a sip of her wine. "My mother was matron at a private school in East London, my father was a veterinarian specialising in wildlife. He was away a lot, doing game counts, capturing animals for re-location, buying wildlife at auctions for the new game lodges springing up all over the Eastern Cape."

Rebecca shuddered. "I'd love to go to Africa, but I'm terrified of snakes and spiders. Ugh! Snakes. Can't even bear to watch them on the telly.

"I met a guy once, quite fancied him. He asked me back to his place for dinner, then told me about his 'pet' – a bloody great snake he lived with. Don't think he had many dates!

"I tried to imagine sitting at the dining room table with half an eye open for something long and silent slithering its way across the floor. Christ, I feel faint even thinking about it."

Buoyed by two glasses of wine, Rebecca took the plunge. "Look, Emily, it's none of my business, but *why* don't you talk about Marcus? It might help you? I know he died, how he died, but not much more? Come on, my girl, talk to me?"

Emily lifted her long hair and rubbed the nape of her neck. "It's too difficult, the way everything happened, I still have nightmares about it."

"Yes, I'm quite sure you do from the little you've told me. But you seem to keep everything bottled up inside, I think it would help if you talked a little more about it all."

Emily took a deep breath. "Marcus had a breakfast meeting at the World Trade Centre.

"Harry Lancaster, his partner at the New York office, phoned me some days later and told me Marcus was missing."

Rebecca frowned. "Why did it take him so long to call you?"

"It was chaos in the city, mobile networks collapsed with the volume of frantic calls being made.

"Then a week later Harry called again, he said Marcus's passport had been found a few blocks from Ground Zero. His luggage was still at the hotel, his credit cards hadn't been used. He was gone."

"What was it like to go through the aftermath?"

Emily rubbed her eyes. "There was an unreality. A feeling you can't accept what happened because you have no tangible truth. It was devastating. Depressing. Surreal in many ways.

"I had to fill out a form for identification. Build, race, eye and hair colour, age, weight, metal implants, facial hair, dominant hand, nail characteristics."

Rebecca raised her eyebrows. "Nail characteristics? You're kidding yeah?"

"No. They needed to know if nails were misshapen, bitten, decorated, tobacco stained.

"Sometimes they found a small bit of a body. Sometimes nothing at all. The authorities put together a list of who worked where, and for which company in the towers, but didn't have a clue who might have been having a breakfast meeting up there in the restaurant."

Rebecca picked up her fork and speared her, now cold, potato and chewed it thinking about how it must have been. "I've heard some interesting stories… speculation about cheating lovers whose affair saved their lives, you know, cancelling a meeting so they could have a few more hours in bed with their lover.

"Sorry Emily, that was insensitive. So, then what happened?"

"I kept in touch with the American Embassy for weeks hoping for some kind of news. I scoured the internet following the aftermath, checking the list of names of those who had been identified, looking for anything to give me some kind of closure."

"The Embassy were very supportive, they sent a grief counsellor to see me once a month, a woman called Megan. It didn't help much."

"Look can we change the subject?"

"Sorry, my girl, of course we can." Rebecca twirled the liquid in her glass, lost for words of comfort.

Emily nudged the silver salt pot with the tip of her finger, saying nothing.

"You can't change your past whichever way you jump." Rebecca said. "Go on a few dates, at least try and make some friends. I mean you don't seem to have any if you don't mind me saying?"

"I had loads of friends at University," Emily said defensively, "but you know how it is, friends go off travelling, get married, have babies. When I got married the few friends I had left, fell by the wayside."

She cupped her chin in her hand. "I've lost touch with my closest friend in South Africa, Janine. We were at school together in East London. My father, and Janine's, used to hunt together on their ranch, at the Wild Coast.

"Janine's mother died when she was eight years old, cancer I think. Her father, I called him *Oupa* Pieter, liked having me around during school holidays to keep her company. He adored her. He was like a second father to me, solid, always in the same place, I'm very fond of him. But, like I said, we lost touch, it happens when you leave the country, when you start to live another life somewhere else, we sort of drifted apart. I'm not even sure where Janine lives now."

"Well it seems to me you're living in the past and that never got anyone anywhere. Try having a date now and again."

"I have tried dating a couple of times," Emily said, her voice taut, "and it was a disaster. No-one wants to hear horror stories, and in my life there seems to have been a few of them. It doesn't make for amusing dinner table conversation I can assure you."

She rubbed the back of her neck again. "I wish I could stop looking for his face in a crowd. I'm always looking over my shoulder, or out of the window, waiting and watching."

Rebecca frowned. "Why?"

"I don't know, it's silly. But something has always bothered me about Marcus's final phone call…"

Rebecca saw how agitated she was getting and stretched across the table, taking her hand.

"He's gone Em, has been for two years, you have to accept it. You said they found some DNA and matched it to him, yeah? You had official notification from the US government. Nothing more final than that. Marcus left the flat to you, you wouldn't have inherited it without the official death certificate."

A vehicle, with its sirens screeching, roared past the flat and they both winced.

Rebecca refilled their glasses. "Okay, let's talk about something else. Have you any plans for next year? You haven't taken any time off since you began working for me at Becoming Books. The first few months of a new year are always dead quiet. Why don't you think about going somewhere? I'll look after Oliver for you, you won't need to put him in a cattery."

"I don't need a holiday Becks, I'm happy spending time in the shop. Anyway, you know I hate flying. I can't do it…"

"If you won't fly, how did you get to the memorial service in New York?"

Emily grinned. "I took a ship, there and back."

Rebecca tried again. "Well why not think about going on a cruise? You could stop off somewhere for a week or so, then join the ship on its return journey. No flying involved. "Here, give me your not so empty plate. You've haven't eaten anything and look how long and hard I slaved over this wretched tasteless turkey! I'll give you some to take home for Oliver."

Emily handed her plate across the table as Rebecca continued. "If you want to be happy again you have to get out there and work on how to achieve it. Life's not like the movies, or the books you've always got your nose buried in."

"Travelling as a single person on a cruise ship won't be any fun, not for any length of time, although I appreciate your suggestion," Emily said hastily. "I'm not sure I could handle all those jolly couples, having a good time. I'd feel an idiot sitting at a table on my own." She picked at some crumbs on the tablecloth, brushing them into a pile.

"Book a private suite that way you could dine in your cabin if you wanted to. Come on, my girl, stop being so negative or I'll get cross with you."

She thought she saw a glimmer of interest in Emily's eyes. Was there a slight indication she was at least thinking the idea through? She patted her friend's arm with encouragement.

"Anyway, don't dismiss the idea of a cruise altogether. Go to a travel agency, you don't have to commit to anything, see what's available and take it from there."

She blew out the candles. "The person who can change things is the one who looks back at you in the mirror. You won't be young and good looking forever, or twenty-six again!"

She stood up. "Come on let's move into the sitting room, I've lit the fire. No, don't worry about clearing the table, I'll do it later."

Rebecca put her arm around her. "I insist you stay here with me tonight, okay? No point in going back home and sitting by yourself with the telly and Oliver for company. I've prepared the guest room, so no arguments."

Over coffee they chatted about authors, old and new, the publishing world, the new best sellers and the book shop.

"I need to have more book signings next year Em; we need a lot more business than we had this year. We must work out how to get more foot fall into the shop. Have a think…" she was interrupted by the ringing of her phone. "That'll be Ben, help yourself to more coffee." She left the room closing the door behind her.

*****

Emily smiled at her friend's thoughtfulness and stared into the fire. She'd met Ben on many occasions and could see why Rebecca was attracted to him. He wasn't much to look at, short and a little overweight, but he made up for this with his huge personality and brilliant sense of humour. He owned an apartment in Paris, which he used as a base for his booming art business, and a not so modest yacht which he berthed in Cannes. She envied their close relationship.

Rebecca returned to the sitting room rubbing her hands together.

"It's snowing in New York City. Ben wants me to fly over for New Year's Eve, and stay on for a while, maybe a couple of weeks. You can run the shop, it'll be dead quiet anyway."

She threw another log on the fire. "I said I would. I know you think it's an odd relationship but it works. I get all the glamour of his jet setting life but don't have to wash his socks or cook his dinner every night!"

12

Emily laughed. "Have you two talked about something more permanent? You've been going out with him for years."

"It's fine the way it is now, and anyway I'd have to give up the shop if I married him, and goodness knows he's asked me enough times. Much as I love Paris I wouldn't want to live there. No, I kind of like joining him wherever he is, especially when he's in the Med on the yacht.

"Anyway, I don't practice my religion anymore. If I married Ben I'd get sucked back into the Jewish thing. Oy, all that tradition, not to mention his mother. Nah, I'm too much of a rebel to do all the Friday night Shabbat stuff, and besides, I'm partial to a bacon sandwich, and I love prawns. It wouldn't go down well I can tell you!"

"So why wear the Jewish necklace if you are a lapsed one, or whatever they call it?"

"Habit, I guess. My parents gave it to me on my twenty-first birthday, and even though they live in Israel, I feel I should wear it, it's what they believe in, so why not. It makes them happy."

Rebecca filled her cup with fresh coffee. "So, what have you decided? Are you going to think about a cruise? I mentioned it to Ben and he thinks it's a great idea."

Emily held her hands up in mock surrender. "I'll think about it."

Chapter Four

As the Christmas decorations were packed away from homes and shops, Emily felt the dragging weight of the season lift from her spirit, now she could return to the reassuring routine of going to work in the morning and returning home in the evening.

She thought about the suggestion of a cruise, the idea did have some appeal, despite her reservations. On her second day back at work, she closed Becoming Books early, then made her way to the travel agency she passed each morning.

The four consultants were busy with customers. Feeling awkward, and not knowing where on earth she wanted to go, she wandered over to the racks of seductive looking brochures.

There were cruises to everywhere. She opened a brochure for Europe. No, that she couldn't face. Getting on and off the ship and then having guided tours around the great cities, like being on a school outing – no it didn't have any appeal whatsoever.

She was about to give up and leave the whole thing for another time when her eyes were caught by another brochure. A giraffe silhouetted against a blood red sunset alongside a tall black tree. She picked it up feeling a ripple of excitement snake down her spine.

Cruise to Kenya, then go on safari. She looked at the white cruise ship anchored some way off an exotic shoreline. Tall palm trees dotted the impossibly white sand, the sea dark blue with curling white foam washing onto the shore. The photographs were so striking she could almost smell the salt in the air and hear the hissing of the sea sucking at the sand.

South Africa held bruising memories it was true, but Kenya might be quite different, with no connections to her past.

One of the consultants finished with her client and looked up from her desk with a bright smile.

She was a woman in her sixties, her white hair held back in a ponytail. "Hi, I'm Caryl. May I help you with anything?"

Pulling out the chair, and shrugging off her coat, Emily sat, the brochure still in her hand. "I don't like flying at all," she said, her voice firm. "So, I was thinking of a cruise." She glanced down and cleared her throat. "This brochure looks interesting?" She said, holding it up.

"Yes, Kenya's a popular destination. It's a three-week cruise to Mombasa, a flight to Nairobi, then a short hop on a small plane to a safari lodge in the Masai Mara Reserve. You can have a couple of days in Nairobi, loads to see there, before the safari. What dates are we looking at here? Is there a budget?"

"I'm flexible with dates, sooner rather than later though, and there's no budget. Well, I haven't worked anything out yet, I just wanted to know what was available."

Rebecca would give her hell if she didn't at least try and plan something.

"I know South Africa well, but I've never been to Kenya."

Caryl smiled at her. "Kenya is quite different to South Africa. Wilder somehow. I stayed in Cape Town for a few weeks and it was more Europe than Africa, it was beautiful, no denying it, but Kenya has a more rough and tumble feel, more African. Will you be travelling alone?"

"Yes. I'm not into anything too social, so going on a safari might not be a good choice." She glanced down at the brochure. "I mean this sort of safari will be all couples, right?"

Caryl smiled. "Yes, there will be couples, but often there are singles. The game rangers mingle with the guests in the evening, so you won't be sitting on your own for dinner. In a lot of the lodges guests eat at the same table. I know it sounds daunting," she said smoothly, "but I can guarantee with all the excitement of the animals, you'd soon be at ease with the other guests."

She pushed another brochure across the desk. "Why not think about it? I've been on safari on my own; it was one of the best holidays I've ever had. No two days are the same and you meet people from all over the world!

"Take the brochures, have a read through, then give me a call if you need any more information." She turned to check something on her computer. "Don't leave it too long though, the next cruise via Kenya is on *The African Star*. It departs from Southampton in four weeks' time, there's not much availability left."

She tapped her keyboard again. "You can return on *The African Prince,* it's *The African Star's* sister ship returning from a cruise to Singapore, calling in at Mombasa, and as you're flexible with dates this would work."

Emily looked down at the glossy brochures then at Caryl, trying to work out how she was going to wriggle out of the whole situation.

"Maybe a few days in Lamu," Caryl murmured, almost to herself. "It's a small island off the Kenyan coast, it would be a shame not to see it when you're in that neck of the woods."

She leaned back and plucked another brochure from the rack behind her and handed it to Emily. "Take your time and if you decide it's for you we can plan the itinerary."

Emily flipped through the brochures in her hand, then pinched the bridge of her nose, feeling a headache clustering. "No, this isn't going to work for me at all. I hate flying and there are two flights here. One from Mombasa to Nairobi and then the 'short hop' you talked about. If I decided to go to Lamu it would be another flight? No, I can't do this." Relieved to have found a reason not to make a decision, she picked up her bag.

Caryl turned to her keyboard again. "Hang on, there is another way of getting to Nairobi, you could take the train from Mombasa. It's not the Orient Express, but I've been on it and it's fun. A bit basic, but you get to see the countryside, which is something you won't do if you fly. The short hop to Honey Badger lodge is about thirty-five minutes."

She glanced at Emily. "The small aircraft the lodges use for transfers don't fly high, so you get a sort of aerial game drive. I'm not a keen flyer myself, even worse since 9/11. I know that sounds a bit crazy, being in this business. She shook her head and laughed. "There's no other way of getting to the lodges…"

*****

Caryl watched Emily leave the agency and turned back to her computer. Honey Badger lodge was perfect for her potential client. She knew the owner, Nick Kennedy, having met him on her last trip to Kenya. She grinned to herself, he would be more than taken with this particular guest, and the charismatic Nick Kennedy wouldn't go unnoticed either.

16

The lodge was one of the most talked about in the country and featured in the brochure Emily had picked up. Yes, if the young woman made up her mind to go she would book her in there.

Satisfied, she turned to the elderly couple sitting opposite her and was soon busy with their request for a round the world cruise in two years' time, marvelling at their optimism they would still be around to enjoy it.

Chapter Five

Emily was tempted. She looked up the web site of Honey Badger Lodge featured in the brochure. It was exquisite with spacious cream tents and en-suite bathrooms, and the dining area with its tall thatched roof surrounded by trees. For the first time in over a year she felt the desire to make a decision and do something, instead of hovering about like a ghost in her own shadow.

She could imagine herself there with the heat and the dust and the animals, feeling the warmth of the campfire, the sparks spitting up towards the canopy of stars above, remembering when her father had taken them into the bush, the simple camps they'd stayed in.

She closed her eyes, letting the memories tumble back. Sitting around a camp fire with Janine, during the school holidays, on *Oupa* Pieter's ranch, watching the chops and sausages spit, sizzle, and hiss as they cooked over the hot embers of the braai, the potatoes nestled in the hot coals. The stillness of the black night and the brilliance of the stars above.

The taste and smell of the succulent lamb chops, tearing at the pink flesh with her fingers and sucking the crispy fat and bones, the hard skin of the baked potato opening to reveal the soft flesh inside, as fluffy as down. So many happy memories – except for one which had almost obliterated all the rest.

Outside there was a screech of brakes and the angry blare of a horn. Emily opened her eyes and sighed, God, London was noisy.

"What do you think Oliver? If I go away for a couple of weeks will you be alright with Becks?"

Oliver paused from vigorously washing his whiskers, gave her a brief look, then carried on with his ablutions.

"I'll take that as a yes then, shall I?"

She turned back to the brochure, the shots were more than seductive. And, oh God, she *did* want to go back to Africa, despite everything.

She opened the drawer and felt for her passport. It was valid for another seven years. So, no excuse there. The last trip she had made was to New York for Marcus's memorial service in December 2001.

Chapter Six

Emily

I'd always been a bit of a loner, preferring my own company rather than spending time with people with whom I had nothing in common with. I found English people polite and kind, but they had no idea of what it was like to be brought up in Southern Africa, and to be honest, not many of them were interested. I felt some of them disapproved of the fact we employed Africans to work in the house and garden. But it's how it was there, and it wasn't as if we didn't pay them to work for us. It was a job just like any other.

At university we were all caught up with the first taste of independence and freedom, the parties, the love affairs, making friends and, yes, studying. I missed my country and my parents. Africa seemed so far away and it was too expensive to fly back there for holidays. As an overseas student the fees were about as much as they could afford.

Whilst my friends went home to their families, I found myself spending a lot of time on my own. Sometimes I would be invited to spend a few days in the country with one or two friends, but that was about it.

The accident happened a year into my studies, I was nineteen. I will never be able to forget it, or the huge gap it left in my life.

When I left university, I found a tiny one-bedroomed flat in Kensington, it was the first time I'd lived on my own. Then one morning, as I was putting the rubbish out, I heard a juddering meow from behind the bin. A tiny black and white kitten, with the most beautiful blue eyes, was crouching there, cold and wet, looking as alone and bereft as I felt.

I adopted the kitten and called him Oliver. Long into the night he would sit on my lap as I applied for job after job. Then curl up on the bed and keep me company until I fell asleep. I think he lost his voice crying behind the dustbin for hours, now he was only capable of juddering his jaws and giving an intermittent squeak now and again.

I didn't realise how difficult it was to find employment, how competitive the market was. Employers were looking for people with experience, my hard-earned first-class degree in English literature didn't elicit any interest at all.

I offered my services, as a freelance editor, to dozens of publishing houses and agents. I had always been a prolific reader, adept at picking out grammatical errors, quick to spot when a story was heading in the wrong direction, or didn't make sense, how it could be improved.

I was prepared to edit manuscripts for no fee, so I could build up confidence in anyone who might be interested in taking me on. My investment in myself paid off and I started to earn money for my editing, and before long had built up a reputation. The manuscripts started coming in on a regular basis.

I worked hard, starting at nine in the morning and sometimes working long into the night to reach deadlines. It was exhausting but kept my mind off other things. My social life during the week dwindled to nothing. I had dates with men - even managed one or two affairs but editing took up most of my time and any romantic potential with a partner floundered – until I met Marcus.

He was a nice-looking guy, Italian by birth, but he'd been brought up in America, he still had a business there in the bewildering, and complex, world of finance.

He was undemanding, fitting in with my schedule, not minding when I had to cancel dates due to meeting deadlines. Having spent so much time alone I found myself attracted to him, he was easy to be with, always cheerful, with the most infectious laugh. Perhaps because both of us were far from our respective countries, there was a bond between us. Six months after we met he asked me to marry him, I said yes, as long as Oliver was included in the partnership.

Oliver didn't like Marcus from the word go.

Marcus's New York partner in the business, Harry, came across for the wedding, a quiet affair. Harry appointed himself as the official photographer. I have yet to see any of the photographs. In fact, I only have one photograph of Marcus, taken on our honeymoon in Paris in 1998. He hated anyone taking photographs of him or taken of us together.

He didn't have any close friends in London, he was happy to be with me, I was enough. We made a few friends, but as he travelled often to the States, or Europe, on business trips, and I was always meeting some kind of deadline with the editing, there wasn't much time for a social life. But everyone who met Marcus loved him, he was entertaining, good company with his jokes and stories, the infectious laugh he had, and his intoxicating charm. He was assertive without being bossy, confident without being smug. But I saw the tough, demanding man who was used to getting what he wanted.

*****

The changes came over a short period of time. He became reclusive, secretive almost. Whereas before we talked for hours about politics, travel, my work, his work, and all the other things young couples talk about when they are on the cusp of a new relationship.

He would disappear someplace, deep inside of him, where nothing I said, or did, seemed to reach him. Sometimes I don't think he was aware we were in the same room. His eyes would become dark and intense, fathomless. His larger than life personality, his infectious laugh and endless jokes ceased. I missed this side of him.

Marcus had a hidden side to him, places where he would not let me in. I put it down to the difference in our cultures, but as the months passed I didn't feel comfortable with him.

The truth hurts. I began to understand, you can be in love and still feel alone. You think you have everything you ever wanted, but then realise you wanted all the wrong things. You can have a husband as smart, sexy, and compassionate as Marcus, but not have him at all.

Two years into the marriage I had lost him. Our lovemaking became sporadic, sometimes I don't think he knew it was me lying in his arms, and he never called out my name. Ever.

Now he was away, more than he was home. I thought he had fallen out of love with me, perhaps he never had been. He wasn't cruel to me, never hit me, he just sort of faded away into himself. Leaving me floundering in the debris of his departing wake.

He spent more and more time at the office, or locked away in his study at the flat, working on his laptop until the early hours of the morning.

Even Oliver sensed the changes coming between us, hissing at Marcus and stalking off if he came into the room.

I began to suspect there was someone else, maybe in New York City, where he was spending more and more time.

My marriage was stumbling towards its predictable end. The man I had fallen in love with had disappeared.

One night, after dinner, he came and sat next to me on the sofa, rubbing the base of my neck with his thumb, as though he needed the warmth and touch of another. Relieved, I snuggled into him and reached for him. He pulled away and stood up with an abruptness which surprised me, as though he had been bitten by a snake, then he locked himself in his study.

I was living with a man I did not know – living with a stranger. I was twenty-four years old.

Our last dinner together, here in the London flat, was over a year ago, the night before Marcus flew to New York for yet another business trip.

It didn't take a genius to work out something was going on. Text messages pinging in night and day, hushed phone calls taken in another room. I had a mental list of the lies he had told me going back months now.

We used a dry-cleaning service not far down the road and, sometimes, as I heaved his clothes into a bin liner, I would catch the hint of a different odour. Sort of dusty and almost sweet, spicy.

I know the smell of heat and dust. It's a different fragrance which seeps into your clothes after spending time outdoors. A fragrance different from any city, warmer somehow.

Sometimes Marcus looked different after a business trip, not as sleek and groomed. But it was more than this – it was as though he had spent a week or so in the bush, or a hot country somewhere, which seemed pretty impossible, but those were my impressions.

I didn't believe every time he left on a business trip he went to New York or Europe.

On that defining day I had been in the kitchen, unpacking the shopping and haphazardly putting it in the cupboards and fridge, the television flickering on mute. Turning on the kettle I leaned against the sink waiting for it to boil, Oliver weaving his way through and around my legs.

Out of the corner of my eye a ball of fire raged on the screen. Scrabbling for the remote I jabbed at the volume, trying to make sense of what was going on, and where. Again, and again the images of a plane slicing through one of the towers played on an apocalyptic loop.

I dropped the remote and fumbled for my phone, stabbing at his number, holding my breath as I watched the terrifying images unfolding before my eyes.

Losing count of how many times I'd tried his number, I made one more attempt.

"Emily! Why have you left me so many messages?"

"Marcus! Where are you! Are you alright?"

"Am I alright? Of course I am! We've just wrapped up the meeting. Love the view from up here – fantastic."

I turned off the phone and leaned back. Stunned.

One lie too many.

*****

Harry called me some days after the collapse of the towers.

"I'm sorry Emily, the news isn't good. Marcus is missing, he had a breakfast meeting at the Twin Towers. It's chaos down there, hundreds and hundreds of people missing and dead. I'll let you know as soon as I have anything. I would have called earlier but all the phone networks were down, overloaded I guess. This terror attack has sent a collective shiver up the spine of the world. I'll be in touch."

There was something about Harry Lancaster I didn't trust.

Chapter Seven

Emily had been surprised at how few people the memorial service, in the sumptuous St Patrick's Cathedral, was attended by. There was Marcus's sister, Adele, Harry, and a handful of other people she'd never met. She'd almost forgotten he had a sister.

Harry introduced her to Adele who had not come to their wedding in London. Heavily dressed in black, Marcus's sister had inclined her head, acknowledging her, before falling silent as the service began, then left with indecent haste as soon as it ended.

Bewildered at Adele's coldness towards her, but excusing her in her obvious grief, she was relieved when Harry suggested they have dinner together.

He was as boisterous as most Americans she'd met, but tonight he was quiet, subdued, and uncomfortable. Looking older than the forty-two years she knew he was, deep worry lines etched his forehead, his pale blue eyes giving nothing away.

Finishing her pasta, she pushed her plate away and leaned back in her chair. "Harry, you knew Marcus better than anyone, you were close. There are questions I need answers to?"

He gave her a wary look. "What kind of work did Marcus do in New York?"

"You *know* what he did Emily. He brokered deals for merging companies. He was good at it, damn good at it. He'll be missed."

"Was that all he did?"

Harry looked around the subdued restaurant, the ghosts of the recently dead filling the empty chairs and tables. Avoiding her eyes, his lips were now a flat line of annoyance. "Yup. It's all he did." His fingers beat a steady rhythm on the snowy white tablecloth, leaving shallow indentations. His face expressionless as though cast in cement.

"I don't believe you Harry, I think he had other interests here. A woman?"

He tapped his fork on his glass, then looked at her, his eyes revealing how annoyed he was. "If he did, I didn't meet her."

"Because you didn't meet her doesn't mean she didn't exist. You see I have a problem with this whole thing. He was up to something. I think you know more than you're telling me. I can't get my head around the fact he's dead. It bothers me a lot."

She narrowed her eyes. "If he'd been such a brilliant negotiator, a deal maker, how come there were so few people at the service this morning – he must have known loads of people in the City?"

Harry ran his hand through his short blond hair, taking a guarded sip of water from his glass. "Look Emily, if you think Marcus was involved with someone else then I can't tell you who she was, I know nothing about it. He's dead, that's the end of it.

"Hundreds of volunteers were drafted in to sift through the rubble, anything identifiable was bagged. They found his smoke damaged passport for God's sake, and the burnt remains of his wallet, with his driver's licence and credit cards, not far from Ground Zero. He never returned to his hotel. His sister has accepted his death. How much more proof do you need, before *you* will?"

"A lot more than you're giving me Harry. Finding his passport doesn't prove a thing," she'd said, her voice tight. "I tried to call him when I saw the towers fall…?"

Harry's fingers stilled.

"Emily, you were overwhelmed with what you saw on television, as millions of people around the world were."

Harry articulated every syllable. "He could have been trying to make it down the stairwell, he could have been anywhere in the building. I doubt anyone fleeing for their lives would stop to answer a phone call. End of story. Why are you making such a big deal out of this for Christ's sake?"

He glanced at his watch. "I'll get the check and see you back to your hotel. I've got a meeting first thing tomorrow."

The taxi pulled up outside the hotel entrance, Harry came around to her door and opened it.

"Goodbye Harry, thanks for dinner. It's doubtful we'll meet again. I won't be coming back here."

He kissed her on the cheek and turned to go.

"By the way, Harry, what do *you* do here in New York?"

26

He turned back to her, his hands deep in the pockets of his jacket, his eyes hardening. "I broker deals Emily, like Marcus did, you know this. We were partners. Have a good trip back."

"Harry, wait. I didn't quite finish telling you about Marcus's phone call. You see in the end he did pick up my last call. He was telling me about the fabulous view from the restaurant – it wouldn't have been possible, I checked the time. He wasn't where he said he was and it makes me somewhat suspicious of what you're telling me."

"As I said, Emily, you were overwhelmed, we all were, you made a mistake, miscalculated the time difference. Phone call or no phone call, he could have been anywhere in the chaos. End of story. Marcus is dead."

*****

The next day she'd sailed home, no closer to the truth than she'd been before she left. For someone who had lost his best friend, his partner, Harry wasn't what she would call grief-stricken.

On her return to London, the first thing she would do was change the locks on her front and back door, install some heavy bolts, then for good measure she would also install sliding bar doors.

*****

Harry told the taxi driver to pull over and let him out. He pulled his phone from his pocket and punched in the London number. The distorted call was answered straight away

"Hey Guv, what's up? How did the memorial service go? How was the grieving widow?

Harry frowned into the phone. "There's a problem with the grieving widow – she's not grieving enough. She's going to be trouble. You have her address and you know what she looks like. I want you to get into her apartment. If she finds anything, which I doubt, she'll blow the whole fucking operation. She'll be back in a weeks' time, got this thing about flying.

"Follow her and get to know her day by day routine. As soon as you get the opportunity, get inside and sort the problem, if there are any photographs of her husband? Get rid of them. Get rid of anything associated with Marcus - got it?"

"Sure Guv, consider it done. Now would be a good time with her being on the high seas?"

"Not a good idea. She might have someone staying there looking after her bloody cat. No, follow her and wait for the opportunity. Don't fuck it up alright?"

Harry stabbed in another number. "Megan? When Emily gets back to London you have a new assignment – grief councillor. Call her and tell her it's a service the Embassy are offering to victim's families. Meet her once a month, keep tabs on what she's thinking."

Harry snapped his phone shut and hurried back to his office. Marcus's so-called sister would be waiting to hear the outcome of the evening, and how they should proceed from here.

Damn Emily Hunter, he'd always known one day she would be a liability.

Chapter Eight

Now Emily watched the blackness of a bitter cold night outside, then turned back to the tantalising brochure, thinking about the year stretching in front of her; loneliness lapped around her settling like a cobweb in a forgotten room. She closed her eyes and took a deep breath.

She bit her bottom lip, tearing off tiny slivers of skin. Why go back to a continent which held bad memories? Why not try Australia or New Zealand, or the Far East somewhere? No. It would take weeks to get there by ship, she couldn't be away for months on end. Emily picked up the brochures and put them in the drawer of her desk. Looking up she saw a fine rain was now falling like mist.

Underneath the street lamp a lone fox sat, its sumptuous red brush curled around the russet pelt of its body, its fur beginning to clump together with dampness.

Unexpected tears filled her eyes. Surely it should be out in the countryside, making its stealthy way through the bushes and fields? How was it such an animal had to resort to scavenging through dustbins in a city?

*****

That afternoon Emily called Rebecca in New York. "Becks? I've been thinking about the cruise idea. I went to the travel agency and looked at all the options - I'm going back to Africa."

"Hey, great news! Any idea of when you'll be leaving?"

"There's a ship leaving in four weeks' time called *The African Star*. It stops in Mombasa, I can get off there and go on safari, go back to the bush. It feels the right thing to do now. You were right, I need a break. I need to go somewhere different, get out of London for a while.

"I was thinking of going shopping over the week-end to get some safari clothes. I'd love you to come with me. You are still coming back on Friday, aren't you?"

"Of course! We'll close Becoming Books, stick a notice on the door saying we're stock taking or something; we'll have lunch then hit the shops, yeah? Nothing like a bit of shopping to get over jet lag!"

"I talked to Oliver and he said he'd enjoy spending time with you – he doesn't fancy a cattery."

Emily picked up the single photograph she had of Marcus, opening the desk drawer she slid the frame inside, face down.

The decision Emily had made would be life-changing. The outcome of which she could never have envisaged or imagined.

Chapter Nine

Ignoring the designer shops, they headed straight for one place specialising in safari clothes. Rebecca pointed out the khaki shorts, trousers and skirts, displayed in the window; she was already caught up in the excitement of Emily's impending holiday.

Emily reached for a jacket, running her hand over the butter-yellow suede with its epaulettes and large pockets. She held it up against herself.

Rebecca gave a soft whistle. "Wow! That's stunning! With your hair and green eyes, I swear it was made for you! It's perfect for evenings when you'll be sitting out in the bush under the stars, enjoying a sun downer - surrounded by gorgeous-looking rangers," she added, pretending to study a leopard print scarf.

Emily rolled her eyes at her friend, then saw the price tag and winced. But knew she was going to buy it.

*****

They left the shop, Emily's safari wardrobe complete. On impulse, she'd bought a soft light-brown leather safari bag to carry her new clothes in. The shop assistant had nodded her head with approval. So much easier to travel with a soft bag rather than an unwieldy suitcase, she suggested, rather wistfully Emily thought.

"Okay that's the safari side sorted out, now what about the cruise? You'll need some glamorous gear, my girl."

Emily dodged around an elderly lady laboriously making her way down the street. "I can't see myself mixing much on the ship. It's a means to an end for me, a way of getting to Africa. I thought just casual things, of which I have plenty."

"You should take one long black dress, just in case, always handy for an unexpected occasion. Let's go to Harvey Nicks and see what they've got?"

Their shopping accomplished, now including a long black dress, Emily had to admit to herself she was looking forward to this trip. Linking arms with Rebecca she suggested a glass of wine in Sloane Square before heading home.

Squeezing into a crowded wine bar, they found a table. Rebecca went to the bar to order their wine, Emily tucked the shopping bags under and around the table and watched Rebecca waiting impatiently to give her order.

Holding the glasses high Rebecca returned to the table. "God, I wish I was coming with you, sometimes these crowded, noisy bars drive me nuts."

Emily raised her glass, the liquid trembled as an underground train growled deep in the belly of the City. "Here's to great adventures and good friends. I'm getting excited…"

Rebecca grinned, her fringe catching on her eyelashes when she blinked, something Emily had always found a little irritating "How does your itinerary look?"

"Three weeks on the boat then overnight on a train from Mombasa to Nairobi. Then a private transfer, it's the bit I'm not looking forward to," she grimaced, "in a small plane out to a lodge called Honey Badger."

Emily wriggled out of her coat. "Thinking about the flight is already freaking me out."

Emily selected a plump olive from a bowl on the table, then proceeded to pursue it with a toothpick before giving up and popping it in her mouth with her fingers.

She grinned at Rebecca. "Food always tastes better eaten with your fingers!

"So, after I've finished my stint in the bush I'm going to be super brave about this flying business and do one small hop to an island called Lamu. It's still in Kenya and sounds wonderful, very biblical."

A police car, its siren howling like a wounded wild beast, sped past them, she waited, covering her ears with her hands.

Emily extracted the olive stone from her mouth and placed it on a saucer. "There are no cars on the island, everyone gets around on donkeys – imagine. The last time I had a donkey ride was when I was about four on a beach in Durban! Then it's back to Mombasa and the cruise home." Emily reached for her wine.

Rebecca lifted her own glass in salute. "It's good to see you looking, and sounding, so positive. Going back to Africa will be good for you. Maybe you could get rid of the rest of the other ghosts in your life, hmm? Stop looking around for dead people?"

Chapter Ten

Marcus

I have a few different names depending on where I'm going, and what Harry wants me to do. It's part of the job. Marcus is my Christian name, but my surname can be anything, and often is.

I move in the dark, dirty, and dangerous underbelly of a changing world, brought about by fanatics and a treacherous religious ambition to change the world. Their ultimate goal is to turn us infidels into good practicing Muslims who would live by their law, Sharia law. They are determined to rule the world with fear, crushing its inhabitants once and for all, with their greedy and relentless pursuit of power and self-indulgence. The world was becoming a highly dangerous place to inhabit.

When I was approached, by Harry, to join the organisation I was flattered, then, when I learned what I would be doing, I hesitated. This particular line of work didn't have what one would call a long shelf life, and I was only thirty-six. But it was considered a great honour to work with Harry. I signed up.

We assist with other law enforcement agencies here in the States, and overseas, when required, but more than often we work alone, unencumbered by rules, regulations and red tape.

Each agent had reached the pinnacle of their specialty, including Megan, who wasn't out in the field, she had another unique talent. The invisible friend.

The agents are hard, yet passionate, who talked to each other without fear or reserve, without bothering with any political correctness. There was no time for niceties in the world we inhabited. We are a tight, highly efficient team, all experts in our respective fields, spread out all over the world.

We agents are some of the most dangerous people on a frightened planet. The only ones more dangerous? The ones we hunted down. I was one of the best in my field, an ex-military man, being able to speak five languages, including Arabic, in which I was fluent, was an asset to the team.

I moved with ease between countries changing passports when necessary, shuffling them like a pack of cards, gathering information about terrorist groups and feeding it back to Harry and his team in New York. I became one of their top agents, a position I was more than proud of.

Things were hotting up all over the world, in particular in East Africa. ISIS were recruiting all over Africa. We had an agent in Cape Town, in South Africa, who was now requesting some back up, he felt another pair of ears and eyes was necessary, he was hearing things he wasn't happy about. He had someone in mind he thought would be ideal.

This was the first time I'd heard the name *Oupa* Pieter. I thought Oupa was his Christian name, but it was a respectful name given to a grandfather, or older man.

He lived near East London in a place called the Wild Coast. The agent suggested we should enlist someone out in the bush in the Eastern part of the country. The rural people, he insisted, sometimes heard things long before people in the cities did. He had heard of *Oupa* Pieter. A fierce warrior of an Afrikaner, who feared nothing and no-one, but God.

He had a large ranch deep in the bush where he ran small hunting safaris two or three times a year. He had fought the bush war in what was then South West Africa, he was as tough as they come. He bred game on his ranch which he sold at auction to re-stock the new game lodges which were springing up in the Eastern Cape.

He had the trust of the locals and they talked to him.

Harry wanted me to make a quick trip to meet *Oupa* Pieter and check him out as a potential agent. I arrived in South Africa and *Oupa* Pieter collected me from the airport in East London, from there he flew me to his ranch.

He was a giant of a man, deeply tanned, his face criss-crossed with lines from the fierce African sun and working outdoors on the ranch all day. He had piercing blue eyes, a white goatee beard, and a full head of white hair, like an Old Testament patriarch. His thick guttural Afrikaans accent was difficult for me to understand at first, but my ears became attuned to it.

Over an excellent dinner of roasted impala, a sort of deer he told me, we talked about the world of terrorism and its long-term impact on the world.

After dinner we sat outside on his sweeping veranda, enjoying a glass of very good South African wine.

He might live on a ranch in the middle of the bush but the old man was well up on the news and what was happening in the world, I could see it troubled him a great deal. He had also heard things from the locals in the various villages scattered in the area. His main source of information came from an old fisherman called Jakub.

Jakub was an elder in one of the villages and heard many things from travellers passing through. Strangers in the cities offering money and a future to young men without jobs. Young men who had lost hope in the promises made by politicians, for a better life in the new South Africa. Young men, ripe for the picking, who had nothing else to lose.

Oupa Pieter knew all about Bin Laden and the Shadow Dancer, he knew South Africa was viewed by them as open territory for recruitment.

I briefed him on our agency, what our goals were, how we worked, but without giving too much away about the way we worked. I didn't want him to disapprove, being a man of God, and turn down the offer.

"The attacks on the Twin Towers and the Pentagon had far reaching effects." I told him. "It blew away all of the police's certitudes, all their investigative and surveillance techniques on a global scale. The secret services, information agencies, police forces and armies of all the countries threatened by Al-Qaeda were on tenterhooks. The politicians were panicking, biting their nails down to the quick. Once more, terrorism had shown its greatest strength was secrecy."

Oupa Pieter said nothing, just stared out into the blackness of the night. A tactic invitation to continue.

So, I did. "Willpower. Madness. Faith. Confronted with a wall of technology and thousands of American agents, a handful of determined men managed to slip through all their surveillance. They didn't care about their own lives, those fanatics, they'd given themselves over to a high power, a higher cause.

"Did you know, Piet, they remove all their body hair before any suicide attacks? Do you know why?"

36

I didn't wait for him to answer. "So as to be perfectly pure at the moment they entered Paradise. And this is what we are now dealing with. Fanatics who have no fear of death.

"So *Oupa* Pieter, would you be interested in the job?"

He took a large mouthful of his wine, almost draining the glass, then puffed on his cigarette for a few moments. "*Ja*, this I will do for you. It would be an honour. I will do it for my country. For my Janine."

Unexpectedly there was a slash of jagged lightening which lit up the black night, followed by the deep rolling, rippling, then the cracking sound of thunder, it even made me jump, and I ducked my head instinctively. Within minutes the rain came down like rods of steel, pounding on the tin roof of the house, making conversation difficult above the noise, large drops of rain ricocheting around our feet like marbles. The wind picked up and roared through the trees and bushes. It was quite something to see, quite something to feel, out here in the middle of nowhere. Almost biblical in its natural fury. We have storms in Manhattan but I'd never seen anything quite so violent as this.

The old man lifted his head and closed his eyes, drinking in the smell of it all.

Then as suddenly as it had arrived the storm abated, leaving a gentle rhythmic patter of rain, and the night sounds of burping frogs and shrill clicks of the cicadas as they welcomed the wetness of the bush; the rain cleansing and refreshing the air.

Oupa Pieter gave me a sad smile. "Whatever we do, whatever we achieve, nothing will change the moon from rising, the ebb and flow of the tides, the mountains. They have seen it all for thousands of years. The earth has the power, Marcus, we have nothing. We will not be remembered, but perhaps the shadows of where we once stood will remain.

"Nature cares nothing for us, we are like ants, dispensable. Africa is an uncaring place, an unforgiving place, but it is unforgettable, like a beautiful woman. But she has no time, or patience, for you or for me.

"Are you married Marcus?"

"No. I was once but it didn't work out – marriage and my line of work made it impossible." No point in mentioning Emily was a South African girl. No point in mentioning her at all.

He refilled his glass again and lit another cigarette. "Out here in the bush one feels close to God, close to nature. When there is a storm, like now, you can feel the Almighty's anger against the world and its inhabitants.

"Are you a religious man, Marcus, or have you seen too much to even believe there is a God?"

"I'm a Roman Catholic, Piet, I don't practice my religion, and, yes, it is hard to sometimes believe there is a God. But, as they say, once a Catholic, always a Catholic!"

The old man nodded. "So, Marcus, you think you will find this scum called the Shadow Dancer, or this Bin Laden?"

I grinned at him. "Sure we will, Piet, we'll get both of the bastards one day. It's what we specialise in, it's our job, our vocation."

The next morning, he gave me a tour of his ranch. He lived in one of the nicest places I have seen so far. I told him I hoped to return again one day, spend more time exploring the country.

He flew me back to East London where I caught my flight to Johannesburg, then home to New York.

He was a nice old boy and would be a valuable asset to the agency. I liked him. He seemed deeply lonely though, his wife had died and his sole child, Janine, had died on 9/11, two years ago. She had been on the flight from Boston to Los Angeles when it was highjacked and ploughed into the North tower. He had a deep hunger, and an insatiable thirst for revenge.

Harry was pleased with the outcome of the meeting. Another corner of the world sewn up, watched over by good people. Nice place South Africa.

Chapter Eleven

Marcus

My next assignment was in London, where we anticipated another terrorist attack. There I would create, as Harry had ordered, the required persona now called Marcus Hunter – I liked the surname Harry had decided on.

It isn't difficult to change ones looks. Contact lens', facial hair, different style and colour, different walk, different accent. I sometimes had a hard job recognizing myself in the mirror.

An office was organized, a small one, in an annex of the American Embassy in Mayfair, and I set myself up as a mergers and acquisitions consultant. I was assigned a short, stout, plain middle-aged woman called Megan, as my assistant.

To succeed with the assignment, I had to ingratiate myself into the London scene. To do this I needed to buy an apartment, this Megan organized for me. A neat place in Chelsea.

I had to become a British subject, which meant getting married to an English girl in order to get this status. Someone who was a bit of a loner, preferably with no family. I didn't want anyone with a big circle of friends - too dangerous.

I began to frequent bars and restaurants looking for suitable women. One by one I seduced them, found out as much as I could about each one, then handed the information over to Megan who with great diligence passed it over to the Agency who processed everything.

One woman passed all the tests – her name was Emily Brandmore.

Born in South Africa, she worked as a freelance editor from her apartment in Kensington. With her parents being British, she was as well, despite being born in Africa. Emily met the required criteria.

I met her in a small French restaurant in Notting Hill. Settling myself at the table next to hers I watched her from behind the menu.

She was more than attractive, tall, with long dark hair. She sat there alone, reading a French magazine, expensive glasses perched precariously on the end of her nose.

"Excuse me ma'am," I said, "would you be able to help me out here, do you speak French by any chance, I can't figure out this menu whichever way I jump?"

She turned with a quick frown, then smiled and nodded.

We ended up having lunch together and I explained I was new in town but anxious to make friends etc. etc. As I said, I'm not going to be asked to appear on the front cover of a magazine, but I'm not unattractive, I can be more than charming if it's called for, which isn't very often.

We arranged to meet for a drink the following evening. When I returned to the office, the next morning, Megan had more than enough information to check Emily out.

She would do nicely. Harry gave me the go-ahead.

We began to see each other on a regular basis; drinks, dinner, theatre. Just the two of us. She assumed all my friends were in the States, so I made a few up and told her about my 'best friend' Harry. Emily didn't seem to have any close friends, I guess being South African, and coming from another country wasn't as easy as having been born in the UK. She was lonely, far from home, looking for love in an uncaring and indifferent city.

After six months of being together, sleeping together, I asked her to marry me and move into my apartment in Chelsea.

Harry came over for the wedding, and between us we managed to rustle up half a dozen friends. Megan arranged all this. Harry was happy with the way things were panning out.

Being married to Emily gave me the credibility I needed. A good hard-working husband running a busy office in London. Seamless cover to continue my hunt for the bad guys out there.

We had been married two years when the world changed forever.

On that cloudless blue-skied morning in September, the perfect solution presented itself. I was in New York City for my meeting with Harry. We watched with increasing fury and shock. We had heard the 'chatter' of an impending hit on New York City, but none of us could ever have imagined the scale of it, the audacity of it. It was a perfect military operation when you think about it.

40

People were staggering out of the burning buildings like grey ghosts, covered in ash and debris looking dazed, staring around with disbelief on their terrified faces.

I knew what Harry was going to say before he opened his mouth.

"It's an opportunity Marcus – too good to miss. It will be chaos out there for weeks to come, the death toll will be beyond belief."

He didn't take his eyes off the television screen as the horror of the attack became apparent, unfolding minute by minute. Then the second plane hit the South Tower and we were both silent.

A massive ball of orange flames, erupted from near the top of the South Tower, stark against the deep blue of a cloudless sky.

"Jesus Christ, Marcus, people are jumping…" Harry closed his eyes briefly as slabs of wood, desks, phones and filing cabinets exploded on the pavements, thousands of pieces of paper floated like feathers from the shattered windows of the burning Towers.

The foul choking air was thick with noise now. Screams, sirens, cries, the overhead thwack thwack of helicopter blades. Police and fire officers were running towards the buildings, fire engines honk honk honking, screaming into place, fire officers tumbling out and breaking into a run, towards the jaws of death.

Harry pinched the bridge of his nose. "One plane might have been an accident, but two. He shook his head.

"Without any doubt," Harry murmured, "this is a terrorist attack, the likes of which the world has never seen before. And we both know who's behind it."

At that moment the Shadow Dancer became enemy number one. He was going to be a tricky bastard to find. But, as Harry said, it was a perfect opportunity.

The Shadow Dancer was the most dangerous terrorist on our hit list. We had been tracking his activities for two years, watching him move up in the ranks, becoming powerful and unpredictable, his hatred of the United States, what it represented, fueling his rhetoric.

Harry, with his back to me, studied the map of the Middle East and Africa which covered one wall of his office.

"Emily thinks you're having a business breakfast at The Window on the World – correct?"

"Correct yes."

Harry turned back to me as the murderous mushroom clouds of thick smoke and dust blotted out the bright sunshine of what had started out as a perfect September morning.

"We'll get you to the safe apartment in the City, your suitcase will be found at your hotel, your British passport will be retrieved from the rubble when things have settled a bit and I can get someone in there, I'll need your wallet as well. It's going to be a fucking nightmare."

He paused for a moment, his hands shaking with uncontrolled anger, thinking his plan through. "I'll fix the travel documents. The passports you already have. I want you to find this bastard and give him a slow death, as painful as possible. Hunt him down, Marcus, hunt the Shadow Dancer down and anyone you find with him.

The phone on his desk chirped. Without hesitation he picked up the hot line and listened intently. Then turned back to Marcus.

"All commercial flights have been grounded throughout the country, incoming flights have been turned back. Only military aircraft will be allowed to fly the skies in the foreseeable future. Once the ban is lifted I need you on the first flight to anywhere, use your US passport to get out. Then find the bastard responsible for this.

"Start on the Kenya Somalia border where you said he was heard of last. You might be gone weeks, maybe months, don't come back 'til you find him, follow him to the ends of the earth – but find him. Use the digital voice distorter when you call me, but only if it's an emergency, or if you've found him and killed him. Otherwise I'll be in touch when I need an update or a meeting."

He looked directly at me but didn't falter. "Emily has now become a problem which must be resolved. She'll be informed you are missing, presumed dead. Then, when the time is right, I'll call and tell her your passport and wallet has been found but you haven't.

"She thinks you have a sister. Not true as we know. Leave it to me – I'll use some of our guys at the memorial service for you.

"We're going to need more than your passport and wallet being found – I'll need some DNA. Irrefutable evidence you are indeed deceased. The Bloodhound can sort this out and, when he thinks a suitable amount of time has passed, he will issue an official document confirming the match, which will be passed on to Emily, along with your death certificate.

I nodded as Harry planned our revenge for the attack taking place before our disbelieving eyes.

"Don't forget to give me a nice Catholic send-off Harry – I need some guarantees the other end! St Patrick's will do – always liked the place." He gave me a wintery smile.

42

If I survived this mission, I would be an invaluable asset to Harry, because I would have become invisible. A dead person, with the top of my little finger missing.

Emily was beginning to suspect something was going on with the frequent trips I was making. I would have no explanation for being away for months and not contacting her. Emily was no fool. So far, she was not a threat. If she became one I would know straight away. I'd already planted a bug in the apartment which would pick up any conversations she might have, and her phone was fixed so each incoming and outgoing call would be eliminated from the call register. Through the phone I could track her wherever she went.

The man in the hoodie used by Harry to carry out his dirty work was also under surveillance by me, as Harry knew. I knew where he was at all times. I'd fixed his phone too. I didn't trust him, hell, I didn't trust anyone. But I did trust Harry.

It wasn't something I was worried about as I mentally prepared for my mission to hunt down and kill, the Shadow Dancer. There would be no high-profile trial for him.

Emily would be the so called sacrificial lamb, a small price to pay in the greater scheme of things in a world where history had just been made. I hadn't married her for love, I'm not the kind of man who has any kind of expectations out of life. Hell, I don't even buy anything with a sell-by date!

I wrote her out of my life. I had to if the mission was to succeed.

As I left Harry's office I passed the Bloodhound, hurrying along the passage way, head down, no doubt lost in his world of DNA samples. His real name was Brett, but he was one of the best scientists in the country, and he was on our team. I swear he could match DNA samples just by sniffing at them.

"Hey Bloodhound!"

He looked up, startled. "Hey Marcus – bad bloody day all round, not so?"

"Sure is – should keep you busy for years to come. Got a job for you, urgent one. Need you to take some DNA from me. Then I'm going to be a dead person."

Brett nodded, nothing seemed to shake him, not even the horror of the day. "Come with me then."

*****

Harry sat on the edge of his bed, it was 2 a.m. in the morning. Sleep was impossible. When he closed his eyes he saw the murderous mushroom cloud gathering speed through downtown Manhattan, the grey ghosts of people fleeing, arms and legs streaked with blood caking the death ash, faces etched with panic and disbelief. The vision of the people screaming as they ran for their lives, the falling exploding people, the thundering rumbling in his ears, in his heart and searing his soul. Ordinary New Yorkers undefined by colour, age or religion, just stampeding grey ghosts brought together by hell on earth.

The wind had changed direction early in the evening, the smell of burnt hair and flesh stank in his nostrils. He thought of the ripple effect of the thousands now in mourning or searching frantically for their loved ones. Their bodies alive one moment, then exploding and disintegrating as they hit the sidewalk.

Harry had seen some bad stuff in his life but this was biblical in comparison, almost beyond comprehension.

He remembered a line from a poem by Kipling "*If you can keep your head when all about you are losing theirs…*"

Marcus was the best agent he had ever had. Marcus would be relentless in his pursuit of the murdering bastards responsible for changing the world forever. There was no-one else on his team scattered around the world who was more qualified.

Harry fell into an uneasy sleep. Tomorrow the real work would begin. He wanted revenge at whatever price. A price he was more than prepared to pay.

Chapter Twelve

The elegant white liner pulled smoothly away from the grey docks. Emily stood under the umbrella watching the distance grow between the land, the oily iridescent sea and the receding figure of Rebecca. She bunched her toes in her shoes to keep them warm then, with a final wave, went back to the comfort of her cabin.

It was large and airy like a luxury suite in a hotel. A writing bureau stood in one corner, her luggage positioned beside it by her steward; a double bed, with several plump pillows and cushions, looked out over her private deck.

Sipping her hot chocolate, she watched England disappear from view. The rain streaked against the glass windows as the ship picked up speed. As the darkness swallowed the retreating coastline, she prayed she'd made the right decision to leave her predictable life behind to embark on this trip back to Africa.

*****

For the following three weeks Emily slipped into her own routine. During the day, she found shelter on her small deck and with a blanket wrapped around her legs she would read, or make notes in her diary, glancing up now and again at the wide expanse of sea, dipping and swelling around the ship.

After 9/11 there had been months of endless questions which had exhausted her.

Had she ever been in love with him? No, she had been in love with the idea of being in love, she had been lonely in London. Marcus had blown into her life when she had been at her most vulnerable.

She leaned back and lifted her face to the sun. A whole new chapter in her life was about to begin, and she was going to grab it with both hands.

She knew her parents would be proud of her. They would be waiting for her.

Emily was going home.

Chapter Thirteen

When Emily woke, on the final day of the cruise, the ship was silent. The familiar vibrations of the throbbing engines under her feet had ceased. The ship had docked in Mombasa.

She opened the doors to her deck and stepped out.

Africa. It was beautiful, as only Africa can be. The older she got the more beautiful she became, possessed by no-one, belonging to no-one. Emily shivered with emotion.

The sun was coming up, the sky was creamy and pink, promising to deepen into the turquoise blue of the days she'd grown familiar with on the cruise. There they were, the tall wavering palm trees, the placid sea and the dazzling white sand – just as she'd seen in the brochure. She took a deep breath; warm and dusty with a hint of spice – she was home.

Emily dressed and packed her last few things in her capacious safari bag. Her main luggage, with her winter clothes and coat, had been taken the night before, ready to be transferred to customs for collection. The shipping agent would store it for her until her return cruise to England.

Taking a last glance around the cabin she picked up her handbag and straw hat, left a generous tip for her steward, and joined the queue of disembarking passengers

With immigration and custom formalities completed, she headed for the exit door, spotting a smiling driver with her name on his board, waiting to take her on a brief tour of Mombasa and then to the station.

"*Jambo* Miss Hunter, I am your guide for the day, my name is William. Welcome to Kenya."

Emily shook his hand. The young African was dressed in jeans and an immaculate white shirt, his feet thrust into cream canvas shoes. He picked up her luggage and led her out to the car. It had seen better days and the inside smelt of stale cigarette smoke.

As they drove through the busy streets she wound down her window, lifting her chin she inhaled the aroma of Mombasa. The perfume of the frangipani trees; the spices, dried fish and pungent odour of garlic, creating a heady mix in the cloying heat.

The fruit and vegetable sellers lined the pot holed roads, their wares displayed in pyramids. Bike repair shops, internet cafes, shoe shops and material shops, the bolts of cloth, temptingly displayed on tables outside, shimmering with colour in the sunshine.

The heat and humidity drained the energy from her very being. Her thighs stuck to the cheap plastic seat of the wretchedly hot car but she soon forgot her discomfort and watched fascinated as the car crept through the heavy traffic. Motor scooters and bikes wove their way through the lorries and buses, some with live chickens strapped to the pannier, their beaks and combs jerking with each indignant squawk.

They made their way to the departure point for the ferry crossing to the mainland. The old harbour was full of dhows and fishing boats, a scene unchanged for hundreds of years.

They inched their way onto the ferry. Lorries and cars squeezed in next to each other and parked in the hot sun, then the foot passengers boarded. Jammed to capacity the ferry chugged and belched its way across the narrow estuary, landing with an abrupt crunch on the other side.

As the car crept through the heavy traffic, Emily sat and watched, captivated. Young African men tapped on her window as the car ploughed through the crowds, holding up their wares with hopeful, beguiling, smiles. It was noisier here than in London, but somewhat more colourful!

Soon the traders thinned out and the road improved a little. Bowling along at a fair speed, dodging goats, and bony cattle, the car headed in the direction of the many tourist hotels of Diani Beach.

Down muddy alleyways she glimpsed shacks built out of pieces of packing cases and corrugated iron; rags, instead of curtains, hung dejectedly from windows. Emaciated rib thin dogs slunk in the shadows of rusted windowless cars, searching for food. Her own life paled into insignificance at the poverty around her.

She scratched her leg absently then looked down to check the source of the itch. Half a dozen mosquitoes were circling around her feet, with haste she reached for the insect repellent in her handbag, and smiled – yes, she remembered the mosquitoes, and the disease they carried, but she had taken her malaria pills.

The car turned left towards the beaches, the endless shacks now gave way to sprawling white beach front hotels, restaurants and bars. William dropped her at a beachside restaurant.

Emily wriggled her toes in the warm sand as she studied the menu. She chose the catch of the day, then sat back in the cane chair and looked around, the sand felt as soft as baby powder under her feet.

The fish she ordered was cooked to perfection, the chips crisp and golden. Hungrily she began to eat, glancing up as four haughty-looking camels loped past, with a cargo of tourists on their backs. The young man leading them gestured to her, inviting her to join them. Emily shook her head. The camels looked decidedly bad tempered. The thought of rocking back and forth on their unforgiving bodies was an experience she didn't need after weeks at sea.

She checked her watch, paid the bill, and went to look for William.

*****

At the station porters scurried up and down the train platform, showing passengers to their reserved cabins and helping them stow their luggage on the overhead racks. Traders, with trays strung around their necks, walked up and down the outside of the train, selling cold drinks and snacks. Young students clambered into the second-class carriages, with their bulging back packs.

Suddenly the carriage jolted, Emily clutched her hat as she hung out of the window. With a shrill whistle and groaning of carriages, the hissing train pulled out of the station, and a cheer went up from the passengers.

In her cabin, she sipped from a bottle of water, watching the passing countryside change from the tropical landscape of Mombasa to endless miles of dry scrubland. Trees and bushes dotted the landscape as they passed small villages with round huts and thatched roofs. Goats stood on the roofs of rusting cars, or on their hind legs, nibbling at the thorn bushes within their reach. Young children with liquid brown eyes and wide smiles, shouted and waved as the train rumbled past.

*****

The train thundered through the African night, the carriages rocking back and forth. Emily joined her fellow passengers in the dining car. It was hot and noisy in there and difficult to eat or drink with the train lurching over the tracks. She frowned at her food, unable to identify what she was eating.

Giving up with both the noise and the food, she returned to her carriage. Changing into an old tee-shirt she climbed into the narrow bunk bed, as the old train hurtled blindly through the darkness. The motion of the train soon lulling her to sleep.

Chapter Fourteen

Emily dressed in the light beige trousers and the cream shirt she'd bought in London. The new safari boots were as soft as ballet shoes. Shaking out the expensive suede jacket she threw it around her shoulders, then sat down and stared out at the flat landscape speeding past.

As the sun appeared over the Ngong Hills on the outskirts of the city, the train clattered into Nairobi railway station. With a final screech of brakes, it stopped; hissing and spitting above the cacophony of voices on the platform.

Emily gathered her luggage and stepped onto the platform. An African porter, in tattered shorts and a faded shirt, ran up to her pleading to carry her bags. She looked at the jostling crowds around her and nodded to him, not trusting herself to be heard above all the noise. Fanning her face with her hat, she shrugged off her too warm jacket and asked the porter to find her a taxi to take her to Wilson domestic airport, the portal for small aircraft flying passengers to and from the game lodges.

This was the part of the journey she was dreading. It would be a flight of thirty minutes or so, Caryl, the travel agent, had assured her. Her stomach squirmed like a snake trapped in a sack. Emily made a conscious move to unclench her fists.

Weaving through the early morning traffic in the taxi, she was surprised how courteous the drivers were to one another, as they dodged in and out of the teeming traffic. Traders and pedestrians picked their way through cars and trucks. Kenyan women, with bundles of wood balanced precariously on their head, their babies wrapped securely to their backs, walked along the dilapidated pavements, in sharp contrast to the men and women in business suits. Colourful, hand painted, buses, belching black smoke, competed with sleek Mercedes with tinted windows, as they all fought for road space.

Africa, Emily decided, was without a doubt an experience which could never be described, unless you had seen it, breathed it, felt it. Everything was louder, bolder and brighter.

The taxi dropped her at the domestic airport. A polite official requested her ticket, then pointed her into the direction of the departure lounge. She walked over to the window. Her mouth went dry when she saw how small the parked aircraft were. She fumbled in her bag for a sweet, putting it in her mouth and crunching down on it with some force.

Pilots were collecting and dropping off their passengers, stopping now and then to have a hurried conversation with a fellow pilot. Tour guides, in the arrivals area, held up boards with passengers' names. The place was almost as busy as the station had been. Other passengers sat with their luggage, dressed in their safari clothes, studying maps and guide books, cameras slung around their necks.

The heat shimmered off the runway and her heart pitched with fear. She turned from the window and went to stand next to the departure board. She knew she was booked on a private transfer to the lodge but had no idea how she would identify the pilot or the plane.

"Emily Hunter?"

Emily turned at the sound of the deep mellifluous voice. "Nick Kennedy. I'm flying you to the lodge."

Tall, tanned and lean, with dark hair as glossy as a raven's wing, she found herself gazing into a pair of deep blue eyes, his wide mouth and full lips adding to his attractiveness. The sleeves of his khaki safari shirt were rolled back from his wrists, his long legs encased in khaki shorts, a pair of sturdy safari boots on his feet. She held out her hand and smiled at him.

"Yes, I'm Emily. Nice to meet you Nick," she smoothed her hair down with a trembling hand. "I'm not looking forward to this part of my journey…those aircraft look rather small. Is there any other way of getting to the lodge?" she asked, her voice full of hope.

He grinned. "Afraid not. Here let me take your bags and we can be on our way. You'll be there before you know it. It would take days to get to Honey Badger by road and believe me you wouldn't enjoy the experience. Bad roads and big pot holes. Ready to go?"

He picked up her luggage with ease, and strode out of the building, turning to make sure she was keeping up with him. She followed his easy loping stride, her luggage seemed as weightless as paper in his hands, then out onto the airstrip towards the waiting aircraft.

It seemed even smaller up close, as she looked at the maroon and white livery and the lodge's logo on the tail. Nick began loading her luggage, and several small wooden crates waiting next to the plane. Once everything was to his satisfaction he turned back to check his passenger. "Provisions for the lodge," he explained, pointing to the neatly stowed boxes.

"Right, in you get. You can sit up front with me."

She was rooted to the spot. She couldn't do it. With a firm grip he took her elbow and she felt the warmth and strength of his hand through the sleeve of her shirt. Her hands were shaking as he strapped her in. He climbed into the pilot's seat, then patted her clenched white-knuckled fist.

"No need to be nervous, we won't be climbing high. It's a great day for flying. Here… put these on." He clamped a headset over her ears, blocking out the crackle of the radio, the voices from the control tower, and the powering up of the engines as he taxied towards the end of the airstrip. Before she had time to think about anything the plane was airborne and they were soaring into the clear blue sky, the ground falling away beneath them.

They flew low over the rolling plains, leaving the city and suburbs of Nairobi behind. No buildings of any kind blotted the landscape, she saw the occasional rural village with no more than a dozen circular dwellings topped with thatch, looking like pebbles laid out in a pattern on the hot dusty earth, the shadow of the aircraft passing over them. The brown and gold African landscape spread like a giant carpet beneath.

She glanced at Nick and saw he was looking pleased with himself. No doubt she'd made an idiot of herself in front of him, but somehow, she didn't think it was going to matter. Not everyone liked flying, he must have done this hundreds of times with nervous passengers.

She sat back and tried to relax. What more could she ask for than a pilot with the looks of a movie star, flying her across the endless bush. She looked down as Nick pointed out the herds of elephant, the giraffe with their rocking gait, a crocodile sunbathing on the banks of a river, and great herds of buffalo. A group of zebra took off in unhurried rhythm, galloping away from the buzzing of the plane.

Thirty minutes later they began their descent, she looked around in panic for the airport, seeing just a short stretch of cleared bush which seemed to appear from nowhere. Nick patted her hand again to reassure her.

Nick banked the plane and zoomed over a small herd of elephant, they shook their heads and trumpeted at the sound of the engines. Their huge bodies looked small from this height. Emily turned to look at him. He was studying the clouds overhead, his hands, strong and tanned, skilfully guiding the small plane.

As they were coming into land he pointed out a pride of lion, resting beneath the shade of a tree. With all the excitement of seeing so many animals she was amazed she had been distracted from her fear of flying, and at how soon the time had passed.

Out of the corner of her eye she watched him methodically work the toggles, switches and valves, noticing there was no wedding ring. The muscles in his legs tensed as he negotiated the landing. Feeling her face getting hot she looked away.

The aircraft juddered to a halt, spewing up clouds of red dust around them into the hot still air. He did his post-flight checks, his fingers flicking switches and pressing buttons, she removed the headphones and watched, observing the sun-bleached hair on his arms and legs. The engines stopped and there was silence. He grinned at her, pushing his sunglasses up onto his head.

"See, wasn't so bad, was it?"

Sliding open the side window he reached out and opened the door, then came around to her side of the aircraft and lifted her down. Flustered with the nearness of this man, and the feel of his hands around her waist, she dusted down her trousers and shook out her jacket, then followed him to a waiting vehicle and driver, parked under the shade of a tree.

Nick introduced her to the Kenyan driver, Amos, who helped her into the vehicle then reached behind the seat for the cold box; twisting the top off a bottle of water he handed it to her.

The two men turned back to the aircraft and began to off-load the luggage and provisions. Emily drank thirstily from the bottle, wiped her mouth with the back of her hand, and looked around at a panorama of unsurpassed beauty. A palette beyond the imagination of any artist or painter.

A herd of impala grazed near the air strip, their golden pelts shimmering in the heat. Her head buzzed with the silence of the endless miles of fecund bush stretched out in front of her. The scent of parched rocks, baked earth and dusty bushes, the scent of a continent. The scent of Africa, bringing back memories of her childhood. She turned to study Nick Kennedy, surprising herself in the process.

54

He was the first man she'd noticed with considerable interest since Marcus's death over two years ago. Perhaps it was being in the bush which was evoking her interest in him. Or maybe it had been his kindness to her when she'd seized up with fear at the thought of flying in such a small machine.

Amos clambered in the back, Nick slid into the driver's seat next to her, then turned the vehicle around and drove through the bush. On the twenty-minute drive he pointed out different birds, animals, trees and bushes. Emily could hear the love and passion he felt for this country. He stopped the vehicle as two graceful giraffe crossed the path ahead, pausing to nibble at the top of an acacia tree, whose branches flared upwards from the trunk, like the spokes of an umbrella, before bursting into a broad flat canopy of leaves at their top, then the giraffe moved on, with haughty, disdainful, glances at the intruding vehicle and its passengers.

Nick started the engine and put it into gear. "Amos will be at your disposal for the entire time you're at the lodge. Each guest is attended to by a personal butler, Amos is yours."

Emily turned in her seat and smiled at Amos, dazzled by his smile, his ebony skin and impossibly white teeth.

Nick drove on through the bush keeping a wary eye open for any animals they might startle and cause to catapult out in front of the vehicle.

"Most of the game will be resting at this time of the day, it's too hot even for them, but they'll all be out later as the afternoon cools off. Here we are – welcome to my lodge."

Honey Bader lodge was as striking as its owner. A well-swept path, bordered on both sides with rocks painted white, leading to the main part of the lodge which nestled under gnarled trees. Beneath the lofty thatched roof, tables were laid for lunch and ceiling fans clicked and circled, moving the languid air.

"Depending on the weather we either eat inside, or out here under the stars." Nick glanced up at the sky, narrowing his eyes against the sun. "It should be fine enough for dinner *al fresco* tonight, might be a bit of a storm later though," he pointed to the build-up of clouds in the distance.

"There's the bar area over there out on the deck," he gestured to the right of the main building. "Help yourself to anything, there's fresh orange and lemonade, or wine, whatever you feel like. Let me show you the main sitting area and the library."

The sitting room was cool and inviting, the floor covered with animal skins. Hunting trophies glared down from the walls along with black and white photographs of famous, and now departed, hunters with their foot on the head of a dead buffalo or other unfortunate beast.

Shelves of books lined the walls featuring biographies and novels by famous characters who once roamed the vast Serengeti plains looking for game to shoot. White wicker chairs were positioned around the room in small circles, African drums served as side tables.

An old-fashioned record player with a handle stood in one corner, its dented metal horn glinting in a shaft of sunlight. On the wooden deck outside, six long planter's chairs, their extended arms ideal for balancing a cool drink, stood in a row. She spotted a small swimming pool, positioned with discretion, behind a cluster of bushes.

She followed Nick as he set off down a path with Amos and her luggage. Each of the tented suites was set on their individual wooden decks under a canopy of trees; thick bushes giving each one complete privacy. Amos unzipped her tent, depositing her bag on the double bed before leaving them.

Nick turned to her, his slow smile reaching his eyes. "You should have everything you need. There's a bath en-suite, but you might want to try the one out on the deck. It looks basic, it's made of canvas, but it makes for a novel experience. I can send Amos to fill it for you if you'd like to try it?"

Emily eyed the canvas bath. "I've never had a bath out in the open, let alone a canvas one. I'll try it, wash some of the dust off from the journey!"

"Good. Come up to the main lodge when you're ready. Don't forget to zip up your tent when you leave. The monkeys are curious and enjoy nothing better than coming into a tent to check things out.

"They'll go through an open suitcase in seconds, pulling things out and draping them over their heads, like ET. They love bathrooms, turning on the taps and preening themselves in the mirror, it's one of their favourite pastimes."

He stepped off the veranda. "I'll leave you to settle in. Lunch will be served in a short while, then we meet at four for tea before the afternoon game drive. There's no pressure to do anything. Dinner is at eight, with drinks beforehand. Come down when you feel ready."

He pointed to a small cream canvas flag on a stick, lying on a table near the steps. "If you'd like a snack, coffee or sandwiches, just stick the flag here in the holder, and Amos will come down to take your order.

He'll check every half-hour or so, to see if you need anything, but he won't disturb you unless he sees you've raised the flag, so to speak."

Emily thanked him and watched him leave, his nonchalant walk conveying ease and confidence. She wandered out onto the veranda in a trance, pushing her sun glasses up on her head. The canvas bath sat at the end of the wooden deck, the views were breath-taking. Two dark green director's chairs and a low wooden table were set back in the shade. She sat down, suppressing a desire to pinch herself – she was back – she was home.

The bush rolled out in front of her as far as the eye could see, golden grasses rippled and whispered on the warm breeze. Five large antelope, their graceful curling horns glinting in the sun, grazed near the river. The silence of the bush was broken only by the sound of the grass being nibbled, the grunts of the animals and the cooing of the African doves. A long line of red ants marched with determination across the edge of the deck before disappearing over the edge.

Emily thought back to the fox sitting in the rain under the street lamp. Destined to scavenge in dustbins, never free to roam where it wanted to, unlike the animals she was watching now.

She took a deep breath, feeling herself relax. A family of warthogs trotted past in single file, their tails held stiff and high, looking full of self-importance, and she laughed out loud.

A spider's web, perfect in its construction, was strung between two bushes, a hapless moth trapped between the strands. Brushing a persistent buzzing fly away from her face, she ducked back into the suite.

Emily unpacked her luggage, admiring the luxury of her suite. A double bed, swathed in a shroud of mosquito netting dominated the room, at the foot of the bed was an old steamer trunk made of wood and canvas, its faded labels almost impossible to read where it had travelled to and from, and with whom.

There was an en-suite bathroom and an outside shower. An open fire place, already laid with wood, promised a cool evening. It was a far cry from the basic rest camps, the round thatched rooms, she'd stayed in with her parents as a child.

She heard a tap on the door and a low greeting. Amos had come to fill her bath. She would order a sandwich for lunch, then sit back and do nothing, just as the rather attractive owner had suggested.

Chapter Fifteen

Nick glanced at his watch. In a few minutes dinner would be served, but no sign of Emily. He dropped another log on the camp fire, excused himself from his circle of guests and made his way to the kitchen. Amos looked up from preparing a tray.

"Miss Emily asked for dinner in her suite, boss. I tried to persuade her to join everyone else but she said she wants to eat alone." He shrugged his shoulders.

"What?" He said incredulously.

"But she's fine, maybe just tired from her journey."

Nick frowned, perplexed. "Okay Amos. Take her a bottle of wine, make sure there's enough wood for the fire then light it for her, will you?"

Puzzled, he watched Amos walking back to her suite with Emily's dinner balanced on the tray. He'd never had a guest at the lodge who dined alone in their suite.

Yes, she'd been nervous when he picked her up at the airport, but he put it down to her obvious fear of flying. She seemed fine when he'd shown her around the lodge and her suite. Maybe she was shy and found the thought of walking alone into the crowded bar area a bit daunting.

Shaking his head, he joined his guests back at the fire, but found his thoughts straying to the woman sitting alone in her tented suite.

*****

Emily snuggled down into the thick dressing gown, provided by the lodge, staring at the glow, at the prisms of refracted light, from the glass in her hand.

She lifted her head at the low mournful cry of an owl and wandered out onto the deck. The night was closing in, filling the air with different sounds, each animal tuning in from afar. Some she could recognise. The intermittent belly laughs and grunts of hippo, followed by the splash of water as they submerged themselves in the river, the distant low moans of thousands of wildebeests, grazing on the plains, punctuated by the sinister whooping and hysterical cackling laughter of hyena

She stood there, rubbing her arms, disappointed with herself. Her euphoria at being back had suddenly dissipated, making her feel disconnected and somewhat depressed.

A slash of lightning lit up the dark night followed by a deep grumble of distant thunder. Emily could smell the rain coming and looked up as the first heavy drops pattered on the canvas of the tent, making fat dark spots on the deck. Pulling her dressing gown tighter around her, she stood there breathing in the fragrance of the rain, thinking of her parents, how much she missed them.

Without warning the rain increased to a drumming downpour and she returned to the shelter of her suite. As abruptly as it had arrived, the storm passed, the steady drips off the roof of the tent were drowned out by the night sounds of croaking frogs and the shrill sounds of the cicadas as they welcomed the wetness of the bush; the rain cleansing and refreshing the air.

Emily sat outside again, listening to the sounds all around her. The candle sputtered and spat, gathering itself to a wavering then steady light.

She took a deep breath and exhaled. There was no point in coming all this way back to Africa if she was going to mope around in her suite. It would be ridiculous and self-defeating. The leaves on the trees seemed to nod in agreement.

Tomorrow was a new day and she would welcome it, just as the animals, and the bush, had welcomed the downpour – if her thoughts should pounce back to the past, and her unanswered questions, she would make a concerted effort to think of something else. A new chapter, she chided herself, a fresh start to her life.

Standing up she slipped off her gown, lifting her arms to the heavens, feeling the trailing mist of the departing rain, like a widow's veil, on her naked skin. The slight wind blowing her wet hair across her face and into her eyes.

Chapter Sixteen

Emily woke late the next morning. She stuck the flag into the pot and waited for Amos, who appeared like a genie. "*Jambo*, Miss Emily, may I get you some coffee and breakfast?"

She smiled at him. "Yes, thank you Amos. A large pot of coffee and toast would be great. I'm quite hungry!"

She stood under the outside shower, it was a glorious morning. The touch of sun and water raking across her body, lifted her spirits. It felt good to be alive despite her gloomy, negative, thoughts the night before.

She dried herself and dressed in white shorts and a fawn shirt, before going out onto the deck and settling into one of the director's chairs. Amos had laid out her breakfast, adding some sliced sweet melon, mango, and paw paw to her order.

Nibbling her toast, she watched the game down at the water hole, the animals just getting on with life, as I will, she thought with determination.

"Emily?" It was Nick's voice. "Just checking to see how you slept last night. We missed you at dinner."

Flustered she went to the front of the suite. "Morning Nick. Um, a bit tired last night, but feeling fine this morning. I have the most enormous pot of coffee here; would you like some?"

"Thank you but no. I have to fly back to town this morning to collect four more guests. I don't suppose you'd like to come with me, would you?"

She stared at him, the piece of toast in her hand forgotten. "You have to be kidding, right?"

He laughed. "Yes, just kidding, I know you don't like my little plane. Anyway, I hope to see you later. Why not join me for a drink at around six this evening? Amos said you don't want to go on the afternoon game drive, so I thought you might enjoy a glass of wine or something, whilst everyone's out on their drive?

"Sipping a drink and watching the game around the water hole is pretty special. Will you join me – or must I sit there all by myself?"

Emily laughed at the little-boy-lost expression he was trying on. "Alright that would be lovely."

Nick turned to go then looked over his shoulder. "Won't cancel out on me, will you?"

"No, I'll be there at six."

*****

Nick positioned himself at the bar, he took a deep breath as he watched her make her way down the path to the main lodge. Every evening hurricane lamps were placed along the path, ready to be lit, to help guests find their way to and from their suites as darkness fell.

She was a beauty with her long gold-tinged auburn hair and big green leaf shaped eyes. He had noticed how her full lips were often a little apart, as though she might be waiting for something, expecting something.

He wondered why she was travelling alone, if there was a husband somewhere, past or present. He'd noticed her wedding ring and on the booking form she was Mrs Emily Hunter.

He stood up as she entered the sitting room and walked towards her, then led her through the thatched bar and out onto the wooden deck, overlooking the water hole. A sofa and chairs were gathered in a haphazard way around a low table. Emily sat, crossing her legs, looking up at him. He cleared his throat running his hand through his dark hair, feeling distracted.

"Glass of wine?" he indicated the silver bucket with bottles of wine chilling, "or something else?"

She pushed her sunglasses up on her head. "Wine would be great, white please. I seem to have worked up a thirst doing absolutely nothing. Oh, good heavens! How on earth did you manage to get that piano all the way out here?"

"With considerable difficulty." Nick smiled as he passed her a glass. "My mother used to play. It was in our Nairobi home, but with her hectic social life she played less and less, then suggested it would be a novel thing to have at the game lodge. It's never used. I don't suppose you play?"

"Afraid not, no. I can play the Clarinet though – if you happen to have one floating around?"

"Um, no, not the last time I looked."

Emily turned to watch the game coming to drink. A small herd of Thompson's gazelle emerged from the tall grass. With caution they glanced around, then tip toed with daintiness to the water's hoof rutted edge. Some kept watch, black noses lifted to the wind, their white tails flicking with anxiety. Others spread their legs, lowering their heads to drink. The sudden sharp crack of an elephant toppling a tree startled the gazelle, and they bolted from the water hole, their brown bodies vanishing into the grass with a flash of black stripes and white tails.

Nick plucked a leaf off the table and twirled it around in his fingers. "We have twelve guests tonight, but if you'd prefer to eat on your own, no problem. There's a nice group of Americans, but they prefer to eat together in the main dining area.

"The two French couples I flew in today are on honeymoon, I imagine they'll want to be alone. So, why don't I organise a table over there for you?" He pointed with the leaf to where the staff were setting up tables and lanterns under the trees.

"We have fresh lobster on the menu tonight, flown in by me this afternoon, just for you."

"You flew lobster in for me?" she said, her voice incredulous.

"Well, not really… I'm just trying to shame you into joining us for dinner."

She brushed an ant off her trousers. "I think I'll have dinner in my suite."

Nick hesitated, flicking the leaf into the bush. "It seems a shame to spend your second night in the bush eating alone, not under the stars. I'd be more than happy to join you for dinner if you like - if it'll make you feel more comfortable."

He watched, the gamut of emotions in her eyes.

"That would be great," her hesitation was brief, "especially as you went to the trouble of flying the lobster in. I love lobster. It'll also give me the opportunity to bombard you with questions about life in Kenya." She turned back to watch the activity at the water hole.

"Oh, look," she whispered excitedly. "Elephants. It's incredible how quiet they are!"

He chuckled. "They come here every evening to drink, they appear like ghosts, in complete silence. They're supposed to be out and about entertaining my guests…not hanging around here."

"One thing I've never been able to figure out, Nick. How come such magnificent beasts with their huge ears, their great bodies and long trunks have such silly little tails? Why don't they have more sumptuous ones like horses? Do you think God ran out of stock of great big bushy ones and stuck all he had left on the elephant.?"

Nick laughed at her question. "You're right, their tails are a bit on the short side, but it's because they don't really need them. Their ears keep them cool, their trunks they use for feeding and drinking, and for covering their backs with dust when the insects annoy them. Sometimes the babies will hang on to its mother's tail when walking, but that's about it. I think, eventually, in hundreds of years time, elephants won't have tails. Well, that of course is if they haven't been poached out by then and become extinct."

They spent the next hour watching the elephants drinking and playing in the water. A water buck came into view; lifting his head he looked around with caution, then bent and drank, the water rippling against his steady lapping.

Nick lifted his head at the sound of the vehicles returning to the lodge and stood up. "I'll go and check on the others, see how they enjoyed their drive. You won't change your mind about dinner, will you?"

*****

The sound of an African drum beating announced dinner, Nick came to escort her to a table under a tree now festooned with lanterns. Crystal wine glasses and silver cutlery reflected the light of the flickering candles in their glass holders.

"This is so romantic! How do you manage to keep such high standards out here in the middle of nowhere? It must be a logistical nightmare."

He pulled a chair out for her, before settling himself down. "It's not difficult once the systems are in place, I like to create a bit of magic for my guests. They've come a long way to spend time here. I want it to be memorable, something they can look back on when they're fighting their way through the traffic in New York, or wherever they come from, on the way to making even more money than they already have." With some difficulty, he took his eyes off the woman sitting opposite him and looked around at his other guests.

The Americans were oblivious to everyone during dinner. They talked loudly and laughed a lot, the game rangers sat at opposite ends of the table, keeping them amused. The two French couples were content to sit together, as he'd anticipated, speaking to each other in their own language.

Over dinner he answered her questions about life in the bush, what she could expect to see on game drives over the coming days, should she ever decide to go on one. Then, as he did with all his guests, he asked her a little about herself.

"I was born in South Africa, then left and went to university in Scotland. Now I live in London, with my cat, and I work in a book shop. I used to be a freelance editor but gave it up when I got married."

"So, you're a child of Africa then. I don't expect I'll need to tell you a thing about all the animals…" A slight breeze blew a tendril of hair across her face, accentuating her eyes and lips, he felt his mouth go dry.

He watched as she absently ran her finger and thumb down the stem of her glass. "We went into the bush, as a family, a couple of times; my mother didn't enjoy it. But I remember a lot of things about it, and there are endless wildlife documentaries on television, but it's not the same as being close to them, being on their turf, is it?"

He extracted a bedraggled moth from his glass and blew it into the night. "No, it's not the same, you're right.

"If you're born in Africa, or spend years there, it's hard to get it out of your system. You'll never belong anywhere else, no matter how far and fast you run. I'm sure your parents feel the same way?"

She looked up at the now star-studded sky, then back at him. "Yes, my father in particular. He didn't want to be anywhere else in the world. When they married they decided to leave the UK. They didn't want to conform to what society dictated there, the dullness of a predictable safe life, the grey sameness, and the weather of course! They wanted the freedom, adventure and lifestyle Africa offered, so off they went, without a backward glance."

Nick stayed silent. She fiddled with the small silver cross around her neck. "They were in Botswana, celebrating their wedding anniversary, I can't remember which one. It must have taken a bit of persuading on my father's part, to get my Mom to go on safari!

"They were on their way to another lodge, the plane seemed to have taken off with no problem, one of those small ones like yours?"

64

He nodded, now things were beginning to make sense, he knew what was coming.

"The engine stalled and they crashed into a small lake – they were all killed, the pilot, my parents, and two other passengers."

"I'm sorry Emily…"

She shrugged. "Then I met my husband Marcus, in London, he was American." her voice trailed off. Then she tried again. "He died on 9/11."

He stayed silent waiting for her to continue.

"It was a difficult time for me." She took a sip of wine and looked off into the distance as if waiting for something to arrive or appear.

"If it helps to talk about it I'm a good listener?"

She twisted her hair over her shoulder. "I'm not sure if this is the time or the place."

"It's as good a place as any…"

She told him about Marcus but didn't appear to be over emotional about her late husband, or the way he had died. But he felt she was holding something back.

He knew from years of experience with guests how the stillness of the bush, the peace of it, could heal even the deepest wounds. After all, he reminded himself, it had saved his life.

He leaned forward and filled her wine glass. "The long tentacles of terrorism were reaching out to the Western world before 9/11. I believe it all started here in East Africa when the United States embassies in Kenya and Tanzania were hit with the truck bombings in 1998."

He swirled the wine bottle in the ice bucket. "I think the world collectively held their breath, sensing an unfathomable change, it was the first real wave, and it caught the attention of a complacent world. It was the first time we'd ever heard of a terrorist called the Shadow Dancer, or Bin Laden.

"But 9/11 changed the world forever, the most pivotal event in recent history. We had a full lodge, mostly Americans. When the news came through over the radio I didn't know how to handle things. Did I tell my guests the news, and ruin their safari? Or did I not tell them what had happened and deal with the fall out?

"I knew I could get them back to Nairobi if they wanted to return home, but it would have been pointless with the no-fly order in place all over America, they wouldn't be going anywhere. It was a real dilemma."

"What did you decide?"

"I had a moral obligation to tell them, a moment I won't forget. It all seemed to be happening so far away from here. Afterwards it was chaos, they all wanted to go back to the States. The safari was a disaster for them, forgotten in seconds."

Emily shifted in her chair. "I went to New York for Marcus's memorial service. The grief in the city was palpable. So many young people gone. Some of the best financial brains in the world.

"Sorry Nick, I don't know what came over me - talking about my private life, it's something I rarely do."

"The bush has this effect on people – I've heard some interesting stories from my guests over the years, things they haven't shared with anyone else."

Seeing how agitated she was, and sensing there was perhaps more to this story, he sat back in his chair and looked up, feasting his eyes on the beauty of the African night, finding the words of comfort he was searching for.

He turned back to her. "When I was little my mother told me when a person died they went to heaven, then appeared as a star. I found it comforting. I liked to think a loved one was looking down on me, watching over me."

Emily reached for her jacket hanging on the back of her chair, draping it around her shoulders, she looked up, her eyes shining. "I love the idea of my parents being stars."

No star forthcoming for her late husband then. He could see there was more to come.

"Another thing I had to deal with was the failure of my marriage. Marcus wasn't the easiest man to live with – the way he died shocked me more than I thought possible. Shocked me because I didn't believe it, couldn't believe it. It was all hard to cope with."

Nick's eyes traversed her face. Now he was beginning to understand why the idea of Marcus looking down on her, as a star, was not too appealing.

Suddenly a lion roared in the distance, a long guttural rasping, she jumped, looking around, startled by the noise. "Lion?"

He grinned at her. "Yes, a male calling his pride, quite close, but nothing to be nervous about."

Emily pushed back her chair and stood up. "I'm sorry, I shouldn't have off loaded all of this on you, I mean… I don't even know you."

She picked up her bag. "I think I'll have an early night. I'm feeling a bit spooked."

He stood up. "I'll see you back to your room. It's not a good idea to venture out on your own at night. The animals sometimes come into the lodge grounds, and those lions are nearby. You'll feel better tomorrow after a good night's sleep." He helped her put her arms through the sleeves of her jacket.

They walked back to her suite. She turned to say goodnight and her eyes filled with tears. He hesitated for a brief moment, then put his arms around her and held her. She felt soft and warm, her hair silky and fragrant against his chin.

He lifted her face and cupped it between his hands, brushing her tears away with his thumbs. Saying nothing.

She moved away from him, rummaging in her bag. "I'm sorry, this wasn't meant to happen." She dabbed at her eyes with a tissue. "God knows what you'll think of me now. I feel so embarrassed!"

"Don't be. I'll send Amos with some hot chocolate and a brandy, which should sort you out. If you need anything, just use the buzzer next to your bed. One of the rangers will come straight away."

"Good night Nick, thank you. By the way, dinner was delicious. Imagine Lobster Thermidor in the middle of the bush – quite something."

She touched his hand, then stepped onto her wooden deck, turning her head to look at him for a moment. He saw her safely inside then went back to his other guests.

*****

Alone in her tent Emily spent some time thinking about him, his deep laugh, his blue eyes watching her, his strong capable hands, the way he gesticulated with them when he was making one point or another. She smiled at her ridiculous thoughts about someone she didn't know, but felt she'd known for a lifetime. Perhaps because they had both been born in Africa there was a natural affinity, some kind of bond.

Being held by a man was something she had missed, even though she'd made a complete idiot of herself by crying all over him. How she was going to face him again she had no idea.

Chapter Seventeen

Emily didn't appear for breakfast but ordered coffee in her room. Nick worked in his office, glancing up now and again, knowing she would be feeling awkward about her emotional outburst the night before. He wasn't sure he was comfortable about what had happened either.

By lunch time when she still hadn't appeared, he decided to send her a note.

I hope you're feeling better today. I'll be away this afternoon, and my other guests will no doubt take their normal siesta before their game drive. Why don't we meet around five and I'll take you out for a drive and sun downers? The rangers have found lion tracks not far from the lodge. It looks as though there might be some cubs with the pride. Nick

She read the note. He'd been right, a good night's sleep had been what she needed. She'd woken once, but soon fallen asleep again. She looked out over the water hole and watched the impala and zebra drinking with accustomed caution, darting quick looks in between as if to ensure there were no predators around.

A troop of baboons sauntered arrogantly towards the water, like a gang of playground bullies, the females with babies clinging to their stomachs, or riding on their mother's back.

Idly, she glanced down at the wedding ring on her finger. She'd continued to wear it, not being one hundred percent convinced.

"Goodbye Marcus," she said, her voice firm. "What happened, happened. I can't change the past, but I will change my future. I won't allow you to be part of it in any way."

She slid the ring off her finger, hurling it far out into the bush, the sun glinted off it for a brief moment, before it spun away and disappeared.

Chapter Eighteen

A mos set up two chairs and a table, then unpacked the hamper. He put the wine to cool in a silver ice bucket and set the glasses up on the table. In a round bowl, he arranged a cluster of flowers. The snacks remained in the sturdy, monkey proof, cool box. He glanced at his watch. The boss and Miss Emily would be arriving soon. He took one last look around then drove back to the lodge.

*****

Nick tracked the lions down to a thick area of bush and cut the engine. They sat in the vehicle under the shade of a tree as Emily scanned the bush for a sighting. In the distance a baboon barked a warning; she felt Nick's hand on her bare arm. He was pointing to the left of her. Her heart thumped as she saw the five lioness stretched out asleep, their cream coloured stomachs bloated. Only the occasional twitch of their ears, or a languid swipe at their face with a plate sized paw at the flies buzzing around their blood encrusted whiskers, gave their position away.

To the left of the females the grass was taller and thicker, her mouth formed an 'o' of pleasure as Nick pointed to the small cubs hiding there, their small ears twitching between the golden grasses, as they rolled and played with each other, waiting for their mothers' to wake up. In the stillness of the afternoon heat Emily could hear their soft mewing squeaks.

Nick backed away. Dust spun a fine red cloud and pebbles pinged against the metal chassis of the land cruiser as it topped the hill, a low thorn bush scraped the undercarriage releasing a pungent odour of wild sage.

"Lion are territorial," he said as he navigated the rough track, "so not difficult to find, as you no doubt know. I've watched them choose a mate, have cubs, the cubs grow up, have their own families and the cycle continues. It's the same with all the animals, they never seem to want more than they already have. I wish people were like that."

Nick slowed the vehicle down as they approached their sundowner spot, he parked under a tree and turned off the engine, there was silence except for the faint ticking of the cooling engine.

Emily settled into a chair as he poured her a glass of chilled wine and a glass of lemonade for himself, before sitting and letting his eyes scan the cooling bush for anything else of interest he could point out to her.

He glanced at her as she lifted the glass to her lips, the tip of her tongue moistening the edge before she took a sip. He took a deep breath. He had to do something with his hands and sort his scattered thoughts out. He handed her a dish of baby ribs bathed in barbeque sauce, his hand as steady as he could make it.

They ate with contentment, helping themselves to bite sized salmon tartlets and sausage rolls. He handed her a bowl with what looked like dark wood shavings in it. She raised her eyebrows.

"Dead flies?"

He laughed. "It's called biltong, a sort of dried meat. Babies in Africa are given big chunks to cut their teeth on, as I did. It's a bit salty but tastes good – here, try some, I'm sure you must have tasted it before."

"I'd forgotten all about biltong, its years and years since I had some! I remember it though. It does taste good, but, if I recall, it tends to get stuck in your teeth; not a good look. I prefer the ribs, the meat's softer. I think Oliver would like biltong, I must try and find some in London for him."

He lifted an eyebrow in question. "Oliver?"

"My cat. I love him to bits, he's staying with my friend Rebecca whilst I'm away. I found him behind my dustbin and rescued him. He's so affectionate – they seem to know when they've been saved don't they?"

She leaned across the table to touch the bowl of flowers. "I remember these flowers too, frangipani. When I was little I thought they were made of wax." She ran her finger over the top of the cluster.

He plucked one of the flowers and handed it to her.

"Gorgeous smell and so perfectly formed." Emily gazed at the creamy white petals, shaped like old fashioned aeroplane propellers, with pale yellow melting into its depths.

He rested his ankle on his knee, putting his sunglasses in his pocket. "I fly them in once a week to make a change from the roses we normally have. Roses are way too civilised for me, but they look nice on the tables."

He reached forward for another rib and dunked it in the sauce before popping it into his mouth, removing the bone from the soft meat.

He sucked his thumb and finger, wiping them on a napkin, then leaned forward, picking up his camera. "Ah, here come my favourite couple, Romeo and Juliet."

The giraffe loped into view, pausing to stare at them with disinterest, before moving on.

Nick took some rapid shots and put his camera down on the table. "Seeing giraffe silhouetted against the setting sun is one of the most beautiful sights in all of Africa, somehow they conjure up the essence of it."

Emily pushed her sunglasses up on her head. "Yes, it reminds me of the brochure I picked up at the travel agency. It's the classic shot isn't it? It certainly hooked me and made me want to come back to Africa."

She studied the giraffe through the binoculars. "They remind me of skyscrapers. What must it be like to have such a grand and remote view of life?"

"I think they're quite spiritual," he said, "they don't kill to survive, they just get on with the business of being an elegant giraffe."

She watched them, captivated, then put the binoculars down on the table. "I wonder what they think about when they stare into the distance – important things I would imagine. Lofty thoughts…"

He threw back his head and laughed, and she noticed the small scar on his forehead.

"The wonderful thing about wild animals," he continued, "is they just get on with life, untroubled by world affairs, politics, terrorists, money or anything else."

He scooped up some nuts from the dish and tossed them into his mouth, wiping the salt on his trouser leg. "We can learn a lot from them. Whenever I travel to the great cities of the world I can't wait to get back here. The crowds, the noise, the pollution. Everyone pushing and shoving their way up the corporate ladder. All the social competition – wearing the latest outfits, eating in the latest fashionable restaurant, where the mind buggery prices would bankrupt the average family here for months."

He flicked an insect from the table. "Then there's the latest place to be seen to ski, the latest private island to holiday on. They remind me of ants – except ants have a purpose, they know where they're going. I'm not sure people do.

"Animals need nothing but each other. They have no ambition other than to stay alive for as long as possible.

"All they need to know is tomorrow they can plod around the bush together and eat as much as they want, when they want. Simple. It's enough for them, but, of course, they don't know this."

Emily dragged her eyes from his face and watched the giraffe loping their way through the bush. Nick was right. A ton of money promised nothing. Too much of it seemed to make people want more and more, until they have everything – then what?

"So now you've met Romeo and Juliet, Emily, they're always together, this is their favourite neck of the woods if you'll pardon the pun. I always know where to find them."

"Is life so simple out here Nick?" she gestured around with her hands at the silence, the emptiness of the bush. "Is it enough for you?"

"More than enough. Besides I've nowhere else to go – nowhere else to be who I am. The lifestyle I enjoy here is unmatched anywhere else in the world. One day when I find the right girl, get married, have kids, I'll be living in an ideal world.

"How about you, Emily, would you marry again? What about children?"

"Of course. I would like to get married again...and I'd love to have children, lots of them. But tell me about you," she said, unable to take her eyes off him.

He sat back, his ankle, once again, resting on his knee. "I was born here thirty-two years ago, I have a brother, Jonathan, he's two years older than me. My folks have owned the lodge for over forty years now." He smiled at her.

"I went to school here, as my brother did, then to a boarding school in England, but we returned to Kenya for the holidays. If the holidays were short, we stayed with my godparents at their place in Hertfordshire. I couldn't wait to get back here when I got my degree.

"We'd been coming out here to the lodge, two or three times a year for as long as I can remember. It was far more rustic then, a basic camp, but my parents decided to go commercial with it. They wanted to share our piece of magic so we built more rooms and I ended up running it. In many ways it saved my life."

72

Emily looked at him intrigued. "Oh? How?"

"It's a long story, not something I talk about much. It was a long time ago now."

The sudden change of subject was not lost on her.

"I've entertained all kinds of business tycoons here at the lodge," he told her, leaning over to top up her glass. "The rich and the famous, all trying to outdo each other with how many houses, or successful businesses, they own. The first day they have their mobile phones glued to their ears, desperately searching for a signal."

He waved a lingering fly away from the remaining food. "By the end of day two they couldn't care less about the outside world. Soon enough they're talking about the animals, the stars, what they've seen on their game drive. They become more human without the trappings of the outside world, humbler. The bush brings people to their senses – now there's a sentence with a true meaning."

She nodded, mesmerised, as he continued, wondering again how this place had saved his life. A disastrous love affair came to mind.

"Living in noisy cities dulls the senses. I don't much listen to the news these days, the BBC sounds like an angel of doom piling on the bad news. Terrorists blowing people up and themselves, nightclubs full of teenagers burning to the ground, child soldiers butchering their own in Africa, children massacred in schools in the States. It's all bad news. I know there are natural disasters with high death tolls, but its man's inhumanity to man which bothers me the most."

Emily nodded in agreement, then changed the subject, reaching safer ground. "Is Jonathan involved with the lodge as well?"

"No, he moved to Singapore six years ago, he loves the bush as much as I do, but he found something he loved more."

"Really?"

"Yes. He's an entomologist, specialising in butterflies. He went out to Singapore to do some research, met a beautiful Malay girl, Kim, and that was it!"

"He must miss all this though?"

"He comes back to visit every couple of years but Kim doesn't want to live here. It's tough on my parents, we're a close-knit family, but he loves his life there, he loves his woman, and that's what counts."

Leaning forward she helped herself to the last remaining rib. "So, Nick," she said feigning disinterest, "no women in your life then?"

He pressed his lips together, looking away from her. "There was someone but she died.

"Then there's Natalie. She saw me through a difficult time in my life. We see each other when I go to town, and she comes to the lodge, when I have space. But otherwise, nothing serious."

Emily was tempted to ask about the girl who died but decided against it. Even though she'd been open with him about her personal life she had a feeling he wasn't going to return the favour.

She felt a pang of envy at the sound of Natalie but chided herself for being ridiculous. After all, she lived in another country, and soon she would be heading back to the ship, sailing out of his life. But right now, she didn't want to think of her flat with its tangible scent of loneliness, even though Oliver would be pleased to see her when she arrived back.

She wanted this moment to go on forever. To remember how he held her with his gaze, the way his mouth moved, how it might taste. The way his hair ruffled in the breeze, sometimes exposing the scar on his forehead, making it hard for her to focus on what he was saying.

She caught her breath. What on earth was she thinking? A mosquito landed daintily on her arm, she smacked it harder than she meant to and winced. A sliver of blood remained after she had picked it off with her nails. "Useless buggers," she muttered under her breath, "what's the point of them?"

Nick laughed as he stood up. "I'd have to agree with you on that one. Come on, we'd better get back before the other guests return for dinner, and before the relatives of the dead mosquito start circling, thinking you're theirs."

He folded up their chairs. "For once I wish the lodge was empty, I enjoy spending time with you Emily. If you wouldn't mind putting the glasses and bottle in the hamper," he said, "I'll sort out the rest."

Flustered by his remark she pulled down her sunglasses and stood up, grateful for something to do with her hands.

They pulled up outside the lodge and Nick killed the engine. "Much as I'd like to dine with you, I'm afraid I can't. The Americans will expect me to entertain them. Perhaps you'd join us?

"No, I didn't think so. Shall I ask Mike to join you, he's the manager. I think you've met him, the guy with the beard? He's worked at a few lodges in East Africa, he's good company."

She nodded, disappointed.

"By the way where's your wedding ring? If you left it in your suite I hope you zipped up the tent, or the monkeys will take it, maybe even wear it."

Emily jumped out of the vehicle. "Chucked it in the bush!" she said laughing at him over her shoulder.

She sauntered back to her suite, twirling the frangipani between her fingers. She opened her notebook and, with a final sniff, placed it carefully inside.

Years later, when the pressed flower was found, it would be another clue as to what could have happened to her.

Chapter Nineteen

Mike *was* good company over dinner, telling her about the safari lodges he'd worked in over the years. "A lot of rangers move around a bit," he told her. "Two years at one lodge, three years in another. I've been at Honey Badger for five years now, wouldn't want to be anywhere else on earth."

"It's a gorgeous lodge Mike, but don't you ever long for life in a big city, doesn't it get a bit boring here, doing the same thing day after day. Having to entertain new guests' night after night?"

"Yeah, sometimes it gets a bit much, but to be honest with you I feel safer here than anywhere else. I've been to London and Europe, but I couldn't stand the crowds and the noise. Lots of people, including me, are nervous to travel now, Americans in particular, after the New York tragedy. As I said, I feel safe here. Not likely to get some terrorist creeping through the bush intent on blowing up the lodge. We're too small fry for those guys, anyway they would be attacked and get eaten by a lion before they got anywhere near!"

Emily smiled. "Yes, well I suppose that's true, but what do you do for a social life?"

"My girlfriend lives in Nairobi, so I get into town to see her a couple of times a month. Nick," he nodded in the direction she was already looking in, "is good about letting her stay here. So, as I see it, they can keep the big cities of the world, I'm not going anywhere."

He patted his pockets for his cigarettes, finding them he lit one up, the smoke permeating through his beard like a small grass fire taking hold. His cigarette glowed red like a predator's eye in the dark.

"It humbles me sometimes when a guest sees a real elephant or lion for the first time in their lives. The look of innocent wonder on their faces, no matter how rich or famous they might be. I still get a kick out of it – nature in all its glory, belonging to no-one. It makes a human feel small and insignificant somehow."

She found her moment. "Nick was telling me about his friend Natalie, have you met her?"

He looked surprised at her question. A grey worm of ash from his cigarette quivered and fell on his khaki shirt, he brushed it off with practised ease. "Yes, great girl, lots of fun. Those two have been friends since they were kids. I haven't met a woman yet who hasn't been bowled over by Nick." He stroked his beard, tilting his chin back and exhaling a cloud of smoke. "He seems to have this effect on them!" He looked over and saw Nick excusing himself from his guests.

"Great pleasure having dinner with you, Emily. Goodnight, and thanks for your company."

She gave him a vague nod as she watched Nick approach.

*****

She brushed her teeth by the light of the lantern, marvelling again at the luxury of the tent. On either side of the bed were small carved chests, with two more lanterns, their soft light spilling around the tent. Wild flowers sat in a vase on the dressing table, next to a tall water jug covered with an intricate coat of Masai beading, adding a striking note of colour. By the door was a round, burnt orange, clay pot full of porcupine quills.

Turning down the hurricane lamp in the bathroom she climbed into bed, letting down the gauzy mosquito net. Sitting up and hugging her knees she could hear the night sounds around her. In the distance, she could hear the throaty roar of lion and the deep belly laughs of the hippo.

She closed her eyes and thought about the day - but tried not to dwell too much on the girl called Natalie.

Chapter Twenty

The next morning, Emily looked at her clothes hanging in the wardrobe, choosing a short khaki skirt and white t-shirt. She piled her hair up and caught it with a clip. Slipping her feet into her safari boots, she headed for the main lodge. She saw Nick having breakfast with the Americans, he smiled at her as she passed and lifted his arm, then continued his conversation with his guests.

A shy African waiter took her breakfast order as she sat there sipping her orange juice. Vervet monkeys rustled the leaves of the tree above her, their white faces like ghosts in the dark, building up the courage to dart over to the trestle table, where cereals, fruit and toast were laid out for the guests. The waiter shooed them away with a flick of his cloth, much to the amusement of the guests.

The bush was alive with the sound of birdsong, from the soft dull grey doves to others with their brilliant greens, blues, crimsons and turquoise, the exquisite Malachite kingfishers, swooping and dipping over the river, with their bright iridescent metallic blue feather wear. Emily searched through the trees spotting the bird with the flute like song, deep and glorious, as golden as its feathers, heralding the beginning of another day. She searched her memory - a Golden Oriole.

Everything seemed more defined in the bush, no thick smog and exhaust fumes, no room fresheners belching out their artificial scent of sickening pine or lemon. Here there was the scent of fresh air, eggs and bacon cooking, and the heavenly smell of fresh baked bread.

Emily watched a monkey somersault up into the tree to eat his stolen bread roll. Out of the corner of her eye she watched Nick regale his guests with another of his stories, when he glanced her way she held his gaze for a moment, then turned away.

She put her sunglasses on and turned back to watch him. He had a burnished look about him, a finished, crafted look. Nick, she felt, wouldn't notice, or care much, if things began to change in his physical being as he got older. Unlike some men she'd known, who banked on their good looks, glancing at their reflection in passing windows, seeking validation.

Stress, tension, nerves and depression, she felt, would never feature in Nick's psyche; anger, sadness and frustration at the things he could not control or change in the world, yes.

Nick was right. Animals just got on with things, not giving a damn what they looked like, or how old they might be.

She took another sip of her juice and turned her head. The warthogs seemed to be busy this morning, strutting across the lawns in front of the lodge. They were either down on their knees ripping the grass to shreds, or marching around, single file, with their tails held high looking as though they were off to an important meeting, then they all stopped as if they were queuing for a bus.

Reaching into her bag she pulled out her camera and took some shots, turning slightly so she could get one of Nick.

A large branch cracked, falling to the ground with a heavy thud, a young warthog leapt up in the air, then cantered off with grass hanging out of his mouth. He stopped and looked back in astonishment. Emily collapsed with laughter, tears running down her face

She felt Nick's hand on her shoulder. "Are you alright Emily?"

She looked up still laughing, her face wet. "Sorry," she gasped, "I have a vivid imagination, it's the warthogs..." her body convulsed again.

He grinned at her. "Yes, they're a real comedy act sometimes. It's good to see you laughing at last, really good!"

Chapter Twenty-One

Emily didn't go on the morning game drives but did join the other guests for the afternoon one, marvelling at the wild animals and open plains, the memories of her childhood rushing back, tripping over themselves.

The American guests were charming and didn't ask intrusive questions, as she'd anticipated. 9/11 seemed to be a subject they tried to avoid, not wanting it to sour their safari experience, here in a place so different to the shattered one they'd left behind. It was something she didn't want to talk about either.

Most of all she looked forward to the evenings and spending time with Nick, who somehow managed to weave his way into her thoughts throughout the day.

The following morning Nick announced to his guests that dinner would be out in the bush.

After the game drive, guests went back to their rooms to shower and change, then assembled in the main sitting room as requested, before climbing into the vehicles lined up at the entrance to the lodge.

The night was clear, the stars crowding the skies. Now and again the vehicle lights would pick up a pair of red eyes as night predators came out to hunt. The trackers, sitting on small bucket seats at the front of the vehicles, sweeping the bush with powerful flashlights, pointing out creatures who ventured out under cover of darkness. Twenty minutes later they arrived at their dining venue.

Under a Bedouin style tent, brass lamps gleamed and swung from the roof. Sumptuous swathes of red silk, held back with gold rope, decorated the sides. Low tables, set on Persian rugs, and cushions gave it a distinctive Arabian feel. The long dining table and canvas chairs were the centre piece. White roses decorated its length, the silver and crystal glinting in the candle light.

The mouth-watering smell of prawns, lamb, beef and chicken, hung in the air, as the chef worked on his barbecue. The guests were stunned when they saw the vision created for them.

Splitting into smaller groups they sipped their champagne and cocktails, sinking back on big cushions, waiting for dinner. Emily wandered away from the other guests to gaze at the stars, she sensed Nick coming up behind her and turned.

"The logistics of getting all this," she gestured around with her hand, "out into the bush and set up - it's incredible!"

His eyes were everywhere, checking for perfection, she thought, and finding it; then they settled back on her face.

"It takes a bit of putting together I admit, but it's worth it just to see the astonishment on the guests faces. After dinner, the staff will pack up and there won't even be a chicken bone left to indicate anything's happened here, just pristine bush again." He looked over his shoulder. "Everyone seems to have taken their seats at the table – shall we join them?"

"It's another world…" she said as they joined the other guests.

"Yes, it is, but it can be hard work. Difficult guests sometimes, disgruntled couples, their marriages in various states of decomposition giving a safari the last stab for the survival of their relationship, or the generator breaks down, there's always something to worry about, but I wouldn't have it any other way. I hope the woman I marry loves the lodge, the challenges, as much as I do – no smart shops or restaurants nearby, nowhere to get her hair done…"

Her heart sank. He's thinking of Natalie, she thought as she sat down next to him. *Lucky girl.*

She discarded the shell off a prawn and bit into it. "Have you ever had anyone on safari who didn't enjoy the experience Nick?"

He reached forward for an oyster shell and holding back his head, slid the contents into his mouth. She swallowed hard and reached for her glass of wine.

"Most guests find a safari a life changing experience."

Indeed, it is, Emily thought, as Nick picked up another oyster and downed it in one.

"The strangest couple I ever had here was a lady from the UK with her partner. They'd travelled out in business class, booked a private transfer to the lodge, but didn't mix with any of the guests for the entire three days they were here.

"Her partner didn't say a single word to anyone, not even to her. She fussed over him all the time. Putting a bib around his neck at mealtimes, reading him the menu, discussing the wine list, chatting away to him. She booked a private vehicle for game drives and off they would go, him dressed in his safari gear, binoculars around his neck."

Emily frowned. "Was there something wrong with him then?"

"No, nothing wrong with him, quiet easy-going type. But I think there might have been a lot wrong with her. I mean who goes on safari with their teddy bear – a bloody great big one as well!"

Emily doubled up with laughter, tears streaming down her face, as she tried to imagine it. She rummaged in her bag for a tissue and wiped her eyes.

"So, what did you do when she brought him up to the bar for pre-dinner drinks?"

"Poured him a double gin and tonic, of course. Every guest is treated with the utmost respect here."

He started to laugh with her. "As for the poor ranger who took them out for their game drives – well, I can't imagine what he thought."

Emily wiped the tears from her eyes again. "So, she paid for his seat next to her on the flight out – everything, as if he was a real person. I wonder what she did for a living?"

"Psychiatrist - very well known."

Chapter Twenty-Two

The next morning, Nick said goodbye to the American and French guests, then came and joined her at her table. "I'm expecting fourteen more guests today, all coming in from different lodges, but Mike can handle them."

The waiter filled his cup with fresh coffee. Nick blew on it before taking a tentative sip. "How about coming on a drive with me? I'll organise a picnic. There's a spot down by the river where Jonathan and I used to play and swim, as kids. I'd like to show it to you, it's pretty special."

Emily stood up immediately. "My own private game drive, with a personal game ranger. How lucky can a girl get? I'll get my hat and camera then we can go." She laughed, and scampered back to her suite, side stepping a brightly coloured lizard which, feeling the vibrations of her hurried footsteps, scuttled off the wooden deck and disappeared.

They drove at a slow pace through the bush, she could feel the dryness of it and the now familiar smell of wild herbs, as the vehicle rocked negotiating the shallow river bed.

As the vehicle crested a hill they saw an impressive herd of impala grazing. As the vehicle approached them they scattered, leaping into the air like delicate ballerinas as they fled from the vehicle.

Nick stopped reaching for his camera. "They leap to confuse predators – it doesn't always work, mind you, but it's what they do to spook a lion. Did you know this?"

She shook her head.

"Impala are smart, you'll often see them following a herd of lion preferring this to being in the front."

She frowned. "It's safer, right?"

"Much safer, they can see what the lions are up to, if they were in front they'd be putting bets on who would be eaten first. Animals are clever, they know the order of things. The reason they survive is because they have no emotions – only instincts."

He put his camera down and drove on. "Animals fight sometimes, during the mating season, sometimes over a kill, but they don't go around punching each other, or arguing. They don't know what being unfaithful is and they don't blow each other up. They kill for no other reason than to eat. They're not political or religious, they don't need cars or clothes or a house. They're quite content with what God has provided them with," he slapped at a mosquito on his arm.

"The human race has much to learn from them but it's too late now, greed and power has taken over basic instincts."

Driving on Nick pulled up next to a herd of elephant drinking at a water hole. He put his finger to his lips warning her to be quiet. It was a breeding herd with small babies hiding beneath their mother's great bellies. On occasion, feeling brave, one or two would dart out on unsteady legs to splash in the water, squealing and waving their rubbery trunks in the air.

After an hour, Nick reversed the vehicle, moving away from them. Lost for words she reached for his hand in appreciation for showing her the elephants and their calves, his fingers covered hers in response.

London seemed a million miles away with its honking, belching trucks, sirens wailing, music pulsing from open windows and the endless streams of people pushing their way through the crowded pavements, or squeezing onto tube trains. She couldn't bear the thought of going back.

They stopped for lunch under a towering pepper tree, at the edge of the river. Nick put down a blanket and unpacked the hamper the chef had prepared for them. They chatted, at ease with each other, whilst they ate chilled prawns and chicken legs. He pointed out the different birds to her, handing her the binoculars to study them. The radio crackled in the vehicle, Nick ignored it.

"I have great respect for two things in life," he said, chewing on a chicken leg, "wild animals and beautiful women."

She raised her eyebrow in question, waving away another persistent fly with her hand.

"They're both unpredictable. It's the reason they fascinate me," he said, wiping his mouth on a napkin and smiling.

"Well you certainly know enough about wild animals."

"I want to know more about you…" His voice trailed off as he reached for his camera. "May I?"

84

"What? Know more about me, or take my photo?"

"Both."

She looked steadily at him as he took his shots, then rested her back against the tree closing her eyes. Emily knew he wanted to touch her, as she wanted to touch him, a physical yearning overriding any logic in her head.

He leaned over to remove a twig tangled in her hair. Her eyes flew open at his touch.

"Nick…" she felt the brush of his lips across the length of hers.

Hearing the growl of a vehicle in the distance, Nick cursed, moving away from her. A cloud of dust heralded the arrival of Mike Connelly.

"Sorry, boss. I tried to get you on the radio but it doesn't seem to be working," he looked at them innocently, stroking his beard. "The generator's broken down. I thought I should let you know."

Nick sighed. "Okay, thanks, we'll just finish up here then head back."

He lifted the hamper into the back of the vehicle and climbed into the driver's seat. Emily hopped in beside him.

Nick gave her a rueful smile. "I'll never be able to concentrate on fixing the generator now. I wanted to kiss you. It's all I'll be able to think about for the rest of the day. He changed gear inching the vehicle over the shallow river bed.

She reached for his hand and left it there. He curled his fingers around hers and navigated his way back to the lodge with one hand on the wheel, the other covering hers.

Chapter Twenty-Three

The sun was going down, a huge sizzling red orb sinking behind the trees, leaving only their dark, mute, silhouettes; a smattering of stars began to appear. Emily soaped her body under the outside shower feeling the cooling air on her skin. As the water cascaded over her, she closed her eyes. Her tumbled thoughts were of Nick, how startled she'd been when she opened her eyes finding his face so close to hers, how much she'd wanted him to kiss her. He hadn't let go of her hand until they reached the lodge.

She turned off the shower and dried herself. Opening a pot of body cream, she scooped up a handful, feeling her warm skin absorbing it. Inhaling its perfume, she opened her wardrobe door.

She chose the long suede skirt and soft cream shirt, then brushed her hair until it crackled and shone in the light from the lamp. Throwing a pale-yellow pashmina around her shoulders she picked up her bag and left the tent.

The sound of drums announced dinner was about to be served. Nick was waiting for her. As soon as the other guests were seated at their tables he joined her. She unfolded her napkin placing it over her lap. Without thinking she reached across the table and squeezed his hand, then hastily withdrew it.

*****

After dinner she leaned back in her chair sighing with contentment, then looked up at the inky sky and the millions of stars above. "The stars are incredible tonight, Nick. I feel I could almost touch them, they're so low. Would you teach me about them?

"My Dad could bring down a rhino with a single well-placed dart, but he didn't have a clue about the galaxy."

"Of course. After we've eaten I'll see if anyone else would care to join us – I'm hoping there won't be any takers…"

After dinner Nick made the rounds of his other guests. Rubbing his hands together, he came back to her. "It seems it's just the two of us after all. My guests seem to be having a bit of a party."

He collected the telescope from the library, then picked up a lit hurricane lamp and walked with her to the perimeter of the lodge. He set the heavy telescope on the tripod, then pointed it up at the stars. He turned down the lamp and the blackness of the night surrounded them. He reached out his hand and found her own waiting for him. Together they took in the staggering sight of the shimmering heavens above them.

Not letting go of her hand he pointed upwards. "The three stars lined up in a row are known as Orion's Belt." He waited, watching her searching the skies before locating them.

"See his sword and shoulders? That's Bellatrix and Betelgeuse. If you look you can see his faithful dog, Sirius, at his heel." He showed her the Southern Cross and the Seven Sisters.

"Once you can read the stars and identify them, you can use them as a sort of compass so, if you ever got lost, you can find your way home. It takes a bit of practice but it's doable."

She giggled. "I doubt they would help me in England, far too much cloud cover."

"Maybe you should think about coming back to Africa, where your roots are. It's a good life…" he said casually.

He cleared his throat, trying to concentrate on the heavens above, acutely aware of the softness and warmth of her hand in his. Distracted he continued. "The reason the stars are clear is because there's no artificial lights anywhere in the area, so they sparkle up there in all their glory, as they were meant to. There's Venus, not a star as you know, but she fits up there in all her shimmering beauty, with the others."

He put his arms around her. "Bugger the stars…" pulling her towards him he tentatively kissed her, and she responded.

He knew then, without any doubt, the woman he was holding in his arms was holding his future.

Breathlessly they pulled apart and he tried to turn his attention back to the star filled sky. He hadn't meant to kiss her, especially with the other guests within shouting distance. "Bugger the stars," he muttered again as he kissed her, tasting her on his lips.

She opened her eyes. "I've been out in a wilderness of my own, for so long, with no stars to help me. But I think I might have found my way now.

"Just as well because I can't remember a single name of any of the stars you've told me about." She gave a nervous laugh. "I'm all over the place..." Putting her hand around his neck she pulled him back to her lips.

"I'm crazy about you," he said, between kisses, "you've thrown my well-ordered life into chaos. I didn't expect this. When I saw you at the airport, looking lost, I felt something I haven't felt before. It was as though I'd been holding my breath all my life, until that moment, and I thought, well there you are at last, where have you been? What kept you?"

He cupped her face in his hands. "I think we'd be good together. I know it's all a bit sudden but it feels right."

He kissed her languidly, then with reluctance pulled away from her. "I suppose we'd better get back, before someone comes searching for us." He dismantled the telescope, then pulled her into his arms again. "I want to help you bury your past - I need to bury mine – we can help each other."

She reached up and kissed him, then traced his eyebrows and lips with her fingers. "I have to go back to London, but I don't want to think about it at the moment."

He held her hand as they walked back to the lodge. "Just an idea - why don't we take a few days before your trip back to London and go to Lamu? You mentioned you were going there, and I've been often over the years. It'll give us some time together, away from the lodge and all the other guests. I want to have you to myself for a few days."

"Yes," she said without hesitation, "I'd love to."

They returned to the other guests.

"See anything interesting out there?" one of them called out.

She gave him her wide smile. "Yes, I did! I saw something I liked very much indeed."

She turned back to Nick. "Please don't tell me you took the mad psychiatrist and her bear out for a bit of star gazing?"

"Course I did! He didn't say a word. But must have been as impressed as you were with my knowledge of the heavens and the galaxy. He was struck dumb."

Chapter Twenty-Four

The following day more guests were flown in. The lodge was full, and Nick was kept busy entertaining the new arrivals. It wasn't possible for him to dine alone with Emily that night, the new guests would expect him to sit with them. They paid good money to stay at the lodge, he had told her, expecting a lot of his time and attention.

It wouldn't have gone unnoticed he escorted Emily back to her suite each evening. To compromise, and happy with the knowledge that tomorrow he would have her to himself in Lamu, he sat everyone at one big table, making sure the waiter would seat Emily as close to him as he could manage.

*****

Emily saw two of the new guests sitting around the camp fire. Smiling, and full of a new-found confidence, she went to join them. This, if everything worked out, would be her job in the future.

She pulled out a chair next to the fire, introducing herself. The two-middle aged American women, Joanna and Meredith, talked about the animals they'd seen and the other lodges they'd stayed at on their various safaris to Kenya. Emily listened dreamily, trying to imagine herself as Nick's partner.

He would expect her to get involved with entertaining their guests, and she was more than willing to learn the ropes. She tuned back into the conversation between the two women, eager to embrace this tentative, but promising, new life.

Nick walked over to check their drinks. Discreetly he ran his finger over Emily's shoulder, then returned to the bar and the small crowd gathered there.

"My, but our host is gorgeous," Meredith purred, watching his retreating figure. "Where do they find all these divine game rangers. Do you think they're picked for their good looks?"

Joanne giggled. "I guess they must be. There's something about a tanned young man, dressed in khaki which turns me on. Maybe it's because they appear fearless, so knowledgeable about the bush, all the wild animals. They seem more masculine than the guys you see in New York City, they make me feel all kinda cute and feminine."

Meredith bent forward reaching for her glass, her diamond rings flashing in the firelight. "It's one of the reasons I come out here every year. I can't think of any other kind of holiday where a single woman is the centre of attention." She wiggled her fingers when she saw Nick looking towards them from the bar.

"Oh, my God, I think he's looking at me," she squeaked, "anyway, where was I? Oh yeah, so on safari the game rangers make sure you're not left sitting on your own, feeling like a leper. I just love all the attention especially at my age!"

Meredith looked over at Nick and laughed. "At fifty-seven I guess I don't stand much of a chance with him, but no harm in dreaming."

Emily smiled politely, taking a sip of her wine. Meredith may well be in her mid-fifties but looked years younger; she must have had work done.

Meredith wriggled back in her chair making herself comfortable. "This is my fourth visit to Kenya and I've stayed at a few lodges. On my first trip I came alone. I have to admit I was apprehensive, but it was the best thing I'd ever done.

"They call it khaki fever over here. Guests falling in love with the game rangers, at the drop of a bush hat. I fell in love with one at a lodge here in the Mara. It was a fabulous affair - he was almost as gorgeous as Nick.

"He'd come to my suite when all the other guests were asleep, leaving early in the morning. I thought this was it - the big love affair of my life. Nothing like sex in the bush with the lions roaring in the distance. Brings out your basic animal instincts!"

Joanna leaned forward hanging onto her every word. "So, what happened?"

Meredith looked out over the dark bush, taking another sip of her martini, ignoring the question. "What I didn't realise was these guys spend a lot of time out here on their own. When they see a single woman they fancy, they pretty much know they can have her."

Joanna laughed nodding in agreement. "Yup, happened to me as well!"

Emily held her breath. The two thwarted women seemed to have a lot of knowledge about this particular scenario.

A shiny hard-shelled beetle crash landed on the table next to her, flipping over onto its back. She flicked it over and away with more force than she intended. She sat back sucking her throbbing finger.

Meredith continued. "If she's willing and let me tell you most of the single ones are, they know they can have her at the click of their fingers. I thought my ranger was serious about me. He told me he loved me, for heaven's sake. Hadn't met anyone else like me and I believed him!" She rolled her eyes heavenward.

"He even asked me to come and live here. Told me he was crazy about me, that we'd be good together. But," she sighed dramatically, "it was nothing more than a brief affair for him. God knows how many other women he'd fooled. I was never stupid enough to do it again...but having said that Nick Kennedy could make me waver – I wonder if he's up for it?"

Her friend interrupted her. "Hey, maybe he's married?"

"So what!" Meredith retorted. "That's never stopped them. I don't see a wife around anywhere. If he has got one she's probably in Nairobi looking after the kids, in which case he would have a clear run at anything taking his fancy! And I think someone already has judging by the amount of attention he's paying the woman at the bar – ah well, too bad then. I bet he'd be like a wild animal in bed!"

Emily glanced over at Nick, standing at the bar chatting to an attractive blonde who appeared to be on her own. He dipped his head towards her, laughing at something. Was this all part of a tried and tested routine? He wanted her, yes, she knew that. He wanted the blonde as well by the look of things.

She stared out into the black night, dismayed at this revelation. Was this how it all worked then?

The two American women chatted on, unaware of Emily's discomfort at their previous conversation. *I'm being stupid*, she thought, *he has to be nice to all his guests*. But Meredith and Joanna had planted a fat seed of doubt.

*****

During dinner Nick watched her across the dinner table. The waiter had failed with the seating arrangements, Emily had been too quick for him. The blonde, Bonnie, was sitting next to him, Emily had ended up next to Meredith.

His powers of observation, honed to perfection in the bush, made him an astute judge of people, their emotions - their body language. He could see Emily was disturbed about something. He didn't think it was her past this time.

Bonnie, began to irritate him. The shrill nasal American accent was putting his teeth on edge. He sighed. Well, it went with the territory. He was expected to be nice to all his guests, no matter how irritating, or boring, they were. Bonnie was available, she'd hinted as much in the bar, coming onto him blatantly.

He looked at Emily again. This was something she would have to learn to deal with. In his experience women seemed to lose their inhibitions at a safari lodge. She would have to trust him. Girls like Natalie understood how it all worked, it was something Emily would have to accept and get used to.

His ear tuned back to Bonnie. She had her hand on his arm. "Honey, would you mind walking me back to my tent, I'm ready for bed…" He tensed, knowing where this was heading.

Emily was watching him. He gestured to Mike sitting at the end of the table. "Would you see Bonnie to her tent, Mike?" He turned back to his guest. "Sorry Bonnie, I have something else needing my attention in the bar. Goodnight."

Nick glanced at Emily, but she was staring out into the night, her face devoid of expression. As he passed her chair, he bent his head and whispered to her.

"Wait for me, I'll join you as soon as everyone has gone to bed. A few more hours, then we'll be away from here."

Meredith leaned towards Emily, pointing at Mike and Bonnie's retreating backs. "See, what did I tell you? By the way, what was Nick whispering in your ear about? Has he singled you out for later?"

Meredith shrugged. "I'll put bets on the blonde in the bar or you. God, I hate getting old, even by candle light I don't think I'm in the running anymore."

Emily glared at her then stared out into the black night, refusing to comment.

Emily sat next to the dying embers of the camp fire, most of the other guests having now retired for the night, except for Meredith. Emily took her diary out of her bag, put her glasses on, and flicked through what she'd written. How happily she'd described her feelings for him. She closed it hugging it to her chest.

It would all work out, she trusted him. He said when the last guest had gone to bed he would come and sit with her. She poked the fire with a stick to get more heat and waited, trying to ignore Meredith.

*****

Nick had been watching her whilst he waited for his last guest to leave the bar. Now he wiped his hands on a towel and walked towards the fire.

Mike came hurrying down the path, stopping him en-route. "Sorry, boss," he said breathlessly, "the guest I walked to her tent, Bonnie? She's just buzzed me. She's adamant her necklace has been stolen. She refuses to let me help her find it, insists she wants the owner to sort it out – no one else will do. You'd better go, she looks the type who might sue if you don't find it…" he said cheerfully.

Nick cursed under his breath. Taking a lingering look at Emily, he strode towards the woman's suite.

Meredith nudged Emily. "See, I told you he was up for it! Same old, same old. Anyway, I'm off, Emily. Goodnight."

*****

Emily began to feel cold, the fire was almost out. He hadn't come to sit with her as he'd promised. She could feel a headache crowning the top of her head. Surprised, and somewhat annoyed, she stood up. He might at least have checked on her before going off to wherever he'd gone. She wrapped her jacket around her shoulders and picked up her bag and diary. With trepidation she looked from right to left for animals, as she made her way along the path. All the staff had retired, so much for Nick's advice of always being walked back to your tent, she thought bitterly.

She saw the shadow of two people, lit by a lamp inside. Suddenly the tent flap was thrust aside and Nick strode out, tucking his shirt into his long trousers, pulling up his zip and adjusting his belt.

Bonnie stepped out watching him go, then stretched her slim body, the negligee hiding nothing of her naked body. A sob rose from Emily's throat as she stumbled towards her own tent. With scrabbling fingers, she pulled the zip up and sat down on the edge of the bed.

A jackal howled outside, a long forlorn sound. She buried her face into the pillow, chastising herself for being stupid enough to fall in love with someone who was unsuitable and untrustworthy. Once again, she'd made a complete and utter idiot of herself.

The *whoop, whoop, whoop,* followed by the hideous cackling laughter of a hyena, adding to her misery.

Chapter Twenty-Five

Nick waited for Emily to appear for breakfast. He'd hurried back to the fire last night, hoping to find her there, waiting for him, but there was no sign of her, her suite had been shrouded in darkness.

Now he watched her approach with a smile, which faded as he studied her body language.

She marched up to him, sunglasses covering her eyes, her body stiff with anger. "I'm leaving today. I'm going to Lamu – alone," she said in a tight voice. "Please arrange to have someone fly me there. I don't care what it costs, or if it's inconvenient."

"Look, if this is about last night, I can explain…" he said.

She cut him off. "I don't need you to explain anything to me, you owe me nothing! Just get me on a plane." With a toss of her head she threw her hat down on a chair and sat down in the other one, ignoring him, her foot beating a rapid tattoo on the wooden deck.

He hesitated then stood up and made his way to the office. There was no point in trying to explain anything to her whilst she was as wound up as she was, with the other guests within earshot. An argument with one of his guests would be unforgivable.

He made the necessary arrangements to fly her out. A pilot bringing in guests to another lodge was returning to Nairobi with no passengers, he was happy to make a detour to Honey Badger to collect another one.

Nick could tell by the way she sat drumming her fingers on the arm of the chair, she was beyond furious.

"The plane will be here in half an hour," he said to her, "the pilot has changed his flight plan and will take you to Manda Island, you'll have to catch the dhow from there to Lamu…"

"Don't trouble yourself with my travel arrangements," she snapped, "I don't need your help or assistance with anything after I leave here."

"I'll send someone to collect your luggage and drive you to the air strip." he said abruptly. He looked at her with dismay, so hostile and cold, so different from the warm, loving, woman he'd held with so much hope, in his arms.

She drummed her foot on the deck. "Coming back to Africa was the worst thing I could have done...why is it so damn hard to trust anyone anymore?"

His heart sank, she was putting him in the same bracket as her difficult dead husband. This wasn't going to be easy.

The vehicle pulled up in front of the lodge and the driver loaded her luggage into the vehicle. Nick opened the passenger door for her. Shrugging off his outstretched hand to help her, she got in and folded her arms, fisting her hands.

"Emily, please don't leave like this, let me explain. Guests can sometimes be very demanding..."

She jammed her sunglasses on, hiding her eyes, cutting him off mid-sentence. "I found you attractive, Nick, but you know something? You're not my type at all. It was fun flirting with you, it helped pass the time. I'd no intention of taking this relationship anywhere. Sorry if you thought otherwise. The last thing I would want to do is spend the rest of my life in the middle of nowhere. No thank you."

"I don't believe that's true Emily."

"If I were you I'd get back to your guests," she said with a tight smile, "I'm sure you're needed there, one way or another."

He watched the plane as it flew low over the lodge. His throat tightened as he half lifted his arm in farewell. They could have been good together - or maybe not, judging by her reaction to him this morning. He watched until the aircraft was a speck in the sky, and she was gone.

He checked his watch – too soon for a drink. No, he thought with bitterness, it wasn't going to be the answer. It never had been.

Chapter Twenty Six

Barely registering her fear of flying Emily stared through the window as the plane began its descent on its approach to Manda Island, here the dhow would take her across to Lamu. She mumbled her thanks to the pilot and collected her luggage.

She knew the name of the hotel where she and Nick were supposed to have stayed and was confident the reservation would still be in place. She descended the crumbling steps of the dock and boarded the old wooden dhow. The ride across the channel took little more than ten minutes. En-route they passed other ancient wooden dhows gliding past in silence, with timeless elegance, their single sails turning to seduce the wind.

The dhow docked disgorging its passengers onto the dirt quayside street. Open-air restaurants faced the water where people sat watching the ceaseless traffic on the water. Gentle, sad faced, donkeys struggled with their burdens as they daintily picked their way through the crowds of fisherman.

A young porter, wearing a ragged shirt and shorts, gave her a beguiling smile, begging to be allowed to carry her luggage. Exhausted by emotion she nodded, giving him the name of the hotel. He trotted ahead of her, her bag balanced on his head, glancing back to make sure she was keeping up. He turned into a narrow, dark cobbled, passageway beckoning her to follow him.

They wove their way up and across the wide, shady town square. She saw shops down darkened alleyways with their doors flung open, selling fruit, silver jewellery, spices and freshly squeezed fruit juice. An old man tended his meat on a brazier, calling out for customers.

They edged past numerous donkeys, loaded with goods, some with riders, some ambling along on their own.

"Plenty donkey on Lamu!" the porter called out cheerfully. "No cars on island, everything carried by donkey."

A one eyed, bone thin, ginger cat sat in a single puddle of sunlight, washing his body languidly. A group of men, dressed in long white robes, wearing tiny embroidered caps, sat sipping what she presumed was their strong Arabic coffee, under a mango tree. Honey-coloured Arab women swathed in black buibui glided past, their eyes dark and kohl rimmed, on their way back from the market, their baskets looped over their arms.

The porter stopped outside two immense carved doors, studded with brass, and off-loaded her bag from his head, wiping away the sweat from his brow with a ragged sleeve.

"Memsahib, here is your hotel." He pushed open the door and gestured for her to enter. As she did so, another man materialised from the cool archways of the courtyard.

"*Jambo*, Miss Hunter, welcome. I am Azzam, the manager." he looked over her shoulder. "Mr Kennedy?"

"Mr Kennedy won't be joining me." She told him in a tight voice, unable to conjure up a smile.

She paid off the porter and thanked him, before she followed the surprised Azzam. A fountain trickled in the centre of the big white courtyard, sculptures and urns nestled in recessed niches. The floors were made from slabs of cool stone. The ubiquitous scarlet bougainvillea cascaded down the walls. Stone steps led to the three levels of the small boutique hotel with the traditional open-air roof garden at the top.

Azzam stopped on the third level, opening the door to her room, depositing her luggage, he bowed and glided away on soundless bare feet.

She looked around. A four-poster bed filled most of the room, its billowing cotton mosquito nets tied back with cream ribbons. At the foot of the bed sat a large Zanzibar chest, its leather surface faded in places, the intricate brass work and studs now dull with age.

A claw footed bath, its brass taps polished and gleaming, stood in one corner.

Emily threw open the balcony doors squinting at the sunlight. The room looked out over the rooftops of the old town and the sea. A blood red hibiscus tree leaned against the left of the balcony, the air heavy with the cloying scent of jasmine and jacaranda. She took a deep breath – the ideal place to begin the process of getting over Nick bloody Kennedy.

She turned, eyeing the bed, feeling the tears mounting, she lifted her head to stem the flow, thinking of how humiliated she felt. She closed the doors and lay on the bed. In the cool of the room she drifted off into an exhausted sleep, warm tears slithering into her hair.

In the early evening, Emily awoke and took a bath. Changing into a long cotton dress, she made her way up to the deserted roof garden. Taking the camera out of her bag she deleted every photo she'd taken of Nick.

Now her rage over Nick's infidelity had subsided she was left with a deep ache and longing for what had looked so promising. But more than anything else she was mortified. She'd shared so much personal information with him, her life with Marcus, the empty years in London, until she summoned up enough courage to take this trip to Kenya.

She cringed when she thought of the words of love she'd spoken to him. He must have been laughing at her. How stupid she'd been to trust him. How well did she know him? He hadn't talked about the girl who died, and she wondered why. Something else she'd noticed – he didn't drink anything alcoholic, not even a glass of wine with dinner. Whatever his problems were, and it was clear he had some, they were not hers anymore, and never had been.

Now as evening fell, she sat on the rooftop of the hotel nursing a cold glass of lemonade she'd brought from her room. Feeling a little steadier, she contemplated her future. She would spend three days in Lamu then head back to Mombasa, where the ship would be waiting to carry her home.

Azzam padded up the stairs to the roof garden, bearing a bottle of cold wine in an ice bucket and a platter of papaya, dates, samosas and cold prawns.

"Will Memsahib be eating in the hotel tonight, or perhaps in town?"

She eyed the platter forcing a smile. "I'm sure this will be as much as I can eat, thank you Azzam. I think I'll sit up here and watch the night life."

"Very good. You are the only guest tonight." She looked up at him in surprise.

"Mr Kennedy wished for you both to be the only guests in the hotel for three days for which he paid accordingly. He made many plans to entertain you…" he shrugged his shoulders. "It is the will of Allah."

"More like the will of Nick bloody Kennedy," she muttered under her breath.

"Should you require anything please be pulling this cord and I will return. Otherwise I wish you *Lala Salama*, good night, I will see you in the morning. You may wish to have your breakfast in your room or perhaps up here. I will look for you tomorrow."

Emily sipped her drink, leaning over the warm, well-worn, ledge of the roof top. She looked down over the open roofs, watching families having their evening meal, crouching women sweeping out their backyards with short tied together sticks, children playing in the dust, the haunting cry of the Muezzin, calling the faithful to prayer. On other rooftops she could see couples dining by the flickering light of ornate lamps. A young man swinging in his hammock, a middle-aged man silhouetted by wooden shutters, head bent, writing into the night.

A moth flitted against the roof garden lamp, pinging against the bulb, drawn to something it could never have. The parallel was not lost on her.

She heard the music from the opera, La Boheme, emanating from one of the rooftops around her; the lovers' chorus brought an unexpected lump to her throat. She looked around for the source of the music and located it. A woman sat motionless on her own roof top, a cigarette smouldering between her fingers.

Emily shivered, sensing the woman's loneliness seeping across the roof tops. Now she knew why she didn't like opera…thwarted love, broken dreams and untimely deaths.

Love was like childhood, something she would not have again. A child-like sob escaped from her lips as she turned and went back to her room.

*****

It was still dark when she was awakened by the amplified call to prayer. She listened, lulled by the timeless sound as it echoed through the town. The Holy men, the *muezzins* chanting from the minarets, a haunting melodic string of vocal sounds, which came to an abrupt end.

She watched the darkness turn to a pale grey as the morning light crept through the shuttered doors, illuminating the old uneven stone walls with its softness. She burrowed down into the bed, imagining life probably hadn't changed here for hundreds of years, unlike hers which seemed to make a habit of it.

Emily spent the days listlessly visiting the fish and produce market and exploring the tiny dark shops down the myriad of alleyways.

In one of the jewellery shops she bought a silver and amber ring for Rebecca and an ornate snuff box for Ben.

Coming out of the shop she noticed a torn poster stuck to the side of a crumbling wall. It was a black and white picture of George Bush, offering one million dollars for his capture. She shuddered. There were posters all over America with the same message, but different faces – Osama Bin Laden and the Shadow Dancer.

Stopping at a street café for coffee, she overheard two English men discussing the Twin Towers, how the news of the assault on America was known in Lamu, one of the oldest Muslim communities in the world, before the international press got hold of it. It was disturbing to say the least. With an unexpected suddenness, she'd felt the need to get off the island and return to London.

She thought back to Nick talking about the Shadow Dancer and Bin Laden. Just what kind of animals were they? What kind of religion allowed these people to be so barbaric? And yet, these island Muslims seemed kind and gentle, humble. She knew it was wrong to judge them all by the actions of a few fanatics bent on death and destruction.

*****

On her last evening, she strolled down to the quayside for supper, the air heavy with the aroma of grilled fish and garlic. Sitting alone amongst the busy tables she tried not to think about how her life in London would seem now. She would miss the animals, the bush and the light here, the friendliness of the people and their ready smiles. So many things. The sky now hung with swollen rain clouds, through which shafts of fading sunlight rendered them almost biblical.

She would miss the shadows of Africa, the colours of the sunsets, the warmth of the days, and the spectacular skies at night, brimming over with brilliant stars. The sky by day seemed bigger and higher than any other sky she had ever seen.

Emily felt she had lost everything, not just Nick. Recent events had shattered the silly dream she had had of living in Africa again. About a new life in a place where she had always been happy and free, who she really was, and her longing to go back to her childhood, to the same innocence when everything was possible. Africa, it was true could be heaven, but it could also be hell. Unforgiving but irreplaceable.

*****

The journey back to England seemed endless. The difference this time was she had nothing to look forward to, unlike her journey out, when she'd been optimistic and hopeful of a fresh start in life.

She saw him when she closed her eyes, she dreamed about him, tormented by the memory of him. She'd fallen in love; but more disturbing was the realisation, she had not loved Marcus. How she felt about Nick was quite different, more intense, as if she had always known him.

She sat in a deckchair, her coat wrapped around her, a blanket around her legs watching as the grey, ghostly, outline of England loomed into view.

She would throw herself into her job, at Becoming Books. Forget all about him, forget all about Kenya. Forget about the triumphant grin on Bonnie's face when she had passed her on the way to reception, before checking out. She rubbed the corner of her eye with her finger, the bitter wind making her eyes stream again. The navy of an equatorial sky already becoming a distant memory.

Chapter Twenty-Seven

Rebecca was there to meet her when she disembarked. On the drive back to London, Emily talked briefly about the safari and the boat trip, but nothing else. Then lapsed into silence.

Rebecca glanced at her, noticing how wonderful she looked. "No flirting with the game rangers then Em?"

Emily stared out of the window then turned to look at Rebecca. "A brief mild flirtation, nothing more. The bush can make anything romantic, but not for me. No, I didn't meet anyone memorable."

Rebecca indicated she was turning left, before glancing at her again. Emily seemed to be unhappier now than she was when she left on her journey. Perhaps she'd been wrong to suggest the trip in the first place.

"Was it good to be back in Africa though? Back where you belong?"

"I don't belong there anymore Becks. I never want to go back. It wasn't how I imagined it would be at all. Not how I remembered it. It was like being slapped in the face.

"Anyway, how's business at Becoming Books?"

*****

Emily unpacked her suitcase, Oliver rubbed against her legs, happy to have her home. What should she do with all the safari clothes she would never wear again? She held the diary close to her chest, willing herself not to read the words she'd written with such passion. The frangipani flower slipped from between the pages and she bent to pick it up, her cheeks wet. It still held a faint perfume – she placed it back inside, burying the book at the back of the cupboard before slamming the door shut, making Oliver leap back in alarm, his tail frizzing up like a Christmas tree.

Chapter Twenty-Eight

Emily sat waiting for her hairdresser to finish with his client, before attending to her. She flicked through an old edition of a society magazine. Licking her finger, she turned the page over. She bit her lip, tasting the tinny warmth of blood.

Pages of photographs leapt out at her. *'Well known Kenyan family announce the engagement of their youngest son.'* Nick Kennedy and Natalie.

She studied the photographs, then searched for the date of the magazine. A year after she'd left. The photo shoot had been held at the game lodge.

The pictures blurred in front of her. He was going to marry, or had married, the girl he'd known all his life. Well good luck to her, she thought bitterly, there won't be any happy ever after in that marriage.

Emily had received emails from Nick, begging her to let him explain about the episode at the lodge. But she'd deleted them without responding, until they'd stopped coming.

She sipped her now cold coffee and stared at the photograph of Natalie. A pretty girl, slender and blonde, with the healthy look of someone who spent a lot of time outdoors.

She studied each photograph. A group shot featured a good-looking man standing next to a small slight woman looking shyly at the camera from under her eyelashes. This must be his brother Jonathan and his wife Kim. The tall aristocratic man with his arm around a striking looking woman – his parents she presumed.

She took off her glasses and closed the magazine, throwing it back on the table next to her. Natalie would have to keep her eyes open for any two-legged predators, yes, good luck to her!

*****

Emily walked back to her flat, from the book shop. It was cold and wet, the rain slashed down soaking her legs and feet. The wind was picking up as she let herself in. Peeling off her wet clothes, she put on her dressing gown, burrowing down into its warmth. She went through to the sitting room and looked out of the window, wet leaves stuck to the glass, she felt her spirits start to sink, as they often did at the beginning of November.

She dreaded the short days, the long nights of winter, the emptiness and the memories snaking under the front door. The loneliness taking up more space than she thought possible.

With Oliver on her lap, the warmth of him seeping through her bath robe, she watched the trees bend in the storm, thinking about another world, hot and dry, with blood red, fiery sunsets, another place with brilliant star filled skies and pearl grey mornings – and her memories of him.

Emily turned on the lamp on the table, imagining Nick at the lodge, with things running like clockwork. Natalie had probably taken over some of the duties. They did have a lot in common, the same background, the same love of the bush. She knew living in Kenya would have been different, but no point in even thinking about it now. She pulled Oliver closer, hearing his deep purr as he butted her chin with his head. And what would she have done with Oliver?

*****

Emily was working on the Becoming Books monthly newsletter. Outside the rain spat against the glass like hot fat in a chip pan, the wind rattled the shop windows jangling her nerves. She saw Rebecca beckoning her to her office.

"Bloody awful weather forecast for the week - and worse for the rest of the month. I've been trying to think of a way to cheer things up a bit. God knows the world needs it with all the terror threats and the bloody Shadow Dancer, adding to everyone's fears. Even I don't like going to crowded places anymore, you never know when the bastard or Bin Laden will hit again and believe you me they're not done with us yet!

"The attack on London last July was just the beginning. I don't think I'll ever be brave enough to go on the Underground or catch another bus, ever again."

She grinned at Emily. "Pity, Bin Laden is a terrorist though. Put him in a good suit, chop off his beard and he's not bad looking when you think about it." Rebecca took a sip of her tea and scratched her head with a pencil.

"Anyway, I think we should have another book signing. Lord knows there are enough new authors around who would kill for one. Christmas will be here before we know it - we have to do something to generate sales."

Rebecca paced her small office. "I thought we could pull the crowds in with a good coffee table book. Something a bit different. Maybe a book about India, or the Seychelles, or anywhere exotic, anywhere warm. What do you think?"

Emily pushed her glasses on top of her hair, giving it some thought. "Yes. Good idea. We could run a theme through the store to complement the book, build up the atmosphere."

Rebecca grinned at her. "Sounds good, anything come to mind?"

"Well maybe we can find a book about fabulous islands, the Maldives or somewhere, cover the floor with sand, hire some artificial palm trees, then on the evening of the signing we could serve exotic cocktails in coconut shells to match the mood."

Rebecca laughed. "Then all we would need is some hot sunshine to go with it plus a hot barman to mix the cocktails but, hey, I like the way your mind's working on this. Let's find a fabulous book and get to work on the publicity.

"We do need to woof up the book sales a bit," she said looking around the now empty shop. "Things have been quiet for most of the year, it's worrying to say the least. When the accountant starts to look like an undertaker I know we're in trouble…"

Emily headed back to her desk, glad of a project to keep her mind occupied.

For the next two hours, she went through the non-fiction books they stocked. India, China, France, Australia. They were all impressive with their excellent photography. It would be difficult to make a choice. Of course, it would make life a lot easier if the author lived in England. It would be the deciding factor, she thought, as her mind filtered through various ideas.

She looked out of the window seeing a sparrow, its feathers clumped together with rain, looking as depressed as she felt.

The next morning Rebecca burst into the shop. "Hey, I've found the perfect book," she shouted to Emily who was making some tea at the back of the shop. "It's perfect. We don't stock any of them but it's not a problem, the publisher's in London, we can order on consignment." She waved a piece of paper under Emily's nose.

"I looked at it on the internet last night. It's called *'Timeless Africa'* and the photographer, Anthony Edmunds, lives in London, the photographs are fabulous. I wanted to jump on a plane and whizz off to Tanzania straight away. Didn't like the shots of snakes though," she shuddered. "On second thoughts it would put me off jumping on a plane!"

Emily pulled her glasses down from the top of her head and studied the fuzzy print out from the internet. If these shots were anything to go by, then the book was just what they were looking for. She looked up at Rebecca and grinned.

"Yup. This should crack it. I know all about safaris… I should be able to conjure up some bush atmosphere in the shop. We can get some South African wine and plates of bugs for snacks, then finish off with some of that famous East African coffee."

Rebecca laughed, whipping the pages out of Emily's hand. "No bugs, thank you, my girl. I think they have something called biltong, I'm sure we can get it somewhere in London. I'll leave you to organise the food and booze. I'm going to get onto the publishers right away, see if the author is available."

"Yes, I know what biltong is – it gets stuck in your teeth!"

Chapter Twenty-Nine

Emily was busy. The author had agreed to the book signing. The Tanzanian Tourist Board promised her posters of animals, sunsets, trees and birds to decorate the walls of the shop. She tracked down a supplier of South African wine, and Rebecca delighted the publisher by ordering fifty books – sale or return.

Emily was enjoying arranging the event – despite her memories she found the theme of Africa was fun and uplifting. Happy with what she'd achieved during the day, she left the shop, heading home.

*****

Rebecca slammed down the telephone in despair, putting her head in her hands. "Hey what's up?" Emily called out to her, looking up from the pile of books she was cataloguing.

"Oy! Disaster, is what. The photographer won't be able to make the book signing, after all. He's gone on an assignment in West Africa, last minute thing apparently, no doubt for a bucket load of money. Now what are we going to do?" she wailed.

Emily thought quickly. "The invitations haven't gone out yet so it's not a train smash. We'll keep the theme the same, find another author who specialised in Africa. Come on, get onto it, we can't waste any time. Do some research, let's see how we can retrieve the situation. We've still got time, not much I admit, but enough to turn this around."

Emily went back to her desk confident Rebecca would come up with an alternative. There were lots of books on wildlife. She'd find something.

Three hours later Rebecca had solved the problem. "Okay I've found another book. It's called '*Beneath the Shimmering Stars,*' and, to be honest, it's far better than our first choice. All the shots have been taken in, um, Tanzania I think, so we don't have to send all the publicity material back to the tourist board.

"I've spoken to the publishers and by pure chance the author will be in London two weeks before Christmas, he's agreed to do a book signing. Now we have our fabulous event back! Everything's fixed and I've been onto the printers to change the title and author.

"Phew, that was a close call – we're back on track."

Emily smiled at her friend, pleased with the news. "I've got a pile of work to get through, so I'm going to leave you to it. I knew you'd come up with something!"

Rebecca snatched up her bag. "I'm going out for a couple of hours; all this stress has freaked me out. I'll see you tomorrow. Nothing like a bit of shopping to calm the nerves!"

* * * * *

The next morning Emily wandered into Rebecca's office and poured herself a cup of coffee. "Would you like a top up Becks, it's still hot?"

Rebecca shook her head. "No thanks, I'm still a bit hyped up from yesterday. I'm going down to the publishers to sort some things out. Then onto the printers to pick up the new invitations. I'll be back after lunch, okay?"

Rebecca bounced back into the shop after lunch, her eyes shining. "Whoa, this gets better and better – wait 'til you see what the author looks like!"

Emily took off her glasses and looked up with interest. "What's his name then, the author from Tanzania?"

"The gorgeous, gorgeous, author, who will have the women swooning and grovelling at his feet, is not from Tanzania, the publisher corrected me on this - he's from Kenya. His name's Nick Kennedy."

Emily felt the colour draining from her face, as she held onto to the edge of the table. *Oh God!*

Rebecca continued, oblivious to her friend's stricken face, her voice full of excitement. "I've already got the printing company standing by to do some blow up shots of Nick. We'll use the one featured on the inside of the book. I'll get an extra copy for myself which I shall pin up next to my bed – well, only if my darling Ben isn't around." Humming happily, she picked up the phone.

Emily managed to get back to her own desk before her knees buckled. It was too late to stop things now. How could she even begin to explain about Nick to Rebecca. How was she going to get out of the book signing?

Dozens of thoughts swirled around her mind. The pencil snapped in half in her hands, her armpits prickled with anxiety. She needed to make a plan. Even if it meant losing her job, the job she loved so much. Rebecca would never forgive her or understand the reasons why. But she *must* come up with something over the week-end. A reason why she couldn't be there for the signing. She put her hands between her knees to stop them shaking.

*****

By Monday morning Emily had failed to come up with any feasible excuse. She knew she couldn't let Rebecca down, not at the last minute.

On Tuesday, she collected posters from the Kenyan Tourist Board and trudged back to the shop hoping the soaking rain wouldn't damage them. She'd already returned the other posters to the Tanzanian Tourism office, despite Rebecca's protests that lions are lions, wherever they are, they all looked the same to her. Emily knew otherwise.

She arrived at the shop and stopped dead. His eyes followed her as she moved to the front door. Her heart turned over at the sight of him again. She felt the blood singing in her ears as her legs began to shake.

Rebecca had been busy. His photograph in the window was already attracting glances from the women passing by. He was still impossibly handsome, his startling sapphire blue eyes seemed to penetrate hers, taking her breath away as they'd done the first time she'd met him at the airport in Nairobi.

Arranged in the window were his books, creating a kaleidoscope of colours on a cold grey winter's morning. On the front cover was a magnificent shot of a leopard lying languidly along the branch of a tree, its green eyes almost the same colour as hers.

"What do you think?" Rebecca called out cheerfully. "If his face doesn't pull the crowds in, nothing will. I've put a copy of his book on your desk. Your own personal copy to lust over. They arrived from the publisher this morning."

Emily sat down, opening the book '*Beneath the Shimmering Stars.*' The photographs were sensitive, evocative, much like the man himself, she thought miserably. To indicate the end of a chapter Nick had used a shot of a frangipani flower.

Pulling herself together she sat up straight. He was married, that was the end of it. She would go through with the book signing but keep as far away from him as possible. Anyway, it was just one evening, she would manage, would have to manage, no doubt he would have Natalie in tow.

*****

The day she was dreading arrived. Nick Kennedy had landed in London two days before. He'd phoned Rebecca from the hotel, telling her he'd be at the shop around five.

Emily dressed with care. She chose a long grey skirt with a matching short jacket, her favourite shell pink jumper and grey boots. She stood back from the mirror, studying herself. Her hair curled around the collar of her jacket, her eyes looked calmly back at her.

"Hey Oliver, what do you think – how do I look?" Oliver looked up at the sound of his name, he juddered his whiskers and squeaked at her, before curling up on the pillow and burrowing his head under his tail.

If she could get her heart back to a regular beat, stop her hands from shaking, she would be able to handle things. Anyway, he would no doubt bring his wife with him, just how much worse could the situation get?

Throughout the day she cast surreptitious glances at the clock, willing time to slow down so she could get her thoughts in order. The caterers arrived with the food and wine. The store was alive with the colours of Africa depicted by the posters, people were already pouring into the shop. Instead of Christmas carols she'd chosen some haunting African music, she shivered even though the shop was warm. She checked everything was ready then stood next to her desk fiddling with the books and shuffling files around.

She sensed his presence as soon as he entered the shop. He was wearing his usual khaki trousers and shirt, a soft suede jacket thrown around his shoulders. Nick looked as if he came from another world, a world far removed from rain splashed London.

Emily watched him make his way through the crowds of admiring women, not seeing her. Then he stopped and looked around. She held her breath. His eyes searched the crowd, the same way they did when he was searching for a particular animal in the bush, his body held still, his head up.

Then he saw her.

It seemed to Emily the entire room went quiet and everyone had disappeared, leaving the two of them alone. Their eyes locked, neither of them moved. Then he was striding towards her.

*****

"Emily." He looked into her eyes, not daring to touch her for fear of what it might do to him. She was more beautiful, if it was possible, than when he'd last seen her over two years ago. She was watching him warily, like a wild animal sensing a predator close by.

She straightened her back and held out her hand.

"Hello Nick. How are you?" she said coolly, looking up at him for a brief moment. He held onto her hand. Not a day went by when he hadn't thought about her. He'd sent emails to which she hadn't replied. He was sure someone as gorgeous as Emily would have found a man by now and married him. He checked her finger, no wedding ring, no engagement ring either. He smiled into her eyes.

"I had no idea this was your book shop. It's wonderful to see you, you're looking as gorgeous as the day I flew you across the bush. I want to hear all your news. Perhaps I could take you out for dinner after the book signing? No husband hanging around anywhere?" He held his breath and looked at her hearing the hopefulness in his voice.

"No Nick, I'm afraid it won't be possible," she glanced over his shoulder. "No wife hanging around anywhere?"

She pulled her hand away from his. "Let's catch up some other time. Meanwhile put all these women out of their misery. Sign their books for them." She waved him away, muttering something about checking on the caterers.

*****

The evening was a success. In between signing the books, she noticed Nick looked up often to see where she was. She was always in the same place, watching him watching her. The familiar touch of his hand in hers had sent a bolt through her. She'd not anticipated feeling this way, not after all this time, but she did. She'd fallen in love with

112

him and stayed that way. But he was now married. There was nothing she could do to change the situation.

*****

Nick's hand was beginning to ache. He lifted his head and groaned, the queue was still long. He couldn't believe his eyes when he saw her there. He knew she worked in a book shop but there were hundreds of them in London, and he'd been lucky enough to end up in hers. Distracted, he handed over a book and received another one.

He was ridiculously pleased to see her, even though she'd hadn't given him what could be described as a warm and welcoming greeting. But he would sort this out later when he'd have some time alone with her. He would find a way.

With the last customer out of the door, Rebecca thanked Nick for a successful evening, shooing them both out of the shop. The rain had stopped and a watery moon floated above them.

They stood on the wet pavement, the passing car lights reflecting in the puddles, the only sound was the hissing of wet tyres passing. Emily stared down at her boots as if she'd never seen them before.

Nick cleared his throat. "Are you sure you won't change your mind about dinner, Emily? We both have to eat, it seems pointless to eat alone. I want to hear what you've been up to."

"No. I'm having dinner with someone at my place, I hope you enjoy the rest of your stay in London. Goodbye Nick."

He stared at her stiff retreating back, then turned around and walked back to his hotel.

Chapter Thirty

Nick returned to the book store late in the afternoon. Rebecca looked up from her computer. "No more books to sign Nick, or did you forget something?"

"Yes," he said, perching on the edge of her desk. "Where's Emily?"

"She called in sick, must have been something she ate, maybe the biltong – I didn't like the look of it myself. Hey, did you two have dinner last night?"

"No, she turned me down flat."

"She turned you down!" Rebecca squeaked.

"Said she was having dinner with someone at her place."

Rebecca tried to stifle a laugh. "Ah, yes, she has dinner with him every night – his name's Oliver."

A faint smile crossed his face. "Her cat, right?"

Rebecca looked at him sharply and frowned. "Yeah, but how did you know she has a cat? What's going on here?"

"Now look Rebecca, I need your help. I have a couple of days left in London and I need to speak to Emily, it's important."

"Nick, I don't know what's going on, but I'm happy to call her and tell her you're here," she picked up the phone. "It will have to be her decision whether she wants to speak to you. Hello Emily?"

He leaned across, taking the phone from Rebecca's hand.

"Emily, It's Nick. The least you can do is hear my side of things. Let's have dinner and sort this whole thing out. Neither of us has anything to lose. Please?"

He handed back the phone satisfied. This time she could not fly off into the sky without hearing him out.

"Thanks Rebecca. I know you're curious and there is a story here. I need to see Emily and explain things. She's agreed to meet me for dinner at the Italian restaurant around the corner."

Rebecca nodded. "Good. I hope for your sake she doesn't cancel at the last minute! I had a feeling you two had met somewhere before. So, you met her in Kenya…she wasn't happy when she came back to London. I'm thinking it might have had something to do with you, right?"

"It did. I intend to sort the whole thing out." He kissed her cheek, then strode out of the door, whistling with happiness through his teeth.

He found the small restaurant, booked a table, then went back to the hotel to shower and change.

At quarter to seven he was back. He stared fixedly at the door waiting for her to appear. He hoped she wouldn't change her mind. So far, she'd proved to be somewhat capricious.

Then there she was, wearing a black coat with a vivid crimson lining and a matching scarf. He rose from his seat and held out her chair. Taking her coat and scarf, he handed them, unseeingly, to the waiter.

The waiter returned to take their drinks order. Emily asked for a glass of wine. They looked at each other, saying nothing. Without thinking he reached for her hand across the table. She snatched it back as if he'd set fire to it.

Emily took a deep breath ignoring what he'd hoped would be a beguiling smile.

"So, Nick, whatever we thought we had together wasn't there after all, was it? Despite *the magic of the bush* you were always banging on about.

"I saw the coverage of your engagement in a magazine. You married Natalie. Congratulations. I hope she manages to keep you out of your guest's bedrooms."

He saw the anger flash across her face as she continued.

"I made an absolute fool of myself. I thought we had something…" her voice trailed off. She took another deep breath. "Have you got children?"

Without waiting for a reply, she opened her menu, feigning a great deal of interest in what was on offer. He rubbed his eyes carelessly.

The waiter appeared, then rolled his eyes as Nick waved him away. Nick leaned across the table and removed the menu from her hand, putting it to one side. He turned her face towards him.

"I wanted to explain to you about that bloody awful American woman but you were furious and left in such a hurry. I fell in love with you, Emily. I don't know what else to say."

His words didn't seem to touch her as she looked at him, a stony expression on her face.

"I know how it must have appeared. American clients can be tricky, they have a habit of suing for anything if it doesn't go right. She'd lost her necklace which fortunately I found."

Emily glanced around the restaurant, a look of disinterest on her face. "Really? Good for you, I'm sure she was thrilled to bits. Did she reward you, one way or another, for your hard work? Take you to her bed perhaps? Because it's what it looked like to me!"

"For God's sake *look* at me, what do I have to say to make you believe me?"

"Try goodbye – that always seems to work."

Nick shook his head with frustration. "It often happens with single women on safari, they want a bit of romance. But we know how to handle those situations. I'm not the kind of man who has affairs Emily. Why would I have jeopardised a future with you for a one-night stand with one of my guests? Even you must be able to see it wouldn't make any sense?"

She was watching him with dark untrusting eyes. "So, what difference does any of this make now? You're married, so none of what happened matters anyway. It didn't take you long to replace me with Natalie did it?"

"I didn't marry Natalie. In many ways, we were too close as friends, too much like siblings. I felt she would be a safe bet after you tipped my life upside down. But in the end, I couldn't go through with it. Natalie deserved someone who would love her far more than I could. I couldn't marry her when I was in love with someone else."

He sat back exhausted. "I'm telling you the truth, I need you to believe me."

He watched the slight smile lighting up her eyes. "When I saw you coming out of her tent, with your shirt hanging out, adjusting your belt, and she with just about nothing on, well, what do you think I thought Nick!"

He smiled with relief, she believed him. "It's rare for game rangers to have affairs with their guests. If they do they're fired – it's not worth the risk."

He fluttered his fingers at the still hovering waiter, waving him away again. "I tried to explain this to you in my emails but you ignored them. Why?"

116

"I was angry with you. I didn't think you were telling me the truth – it's easy to write things, try and explain things. I didn't believe you."

"But you do now – why?"

"Because I can see in your eyes you're telling me the truth Nick. It's what made me trust you when I first met you – your eyes."

He shook his head at the memory, stretching across the table to take her hand. This time she didn't pull away. "I had to crawl all over the bloody tent, check behind the bed and all the other furniture, no wonder my shirt was hanging out. I was furious. But you were so mad with me, you wouldn't give me the chance to explain anything. Remind me in the future never to get on the wrong side of you." He reached for her other hand. "There will be one won't there?"

Her eyes filled with tears, as she nodded and gave him a wobbly smile.

Nick turned and raised his hand at the waiter who had given up trying to take their order for dinner. "A bottle of your best champagne please."

She still loved him and God, he loved her.

After a dinner neither one of them would recall eating, the champagne remaining untouched, he helped her on with her coat and they left the restaurant. He hailed a taxi and Emily gave the driver her address. He put his arms around her, holding her. "I want to stay with you," he whispered into her hair, "I want to wake up in the morning with you in my arms."

"I want you to stay Nick…I'm terrified you'll disappear and it'll all go wrong again."

"Nothing will go wrong, I promise you. I'm not going to let you escape again!"

Chapter Thirty-One

After coffee and toast the next morning, Nick reluctantly took a shower and dressed.

"I'd better get back to the hotel and pack. I'll come back to the shop after the meeting with my publisher. I don't think he'll get much sense out of me though. You've worn me out! He gave her a lingering kiss before shrugging on his jacket.

"I'll see you later. Don't go running off again Emily...I'll never be able to find you in London. I could track you down in the bush with no problem, but here would be more than a challenge."

"I'm not going anywhere without you," she said nuzzling into his neck. "I'd better take a shower and get dressed as well. I can't wait to tell Rebecca the news."

They had talked long into the early hours of the morning. He'd told her about Pippa, his guilt at the loss of her life which he felt responsible for, then the steady spiral into alcoholism. His life out of control.

"Did you love her?"

He had folded her back into his arms pulling the duvet over them, Oliver clinging with grim determination to the cover. "I thought I did, although now I realise it wasn't love. You are love. Now I understand what it means. It's why I want to marry you Emily. I know I can make you happy. I'll look after you. Will you think about it?"

"No, Nick, I won't think about it."

He had pulled away from her, holding her at arm's length. "Why not? Is it me or Kenya? You don't want to live there? I don't understand. I love you and you love me – it's all very simple..."

"Oh, Nick, my love, I don't need to think about it – not for a second. Of course, I'll marry you. Tomorrow if you like!"

He had pulled her close again. "You have a weird sense of humour Emily Hunter, you got me there. I'd get down on one knee in any other

118

country with a decent climate, but I'm buggered if I'm going to do it here, your bedroom is freezing! Let's think of another way of sealing this commitment we've just made to each other…"

Making love again had felt different, as though something in the world had shifted, making it feel like an almost out of body experience. Afterwards she had lain on his chest, hearing the steady beat of his heart.

"Nick?"

"Yes, my darling?"

"What about Oliver? May I bring him with me to the lodge?"

Oliver moved up the duvet and sat on Nick's chest, staring at him, his whiskers juddering, a slight squeak emanating from his mouth, his big blue eyes round with interest.

"Of course you can, but it might be a bit of a problem, Emily. There are too many wild animals around the lodge. He could get taken out by any one of them. We'd have to keep him locked up in a room, which I don't think you would like, any more than I would.

"I think you'll have to put his future first. He's a handsome fellow, it shouldn't be too hard to re-home him. Now, come on, don't get upset, we'll make a plan for Oliver. Maybe Rebecca would take him?"

*****

Emily was confident Rebecca would be more than happy to give her a few hours off to finalise the plans with Nick. Her whole future, which the day before was so grey and desolate, now glittered ahead like the sun on the ocean. Humming, she pushed open the door to the book shop.

"Hey, Emily," Rebecca called out. "Did you have dinner with Nick? Or did you cancel at the last minute as you're inclined to do?" She glanced up. "Wow, you look fantastic this morning."

She narrowed her eyes. "Did you spend the night with him then? You're looking rather smug I must say?"

Feeling highly emotional she flung her arms around Rebecca. "I'm going to live in Kenya, we're getting married there. I'm still reeling with shock. And, yes, we did spend the night together. When I woke up I couldn't believe he was lying next to me," she grinned at her friend. "He looks more than cute first thing in the morning with his hair all mussed up…"

"Your eyes are glazing over Emily… but why didn't you tell me you'd already met him before the book signing?"

Emily told her about how they met, how they parted. It was a good story, now it would have the perfect ending.

"He's flying out to Kenya tonight. His manager, Mike, is going on leave so he has to get back to the lodge. We've so much we need to go through, there's a lot to plan. I'll have to sell my flat and give up my job here - sorry Becks. It'll take a couple of months to sort things out. Would it be alright if I have a couple of hours off this afternoon? After the book signing, the marriage proposal, and, er, last night, I'm exhausted. I want to spend a few precious hours with him before he leaves tonight."

"Of course! Take the whole day if you want. It's a nice one for a change, freezing but sunny, go take a walk in the park. Come back tomorrow and don't feel bad about resigning. I've been trying to find the right moment to tell you. I'm going to sell the shop and join Ben in France, I have someone keen to buy. I don't want to struggle with it anymore. I also want some fun in my life!"

*****

Hand in hand they walked through the park, stopping often to kiss and hold each other, oblivious to everything and everyone.

"I'll have to rely on all your friends and family for the wedding." she said. "I only have Rebecca, I'm sure she'd love a trip to Kenya with Ben!"

"I've enough friends and family for two, my darling. You won't feel alone at all. Now, about the actual ceremony itself, what would you prefer? A beach, or bush, wedding?"

Emily felt dizzy with the possibilities. "On the beach, I think. Yes, a beach wedding would be wonderful."

He gathered her into the warmth of his arms. "Then a beach wedding it'll be. There are some great spots down on the coast; we have a house there. I've called my parents, they're over the moon and dying to meet you. There won't be any kind of announcement made until you arrive in the country."

He hugged her. "Now, let's set a date shall we – how about May fourteenth? My birthday, which means I'll always have happy ones afterwards, remembering the day I married you.

"It'll give you four months before we get married, enough time to tie everything up here in London and sell your flat. I'll do my best to fly

120

back here if I can. It'll depend on how the bookings look at the lodge, its high season so they'll be back to back."

He cupped her face in his hands and kissed her. She wound her arms around him snuggling into the warmth of his jacket as he continued. "Once I've introduced you to my parents and a few close friends in Nairobi, I'll take you down to Mombasa to our house there and you can ready yourself for the wedding.

"Now where shall we go on honeymoon? You can choose anywhere in the whole world, I don't care where. We'll have to be back at Honey Badger the end of the first week in June though."

Emily looked up at him. "Oh? Mike does a good job of running it when you're away doesn't he?"

"Yes, he does, but the whole lodge has been taken over by a VIP party. It was booked eighteen months ago, members of the Royal family here. A huge amount of security is involved, plus all the other things associated with hosting a Royal or two. I have to ensure everything runs like clockwork. The Palace insist I'm there. We need all the publicity we can get in Kenya at the moment, these terrorist attacks, Bin Laden and the Shadow Dancer are claiming responsibility for, are having a bad effect on tourism, people are frightened to travel. So, it's important I'm there – we're both there."

He pulled her close and kissed the top of her head. "A baptism of fire for you, my darling, but together we'll give them a safari they'll never forget."

Emily looked up at him again and laughed. "Whoa, slow down sweetheart. It's all going too fast for me, all a bit overwhelming." She gestured towards a damp bench. "I need to sit down for a minute."

"Sorry, I'm getting carried away. Let's take it step by step. You'll need to get your wedding dress here, there's not much of a selection in Nairobi!

"I'm sorry I won't be here with you to choose your engagement ring. When you find the one you want, get the jeweller to courier it to me at my club. I'll have it with me at the airport when you arrive, in case I can't manage to get back to London before then."

He held up his hands and smiled. "There I go again, getting carried away."

Emily kissed him. Oh, God she loved this man. "Things are happening so fast, but once I come back down to earth I'll organise everything. The first thing is to put the flat on the market. Then I must find a home for Oliver, Rebecca won't be able to take him, she's going to move to France to be with Ben, her partner. It's going to be hard for me, I do so love Oliver."

She bit her lip as tears flooded her eyes. He pulled her close. "But you're right," her voice was muffled next to his chest, "he wouldn't be happy out in the bush surrounded by strange scents and animals, cooped up in a room for his own safety. I must put his welfare first, but it's going to break my heart."

They walked and talked until the watery sun disappeared and the afternoon sky began to darken. Holding her close, in the back of the taxi, he kissed her neck. "I'll miss you, you have no idea how much…"

When the taxi pulled up outside her flat, she turned to him. "I'll be with you as soon as possible, sweetheart. Once I get a buyer for my flat I'll wing my way to you." She kissed him, not wanting to let him go, then opened the taxi door. "Oh, by the way, something I keep meaning to ask you…why did you call your book *Beneath the Shimmering Stars*, it's a beautiful title?"

He stood next to her on the pavement, the taxi's engine idling next to them. "When I thought about you, which was all the time, I remembered telling you the story about when people die they re-appear as a star. The first time I kissed you out in the bush, when I pointed out the stars you wanted to know about. The stars will always remind me of falling in love with you. I used the frangipani flower at the end of each chapter because it reminded me of our picnic in the bush – I never forgot you, I never stopped loving you," he kissed her. "I never will."

He patted his pocket, pulling out an envelope. "Here are all my contact details, my lodge location, my folks address and their phone numbers. You'll need all these details when you arrive in Nairobi and complete the arrival forms. Keep them somewhere safe!"

*****

Emily watched the rear lights of the taxi disappear, the red of them reflecting on the wet road, taking him back to the hotel for his luggage, then out to the airport. Clutching her envelope, she hurried inside with happy tears.

Tomorrow she would call the estate agency. She was longing to be out under those shimmering stars with him again, even though, after their honeymoon, she would have to share him with the Royal party for a week. Nothing like being thrown in at the deep end, but she could do it with Nick showing her the ropes. She hugged her own shoulders, shivering with nerves and excitement.

Tomorrow she would also start to look for her wedding dress – then buy a book on the correct protocol required for dealing with a Royal or two.

She scooped up Oliver from the bed and hugged him. "I promise I'll find you the best home ever Oliver. You wouldn't like Africa, it smells different and you might get eaten by a wild animal. You wouldn't be happy there, you'd be scared and it would be way too hot for you." She kissed the top of his head, now damp with tears.

Chapter Thirty-Two

The next few weeks crawled past. Potential buyers came to see the flat, but there were no offers. Christmas came and went but she didn't mind being alone. Every Christmas, from now on, would be with Nick. He'd spent the holiday at the lodge with his guests, phoning her as often as he could. Rebecca had flown to Paris to be with Ben.

The trip Nick planned back to England was cancelled at the last moment. He'd called, explaining his father had had what the doctors suspected was a mild stroke, he didn't feel he could leave his mother to cope on her own.

Understanding the closeness of the family Emily had assured him they would be together soon. He must stay put and support his mother.

Rebecca had finalised the deal with the potential buyer for the book shop. She was going to move in with Ben and write her own book. Something she'd been itching to do for years.

"I'm sorry we'll miss your wedding Emily." She said over their farewell lunch, at the end of January. "Ben's taking a break from his business, he's planning a three-month cruise around the Med. We're leaving mid-February. He's also talking about buying a property in the South of France to use as a base, rather than Paris."

She reached over and squeezed her friend's hand. "Nick's a good man. You can say goodbye to all your bad memories, and ghosts, and start a new life with a new man, in a new country. I promise we'll come and see you both. I can't wait to go on a safari after all the excitement of yours!"

At first Emily missed going to work each day, but there was plenty of things to keep her busy. With glee, she bundled up all her winter clothes, the heavy boots and warm hats – she wouldn't need anything warm where she was going, they could all be donated to a charity shop. As she rummaged through the cupboards she came across the box she'd packed her safari clothes in. She shook out the soft suede jacket. That was a definite, she was going to take the jacket. The safari boots were almost new, she put them to one side; she would be doing something she once thought would be impossible. Retracing her footsteps in them.

Clearing the drawers, she came across the book she'd kept her notes in on her first trip to Kenya. Flicking through the pages she found the pressed frangipani, now brown and flat but still with the faint hint of the memory of its perfume. She would put it in her passport and take it back home where it belonged.

Oh God, it was wonderful to be in love, everything in the world looked different, people seemed friendlier somehow, even food was more piquant, the world was a beautiful place to be in. And, oh God, she loved this man called Nick Kennedy.

With no offers on the flat Emily decided to drop the asking price. She couldn't wait any longer. When a young couple made an offer, she accepted without hesitation.

The buyers wanted to purchase all the furniture so there wasn't much left to pack and store, just a few treasured pieces, including the journal she'd kept when she had first met Nick, her old laptop, bank statements, tax returns, her marriage certificate and the death certificate for Marcus, his photograph, and other personal papers. She needed a new laptop and Nick assured her he would get her one in Nairobi. There was an internet café down the road which she would use in the interim.

But the best thing of all was the new owners wanted to take Oliver. They'd fallen for him as soon as he had strolled into the sitting room, looking his most adorable best.

Emily called the removal company making the arrangements for her things to be collected. Not knowing how long they would be in storage she paid them up front for six months, telling them she would let them know when, and where, they should send her boxes to, and if there was a balance outstanding she would settle it before they shipped her things.

Nick called her as often as he could, although it was difficult out there in the bush. Emails were sporadic and the lines went down often, either because of the elephants pushing over the telegraph poles, or the erratic electricity supply. Finally, she was able to book her flight, on Nick's credit card.

"I'll be arriving in seven days' time, on Kenya Airways!" She told him excitedly over the phone "I can't wait to see you, it seems like an eternity since you were in London. I arrive on the fourteen of April at some ungodly hour in the morning. You should be proud of me, I used to be terrified of flying, as you may remember. You've made me brave and fearless. I love you Nicholas Kennedy!"

Across the miles she heard the relief in his voice. "I'll be here waiting for you at the airport. It's been the longest three and a half months of my life. I'm bringing your engagement ring with me, it arrived by courier from the jewellers.

"Ma has organised something spectacular for a beach wedding. When you arrive, she'll send out the invitations telling the guests where and when. Jonathan and Kim are arriving a week after you, they're staying for a month. I've never seen my parents as happy as they are at the moment…"

"Isn't it cutting things a bit fine, sweetheart, with the invitations I mean? Maybe you should send them out now, give people a bit more time?"

He laughed. "There'll be a stampede to get to our wedding, it will be the highlight of the social calendar, everyone will drop everything to be seen there, and to come and check you out! Now hurry up and get over here!"

She heard the slight hesitation in his voice. "You won't change your mind will you Emily?"

"Are you mad! Of course I won't change my mind! If I don't pitch up it will mean I've met a man who's even more fabulous than you – which would be impossible because I love you too much!

"How are the plans going for the Royal safari?"

He groaned down the phone. "It's challenging to say the least, apart from the Royals there are bodyguards, personal doctors, press secretaries, personal secretaries, a nanny or two, hairdressers, and all sorts of other staff necessary for the trip. God knows why they need bodyguards in the bush, it's the safest place for them to be. They're not going to get knocked off in the middle of nowhere but, no, the bodyguards are not negotiable! Bit of a nightmare, but we're getting there, I'm working with the British High Commission here in Nairobi to make sure I give them everything they demand.

"I think you'll enjoy it though – it will be a unique experience."

She laughed as she tried to imagine it all, then put the phone down and danced around the room. One week to go. She'd chosen her wedding dress, which needed some slight alterations; all she had to do now was collect it. She had a first-class ticket so she could carry her dress with her, and have it taken care of during the flight.

Emily had given a set of keys to the estate agent for the new owners, she'd post hers through the letter box when she left for the airport.

Chapter Thirty-Three

Deborah Kennedy put the receiver down smiling to herself. She'd never heard her son sound so happy. Emily would be arriving in a weeks' time. She glanced at the framed photographs of her sons clustered next to the phone. Nick astride one of his polo ponies; another playing rugby, one with his arm around a pretty girl, whose name she could not recall, after a tennis match. Nick standing with pride next to his first Cessna aircraft. So many memories…

She checked herself in the mirror above the telephone. Her dark sapphire blue eyes looked back at her, her high cheek bones catching the light as she turned her head. Her ash blonde hair pulled back to the nape of her neck in a velvet clasp.

Satisfied, Deborah turned away, her thoughts still with her son.

Nick's road to recovery had been fraught with difficulties after his girlfriend Pippa died.

He'd been driving Pippa home to her family ranch after a party in town, having had too much to drink.

The male water buck appeared from nowhere. Startled by the lights of the vehicle it leapt across the road colliding with the bonnet, Nick swerved to avoid it and crashed into a tree. Pippa was killed.

After being released from hospital, his only injury being a deep gash on his forehead, Nick spiralled into depression. Blaming himself for Pippa's death, he began to drink heavily.

He'd become a fixture at all the popular bars in town and at the club, until, one by one, his friends dropped him and the club banned him from the bar. Natalie had been the only one able to persuade him to go into a rehab centre in South Africa.

When he came home, his father's suggestion that Nick should take over the running of the lodge was a stroke of genius. It had steered Nick away from any temptations, given him a purpose in life, and Mike Connelly had kept an eye on him out there in the bush.

Now he had Emily she could stop worrying about him. He would be alright. Emily, had lost her own husband, there would be empathy, understanding, between them. Coming from South Africa her own roots, like Nick's, were deeply embedded in the African soil. She sounded perfect.

Deborah walked through the sitting room, stopping to straighten a picture. She looked around the familiar room with its heavy upholstered cream cushioned armchairs, and tasselled skirts. The low square table, polished to a high sheen, crowded with books and magazines, a bowl of apricot roses at its centre. At the tall windows, long cream velvet curtains brushed the surface of the floor, held back by navy blue sashes.

Picking a pale grey feather off the carpet she went in search of her husband. "Hugh! Where are you? I have wonderful news."

"On the veranda darling - ready for a gin and tonic! What are you sounding so excited about?"

"That was Nick on the phone. Emily will be arriving in Nairobi in a week's time. There's so much still to be done! Now, did you mention a gin and tonic? I could certainly murder one. William!"

William appeared, looking cool and regal in his floor length white *kanzu*, embroidered waistcoat and red fez on his head, bearing a tray with two glasses, an ice bucket already beading, a bottle of gin, tonic water, sliced limes and a pair of silver ice tongs.

"Ah, thank you William, it's such a gorgeous evening and we're in the mood to celebrate! Nick's bride will arrive soon. I can't believe it."

William's familiar smile broadened with the news. "Yes, such happy news. There will be much celebrating in Nairobi. Allah Akbar. God is good." He put the tray down, then padded away on bare feet, back into the cool shadows of the house, humming tunelessly.

Hugh made swift work of mixing their drinks. Handing his wife hers, he sank into a cane chair, which creaked in protest, and looked out over the immaculate lawns and gardens of their home.

He gave a contented sigh. "With another wedding in the family, maybe it'll lead to some much-needed grandchildren. Jonathan and Kim seem to be taking their time about coming up with any – maybe Nick and Emily will beat them to it! Cheers"

"Cheers!" screamed the African Grey parrot from his perch in the corner. "*Jambo* Debs!"

Hugh rolled his eyes. "Damn bird, can't believe we've had him for forty odd years, and not given him a name. Let's hope when Emily gets here he doesn't use any bad language in her presence. Where did he learn all those swear words anyway?"

She raised her eyebrow. "Why Nick and Jonathan of course – and their friends from school. Parrots always seem to evoke the devil in children. They whisper all the naughty words to them, thinking no one will ever know, then one day they open their beak and out it all comes. Yes, we can hold our boys, and their chums, responsible for the bad language."

Deborah glanced at her husband. He was, and always would be, the beacon of her life, the love of her life. She'd met him here in Nairobi when she was twenty years old, he was twenty-eight. She was visiting Kenya from England, staying with an old-school friend in Nairobi, and had been introduced to Hugh at the club. At first, she'd been in awe of the famous aristocratic family but Hugh was down to earth and unassuming. Tall, dark haired, and most attractive, she'd fallen in love with him within weeks. They married three months later.

Deborah and Hugh Kennedy, with their privileged lifestyle, and Hugh's fortune inherited from his father, were not oblivious to the poverty around them, and worked long and hard to improve the lives of others. There were fewer parties these days as they put all their energy into their many charities.

She reached for Hugh's hand. "Nick has some photographs of Emily, he wanted to show them to us when he came back from London, but we were in Mombasa and missed his return, if you remember?

"He wants to send some pegs, or something, to the computer, so we can see what she looks like. I told him we'd rather have some nice printed photos. He's going to bring them when he comes through to Nairobi to collect Emily. He's bringing her here for lunch. She'll be staying at the Norfolk but if she feels comfortable enough with the idea, I'll suggest she stays here with us, in the guest cottage. What do you think, darling?"

Hugh looked up puzzled. "Good idea, but what the devil are pegs Debs?"

"I have no idea. Milly does all those sorts of things, we'll have to ask her."

Milly, Deborah's personal assistant, spent three mornings a week helping with the paperwork for her various charities. Deborah never touched the computer, it was all way beyond her.

130

"Anyway Hugh," she said now, "there's a lot to be organised for the wedding. We need to finalise the list of guests to be invited." She wrote something in her note book." I'll do the social side and leave business and political invitations to you. Gladys and Arthur have already been invited, of course. It's years since our last trip to the UK to see them." She shuddered and took a sip of her drink.

"It's a beautiful old estate and the house is heavenly but oh, the terrible cold and dampness seeping through the walls! There'll be no excuse for them not to visit us for a change, as long as Arthur can be persuaded to fly – after all it's their godson who's getting married." She scribbled something on her list. "I hope Arthur behaves himself though, the gardeners at the club won't take kindly to him swiping the heads off the roses with his walking stick."

She scribbled another note. "Gladys wanted to invite Emily out to their place for a week-end, to get to know her, but Nick didn't think it was a good idea and I had to agree with him. Arthur can be a bit, shall we say, overwhelming, if you don't know him well. Nick said he didn't want Emily to bolt with fright and call the whole thing off!"

Hugh laughed and sipped his drink, fondling the warm ears of their Labrador, Barney, listening to the plans for the wedding and how Deborah was planning to launch Emily into Nairobi society.

"Bit short notice for the invitations to go out isn't it darling?" he said mildly, putting his glass down, with practiced ease, on the table at his side.

"Nonsense Hugh! There's not a single person on my list who won't drop everything to be seen at the wedding and watch Nick get married, or more to the point see what the bride looks like. Trust me I know what I'm talking about. The day Emily steps foot on Kenyan soil, Milly will send out all the invitations."

She scribbled something else on her list. "Oh, one more thing darling, Nick insists we make no announcements about the wedding, or tell anyone her name. He wants to ease her in gently, as he told me, he seems more than protective of her. So, don't go trumpeting it around the club, will you? I don't want the local press to be swarming around her when she arrives. It'll be too much for her."

William appeared to take the drinks tray away. "Dinner is served Memsahib."

Deborah helped herself to the salad before pushing the bowl towards her husband. "In a way, it was a good thing Natalie and Nick didn't get married. I love her dearly, goodness knows, I've known her since she was a baby, but she wasn't right for him, not as a wife. Still, it all worked out for the best, and the money the glossy magazine paid for the engagement announcement paid for another rural clinic."

They took coffee in the sitting room, where the log fire hissed and crackled with the damp wood. Hugh sat in his favourite chair and sighed with content.

"Funny thing about possessions," he mused. "You don't own them at all. They possess you in the end. Look at all these things," he gestured around the room. "I inherited from my father and no doubt he did from his.

"The boys won't want all this furniture when we go y'know. Maybe the odd thing or two for memories sake… but young people want their own things, not all this ancient stuff they call antiques these days." He shook his head. "A bit like us I suppose.

"The only positive thing about getting old is I won't have to see the ugly face of terrorism, or Bin Laden and the bloody Shadow Dancer, destroying our world. It won't get any better Debs, that I can tell you. Not sure I want to be around as the world becomes more dangerous. I worry about our boys and their future."

"Come on darling, you're getting maudlin. Yes, Nick getting married is a big step, not our little boy anymore. It's how it is, the wheel of life or whatever it's called. We won't need to worry about a relapse now. Whatever we think about the world, there is nothing we can do to change it, so no point in worrying about it."

Hugh stood up stiffly. "Come on, old girl, time for bed." He held out his hand for hers but she continued to stare into the fire. "Debs?"

He saw confusion in her eyes. "Are you alright?"

"Yes, of course! I seem to be forgetting things, like the names of people I should invite to the wedding…maybe I've too much on my mind at the moment. Oh, it will be so good to have our boys together again. I miss Jonathan, Singapore seems so far away."

Hugh stroked her hair. "Milly will help you with all the wedding plans, stop worrying about things. There's a storm coming, let's get settled in bed before the power goes off again.

Chapter Thirty-Four

Emily was leaving England the following evening. Her suitcase was packed; her passport zipped into the side pocket, her ticket in her handbag. Oliver had been delivered to the cattery, he would be collected by the new owners of the flat at the end of the week. She had cried all the way home, still seeing his big blue eyes staring at her accusingly as she handed him over.

Now all she had to do was collect her wedding dress. She ran down the stairs, paused, then went back up.

It would be safer to put the suitcase under the bed, she didn't want anyone to break in and run off with her passport. She knew she was being neurotic but she wasn't going to take any chances. She had waited too long for Nick, things had had a bad habit of going wrong in the past. She wasn't going to tempt fate in any way.

Emily heaved the suitcase off the bed, lifted the bedspread and pushed the case under the bed. Halfway in it jammed against something. Emily pulled it out and tried again, it still wouldn't go under. Swearing under her breath she pulled it out again, then bent down to see what was blocking it. Pushing back the carpet she saw part of a raised floorboard and the corner of what looked like a CD cover, she pulled it out and opened it.

Putting on her glasses she stared at the four passports. All had different names; all issued in different countries, all with different birth dates. All belonged to Marcus.

Emily felt for the chair behind her and sat down trying to make some sense of what she was holding in her hands.

She flipped through the pages checking the immigration stamps. Somalia, Sudan, Pakistan, Iran, Syria, Kenya and Lamu. Dates going back years. So out of the five passports he owned, including the one he'd travelled to New York on, what was his real name?

Only one person could tell her.

She picked up her phone punching in his number. "Harry? It's me Emily."

Not waiting for him to speak she continued. "So, what was his real name, and more to the point what is *my* real surname?"

There was a slight pause. "What kind of a dumb question is this Emily. Have you been drinking?"

"Don't patronise me Harry. I'm holding four different passports in my hand. I know you know all about this, tell me what his real name was?"

"He's dead. Get over it."

"Is he? Look Harry, I'm getting married again. I *have* to know the truth, even you must be able to see the ramifications of all of this?"

There was another long silence at the end of the phone. "Look, if you won't help me then tomorrow I'm going to take these passports down to the American Embassy and ask them to investigate! I don't understand any of this Harry, and I don't like it. It raises questions I don't want to think about. Why would someone in the world of finance need five different passports and five different names?"

"He's dead. End of story. Go get married, good luck to you."

"Well I don't trust you or believe you. Goodbye Harry, if this is *your* real name."

Locking her suitcase, she pushed it under the bed with shaking hands. Marriage to Nick would not be possible until she knew for absolute certainty she was free to marry again. The doubts she had always had, but managed to smother after meeting Nick, began to claw their way to the surface of her mind again.

Fate has an uncanny way of finding its next victim.

Chapter Thirty-Five

Harry looked out of the window at the endless New York traffic below, the screaming of sirens, the never-ending road works and their noisy hammering. The office was cool but he could feel the sweat running down the centre of his back. He would have to make the decision, he had no other alternative, given the circumstances. He didn't want to risk anything happening to Marcus out in the field, he was absolutely vital to the operation.

He picked up his phone again. A distorted voice answered immediately.

The man in the hoodie. "Yes Guv?"

"Job for you and you need to be quick. Emily Hunter is going to the American Embassy tomorrow, as soon as it opens I would think. Get to her before she gets there. She must be stopped; she has things in her possession, in her purse. I need them. She could blow the whole fucking operation. I don't care how you do it – make it permanent okay!"

Harry put down the phone and stared out of the window, then turned and studied the map on the wall, his eyes travelling over it until he came to Africa. He traced the coast of East Africa with his finger. Kenya, Lamu, Somalia. Some of Marcus's turf in pursuit of the Shadow Dancer.

Emily had travelled to Kenya and Lamu. They'd been keeping track of her movements.

Why, out of the blue, had she decided to go to East Africa two years ago?

He'd had five de-briefing sessions with Marcus over the past two years, all of them had taken place in London. Security in the States had cranked up considerably since 9/11, less questions were asked by the British authorities. Marcus's pursuit of the Shadow Dancer had produced more information about the dangerous world the terrorist lived in, a profile, thanks to Marcus, was beginning to take shape.

Finally, Marcus had a photograph of The Shadow Dancer, this was a major step forward, he also had his name. Aaquib Salim Ahad.

They were moving in on him. Marcus was doing a fantastic, but dangerous, job – but he was closing the gap, gaining ground. He would find him.

Emily, in pursuit of whatever truth she was looking for, could blow the entire operation if she wasn't stopped. He needed to get his hands on those damn passports.

Chapter Thirty-Six

Mayfair was teeming with pedestrians, the traffic relentless, the wind and rain compounding the chaos. Emily struggled with her umbrella praying it wouldn't turn inside out.

Hurriedly she made to step off the pavement, heading towards Grosvenor Square, and the American embassy, and, as she did so the side of her umbrella blew in, obscuring her view.

She felt a punch in her back and staggered half turning in pain, then another violent punch, and her legs gave way as she struggled to stay upright. Emily toppled forward headlong into the traffic. She didn't see the car speeding towards her, the driver swerving, trying to avoid her, the frantic blare of a horn, the screams from other pedestrians. Emily heard the screech of brakes, a black flame seared across her body, her arms and legs crashed down from the car. Pain exploded in a hundred places, her legs shot up over her head, her chin pressed down on her ribcage, taking the air out of her lungs. Then everything went from red, to dark grey, to black. Then nothing.

In the chaos which followed no one noticed the man in the hoodie running down a side street with her handbag tucked inside his coat, lost in a sea of umbrellas and dense traffic.

Emily's ankle bracelet lay in a puddle - as broken as she was.

*****

Harry checked his watch again, his fingers drumming a steady beat on his desk.

He snatched up the phone on the first ring.

"All done, Guv. She got hit by a car. Doubt she'll survive."

"Good job, my man. What was in the purse?"

"A ticket to Kenya, departing tonight, four foreign looking passports. Dunno who the dude is though."

There was a silence at the end of the phone, then. "What else?"

"Usual things women carry around with them, oh yeah, a camera and a mobile phone. I checked out the camera. Shots taken in London with the man in her life. There was an envelope with some contact details. Nick Kennedy ain't gonna be happy when his lady don't pitch at the airport in Nairobi, wherever that is."

"Okay FedEx them to me then disappear. I want the purse to disappear as well. Send it to me with the passports and the camera. Destroy the mobile. Keep your ears and eyes open, pal, we need to know for sure she's dead."

Harry's eyes once more traversed the map on his wall. So, Emily had been going back to Kenya again. Interesting.

*****

The man in the hoodie jogged down a side street, filled with bulging refuse bags waiting for collection. Ducking into a dark doorway he re-checked the contents of the bag, feeling in its depths for the mobile phone. Pulling out the sim card he looked around furtively before picking up a broken brick and smashing the phone. He threw it deep into the pile of rubbish bags, along with the sim card.

Zipping up Emily's bag he didn't sense the dark shape behind him, only the searing pain as the knife buried itself deep to the left of his spine, before being jerked up towards his heart and lungs. He felt the bag leave his hands, then nothing.

Chapter Thirty-Seven

Marcus

As I told you, I think, my parents emigrated to the States when I was just a baby, I was an only child.

My schools, as I grew up, were hand-picked for their excellence. My college, was one of the best the States could offer. With my first-class degree I was head hunted by US military intelligence.

They had a rigorous and selective screening process which I passed with little effort. I started on the bottom rung, as did the other agents, where they taught us everything necessary to become a superior agent; operations planning, physical and electronic surveillance, undercover covert operations, interrogation, counter terrorism, forensic science, cyber intelligence and all the other skills we would need to operate in the field. I was a natural.

My parents didn't live to see me achieve excellence, didn't watch me work my way up through the ranks until I was up there with the best. They died a year before I was chosen to work alongside Harry.

They were good parents, good people, and achieved everything they had set out to do for their son. I know they were more than proud of me, very proud of me.

Working with Harry was the ultimate dream job. Using all the skills I had learned I was soon out in the field, pursuing shadowy figures all over East Africa, the Middle East and Pakistan. The kill rate was impressive. No explanations were necessary, only Harry needed to know. What he did with the information was up to him, no one asked him any questions – he was the boss, with a direct line to the White House.

We were all kept busy chasing up contacts all over the world, meeting informers, dissecting intelligence. Extracting important information from casual conversations.

The Shadow Dancer left a distinct thread behind him, I knew more about him than anyone else, I now knew what he looked like, I knew his name – Aaquib Salim Ahad.

When we agents were out in the field all contact with Harry was forbidden. De-briefing sessions were held in person, face to face. Harry was the only one with the authority to contact an agent if it was absolutely necessary.

The man in the hoodie was not an agent, just someone who was used to carry out some of the small time dirty work for Harry.

Not many tears were shed when he was found dead. The Agency didn't come forward to claim his body – nor did anyone else. We would easily be able to replace him with some other small-time crook.

Chapter Thirty-Eight

In the bridal department of the shop the assistant glanced at her watch. She knew Miss Hunter was leaving the country today. Her wedding gown was packed and ready to go. If she didn't arrive in the next ten minutes the shop would be closed, and Miss Hunter would have to fly off without her dress.

The security guard stood in the doorway, tapping his watch – time to close up. She frowned, looking again at her own watch. Maybe something had happened to delay her customer. Maybe she'd changed her flight and would call in, in a day or two.

Chapter Thirty-Nine

Dawn crept over the hills of Nairobi, the pink sky held the promise of a beautiful day. Nick hummed to himself as he drove to the airport. He had piloted his plane in yesterday, collected his vehicle from the car park, where he always left it, then driven to his club in town. He repeatedly felt in his pocket, checking the box containing her ring was still there.

He would slip it on her finger the moment he had his arms around her again. He'd tried, but failed, to make contact with her last night, wanting to hear her voice, to wish her a safe journey to him, but her mobile phone was dead.

He parked the vehicle and made his way into the arrivals hall. Her flight had landed. He watched the bustling crowds, the kissing, the hugging and the emotion. As he had the advantage of being tall, he could see over the passengers streaming into the arrivals hall, pushing squeaky carts, with wobbling misdirected wheels, loaded with luggage; their faces full of expectation.

In a weeks' time his brother, Jonathan, and Kim would arrive and he would be there to meet them too. He turned around at the sound of his name.

"Hey Nick, nice to see you again – who are you meeting – clients?"

He grinned at the young woman. "Hello Charlotte! How are you?"

Charlotte raised her eyebrow. "I hear someone interesting is coming in…we're all dying to know who she is!"

Nick sighed – nothing was ever a secret in Nairobi. "Just a friend…see you around."

He watched, his stomach tight with excitement, his eyes searching for her face. Now there was just a trickle of passengers – then no one else. Perplexed he wondered if she'd been caught up in customs or experiencing problems with her visa. He tapped his foot with impatience as he leaned on the barrier in front of the arrivals hall. There were no more passengers coming through.

Not unduly worried he walked up to the Kenya Airways representative, asking if all the passengers had disembarked. The official assured him they had, but he would go and check customs and immigration, see if there was anyone stuck there. A few moments later he came back, shaking his head.

Nick drove back into Nairobi, stopping at the Kenya Airways office. He explained his fiancée, was supposed to be on their flight this morning, would they check the manifesto for him?

The clerk checked. Shrugging his shoulders, he told Nick she was on the manifesto but had not checked in at Heathrow.

He walked back to his car disappointed. She would be on the next flight out of London, due to land the following morning. Nothing to worry about he assured himself, for some reason she had missed her flight – it happened. He would call his Mother and tell her to cancel lunch.

He stayed overnight at his club, then went back to the airport the next morning. There would be a logical reason for her missing the flight yesterday, he rationalised. He'd tried calling her several times on her mobile, but it was silent. Maybe Oliver had gone missing?

There was no sign of her on the flight the next morning – or the day after.

He called his mother again to let her know there was still no sign of Emily. "What on earth do you mean, Nicholas? Missing her flight was one thing, but now what are we supposed to think and do? What about all the arrangements we've made? And Jonathan and Kim are coming all the way from Singapore for the wedding! It's too bad she hasn't called to explain. I don't know what to say.

"And what about Arthur and Gladys? They've booked their tickets, what will I tell them? What are you going to do?"

"I'm going back out to the lodge to collect my passport, then I'm going to fly to London and find her. Tell Arthur and Gladys the wedding has been postponed, it's all you have to say. Blame it on the Royal safari party, you'll think of something Ma.

"She must have changed her mind, it's all I can come up with." He told her, his voice ragged with emotion. "Maybe I don't know Emily as well as I thought. She can be unpredictable. I can't think straight at the moment. Anyway, I'm going to find her.

"I think you should postpone all the arrangements – don't cancel them. I don't know what else to suggest. Maybe I pushed her too hard, and the thought of living in Kenya and giving up her life in London was something she decided she didn't want to do after all – I have no idea."

Nick put down the phone, he needed a walk. He strode with resolution past the club bar then hesitated; turning on his heel he went up to the barman and ordered a double whisky.

*****

Deborah sat at her desk, staring out into the gardens. Somehow there had to be an explanation for this business with Emily. She picked up her private address book. Kitty Matthews, who had introduced her to Hugh all those years ago, now lived in London; she would ask her for her help. With Kitty being as well connected as she was, there must be something she would be able to do?

"Mrs Matthews's residence."

"Jennifer? It's Deborah Kennedy. Is Mrs Matthews at home?"

"I'm afraid not, Mrs Kennedy. Mr and Mrs Matthews went on a cruise two days ago, they're spending a few months in New Zealand before returning home. May I take a message for her?"

"Perhaps you'd be good enough to ask her to call me on her return. Thank you."

She tapped her rings on the side of the table. Maybe she should call Gladys and Arthur, see if they could assist in some way.

No, Nick would be furious if she got them involved. But she'd have to tell them the wedding was postponed.

Defeated, Deborah closed her address book and went to look for her husband.

Chapter Forty

Nick flew back to Honey Badger, still nursing the hope, and a hangover, Emily would call him to explain what had happened, tell him she had collected her dress and was on her way.

He'd called the book shop but the phone was as dead as he felt inside. He knew her friend, Rebecca, had left the country and was somewhere in the Med on a yacht.

He emailed, then when he received no response, he wrote to her at her old address, maybe she had given the new owners some other address for any letter or bills and they would forward his. If she was still in England she would pick up her mail at some point.

He flew himself back to Nairobi, two days later, posted the letter, then called in at his club, where any mail for him was always delivered – there was nothing.

She'd stormed out of his lodge like a wounded lioness after the incident with the American; maybe she was a bit highly strung, after all how well *did* he know her?

Know her or not, he'd made up his mind. Tomorrow night he would be on the flight to London to find her. When he did, he would tell her he'd postponed the wedding to give her more time. They would work together on another date which would make her more comfortable. He would bring her back with him and start all over again – but she was worth it. He had pushed her too hard trying to juggle the wedding date with his upcoming Royal safari party.

He would collect his brother and Kim from the airport tomorrow morning, and explain everything to them, before flying off himself that evening.

He rubbed his eyes and pinched the bridge of his nose. What he needed now was a stiff drink and a good night's sleep.

The bar at the club was hot and noisy, but he was in no mood to talk to anyone. He was sure the rumours and gossip were already whispering their way around the social circuit. He turned on his heel and went back to his car. He would head for one of the International hotels in town where he was unlikely to bump into anyone he knew.

*****

Nick sat at the bar and ordered a double whisky. God, he was tired, too tired to even think straight. The room was quiet with just the low murmurs of groups of business men and women, sitting around small tables. At the bar, there were four other men watching CNN as they nursed their drinks.

He half watched the journalist as she reported on the dire plight of refugees, some place in the Middle East, waiting for urgent relief from the rest of the world. When the ads came on he turned away, remembering the soft curve of her neck, the tumble of long curls on the pillow, the soft feel of her in his arms as she sighed, pulling his arms tighter around her.

He was going to find her no matter what the outcome might be. He had to see her again.

His eyes burned as he swirled the ice cubes in his now empty glass – he needed another drink.

He raised his arm catching the attention of the barman. He ordered another whisky, drumming his fingers on the side of his leather bar seat. With reluctance, his eyes turned back to the television – the CNN *Breaking News* banner was up, the anchor was reading something from his laptop. The barman brought his drink and Nick took a sip before turning back to the television.

A plane had disappeared off the radar on a flight from Singapore to London.

Nick stood up, moving closer to the screen, asking the barman to turn up the volume.

Kelong Airlines flight 642 was en-route from Singapore to London when it disappeared. It is thought, though not confirmed, the aircraft went down somewhere in the Indian Ocean. There was no Mayday call from the flight deck. The CEO of Kelong Airlines has told CNN, rescue ships are on their way to search for survivors.

Flight 642 was carrying two hundred and thirty passengers plus twenty crew. CNN will bring you more news on this breaking story as we get it.

Nick stared at the screen, then looked wildly around the room as though it might confirm he hadn't seen what he'd watched on the news.

He sat down in his chair, reaching for his drink. His mind scrambling to make some sense of the news. Yes, his brother and Kim, had been on a flight from Singapore with Kelong Airlines, but maybe they had two or three flights a day to London?

He patted his shirt pocket, pulling out a piece of paper – flight 642. He looked back at the screen where they were repeating the news over and over, showing a similar aircraft to the one which had gone down, and the crowds of bewildered and distraught relatives at the airport in Singapore.

Throwing some money down on the bar he stumbled out of the room, out of the hotel and into his car. He hit the steering wheel with his fist, then lowered his head onto his arms, his shoulders heaving with the enormity of what had happened. He would have to go to his parents' house and tell them. He shuddered at the thought of their once happy faces reduced to ones of unspeakable grief.

Chapter Forty-One

Nick boarded the flight for London the following evening, leaving his shattered parents to cope with their grief, as he had to cope with his own. Unable to comprehend the devastation which had so swiftly overtaken their lives now irrevocably changed, diminished, by the death of their son, his brother, Jonathan.

He had booked a return ticket to Singapore, via London, and would wait there at the airport, with all the other relatives and friends, for news of the doomed plane and any possible survivors.

Arriving in London early the next morning he looked out of the aircraft window knowing Emily was down there somewhere.

His flight to Singapore didn't leave until after lunch giving him enough time to get to Emily's flat and the bookshop. He joined the queue for a taxi, cursing at the length of it, relieved he had checked his luggage through to Singapore.

The taxi stopped outside Emily's flat. He paid the fare, and, climbing out, looked up at the windows. The place had a deserted air about it but it was still worth a try. He rang the doorbell, waited, then beat on the door with his fist.

A window opened from a basement apartment, a young man poked his head out. "No point in beating on the door mate, no one lives there."

Nick turned to the sound of the voice. "Did you know the woman who lived here before, tall, long dark curly hair?"

"Sorry mate, I haven't been here long, but I can tell you no one lives there – curly hair or not. The place was sold, saw the sign outside when I moved in meself. Mind you you're not the only one who's been looking for her."

Nick frowned at him. "What do you mean?"

"Another bloke was here a few days ago, a Yank he sounded like. He couldn't get in either."

148

Nick cursed and went back to the road to flag down another taxi. He sat in the back, his mind spinning. An *American* had been looking for her? *Marcus*? Despite everything had he maybe survived 9/11? If she was still married then it would go a long way to explaining why she'd called the whole thing off.

No, it was an impossible scenario.

His next stop was the bookshop – maybe the new owner could give him the information he so desperately needed. It was a slight hope, but it was all he had.

The taxi dropped him a block away and drove off. Nick's heart was beating rapidly as he pushed his way through the crowds.

Hopeless. The windows of the shop were blanked, a sign on the door told him the shop was closed due to new ownership and stocktaking.

A plane roared overhead and he looked up, feeling a wetness on his face.

Jesus, nothing was going his way in his search for her. There was one other place he could try. The bridal department at Harrods. He would walk there.

The young girl manning the desk was busy chatting on the phone, admiring her nails. He glared at her and she rang off hastily.

"Yes, sir, may I help you?"

"Emily Hunter bought a wedding dress from you. I need to know if she collected it?"

"Um, look I'm only a temp, here for two weeks, I'm not sure I'll be able to help you."

"*Well call the bloody manager then!*" He ran his fingers through his hair. "Look, I'm sorry, I don't have much time. I need to know if she collected her dress?"

He watched the girl tapping the keys on her computer. "What date am I looking for here, when was she supposed to have collected it?"

"Sometime before mid-April – I don't have the exact date." Nick rubbed the back of his hand across his forehead – he couldn't think straight.

The girl tapped on the keyboard. "Ah, yes, here it is. Although it was paid for she didn't take it with her, it needed some alterations done."

"*I don't care about the bloody alterations! Did she pick it up, or not!*"

"I'm sorry sir, all I can tell you is, no, she didn't pick it up – it's still here."

Jesus. "May I see it?"

"I'm afraid not, the dress belongs to Miss Hunter. It would be against store policy for me to show it to you. Sorry. Only the manager can override that decision and I'm afraid she's away on holiday – that's why I'm here."

Nick turned and walked away.

*****

Poor bugger, the girl thought. He looked as though he'd been crying, the bride must have called the whole thing off. What a state the man was in. Nice looking though, definitely didn't get the tan here.

She picked up her phone to resume the conversation with her friend then paused. Maybe she should have asked him his name. She shrugged, she was just a temp, what did it matter. She would be moving on to another job after this one.

Chapter Forty-Two

Nick waited at the airport in Singapore with the other distraught relatives and friends. Finally, the CEO of the airline informed them the wreckage of the aircraft had been found - there were no survivors. There was speculation the flight had been the target of a terrorist attack, a bomb on board. No one had claimed responsibility as yet.

Numb with disbelief, Nick checked into a hotel before catching a taxi to the block of flats where Jonathan and Kim had lived. He collected the key from the caretaker and let himself into their home.

Finding himself now alone, surrounded by furniture and personal belongings which had made up his brother's life in Singapore, he gave into his grief.

The next few days he was kept busy arranging for the packing and shipment of his brother's personal belongings back to Kenya.

He paid his respects to Kim's shattered parents and family, then made a courtesy call at Jonathan's work place.

When there was nothing more he could do, Nick checked out of his hotel and returned to the airport for his flight back to Nairobi, via London, to give what little comfort and support he could to his parents.

*****

The memorial service, in Nairobi, for Jonathan had been crowded and emotional. The hot African sun seared through the stained-glass windows of the church, spilling a kaleidoscope of vivid colours over the hundreds of sombrely dressed mourners.

His parents seemed to have aged, his father now stooped, his mother's face carved with untold grief. But he knew they were strong and, in time, the raw pain of losing their son would diminish. The world, a world which cared for no one, would go relentlessly on.

Supporting his parents and having to remain strong for them, despite having to deal with his own grief at losing his brother, and Emily's silence, had drained him.

Through the long nights, at his childhood home, he lay in his bed wrestling with his imagination. Was it quick, or did Jonathan and Kim have minutes of unimaginable terror knowing they were going to crash. There'd been a fire, his thoughts veered away from the horror of that. He imagined the oxygen masks swinging down, the screaming, the fear, then the sickening shuddering thud as the aircraft hit water. Sucked into nothingness.

Oh, God but he needed Emily now, to give him something to hold onto in his fallen apart world.

He would go back to the bush - back to a more predictable world.

*****

Mike Connelly welcomed him back, offering his condolences, suggesting, with some diplomacy, it might be easier for Nick to welcome the new guests when they arrived, but leave the entertaining to him and the rangers.

Nick had agreed with him. He spent most of the time in the office preparing and planning for the Royal safari which would arrive at the end of the first week in June. Having to concentrate on each tiny detail, harnessed his thoughts, leaving little time for them to become untethered.

His staff, including Mike, noticed the change in him, the once warm and ready smile had gone, and he was more abrupt with them.

"As you know, Mike," he said at their regular morning meeting, "the lodge will be empty of guests as from tomorrow, as scheduled. I want all the staff to take a break for two weeks. You'll have a week to spruce the place up before our VIP's arrive.

"I want the place to myself for a while. I need some space and time…"

Mike hesitated and cleared his throat. "I'm sorry about Emily, Nick, it's a tough call."

Nick didn't answer. One month had passed with still no word from her. Tomorrow should have been the day he married Emily.

Bin Laden had claimed responsibility for the explosion on the flight from Singapore to London.

152

Chapter Forty-Three

Nick sat in the deserted lodge, but after a week he'd had enough of his own company, and the silence of the place.

He packed one of the vehicles with enough provisions for ten days, a small tent, his rifle and cameras. He would keep himself occupied recording the game in the area, stopping when he felt like it. He called his mother before he left.

"Ma, I'm going out into the bush for a couple of weeks, to check on the game, I can't sit around here another day. I need to keep busy with something."

"Would you like us to come out and keep you company? Or, if you prefer, your father could come along with you, help with the game count? A few days in the bush would do him the world of good. He doesn't say more than a dozen words. I'm so worried about him."

"No. I'm not good company at the moment. I need some time on my own."

"I understand darling; it's been difficult for all of us. Don't forget to look up at the stars – Jonathan will be up there somewhere." He heard her stifle a sob and there was silence for a few moments.

Deborah cleared her throat. "Nick I've given this business with Emily a lot of thought. You've always been an excellent judge of character, I can't believe you misjudged her. Something *must* have happened to her."

"Emily had all my contact details. If she was ill or involved in an accident she would have had them with her. Someone would have contacted me. Sorry Ma, she changed her mind - that's it."

He heard his mother sigh again. "Well I don't know what to think anymore…It doesn't look as though we'll be seeing you any time soon. Please send those peg things through, darling, the pictures you took of her in London. We'd both like to see them."

"What's the point Ma?"

"Well there isn't one I suppose, if you've made up your mind about her."

"I've tried everything, Ma; I've made phone calls, checked with the book shop, sent her a letter, emailed dozens of times. Searched London for her in the little time I had there. She didn't even collect her wedding dress Ma. No, it's over, I need to get out into the wilderness. Get her out of my mind. I'll give you a call when I get back."

*****

Each evening Nick set up camp, built a fire and cooked up some food. Weary from all the driving through rough terrain he'd roll out his bed and lie down staring up at the stars, thinking of Jonathan, how the loss of him still left a gaping hole.

He'd had plenty of time to think about love and loss. How when someone you love dies, nothing happens. The sun comes up and goes down, the rivers still flow, the birds continue to sing and lay eggs. People all over the world get up in the morning, work all day, go home for dinner, then go back to bed, and do it all over again the next day.

Newsreaders continue to read news, politicians play with the truth making promises they will never keep, no-one cares if a bomb has gone off in your life when someone you love dies. The hole that's left which cannot be filled with memories, but perhaps with time, the sting is lessened. But impossible to imagine a time like this will eventually come.

With a tin cup of whisky to hand, he mulled through his thoughts and memories trying to find answers. His mind festering with *what ifs* and *maybes.* Loss, in all its guises, was simply a different face of death.

On his last night, he pitched his tent a little distance from a large waterhole. Nursing a beer, he watched the setting sun changing the colour of the bush around him, the yellow, pink and apricot reflecting in the water. Impala, zebra, eland and wildebeest dotted the landscape as far as the eye could see, their shadows lengthening with the fading light.

A row of giraffe heads appeared behind some trees before they emerged, lanky and graceful, heading for the water hole. Planting their long bony forelegs wide astride they lowered their elegant necks, their rumps high in the air. On the opposite side impala, with their majestic curled horns, made their way to the other end of the water hole and stepped with dainty hooves into the mud. Looking around with

154

trepidation, they too bent their heads, quenching their thirst, their bodies reflecting bronze in the rippling water.

Nick reached for his camera then stopped. The impala were scattering and leaping into the air in panic, re-grouping at a distance. The giraffe scrambling to lift their heavy necks before they too disappeared into the bush with a rocking clumsy gait. Nick looked around, nothing was moving. Somewhere to the left of him a baboon gave a warning bark to his troop.

Then out of the bush stalked five lions; a big male and his four tawny females. In no hurry, they loped towards the edge of the water hole and crouched down, ears back and tails twitching, their powerful haunches bulging, yellow flickering eyes missing nothing.

Suddenly the big male jerked his head up, the water dripping from his bearded jaws. Out of the gathering darkness, five huge, grey wrinkled elephants made their ponderous way towards the water, their massive ears moving back and forth.

The five lions, beards dripping, tails twitching, watched them drink on the other side of the water. The lions and the elephants glared at each other for a few minutes, then the male lion rose and loped off, his lioness' following him. The elephants lowered their trunks sucking up the cooling water, curling their trunks up and under, squirting the liquid into their mouths.

The thunder of hooves had him reaching for his binoculars. The four lioness were on the move.

Only the male was visible, his whiskers twitching, as he watched one lioness race across the plains before coming to a crouching halt, her flickering ears visible above the grasses, the other three females fanned out around a hapless impala who had become separated from his herd.

Sensing the lion, the impala became panic stricken, zig zagging across the plain, his hooves thudding in terror, as he tried to outrun the pride.

The tawny female rose up from her hiding place and gave chase, leaping onto the impala's back she brought him down in a cloud of broiling dust. The impala bucked and kicked trying to dislodge its passenger, then collapsed. The lioness buried her jaws in its throat and held still, the other females, arriving amidst the dust, tore into the living flesh of his legs and back.

The impala lay still, blood gushing from its throat and other wounds. The big male stood up from his vantage point and strolled over to his females. Swatting them aside with a paw the size of a frying pan, he settled down, sinking his jaws into the warm belly of the now dead impala and began to feed. The females approached with deference, crouching down on their haunches, waiting for permission to join in the feasting. Tomorrow the hyenas would shadow around the remains, and the vultures would goose-step in the high trees waiting their turn for what was left.

Nick put his camera down, a ghost of a smile flittered across his lips. Who needed to go to the theatre? He had drama all around him right here. At least lions, when they killed, made it quick and clean, unlike Bin Laden and his terrorist entourage who didn't.

He cracked open a can of beer and lay back, looking up at the stars, arriving in their millions above him, the fire crackled and spat next to him; a tin dish, with his dinner, pillowed in its embers. Closing his eyes, he finally felt the healing balm of the wilderness washing over him.

And he knew then, unlike the impala, whose shadow would no longer grace the land, his would. He would survive although the price was going to be high.

It was a decision he didn't want to make. But he had to.

With the game count completed, and sporting a ten-day beard, he headed back to Honey Badger, not looking forward to asking his father to bear another loss.

That evening, nursing his second glass of whisky, Nick called his father telling him, with his consent, he wanted to sell the lodge and do something else with his life.

"If it's what you want to do son, then you have my blessing," his father said weariness and grief, seeping through his voice. "Your mother and I want you to be happy. If selling the lodge will achieve this, then go ahead. I'll call the estate agency in the morning. It will be a wrench not to have it in the family anymore."

There was a pause, then his father cleared his throat. "When do your staff get back to Honey Badger? What about the forward bookings, after the Royal tour?"

"Everyone will be back in a day or two for the Royal safari. After that Mike will run the lodge. Any buyer should want the existing staff to stay on to handle the guests, so I don't anticipate any problems there. It'll be part of the deal with the buyer that he keeps the staff, if they want to stay on."

"Alright son, come and see us soon. By the way your Mother still insists she wants to see a photograph of Emily, I know there seems no point now, but do me a favour and send something Nick. It will make her happy, and God knows she deserves to be after the accident, I'm so worried about her."

*****

The Royal safari was a success. With all the attention to detail it had required, the long hours Nick and his team had worked to make it so, had exhausted them all.

Three weeks later, at the beginning of July, there was a call from the estate agent. With its well-earned international reputation, plus the rumours of a recent Royal safari there, Honey Badger had not been difficult to market. A potential buyer wanted to come out as soon as possible to take a look at the property.

The potential buyer, an Englishman, bored with his predictable life in rural Yorkshire, and looking for adventure, put in an offer and the lodge was sold. He was eager to keep on all the existing members of staff, including Mike Connelly.

Four weeks later Nick was on his way to the coast where he planned to find something to do to keep himself occupied. The only reminder of Emily was the photographs he'd taken of her on their picnic, down by the river in the game reserve, and at the park in London. He made a mental note to send the jpeg of Emily to his mother.

Chapter Forty-Four

The police had contacted the newspapers and asked them to run a short story on the accident in Mayfair, but there was no response from the public. CCTV cameras had revealed nothing of relevance. Witnesses, and the driver of the vehicle, had all been interviewed but could add nothing. The woman appeared to have tripped then fallen in front of the car – perhaps it was as simple as that, a freak accident, and a common thief seizing the opportunity to steal her handbag.

Alongside the article on Emily was another one about a man's body, the victim of a knife attack, found in amongst a pile of garbage bags. Identity unknown. The CCTV cameras had picked up a grainy image of a man in a hoodie leaning over the body, but there was nothing else to give any indication as to what might have happened. London was full of people wearing hoodies, it had become some kind of uniform, making it nearly impossible to identify anyone individually.

*****

Doctor Harrington entered the darkened room, quiet except for the bleeping of the life support machine. He checked the board at the foot of the bed, as he did each day, and studied the cadaver still patient. Who was she? There were no identity documents on her when the ambulance delivered her to the hospital. There was no sign of a handbag. Nothing on her to tell them who she was, not even a tattoo where they could maybe trace the artist.

Maybe, Doctor Harrington thought, she was a tourist, in which case he would have to wait until someone realised she'd not come home and alert the authorities. She'd been in a coma since being admitted four weeks ago.

Her injuries were not as severe as they could have been. The vehicle had hit her hard, causing considerable bruising and some fractured ribs, but the real damage was done by the blow to her head when she bounced off the windscreen, hitting the pavement. The operation, to relieve the resulting pressure on the brain from the contusions, had been successful, but at this point in time he couldn't even begin to guess how long she might take to recover.

He shook his head in puzzlement as he left the room. There must be someone out there who knew her. A mother or father, a husband, or boyfriend? Everyone was connected to someone in this world.

*****

The tall slender African nursing sister checked Emily's pulse as she gazed out of the window at the heavy skies and relentless rain. She loved her job, the fact she was living in London, but she yearned for her home and her family. She missed the warmth and the light there, the smell of warm sand, the salty tang of the sea air, the acrid scent of seaweed.

In her mind, she could see the brilliant colours of the bougainvillea, scarlet, purple, orange and white, tumbling over the walls surrounding the family garden. She inhaled deeply, imagining the smell of the heavy scent of the frangipani trees; she was homesick. She looked back from the window and straightened the patient's bed.

Anna Kiwathe checked all the machines; the ECG monitor was beeping healthily. The read-outs correct. The endotracheal tube was clear, the ventilator was functioning. She folded a large cuff around the girl's arm, checking her blood pressure. Satisfied, she made some notes on the clip board.

"*Eish*, who are you?" Anna whispered, for the hundredth time. "Why has no one come to find you?" She squeezed Emily's hand and left the room. As she turned to close the door she thought she saw the girl's hand move, she returned to the bed. Yes. She was clenching and unclenching her hand, moving her head. Anna pressed the button to call Doctor Harrington.

*****

She struggled to open her eyes, a blackness forcing her backwards away from the dimness of a light she could see. Dazed and disorientated she looked around in confusion, not recognising the stark walls or the bright curtains at the window.

A man stood beside her dressed in a white coat, his face loomed closer to hers. "Don't be frightened, my dear, you're in hospital, there was an accident, but you're doing well. I've taken the tube out of your throat, so it will feel sore. Can you tell me your name?"

Groggily she turned her face towards the voice and felt pain jack-knife through her, the blackness swirled around her as she felt herself reeling back into darkness.

"Lie still, my dear, try not to move."

"Who are you?" she whispered, her voice hoarse. Her throat painful, her lips dry and stiff.

"I'm Doctor Harrington – would you tell me your name?" he repeated.

She ran her tongue over her cracked lips. "My name? My name is…" she frowned, not understanding why she couldn't think of it. But when she tried there was just a confusing blankness – a throbbing in her head which wouldn't go away. "I don't know my name. I can't remember it." Her voice croaked as she felt panic overwhelm her. "What happened to me?"

Doctor Harrington took her hand. "You were involved in an accident. You've suffered a head injury, a concussion, plus a couple of fractured ribs. I'm going to give you something to take away the pain, it will help you sleep, okay?"

She felt a brief sting in her arm, feeling sleep unfolding within her, there was no point in trying to fight it, putting up any resistance. She was being pulled down deep into the sea of forgotten memories.

She heard a faint voice inside her head. *Oupa* Pieter, *Oupa* Pieter!

"Hem-er-lee! Hem-er-lee! Another voice.

Then the voices tip-toed away from her vacant mind.

160

Chapter Forty-Five

S he sat by the window, looking out over the hospital gardens, her mind a blank. It was a still golden June afternoon, and she tried to concentrate on the leaves as they filtered the rays of sunshine, searching her empty mind for some clue as to who she was.

The doctor had explained to her about the accident but she couldn't remember anything about it. He said maybe in time, with enough stimuli, she may get her memory back. She was trapped in a body she knew nothing about, looking in the mirror at the face of a stranger; a face she didn't know.

After coming out of her coma, she had been transferred to the Neuro floor for three weeks, now she was in the rehabilitation wing of the hospital.

Each day she went for her physiotherapy, then sat by the window next to her bed, willing her brain to tell her something, to remember anything at all.

"I'm desperate to know who I am, what I was, where I lived, what I did." She said to Anna, the nursing sister, on one of her daily visits to check on her. "Why hasn't anyone missed me? Why have none of my family, or friends, come to find me?" Her eyes swam with the now too familiar tears.

"There *must* be a place somewhere with my clothes and things?" She took a deep breath, confused and frustrated by the constant blankness; the absence of answers to any questions.

She leaned forward clutching at Anna's arm. "I *have* to find out who I am, Sister Anna! I have this constant compelling feeling I'm supposed to be somewhere. It's important, more than important, it's as if something terrible will happen if I'm not there."

Concern washed over Anna's face as she watched her agitated patient. "Well, let's be positive! You must have family somewhere. They must be frantic with worry about you. You sound English but then again you could be from an English-speaking country, maybe South Africa, or Australia, here on holiday." She rubbed the girl's arm, trying to comfort her.

"Where do you come from Sister Anna?"

"I was born in Tanzania, on the East coast of Africa."

The girl felt something shift in her brain – she remembered a place where it was warm, with African people. Was it a documentary she had watched at some point in her past? She tried to think it through, but the tenuous images dissipated then slid away, and once more her mind emptied. She closed her eyes in despair, the tears clumping her crowded dark lashes.

"The police are waiting to talk to you." Anna said, "They're coming in this afternoon, don't look so worried, everyone is trying to help you."

*****

Anna showed the young policewoman into the girl's room. "Hello, Miss. I'm Constable Catherine Milton, from the Chelsea Police Station. I need to ask you a few questions about your accident?"

The girl sitting on the bed gave her a bleak smile. "I'm afraid it'll only take a few minutes then. I can't remember a thing – my mind is like a blank canvas."

The policewoman smiled. "Well we do have to find out who you are. I suggest we run a photograph of you in the evening papers. Maybe you have a flat mate, perhaps some friends, who will read the article and contact us.

"A family member may come forward, unless you're a visitor to our soggy little island! We must try everything we can. I'm not sure how successful we'll be. But we'll do all we can to help you find your family."

The girl's lips trembled and she bit down, as the Constable continued. "We're presuming you had your handbag with you on the day of the accident. Normally, in a situation like this, a member of the public would have handed it in, but no one has. Invariably a bag will turn up with the money and any other valuables missing. But this hasn't happened," she looked down at her notes. "Let's see if an article with your picture will prompt a reaction from anyone, shall we?"

A photograph of the girl appeared in the newspaper the following week, imploring the public to come forward if anyone recognised her.

But she'd changed. Her hair had been partly shaved to enable the surgeons to work on her injuries. The weeks spent in the hospital had also taken their toll. In the photograph, her face was thin and wan, nothing like the way she'd looked before.

No one came forward. PC Milton returned to the hospital with the disappointing news.

"Here's your case number, Miss. Please keep in touch with me." She handed the girl her card. "If you have any problems with anything, give me a call. You might find yourself in a situation where you need to provide some identification. If this should happen ask them to call me. I'll verify your case history. If we learn anything at all we will, of course, let you know straight away."

She lay back on her pillow feeling alone with the emptiness of her memory, an emptiness she seemed powerless to fill. She turned her face to the window and looked at the darkening sky outside. "Someone, please come and find me?" she whispered.

*****

Harry's new man in London read the article about Emily in the evening newspaper – he would have to let Harry know.

"Hey, mate, you want the good news, or the bad news?"

"Do not call me mate, do you hear? I am not your mate and never will be! You work for me, understand? Come on, I don't have time for games – shoot!"

"The bad news is Emily Hunter still isn't dead, but the good news is she's come out of a coma but can't remember who she is. It's in the newspaper here. Guess I'm done here Sir?"

"Not quite," Harry said sharply. "Follow her progress. Stick close. If she recovers her memory, well, you know what to do."

Then Harry paused, thinking incisively. "No. I have another idea. Keep a watch on her when she's discharged from hospital, whenever that might be. I want to know where she's going to live and if she finds a job. Then you will be removed from the case – got it?

Harry had a much better plan for Emily Hunter.

He never did get his FedEx parcel. Whoever had killed his small-time crook had without doubt taken the purse with the passports, and everything else Emily had had in there.

He tried not to lose sleep over it – but he did. Trying to work out the worst-case scenario, and the consequences.

Harry tapped a number into his phone and made another call.

Chapter Forty-Six

Soon she would have to leave the hospital. Did she have a home somewhere, and if so, where was it?

Anna bustled up to her bed perching on the corner. "Hello my dear," she said in her familiar cheerful voice. "I have good news for you. You're now considered well enough to go back out into the world! Isn't that great?"

"But where will I go, I don't have any money. I don't have any identity. How will I survive out there?" Panic streaked through her rushed words.

"The first thing you must do is rent a furnished apartment and find a job. Social Services will help you with this."

Anna straightened the sheet on the bed, pulling it taut. "When I walked to work this morning, I noticed a sign in the window of a gift shop, it's called Imagine. They need someone temporary to start work there. Why don't you think about applying for the job?"

The girl gave a slight nod, looking down at the hands of a stranger. She must do something, but she was frightened of going back out into the world. The hospital had cocooned her from life outside, for over three months. But the day had now arrived; she would have to start a different life outside of the security of the hospital. The thought of not seeing Anna each day threw her into a complete panic.

"Anna, there's another thing bothering me, it might impact on me getting a job in the gift shop, or anywhere. I've been getting books from the library, but the print is all blurry. I thought it might be something to do with the accident so I haven't been all that bothered, but my eyes haven't improved at all. I'm wondering if maybe I should get my eyes tested, maybe I used to wear glasses?"

*****

Anna hummed to herself as she cooked supper. Soon she would be heading home, back to her family, friends and relatives whom she hadn't seen for almost three years. She was taking three months paid leave due to her, and two months unpaid. Only two weeks to go.

She thought about the girl she'd nursed over the past few months. She was a mystery, it was odd no one had come forward with any information about her.

Anna wondered how she would fare when she was released from the hospital. She was fond of her patient.

She smacked her forehead with the heel of her hand. *Eish*! Of course! Why hadn't she thought about it before? Her patient could stay in her flat whilst she was away, it was a great idea, she doubted the hospital would have any objections.

The next morning Anna strode to work, keen to let the girl know she now had a place to stay for a few months, if Doctor Harrington had no objections. She needed to clear it with him first. Social Services would be there if she needed any additional support.

Doctor Harrington voiced no objections, as long as his patient made regular appointments so he could monitor her progress.

The girl listened, relief washing over her face. "That's wonderful Anna. The next thing will be to find a job. I thought about the gift shop, I think I'd enjoy something like that. I was right, by the way, I do need glasses."

"Good! There are a few things we'll need to do to get you started. First, we need to give you a temporary name until you remember your own. Then get you some clothes, the charity shops have good bargains. Social services will help you with this as well.

"I'm afraid the clothes you arrived at the hospital in had to be cut from you so the injuries could be ascertained. But, luckily, your coat, the one with the scarlet lining, survived. Of course, it was in a bit of a state, needed a dry clean, but it's all fixed now, including the tear in one of the pockets" she nodded towards a cupboard. "It's hanging in there, not that you'll need it until winter.

"I'll show you where all the grocery shops are, you'll be safe and secure in my flat. But the first thing we must do is get the job for you. If you're successful then it'll be brilliant, because you can walk to work from the flat. I promise you'll start to remember things. You need the stimulation a job, and meeting new people, will give you. So, what name are we going to give you?

Her patient gave her a blank look.

166

"How about Diana? It sort of suits you I think. Um…" Anna glanced at the spine of the library book the girl was trying to read. "Foster. This will do until we find out your real name."

She murmured her name. "Diana Foster. Well, now I have a name, a coat, I'm left-handed and I need glasses. It's a start isn't it Anna!"

*****

Doctor Harrington was relieved Anna was prepared to take the girl under her wing by offering her a temporary home. With the backup of Social Services and a possible job she would be fine.

"It's impossible to say when your memory will come back," he'd told his patient at their last appointment before she was discharged.

"But it will come back won't it. My memory?"

He'd leaned back in his chair and studied the agitated woman sitting on the opposite side of his desk, her eyes veiled by her eyelashes.

"I'm sorry my dear, I don't know. It could be today, tomorrow, next week, next month. It will return though, with pieces of your past coming back to you when you least expect it – maybe in chronological order, from the most recent, or maybe the other way around, like pieces of a jigsaw puzzle which fit together in the end."

"But what if none of this happens – what if my memory remains a blank for the rest of my life?"

He was aware of the sharp edge to her voice. Saw the fear in her eyes.

"There have been cases where the patient has never recovered their memory, but it's rare," he hesitated, "however, it's altogether possible you may not remember the events immediately preceding your injury."

"Are you saying all I can do is sit and wait for my memory to come back – if it does?"

"I'm afraid so, yes."

She had stood up and paced the small room. "I can't accept this. There has to be something I can do?"

"You can't force your memory to return. The more you grasp for it, the more elusive it will become. It's better to relax your mind, allow it to return when it's ready – let Mother Nature take its course in other words. I'm going to prescribe some pills for you.

"You might find you have bouts of depression. This could be caused by any number of things, I need to make you aware of this. If this should happen take the anti-depressants I'm going to prescribe. If you have trouble sleeping come off the anti-depressants and take the sleeping pills. Don't take them both together alright?"

She had nodded. He made her promise she would make regular appointment with him, whilst Anna was out of the country.

Chapter Forty-Seven

Anna settled her patient into her flat and busied herself preparing dinner. A chest with brass corners glinted in the light of an ornate lantern, on top of it were two tall wooden carvings of giraffe and a basket full of sun bleached shells. A cream and brown hand-made rug covered the floor.

Anna glanced at her as she added more pepper to the pasta sauce she was making. "It's a beautiful rug, isn't it? It was hand made in a place called Lesotho, they're quite unique. I decided if I was going to live in London, I'd create my own little world of Africa around me, hence the carved animals I seem to have so many of, and the wildlife pictures."

The girl studied a framed photograph of a lone elephant against a thunderous black sky and a snow-capped mountain. "Wow! What a shot. Look how the photographer has captured the lighting – it's impressive."

"Yes, it's dramatic isn't it? I have a few wildlife books. You'll find them in amongst the clutter of what I call my reading corner. You're welcome to read any of them, but don't lend them to anyone. It's one rule I have, never lend books, you never get them back!"

"I won't be doing that Anna, for a start I don't know anyone. Your books will be quite safe with me, I promise."

Anna, it was evident, was passionate about books; they lined one wall of the room. There were more books piled up on the table next to the sofa.

The pale grey sofa was peppered with small cushions decorated with faces of wild animals, and a throw of burnt orange and black design lit up the apartment, filling the area with vibrant colour.

She looked up. "Thanks for letting me stay here Anna. Your flat is great with all these gorgeous colours. I don't know how I'll ever be able to repay you for everything."

"Don't worry about any of that now, just don't forget to water the plants." Anna said blowing on a spoonful of pasta sauce, tasting it with care. "*Eish*! This is a seriously hot sauce, not too hot for you I hope!"

The girl frowned. "It's the silly things which worry me more than the big ones. For instance, do I like pasta sauce hot or seriously hot? What are my favourite foods? Books? My favourite colours? Favourite perfume? Do I speak any other languages? Did I wear make-up – what colour lipstick was my favourite? I don't even know how old I am Anna!"

Anna lifted the pasta onto the plates. "Yes, it's all quite unsettling, though I can't imagine how much. It's funny though, if you look at it another way." She stirred the sauce. "So many people want to forget their past, start anew, and here you are, desperately trying to remember yours!"

She picked up one of the cushions hugging it to her chest as Anna continued.

"Some people would kill for the opportunity to re-invent themselves…why are you looking at me like that? Have I said something wrong?"

"No, not at all, I don't know why but what you just said, well, don't know, it's making me feel odd. It's like the word *Eish* you use quite often. It seems familiar to me. What does it mean Anna?"

Anna laughed. "I picked it up from a guy I met, he was from South Africa. It's a word they use to express frustration, puzzlement, things like that – I got into the habit of using it. It's a good word when you can't think of anything else!"

Anna stirred the pasta sauce, tasted it, then added more pepper. "Listen, my dear, you need to get a tighter grip on yourself if you can, or you'll fall apart under all the pressure of trying to remember. I've had patients with Alzheimer's and Dementia and they don't have a hope in hell of getting their memory back – but you do! Be grateful for this at least. Have a little faith – at least you're alive!"

She giggled. "Faith? Where shall I start? Catholic? Church of England? Maybe I'm Jewish?"

Anna laughed. "You were wearing that silver cross and chain when you were admitted to the hospital, but it doesn't tell us much. Pray to any God who will listen, then you've covered all the bases!

"Now come on, sit down, let's find out how hot you like your pasta sauce!"

Although it was strange to be out in the real world again, she soon settled into her temporary home. Anna was as good as her word, taking her to a local charity shop, where she found three or four outfits which would see her through until she began to make some money.

Anna accompanied her to the gift shop for the interview. Feeling nervous she'd looked around the shop, thankful it was not too big. She straightened her skirt and pushed her spiky hair back out of her face.

"Good luck," Anna whispered as the Manager led her away.

*****

The Manager asked her to give a little information about herself. Unbeknown to her, Anna had spoken to him over the phone, before the interview. She'd explained the situation as she knew her friend would find this part distressing, and with no CV he wouldn't have much to go on.

But he was sympathetic, realising how difficult it must be to have no past at all, she was nice looking, well-spoken, he was happy to give her a chance.

*****

Her first two weeks at the shop was not as difficult as she'd anticipated. The shop sold unusual, but expensive gifts. Scented candles in pastel shades of apricot, fern, cream and pale pink, silver table decorations, hand painted mugs and greeting cards, and in one corner, artists supplies of slender sable brushes, oils, water colours, interspersed with pieces of art, to inspire, or buy.

In the middle, spread out on a long table, handmade chocolates nestled in their beds of white tissue, their sheer cellophane wrapping tied with delicate silver ribbons.

The smell of the small collection of coffee table books, on interior décor, triggered a dim memory which slithered away in seconds.

Her job was in sales and working at the till, wrapping and ringing up purchases. The Manager, who was also the buyer, travelled to France, Italy and Germany to stock the shop, and was soon confident enough to leave his new employee in charge.

*****

Tomorrow Anna would be heading home to her family, she would be alone for the first time. But she was gaining confidence every day, convincing herself that in time, she would remember who she was.

Chapter Forty-Eight

W ould you like this gift-wrapped Joe?"
For the past four months Joe Challis had been a regular visitor to the shop. With Anna out of the country she had felt somewhat alone, she found herself looking forward to seeing his cheerful face.

He often popped in with a coffee for her or persuaded her to take a lunch time walk in the park with him. They talked about the weather, the movies, and what was going on in the world.

Joe seemed to sense she was reticent about discussing her personal life but told her about his family who lived in Devon, where he rarely ventured.

His mother owned a small grocery shop in the local village, his father was a marriage councillor, and his older brother, Patrick, had been living in Australia for five years now.

His work as a researcher for an international pharmaceutical company kept him busy and meant he could work from home.

*****

She worked late on Christmas Eve and by the time she got back to the flat she was exhausted. She poured herself a glass of wine. It was a time for family gatherings, she wondered what her family, if she was part of one, were doing and where.

Anna was right, working at the gift shop, meeting new people, was helping her with the slow process of remembering her past, but it was still hazy, with an occasional caress of a memory. It would invariably be the scent of, or the taste of something, the sound of a piece of classical music, she thought she remembered. Her mind veering between what she thought she recalled, or what she might have seen, on television. It was impossible to separate the two. Hard to work out what was real and what was not.

Her phone rang, making her jump. "Hi, it's me, Joe. I'm kind of knocking around on my own this evening. I wondered if you'd like to go out for a glass or two of wine. We could meet at the wine bar near your shop?" His warm reassuring voice was persuasive.

"Come on, it's Christmas Eve, I don't want to spend it on my own, please come?"

She smiled into the phone. She was desperate for company, desperate for anything which would take her mind off who she was, if only for a few hours.

She took a quick shower, changing into black trousers and a black polo neck sweater. Grabbing her coat, she headed out to meet him.

She kissed him on both cheeks as he helped her off with her coat. Hanging it on the coat rack he went to the bar, ordering two glasses of wine. Carols played softly in the background.

"Thanks for calling, Joe. I wasn't looking forward to staring at the walls tonight. But why are you on your own, where's your family?"

"The folks have taken off for Australia to see my brother. They fancied some wall to wall sunshine and barbecues on the beach – don't blame them either!"

He took a sip of his wine. "So now it's your turn - tell me a bit about yourself?"

She looked down at her hands, a stranger's hands with pale bronze nails, wondering how to tackle his question.

"Come on," he urged, "I want to know more about you, where you went to school, your family, where you were brought up. Unless you've done time in prison for murder or worse, but even that could be interesting… you know all about me, now it's your turn."

She swirled the wine around in her glass staring at it as she contemplated her answer, deciding to tell him the truth, hoping it wouldn't spook him.

"I may well have done time in prison for murder, who knows." She laughed at the shocked expression on his face. "I was knocked over by a car some months ago, I can't remember much at all, I don't even know how old I am, or when my birthday is. Diana isn't my name, I don't know what my name is. I was wearing that coat", she nodded towards the coat rack, "the rest of whatever I was wearing didn't make it back into my lost wardrobe. Some kind soul at the hospital arranged to have it dry cleaned for me. I don't remember it as being mine, but it's my one single tenuous link with my past.

"I wear it all the time, it's like being in the arms of someone who knows all about me, knows where I've been, who I've met. I know it sounds a bit mad, but I find it hugely comforting."

He stared at her. "Wow, I've never met anyone who's lost their memory, I can't imagine what it must be like to have a complete blank where your life should be. It would freak me out. But it's not possible you didn't have someone in your life, if you don't mind me saying, you're quite attractive you know."

She took a sip from her glass, smiling at him. "Sweet of you to say, but I haven't a clue if there was someone in my life, I don't think there could have been, otherwise he would have come looking for me. So, I don't think there was anyone. To be honest, no one came looking for me. It's the hardest thing I've had to come to terms with.

"I remembered a few things though. I was brought up in a town, not sure where. I don't recall having any brothers or sisters, so perhaps I didn't, or they would be trying to find me. I can't remember anything about my parents at all.

"I have a vague recollection of living in London, I recognise a lot of it, so this is what I'm assuming."

She smiled at Joe's intent expression. "I dream a lot, and the dreams are vivid, but I have trouble recollecting them when I wake up. My doctor has given me sleeping pills if I need them, but so far I've resisted taking any, in case I miss something when I'm in a deep sleep. Anyway, I had enough sleep when I was in a coma!"

She took a handful of peanuts from the dish on the table. "Last week I dreamt about a man's funeral, I seemed to have known him. It was one dream I was able to recollect the next day because it was so horrible, there was some kind of accident, a big one, lots of people killed. A bus accident maybe, or an earthquake... something like that."

She brushed back her hair, feeling a little embarrassed. "I shouldn't be telling you all this, but I spend so much time on my own, thinking and thinking about who I am, Joe, who I was. It's good to be able to sit and talk about it."

Joe pushed his glasses up with his finger. "If you were living in London someone would have contacted the police if you hadn't returned home? You can't be a tourist not with your posh British accent..."

"No. Anna suggested I might be from New Zealand or South Africa, maybe Zimbabwe, but I don't have an accent, you're right."

"If you were from another country your folks would have reported you missing to the relevant embassy. They'd be looking for you? If they're still around, of course. He reached across the table, giving her hand a comforting squeeze.

"If you ever feel the need to talk, give me a shout. I think it might help if you chat about your thoughts, your dreams, it could trigger something."

He offered her the bowl of peanuts then took a handful himself, tossing them into his mouth, spilling a few down the front of his jumper. "By the way I was watching you on the computer in the shop the other day, you know how to use one, so it's probable you owned a laptop? It would be a treasure trove of information."

She nibbled on a peanut. "It also crossed my mind, but like everything else there's no trace of it. But I do need to buy a laptop, just not sure which one."

"I'll come and help you choose one, if you like? Help you set it up?"

"Thanks Joe, I would like that. I'll wait until Anna gets back. I need to start getting my own things around me again, now I'm working and earning some money. I'd like to do some research on memory loss, I think it will help. You're good at research, it's what you do, maybe you could help me with that as well!"

*****

That night, buoyed by the two glasses of wine, she sank into a deep sleep. In her dreams, she saw an unfamiliar country, and what looked like a tented camp. A tall man, wearing some kind of uniform, was standing beneath a tree with lantern shaped leaves, his face in shadow. She'd had dreams similar to this before, where faces were always in shadow, making it difficult to work out if they were male or female.

But this one was different. He was beckoning her, calling her to come to him, but when she tried to move her feet, to run to him, they refused to move, then he turned his back on her and walked away.

She woke up groggily, reaching for the water next to her. Who was the tall man in the dream? Surely there was no tree in the world with leaves the shape of lanterns? She tried to remember. Because she knew him, she was sure of it. But the harder she tried to remember, the faster the dream receded until it was gone like a sliver of the moon behind a dark cloud. But the one thing she did remember - he'd called her name. He'd called her Emily.

176

Chapter Forty-Nine

S he pushed her way through the crowded restaurant to meet Joe. Last night he'd insisted they have Christmas Day lunch together. He'd already booked a table for himself, and felt sure they could squeeze her in. Breathless with excitement she sat down beside him.

"Joe! I think I know my name – its Emily! It feels right. It was in a dream. A man calling my name, he called me Emily. He was tall and in some sort of foreign country. I thought it might be India, but I'm not sure. He was standing under a tree, with leaves shaped like lanterns. Do you know of any tree like that, I certainly don't?"

"Excellent news! This is good progress, um, Emily – because it means your memory is coming back. Come on let's have lunch I'm beyond starving."

Joe chased the last of his mince pie around his plate before capturing it with a stab of his fork. He sat back and took a sip of his wine.

"Leaves shaped like lanterns eh? No, I don't know of any trees like that…you think it might be India? That would make sense. The people there are big on lanterns, like they are in the Far East. They use them to celebrate important events, funerals, feasts and religious holidays. Maybe they hang them in trees as well as float them down rivers. You didn't see the man's face?"

"No, his face was in shadow, and, yes, it could have been a tree with lanterns. But what sort of person in India wears a uniform?"

"Well, serving members of the military would, or maybe you were at some sort of safari camp. They have some really stylish ones there where people go and try to spot tigers and things. Maybe the man was a tour guide, or a game ranger? Dunno Emily."

"Some mornings, on the edge of sleep, I think I can see someone else in the shadows, a big man with a white beard, then it's gone in the puddle of all the other lost memories, leaving me staring into a past I can't reach." She shook her head in frustration and he changed the subject.

*****

Emily had grown fond of Joe. He phoned her regularly, coming to the gift shop at least twice a week. He was easy to be with and they'd often have a sandwich in the park together at the week-ends, or go to a concert, or a movie. Every Friday she would meet him at the wine bar – something she looked forward to.

She liked his fresh-faced look, his tousled thatch of blonde hair, the smoky grey eyes, the habit he had of pushing his rimless glasses up with his index finger, or polishing them with enthusiasm when he was excited, or agitated, about something.

He was good company and although she yearned for someone to hold her, wanted him to hold her, she kept her distance, afraid to let anyone close to her until she discovered her identity. She knew he understood, and he didn't push the boundaries of their friendship. He'd invited her to his place for dinner a couple of times, seeming to understand when she politely declined. She hadn't invited him to Anna's flat, after all she was a guest there herself, it wouldn't feel right.

In two days' time Anna would be returning to London, then she would have to do something about finding a place to live.

"I can't afford to rent a place near the shop," she told Joe over lunch at the local pub, "which is a pity as I prefer to walk to work. I'm not sure what to do at the moment. I'll have to share a place which is not an attractive thought – living with complete strangers. It's tough enough living with a stranger myself – me! I should start scanning the newspapers and see what I can come up with."

Joe jumped in with alacrity. "I have a fairly large place, it has two bedrooms, two bathrooms, and it's not far from the gift shop. I've been thinking of getting a flat mate for some time now. It would suit me down to the ground to have someone like you. Why not think about it as an option? We could have a few ground rules so we don't trip over each other – I think it could work, at least we know each other now and we're friends?"

Reaching across the table she took his hand. "Where would I be without you Joe?"

He gave her a lop-sided smile. "I'm not sure where you *could* have been without me, all I know is I'm glad you're here with me now, very glad."

Chapter Fifty

Nick Kennedy raked the white sand around the bar, straightening the chairs and tables set in the sand under the thatched umbrellas. He glanced at his watch. Customers would soon start to arrive after a day in the office, or on the beach. The bar was a popular spot for tourists and locals alike, he was busy every night.

Propping the rake against a palm tree he went behind the bar, setting up for the evening ahead.

After selling Honey Badger Lodge he'd cast around for a business to start, or buy, in Mombasa. He hadn't considered purchasing a beach bar, given his history, but the endless nights on his own drove him to make the decision to buy this one, down on the south coast, not far from the family beach house where he now lived. He ran and managed the bar himself. It kept him busy, harnessing in his thoughts of Emily. The memories stronger than the life he was now living. He allowed himself two glasses of wine a night, keeping well away from the whisky.

There were plenty of women he could have had relationships with. They came to the bar in the evening eager to attract his attention, and when his physical needs overcame him he would give in to them, steering clear of any involvement of any kind. He would never put himself in such a vulnerable position again. If this meant being on his own for the rest of his life, then so be it.

Chapter Fifty-One

Emily pushed open the door to Harrods, the icy January air snaking in behind her. Pulling off her glove with her teeth she punched the button in the lift to the fashion floor. This was now her favourite shop, she spent hours there wandering through the various departments. Without thinking she felt herself drawn to the bridal section. Mystified she followed her instincts. Whenever she felt an urge to do something inexplicable, she did it, hoping it might stir a memory.

*****

An assistant looked up from her paperwork, watching the woman touching the transparent covers of the wedding dresses. She frowned. Wasn't this the woman who paid for her wedding gown but failed to collect it? She had a good memory for faces, and she was sure she was right. She hesitated. What if she was wrong? It could be embarrassing for both of them. Despite her slight doubts, she approached Emily.

"May I help you, madam? "

Emily turned to her and smiled. "Um, no thank you. These gowns are so…" her voice trailed off.

The assistant studied her. She chose her next words with care.

"When is madam planning to get married?"

"Oh, I'm not planning to get married at all. I just wanted to take a look around."

The assistant returned to her desk, pondering her next move. Something must have gone wrong with the woman's wedding plans, but it was none of her business. She watched Emily turn and leave the room in somewhat of a hurry. Shrugging her shoulders, she went back to her computer, tapping into the data base.

Yes, Emily Hunter, that was her name. She was supposed to have been married somewhere overseas – well it obviously hadn't happened.

The dress was supposed to have been collected in April last year, instead of hanging in the store room where it was now.

She closed down the computer and went back to her paperwork. Maybe it was just someone who looked like her.

*****

Emily sat down in a café opposite Harrods. Her legs trembling as thoughts, like frightened bats, flew haphazardly around her mind. A wedding dress – she remembered trying one on, having it altered. But where? And if this was the case where was the man she was going to marry?

There were too many questions swirling through her brain. She blew on her coffee taking tiny sips. It would all come back to her in time; she knew she had to be patient as Doctor Harrington had cautioned her.

A woman walked past with her dog on a lead. Emily sucked in her breath. Oh, my God, suppose she'd owned a dog! She tried not to think of what might have happened to it if she'd never returned home. The English were a nation of dog lovers, someone would have saved it, heard it barking, or whining. She couldn't think about this now, not on top of everything else she was struggling with.

Feeling through her memories was like a delicate knotted chain, trying to find the link, through the links, which would untangle them, and lay them out flat.

She put her face in her hands, sometimes she thought she would go mad with all the *what ifs*. Sitting up straight she drained her coffee cup. It would all work out, one day she would remember who she was, where she came from. Some days were just more difficult to deal with. Maybe taking some of the anti-depressants, Doctor Harrington had prescribed, would help.

At times she felt as though someone was holding her head underwater and her brain would burst with the pressure.

Chapter Fifty-Two

Nick parked under the shade of a tree; it was a scorcher in Mombasa today. He wanted to finish his grocery shopping as soon as possible and be back down on the beach where there was a cool breeze.

The store was busy. Stopping to chat with a few friends and acquaintances, he filled his trolley and waited in line at the check-out.

"Hello Nick!" He turned at the sound of his name.

"Anna! What are you doing here? I thought you were in London! It's good to see you again." He hugged her.

"I had three months' holiday accumulated, and took another two months unpaid, so I could come home to see the family. It's good to be back. I was so sorry to hear about Jonathan. What a terrible thing to have happened."

He nodded at her, saying nothing.

"But Nick what are you doing here on the coast? Why aren't you at your lodge? The tourists are here in their droves!"

"It's a long story, Anna...but I want to hear all your news. Let's go grab a coffee when we've finished here."

He'd known Anna, and her parents, for years. Her father had been one of the finest doctors in Tanzania. When he retired, the family had relocated to Mombasa.

Nick packed his groceries in the boot of the car, then headed for the coffee shop. Anna was waiting for him. They ordered their coffee.

"Now, Anna, tell me all about London and your life there."

She smiled at him. "I like London, but not the winters there. I loved having Christmas here! I enjoy my job though. I work at the Chelsea and Westminster Hospital, which is huge. I have a flat not far from there, it's not big, but its close enough for me to walk to work. It's an expensive city so I don't socialize much."

"No man in your life then," he teased her.

"A couple of good friends, that's all. I don't have time for anything more, with all the shift work at the hospital. Besides, I want to come back home one day, in the not too distant future. I don't want to live in England for the rest of my life."

She took a tentative sip of her coffee. "I heard you didn't marry Natalie after all – how come?"

He sighed. "It didn't work out. Natalie and I are good friends, as you know, we still are. We thought marriage might work for us but changed our minds."

"Just as well I manage to keep up with all the gossip!" She grinned at him. "No new love in your life then, Nick? I can't believe you're still single. You're one of the hottest bachelors in East Africa."

She watched as he placed his cup back on the saucer with care. "There was someone. I met her at my lodge. She was unlike anyone I'd ever met, I fell for her, Anna."

Anna sat back in her chair and laughed. "Come on Nick, we all know the stories about romance under the stars and the moon, handsome game rangers, khaki fever etc. It's why people go on safari, they're looking for a bit of romance. I'm surprised *you* fell for it."

He shook his head. "No," he insisted, "she was different." For a split second, he was tempted to show her the photograph of Emily which he always carried in his wallet but decided against it. There was no point now, what would it achieve?

"I felt something for her as soon as I saw her. It's never happened to me before. I used to laugh when people told me they 'fell in love instantly'. But she was special – unusual."

"So, what happened? What was her name? Where was she from?"

"Nothing happened. It didn't work out. It was a bad time in my life; then I lost my brother."

Anne stirred her coffee. "Maybe she didn't feel the same way about you, Nick. Though God knows why, you're a real catch! Maybe she decided she didn't want to live in Kenya for the rest of her life, not everyone wants to make that sort of major move."

Diplomatically she changed the subject.

"I have an interesting person staying in my flat at the moment. Diana. We met at the hospital. She's looking after my place until I get back. I hope she remembers to water the plants, she can be forgetful sometimes. She's a mystery though."

She took another sip of her coffee, eyeing him over the brim of her cup. He was miles away, fiddling with his coffee spoon, not listening

184

to her. She saw the loss in his eyes, the stillness in him, and her own eyes filled with sadness.

She shook her head, gathered up her sunglasses and handbag and stood to leave.

"Thanks for the coffee, Nick. I must get back to the house, pack up my things. I'm off back to London at the week-end. I'm eager to see how Diana survived without me."

Nick looked perplexed. "Diana?"

"For goodness sake Nick," she said exasperated, as she stood up. "I've just told you about her, but you weren't listening." She looked at her watch. "I have to go." He pushed his chair back and stood up.

She stood on her toes, kissing him on the cheek. "No one ever died of a broken heart you know, trust me I'm a nurse. You'll find someone else, give it time. One day another woman will stroll into your lodge and you'll fall in love all over again."

"It's just not going to happen, Anna. I sold Honey Badger six months ago and bought a beach bar here. I have a new life. Now, off you go. Next time you visit you must come see the bar – I'll stand you a drink." He hesitated then took her hand.

"I'd appreciate if you didn't tell anyone about all this. It was a private matter and I wouldn't want to be the subject of speculation around the dinner table – you know how it is here?"

"Of course, Nick. Apart from the fact you've told me nothing about her, anyway my lips are sealed, I won't breathe a word to anyone. Oh, I almost forgot. Congratulations on your book, *Beneath the Shimmering Stars*. It's stunning. You should think about doing another one." She hugged him again and began to walk towards her car. Then, half turning she called back to him.

"Why did you choose that particular title for your book, it conjures up all sorts of things?"

"When I think of her I think of the stars – just a story I told her once."

Anna drove home thinking of her conversation with him. Well whoever she was she'd knocked him for six and, if she was not mistaken, he was still in love with her.

*****

"I saw Nick Kennedy in the store today, we had coffee together." Anna said to her father over dinner. "He seemed a bit morose, nothing like his old self. I mean I know the family have gone through hell with the death of Jonathan, but there's something else. Have I missed out on some gossip?

"Not really. He met someone, but it didn't work out in the end.

"Only a handful of people knew Nick's plans, the Kennedy's are a powerful, intensely private family, as you well know. The subject was never brought up again. Nick closed his lodge to the public, spent some time there on his own apparently. The death of Jonathan shattered him, over and above losing the girl."

Anna felt a wave of sympathy for her old friend. "Then what happened to him Daddy?"

"Well, then he sold up, came here to Mombasa, bought a bar and moved into the family house. I've seen him on a couple of occasions but didn't bring up the subject of the girl. You remember the look he can give if someone gets too close to something he doesn't want to talk about; I've seen that expression many times."

He smiled at his daughter. "Yes, I know, with his history buying a beach bar was maybe not such a good idea…but think about it. It was almost as if he wanted to confront his demons head on – what else did he have to lose?"

Anna passed the salad bowl to her father's outstretched hands, intrigued with the story. "So why didn't you tell me all this?"

"There didn't seem any reason to. I knew you would come home at some point, and decided I'd leave it up to Nick if he wanted to discuss it, which clearly he didn't when you had coffee with him."

"What was the woman's name?"

Her father shook his head. "I can't remember to tell the truth. The bottom line was the whole thing turned out to be a non-event. It was embarrassing for the family, especially after he and Natalie broke off their engagement - there were plenty of rumours flying around."

Glancing at his watch he pushed his chair back. "Better phone your mother and see how she's enjoying her shopping trip in Nairobi, it's time for her to come home, before she bankrupts me!"

Anna finished washing up and dried her hands, cursing herself for being so insensitive to Nick's mood when she'd seen him that morning. It was obvious he was still hurting over the love affair which had come to an abrupt end. Knowing him as she did he would have been devastated, embarrassed, by what had happened. Maybe one day he would tell her about it.

186

She rubbed cream into her hands as she looked out over the darkening garden. Love could be so destructive, something not to be played around with. God knows she'd seen it happen so many times with her friends, and some of her patients. How damaging love can be, how powerful when it all goes wrong. One going on with a new life, the other left behind with the devastation – the hopelessness.

She knew what depression looked like, she knew what broken looked like. Nick was going through a rough patch. Someone should invent a pill against falling in love – but would anyone take it?

She smiled to herself – what a very odd expression it was "*falling in love*," why not leaping into love? Or, jumping into love? Surely the very fact that *falling* usually meant the end result would be getting hurt?

She took off her apron, turned off the kitchen lights and went to join her father on the veranda.

Chapter Fifty-Three

Emily sat curled up in her chair listening to some classical music. Anna would be back tomorrow, she couldn't wait to see her and hear about her holiday. She picked up the novel she was reading, trying to concentrate. Memories, like the rustle of leaves on a tree, distracted her again. Exasperated, she closed the book, pulled back the curtains and stared out into the brittle January night.

She was no closer to knowing who she was than five months ago, when Anna left. Yes, she'd cobbled some memories together, had fleeting images of others, but still she didn't have anywhere near the full picture. But she was now sure her name was Emily. She'd phoned the police woman and fed her this scrap of information.

She reached over and picked up one of the glossy books from the table. Idly, she flicked through the pages, beautiful pictures of unusual houses in America. Bored she reached for the next one. As she pulled it towards her she knocked another one onto the floor. Cursing, she picked it up, hoping she hadn't damaged it in any way. She glanced at the title: *Beneath the Shimmering Stars.* Settling back, she opened it.

The photographer certainly knew his job. The photographs were magnificent. She stared at the pride of lions, the lioness sitting on a rock scanning the horizon, her young cubs asleep around her. The shot was so clear she could almost see the cat's whiskers twitching. The blood red sky of the sunset made a dramatic backdrop to the tableau on and around the rock.

Turning the last page, she went back to the beginning. She was curious to see who the author and photographer was. She opened the inside front cover. His eyes... She felt her scalp prickle.

She studied his photograph. Did she know him? Had he been into the gift shop? She shook her head. There was no way she would have forgotten a man as attractive as this one.

Emily closed her eyes against the hopeless, fragmented, memories and images, but inside her lids they rose up again, the same images, determined and undiminished, invisible trails in the air.

Glancing at the clock she decided to go to bed. She wanted to clean up the flat before Anna arrived home. She put the book back where she'd found it, before heading for her bedroom.

Sleep eluded her, with reluctance she took a sleeping tablet. All she could see in the dark was the image of his face, but nothing else. She tossed and turned, despite the pill, unable to get Nicholas Kennedy out of her thoughts, finally she fell into a restless sleep, holding him with her into her dreams.

The next morning, she awoke tired and tense. Her dreams vivid, Nicholas Kennedy woven through each one of them.

Frustrated she jumped out of bed and went to make some coffee. She couldn't get him out of her head.

Emily vacuumed the flat, cleaned the kitchen floor vigorously, then washed up the dishes before dashing out to buy some flowers. She stopped off at Sainsbury's, buying enough food to fill the fridge. Tonight, she'd cook dinner for Anna, who would be tired after her long flight.

Satisfied she had all she needed, Emily returned to the flat, unpacked the bags, and put everything away.

Sitting with a mug of coffee her eyes strayed to the spine of the book she'd pored over last night. Firmly she put the picture of him out of her mind. It was ridiculous to think she knew this man – she didn't. She put the radio on, turning up the volume.

*****

Anna smiled at her friend across the table. "Another thing we now know is you can cook. Dinner was delicious Di… sorry I mean Emily. I have to say you're looking good, so much better than when I last saw you. Your hair has really grown!"

The two friends moved away from the table and sat in the chairs in Anna's book corner. "I brought back some of our world-renowned coffee, let me make some, then I'll tell you all about my trip."

Anna regaled her with stories of her family, and how they'd prepared such a warm welcome home for her.

"There must have been over thirty of us around the table for dinner on my first night back. I'd forgotten what a large family we are. I was shattered after the flight to Nairobi and the overnight train to Mombasa but had to stay awake so as not to offend anyone."

"Oh, I assumed you went back to your home in Tanzania!"

Anna smiled. "No, I was born there, lived there with my parents until I was twelve, my father had a practice there. When it was time for me to get a further education, they decided to go back to Kenya, where my parents came from.

"He started a practice in Nairobi until he retired, then they went to live in Mombasa. Anyway, as I was saying, my father sat at the head of the table, as always, telling anyone who would listen, who hadn't already heard him say it over and over again, how proud he was of me for following in his footsteps, studying medicine.

"My mother spent all her time hauling huge platters of food out of the kitchen. It was after two in the morning before everyone left and I could get to bed. But it was great to be home again." She stopped, putting her hand over her mouth, stricken.

"Oh, I'm sorry! I wasn't thinking, you know me when I get going. How insensitive to talk about my family when you've spent so long wondering if you even have one. Let's change the subject; it's your turn to tell me all your news."

Emily brought her up to date on what had been happening at the gift shop for the past months. She told her about Joe, his offer to flat share with her, and she was going around to see it in the morning. Anna gave an approving nod. Then she told her about the bridal shop at Harrods, how she remembered being fitted for a wedding gown, though she couldn't remember which shop.

Anna's large brown eyes opened wider. "You were going to marry someone? Oh, my goodness, where is he then?"

Anna gave into another stifled yawn. "Anyway, because you remembered trying on a wedding dress doesn't mean you were getting married. You might have modelled one somewhere, you could have been a model with your looks. I wouldn't read too much into it if I were you. I must go to bed, before I fall over. Sleep well Emily. We can clear up in the morning. Thank you for dinner and the flowers, what a home coming! I shall miss you when you move out."

Emily's mind was in turmoil. Maybe Anna was right, the dress she thought she remembered being fitted for might not have been hers at all.

She sighed. She would put this question in her "possibility bank" along with all the others she had accumulated.

She had to stop all the questions spinning around in her head, let her brain work its way through what might have happened, or what did happen.

She would take another one of her sleeping pills and try to get a good night's sleep.

*****

The next day Emily left Anna to sleep off her jet lag, she was going to take a look at what could be her next home.

Joe was expecting her and the coffee was brewing. She stepped into the front room. With its high ceilings, big picture windows and wooden floors, the room was full of morning sunshine. An old-fashioned fireplace held logs and fir cones. A large flat-screen television sat in the corner. The cream linen sofa and matching chairs looked seductive; she could imagine herself spending hours curled up with a book, warmed by a crackling fire, Joe beside her for company. The sitting room led onto a dining room, with enough chairs to accommodate six hungry people.

Upstairs her proposed bedroom was bright and sunny. Joe, it seemed, preferred as little colour in the rooms as possible. The double bed and bed linen were all white, as was the dressing table and mirror. Two turquoise cushions were his single concession to colour here. The bathroom was white and spacious. She loved everything about the place. Joe followed her around like a puppy looking for a home, as she made her way through the rooms.

"Well, what do you think? Will it do? Does it pass muster?" He pushed his glasses up his nose, then took them off, rubbing them vigorously. His face awash with hope.

She hugged him. "I love it, Joe. Let me fetch the coffee then we can get down to the lease, and the rent etc."

For the next hour, they discussed the house rules. If one of them cooked, the other would do the washing up. They would do their own laundry and take it in turns to do the weekly shop and cleaning of the flat. They both agreed should either one of them have a friend they wanted to spend the night with, then it would have to be at the friend's apartment and not here.

Emily knew from her side of things this was never going to happen, she was still too confused to even think about any kind of relationship, and she felt Joe was more than interested in pursuing a relationship with her. She would have to be sensitive to this, not encourage him, or give him any kind of hope.

She returned to Anna's flat. Anna was up and having her first cup of coffee of the day. She told her about Joe's place. "It's about twenty minutes from here, Anna, walking distance. So, I'm hoping we'll visit each other on a regular basis. You'll love Joe, he's great."

"Tell me more about him then."

"Joe's twenty-eight and does research for an international pharmaceutical company, something to do with malaria, and works from home. He's a nice guy, easy to get along with." She told Anna about his family in Devon and his brother in Australia.

"I'm looking forward to meeting him." Anna stretched and rose from her chair.

Emily stood up and hugged her friend. "You've been so good to me, Anna. I don't know how to thank you?"

"One day your memory will come back, it's all the thanks I'll need. I'm as intrigued as you to find out who you are."

Chapter Fifty-Four

That evening whilst Anna caught up with the news on television, Emily packed her few belongings into Anna's suitcase, ready for her move the next day. When she finished, she came and sat down.

Anna glanced up and rolled her eyes. "I can't bear to watch the news these days, all the information running along the bottom of the screen, things flashing all over the place; and not content with just reading the news, the newsreader then has to point to things with a stick and explain everything with visuals, then repeat everything that's been said by putting it up on the screen.

Anna reached the remote. "They treat their viewers as if they're complete idiots and didn't catch things the first time around! Then they play the whole damn thing over again ten minutes later. *Eish*, I'm sick to death of hearing about terrorists, all the foiled attempts and the not so foiled. The world has gone mad. Honestly, if the media didn't give these damn terrorists any publicity, the world would be a better place. All it does is frighten everyone, which is exactly what the bad guys want." She hit the off switch and put on some music.

"All packed?"

Emily rubbed her eyes. "Yes, not much to pack though, but at least it's more than I had when I arrived here, which was precisely nothing. I'll return your suitcase as soon as I can."

Anna laughed. "There's no hurry to return it, I'm not planning on going anywhere after those two long flights. I loathe travelling these days, all the queuing, the crowds of passengers, the endless security checks. Come and sit, I'll make us some hot chocolate before we head off to bed."

When she returned from the kitchen she found Emily looking through one of her books. Putting the mugs down, she glanced at the title her friend was so absorbed in.

"What do you think of that book? It was done by a good friend of mine, in Kenya."

Emily curled her legs under her. "It's incredible, he seems to be able to see more through a lens, than the average photographer. The shots are so real; I expect the animals to leap off the pages."

She frowned, looking up at Anna. "You know this Nicholas Kennedy?"

Anna nodded. "Our families have been friends for years, I used to see Nick during school holidays when we lived in Nairobi. We played tennis with him, and his girlfriend Natalie, at the Muthaiga Club. I lost touch with him for a couple of years when I moved to London."

Anna blew on her hot chocolate, taking a cautious sip. "Funnily enough I saw him last week. I bumped into him at the supermarket, we had coffee together."

"I know it's ridiculous, Anna, but in a strange sort of way he seems familiar to me. I keep telling myself he must have come into the shop at some point, or maybe someone similar to him."

"He does seem to have this effect on women," Anna laughed. "He always has. He rarely comes to England or travels anywhere. When the family opened their game lodge to the public he travelled all over the world promoting it, but I don't think he enjoyed it much, he was always keen to get back home. He went to school here, but the weather drove him mad, he couldn't wait to return to Africa."

She made room for her cup on the table in front of her and continued.

"As soon as he finished his Zoology degree he high tailed it back to Kenya. He was over here for the launch of this book though, the one you're holding. He did a book signing which I missed; I didn't even know he was in town, but he made sure I got a copy as you can see. He took the shot behind you, the one of the elephant?"

Anna began to say something, then stopped. He had made her promise she wouldn't repeat anything about his private life.

She leaned forward and stirred her mug of hot chocolate, then lifted it with both hands. "Everyone knows his family; it's one of the oldest in Kenya."

Anna looked at Nick's magnificent photo of the elephant hanging on the wall behind Emily's head. "Their ranch was one of the largest in Kenya, then Hugh Kennedy, Nick's father, decided to divide the ranch up, sell it off to the local African farmers, who had little land themselves.

"It was a wonderful gesture on his part; giving something back to the people. They bought a place just outside of Nairobi, it's where they live now."

She put her empty mug down on the table. "Hugh travels around the country teaching the African farmers how to get the most out of their land. He does good work."

She smothered a yawn and stood up. "It's time for bed. Sweet dreams Emily. You'll certainly have those if you dream about Nick Kennedy, you and hundreds of other women!"

Chapter Fifty-Five

Emily tapped on the door of the study. "Sorry to interrupt Joe, how did it go today with the research, is it coming together? What are you working on?"

"Yup, I've made good progress. Mosquitoes are canny little buggers, but with a lot of hard work we'll come up with a vaccine one day. It's what I'm working on at the moment.

"I think I've spent enough time in front of this computer." He ran his fingers through his hair and stretched. "Come on, I've cooked dinner for you."

He stirred the casserole, tasted it, then tossed some of his wine in, with some more fresh herbs for good measure.

"Are those potatoes ready, I'm starving?"

She laughed. "Oh, Joe you're always starving! I'll lay the table. We were so busy in the shop today, I just want to eat, take my shoes off and curl up in a chair. What's on television tonight?"

"Nothing much I'm afraid, we're down to documentaries and wild life, but it's better than nothing, all the movies look like rubbish."

*****

Joe fiddled with the remote changing from one station to another. "Well we can either watch a documentary on Wild Dogs, I think it was filmed in Botswana – could be interesting. Or there's one about elephants which I don't fancy. I'm not really interested in watching them plod around the bush, chucking dust over their backs, knocking trees over, and flapping those great ears around. Ah, what about this one," he selected a channel, "it's a half hour programme on the Great Migration in East Africa. Then there's a documentary on 9/11. Shall we try them?"

Emily tucked her feet under her. "Sure, why not. 9/11 is one event I'm grateful I can't remember! The migration could be interesting though."

Joe sipped his beer engrossed in the magnificent spectacle of thousands of wildebeest making their annual migration across the Serengeti.

"This is amazing isn't it? How do they know when to gather in one place like that, then it's like a starter's gun goes off, and they all gallop off? I mean, how do they know where to go?"

"You would have made a good wild animal Joe, just think you could sit around all day doing nothing but eat."

He threw a cushion at her. "Very funny." He said, turning back to the screen. "I'd love to go to Africa one day. Like millions of people in the world I'd like to go on safari, see all this," he gestured at the screen, "for real – it must be fantastic. I know a lot of those wildebeest got chomped as they tried to cross the river, but most of them did get away. I wonder if they suffered from post-traumatic stress afterwards? I mean, I would have if I'd been chased by lions, or just missed the gaping jaws of a crocodile."

Emily laughed. "I think they would just have been grateful, but dreading the return journey, then having to do it all over again the following year."

The credits began to roll and Joe sighed. "I enjoyed that. I'll switch to the 9/11 doccy, and we can lose ourselves in another world with different kinds of animals…"

Twenty minutes into the programme, she suddenly stood up. "I don't want to hear any more about Bin Laden or the damn Shadow Dancer. It makes my skin crawl to think of how many innocent people they killed, the lives of the families they've destroyed. What kind of animals are they?

"I've seen enough thanks, I don't want to watch any more or I'll have nightmares. Goodnight Joe. I'll see you in the morning."

"Goodnight Emily." He watched her leave the room, a puzzled expression on his face.

*****

Joe woke up when he heard her moaning. Intrigued he padded to her bedroom and was about to knock when she screamed.

He went to her side. "Hey, Emily," he murmured, squeezing her shoulder, not wanting to frighten her. "It's alright. It's me, Joe, I'm here, you're having a nightmare that's all… wake up."

He switched on the bedside lamp as she struggled to sit up. When he saw the panic in her eyes, he sat down and put his arms around her.

"Oh God, Joe. Such a terrible dream."

Joe sat on the bed, peering at her myopically. "It's okay it was just a nightmare, tell me what happened, what did you dream about?"

"It must have been the documentary we were watching…I told you it would give me nightmares, people screaming. Horrible."

"Sorry Emily, my fault, we should have watched the plodding elephants instead. Can I get you anything, some tea maybe?"

Emily wrapped her arms around her knees, rocking back and forth. "Would you stay with me for a while?

"I think I'll take one of those sleeping pills, I don't want to go back into the nightmare."

"I'll get one for you – where are they?"

"In the cupboard in the bathroom. Thanks Joe."

He retrieved his glasses from his bedroom, then rummaged around in her cupboard until he found the pills. Checking the dosage, he popped the lid and shook one out into his hand. He picked up another plastic container. Anti-depressants. She hadn't mentioned to him she was on other medication. Filling a glass with water he went back to the bedroom.

"Here we go – I'll stay with you 'til you fall asleep."

"Will you hold me, Joe, I feel so shaken up."

Putting his arms around her again, he rocked her back to sleep.

He lay awake and thought about her dream. Had the 9/11 programme evoked some kind of memory from her past?

He held her close until she fell asleep but fought sleep himself.

Careful not to awake her he sat up straight. He would not sleep, not whilst he had her, warm and soft, in his arms. He would stay with her the whole night in case the nightmares returned. If they did, he would be there right beside her, watching over her. Ready to help and comfort her in any way he could.

Chapter Fifty-Six

The supervisor held up a wedding dress. "Is this the gown the bride - who was it," she glanced at the label on the plastic wrapping. "Emily Hunter, failed to collect?"

The assistant nodded. "Yes. Funnily enough she came here a couple of weeks ago. At first, I wasn't sure if it was her, but I have a good memory for faces. I'm convinced it was Emily Hunter."

The superintendent sighed. She knew the store policy. The dress must be returned to the person who paid for it.

"How did she pay for it?"

The assistant turned to the computer, tapping on the keyboard. "By credit card on the seventh April. It needed some slight alterations. She was due to collect it on, let me see…on the thirteenth of April, almost a year ago."

"Well get onto the credit card company then, see if you can get an address out of them," she said testily. "This dress must be returned one way or another. As you say it's been sitting here for almost a year now."

*****

Frustrated the assistant slammed down the telephone. With all this data protection red tape, it was impossible to get any information on Emily Hunter. Where she lived or where she worked. But they promised to send a letter to her last known address, advising her of the purchase made at Harrods. This was all they were prepared to do.

The letter arrived, joining another postmarked from Kenya.

*****

Emily turned as she heard the front door open. "Hi, it's me," Joe called out. "I've got everything for dinner tonight, but forgot the pasta sauce, sorry."

She rolled her eyes at him then smiled. "Don't worry, I have to go out anyway. Harrods called to say they have the shirt I ordered. I want to wear it tomorrow. I'll whiz into their divine food hall and pick up some pasta sauce."

Humming under her breath she made her way towards the food hall.

"Miss Hunter? Excuse me, Miss Hunter," the assistant called out breathlessly.

Emily carried on, oblivious to the sound of her name. She felt a tap on her shoulder and turned around startled.

"Miss Hunter?"

Emily frowned, she didn't know this woman. "No, I'm sorry, I'm not Miss Hunter."

"You're not Emily Hunter? I'm so sorry, my mistake…"

Emily felt her legs give way beneath her. A chair was produced and a bottle of water hijacked from a passing shopper, who was now watching the drama being played out in front of him.

"I'm sorry I seem to have upset you. You look so similar to the Emily Hunter who paid for her wedding dress in April last year but didn't collect it."

Emily stared at her aghast. "Are you sure it was me?"

"Well yes, I was quite sure up until now, but if you're not Miss Hunter…"

"Look," Emily said, her voice shaking, "it could be my surname, I'm not sure."

The assistant's thin penciled eyebrows crawled upwards in surprise. "If you're feeling a little steadier perhaps we could go up to the bridal department, I'll show you the gown. You signed for it you see; your signature is there."

Emily breathed slowly in and out. If this was true, then it was incredible news. It would mean she was right about her name being Emily, and, if the shop assistant was correct, then her surname was Hunter.

She frowned. If she'd been engaged to be married, where was her engagement ring? She'd been wearing no jewellery except for the slim silver chain and cross around her neck, when she was admitted into the hospital. With some trepidation, she followed the assistant.

200

Emily had signed for her dress using the name Emily Hunter, she signed this name again now – the signatures were identical. There could now be no doubt of her true identity.

*****

Joe heard her come into the apartment. He continued to prepare the salad, waiting for her to come bounding into the kitchen, as she always did. Curious as to what was taking her so long, he wandered into the sitting room.

"Hey, where's the pasta sauce?"

She was sitting in the chair looking shocked. Next to her, wrapped in a transparent plastic clothes bag was something long and white, something as white as the colour of her face and knuckles.

Hastily he returned to the kitchen and poured a glass of brandy. She seemed as though she were in some kind of trance. He placed the glass on the table next to her and took her hands, rubbing them between his own, feeling how cold they were.

"What is it? What's happened? You're scaring me. Did something happen to you, did you remember something which frightened you? Here take a sip of this."

She sipped the brandy he held to her lips. Some colour seeped back into her cheeks.

"My wedding dress," she whispered pointing at the bag next to her. "This is my wedding dress. I bought it a year ago. My name is Emily Hunter," then she burst into tears.

He held her, until she gained control of herself. "What happened then, tell me?"

Rubbing her eyes, she told him.

"I asked the lady in the bridal department if I'd told her where I was going to be married, but she didn't remember. So, it was a dead end." She gave him a shaky smile, taking another sip of her brandy.

He pushed the hair back from her face, kissing her on the forehead. "But this is great news. Now you know your name!"

He gave her his full attention as she told him the story.

He took her hands in his. "The first thing we must do tomorrow is get hold of the police woman, let her know you now have your name. They should be able to tap into a data base, find out more about you. Now let's check out your dress and try to be positive about things."

Emily nodded at him, tears balancing on her lower lashes. "I should take a look. Maybe I'll remember something about my mysterious fiancée."

Joe unzipped the clothes bag and drew the gown out. He whistled. She would have made a stunning bride wearing this. The bodice and tiny shoulder straps were encrusted with Swarovski crystals which shimmered and sparkled in the late afternoon sun. The long skirt cascaded out into a fishtail at the back. It was magnificent.

"Why don't you try it on? It might trigger your memory a bit."

But she shook her head and shuddered, "I don't think I'll be able to handle that. It's all too much at the moment, my mind is reeling. Please take it away Joe, put it somewhere."

With care he placed the gown in its bag and zipped it up. Upstairs he pushed it to the back of his own wardrobe. Better if she didn't have a constant reminder, each time she opened her own.

Joe came back to her carrying two glasses of wine. "Here's to you Emily Hunter, we finally found you!"

Chapter Fifty-Seven

Emily hesitated at the door of her former flat, taking a deep breath to calm herself, before ringing the bell.

Police Constable Milton had provided more information about herself. Emily now knew her date of birth, June 9th, and where she was born, South Africa. She was thirty-two years old. She knew her parent's names, where they were married, and where they died. She'd been married to an Italian/American, Marcus Hunter, who had died on September 11th. She wondered what her marriage had been like; what kind of a husband he'd been, what he had looked like? She and Marcus had lived in this flat in Chelsea. Over a year ago the flat was sold.

They gave her details of her bank account and credit card numbers. Now she had her identity back, and a sizeable bank account, but very little in the memory bank. She was planning to give Anna three thousand pounds to donate to a charity of her choice in Africa. It was the least she could do, after all Anna had done for her, and she could afford it now.

She heard footsteps and the door was thrown open. A young man gave her a questioning look, then, much to her surprise, smiled with pleasure

"I'm sorry to intrude," she said nervously, smoothing her hair back. "My name's Emily, I used to live here. I lost my memory, but it's coming back bit by bit…" She knew she was babbling and tried to slow down.

"I wondered if I might look around, see if I can remember anything," she refrained from peering over his shoulder to see inside. "I know it's a lot to ask, but it's important?"

The young man hesitated, then held out his hand. "I'm Paul Fancourt, of course you may. Come on in." He held the door open and she stepped inside. "I'll make some coffee, then show you around, the sitting room is through there."

Emily sat down gingerly on the edge of the chair. She looked around her. Images came to mind - a man sitting near the window - the two of them sitting down together for dinner, the man, then, must have been Marcus.

She could see the dining room through the alcove. She tried to picture his face… and failed, but now understood why the documentary she and Joe had watched had frightened and disturbed her so much.

Despite all the new information she now had about herself she was still puzzled by one thing. Where were all her things? Her clothes, books, photographs? She wouldn't have left her personal things behind when she sold the flat?

"Here we go Emily, I hope it's not too strong for you." Paul handed her a cup indicating she should help herself to cream and sugar.

She shook her head and smiled at him. "I prefer it black, Paul, well at least I think I do! The police tell me I sold the apartment, so it must have been you I sold it to. When you saw me, you smiled so you must have recognized me?"

It was his turn to shake his head. "No, I didn't buy it from you," he raised an eyebrow. "I would remember if I had!"

"Who did you buy it from then…oh!"

A large black and white cat streaked through the sitting room, leaping onto Emily's lap, butting her chin with his head, purring loudly, his paws kneading into her thighs. She smoothed its fur and laughed. "What a gorgeous cat, and so friendly!"

Paul looked bemused. "He's never done this with any of my other visitors, normally he runs away, hides somewhere, is he bothering you?"

"No, not at all. What's his name?"

"Oliver. I inherited him from the couple who used to live here, they couldn't take him with them.

"I bought this flat from them. They'd been here a couple of months when the husband was offered a contract in Hong Kong. I'd just qualified as a dentist and fell in love with the place, and Oliver of course."

He looked at her. "I bought the flat with everything in it, including Oliver. It was a blessing for me because I didn't have time to shop for furniture and pots and pans. They told me they bought all their things from the previous owner, so it must have been you."

He blew on his coffee. "The other thing I didn't realize was I'd inherited a suitcase, it was under the bed. It was months before I discovered it," he gave a short laugh.

"I was looking for Oliver, and there he was crouched next to the suitcase as if he was guarding it.

"I assumed it belonged to the previous owners. I thought they must have forgotten it in their haste to get to Hong Kong. No doubt they'll send for it at some point. I don't know what's in it, it's locked. Maybe it was things for a charity shop. I should do something about it, but I haven't had time. I'd forgotten all about it until now, so thanks for reminding me!"

Emily's heart sank. She'd been depending on the new owners of the flat for information. She surmised she must have told them she was getting married, where she was going to live. It would have been vital information. Now this too seemed to have slipped through her fingers. Where had she gone when she sold the flat? If she'd checked into a hotel, then her suitcase must be somewhere?

They finished their coffee and Paul stood up. "Sorry to rush you, but I have to be at the practice in half an hour. Let me show you around, or maybe you'd prefer to do it on your own?

"Go ahead, I'll wait for you here." He sat down again.

Emily wandered through the flat, holding the cat, recognizing it all. The furniture, the pale-yellow walls in the bathroom, even the curtains were the same. Not wishing to take up any more of Paul's time she returned to the sitting room, put Oliver down on the sofa, and shrugged on her coat. Picking up her handbag she turned to go, then stopped.

"Paul, may I see the suitcase?"

"Sure. Let me go and get it."

He took the stairs two at a time, reappearing a few moments later.

She stared at the pale brown leather case. It was hers, there was no question in her mind – she'd found her suitcase. Oliver jumped off the sofa, weaving his way around the outside of the case, then sat on top of it staring at her.

She threw her arms around the young dentist and hugged him. "Thank you, thank you so much. It's mine! I've found something which belongs to me!"

*****

Paul closed the front door behind her, then cursed. There had been some letters addressed to her on the hall table, but the former owners had left no forwarding address for her. One he remembered with exotic stamps, had been posted in Africa somewhere. He'd waited a few months, then thrown them away. He'd no idea the recipient would one day pitch up at his door. But it was too late for regret now. He hesitated. Perhaps he should run after her and tell her about the letters. No, he didn't have time; he was already late for his first patient.

"Bye, Oliver, see you later," he called out.

Oliver was staring intently out of the window.

He went over and knelt down in front of the cat. "You recognized her didn't you Oliver?"

Oliver juddered his whiskers then turned back, staring out of the window again.

Chapter Fifty-Eight

Emily hauled the case up the stairs and into the flat. She flopped down on the sofa to catch her breath. The suitcase, seeming quite easy to manage when she set off with it, got heavier as she wheeled it along.

She looked at it, wondering where the keys might be. She poked at the locks with the tail of her comb, then gave up in frustration. She'd have to wait for Joe to help her break the locks. She peered at the chic luggage label hanging from the handle. No name, no forward address – only the name of the travel agency she presumed she must have booked her ticket through, if indeed she was leaving the country. She shrugged her shoulders. Maybe she didn't get around to filling in the details on the label which didn't help her now.

She was in the kitchen when she heard his key in the lock, she popped her head around the door.

"Hey Joe, I'm making tea, would you like some?"

He put his backpack down on the floor. "Sure, that would be great. It's bloody cold out there and I'm, um, starving as usual. Are you planning on going away for a few days? I don't remember you bringing the suitcase I saw in the hall when you moved in, you borrowed Anna's if I remember. Is it new?"

Breathlessly she told him about her visit to her old flat. "The problem is, Joe, there are no keys for it. I've tried to pick the locks but I'm not quite sure how to do it, anyway I gave up and decided to wait for you to give it a try. Would you take a look, see if you can break the locks? I think we can rule out I was a burglar in my former life!"

"It looks like an expensive piece of luggage, I'll try not to wreck it in the process. Shall I take it up to your room?"

Emily hugged him. "Thank you…"

She sat on the bed, watching him fiddle with first one lock, then the other. There was a satisfying clunking sound as one lock flew open, then the second one. Emily held her breath as they stared at each other. In the distance, there was the searing sound of a siren, followed by the hapless barking of a dog.

Joe left the room, closing the door behind him, leaving her to it.

*****

Emily folded the lid of the suitcase back, lifting the first layer of tissue paper. She stared down at the exquisite underwear, all brand new. "My God," she whispered. She lifted a veil, soft and impossibly white, from its nest of tissue, walking to the mirror, she held it over her head, then placed it carefully on the bed.

There were no winter clothes. Everything was new, except for some casual clothes and boots, and a suede jacket, which had been worn at some stage. She must have thrown the winter gear away, or maybe given it to a charity shop. One thing was obvious though, she'd been heading for a country with a warm climate.

She glanced at her watch. She'd promised Anna she'd join her for a walk in the park. She had fifteen minutes to get over there. She popped her head around the door of the sitting room. "I'll be back in a couple of hours, Joe. I'm going for a walk with Anna."

He looked up from his newspaper. "What did you find in the suitcase?"

"Bridal things, shoes, some clothes I must have worn at some point, a pair of boots… I'm no closer to knowing what happened to my husband to be, or where I was supposed to be going with him. I need a walk, need some fresh air, to clear my jumbled thoughts." She gave him a weak smile.

"I'll see you later. I'll invite Anna for dinner, she'll want to see what was inside the suitcase."

*****

Emily and Anna walked arm in arm through Hyde Park. The girls chatted away to each other, their spirits lifted by the warmth of the April sun on their backs. Emily told Anna about the suitcase and its contents. They sat on a bench watching the people around them. Children playing, joggers, dog walkers, and cyclists. Emily was feeling steadier than she'd been for a long time. The pieces of the puzzle were falling into place at last. She put her head back, closing her eyes against the sun.

"I've been thinking, Emily. You must have had a passport and maybe a ticket. Did you search all the compartments in the suitcase?"

Aroused from her reverie Emily opened her eyes. "No, just the main bit, I'll have another look when I get back, I didn't want to be late for our walk. Anyway, even if I can't find my passport, it's not a huge problem. The police gave me the number of it. I'll have to apply for a new one. It would be interesting to find the original though, see where I might have travelled to. As for the ticket, well it was more than likely in my handbag. Maybe my passport was as well.

"Why don't you come back to our place for dinner Anna? I'll show you all the things I found?"

*****

Anna followed her up the stairs to the bedroom, raising her eyebrows when she saw the clothes and shoes strewn across the bed. "Wow! Very sexy indeed! What a waste the invisible man never got to see you in all these beautiful things."

Anna picked up one of the soft boots and examined it. "These are bush boots, safari boots, they've been worn at some point. Maybe you went on safari in South Africa or somewhere. She glanced at the other clothes spread out on the bed. Yes, this is safari gear. Wow! What a great jacket, it must have cost the earth."

Emily unzipped one of the side pockets of the case. She felt the flat square and pulled it out. Her passport!

A pressed flower fluttered to the carpet. Anna bent to pick it up, twirling it in her fingers.

"I recognize the shape of this flower. They're called frangipani, they grow all over Africa. We have frangipani trees in our garden in Mombasa. I wonder where this one came from? Probably South Africa, they have frangipani trees there as well."

"I haven't a clue, let me have a look?" She looked at it then shrugged her shoulders dismissively, handing it back to Anna.

"The next time you come to the flat, Emily, I'll show you what they looked like before being flattened like this one. My photographer friend, Nick, used a shot of the frangipani flower to indicate the end of each chapter in his book, remember?"

Emily flicked through her passport, half listening. "Well, that puts paid to the theory I might have travelled to exotic places," she flipped through the rest of the pages, "I haven't been anywhere exotic. Here's a visa for the States, I must have gone over for Marcus's memorial service, no, wait. There are two stamps here at the back. I'll see if I can work them out later. I'll maybe need a magnifying glass, they're so small."

Emily put the passport down on the bed, continuing her search for anything else she could find. She ran her fingers back across the lining, finding nothing.

Anna fiddled with the luggage tag on the handle of the case. "Why don't you give these people a ring, the travel agency? They might have some record of a ticket they booked for you, it should be in a computer somewhere. They might have booked two tickets, if they did you'll have the name of the invisible man."

"Good thinking, yes I planned to do that." Emily looked at her watch. "I'll go and give them a call, I'll use the land line, my mobile needs recharging." She picked up her passport and left the room, Joe's eyes following her as she passed by the sitting room.

Joe and Anna waited in the sitting room, keen to hear the outcome of the phone call. After a few moments, Emily came back. "The travel agency no longer exists. Like many others, it went under. So that's the end of a good idea. What shall we do next?"

Joe stood up and hugged her. "I've made supper, let's eat. Then we can watch a movie and forget about this for an hour or so. How does that sound? Clear our heads a bit," he headed for the kitchen, then turned. "Must be great to have your passport back Emily, it should bring back some more memories!"

Emily lifted her shoulders and shrugged. "Not yet, but I'm hopeful."

"You were right about Joe," Anna said, putting her half full cup of coffee down on the table, "he's cute, and he's nuts about you. How do you feel about him?"

"I'm fond of him, more than fond of him, but I can't afford to play with another man's feelings, not until the last piece of this puzzle is in place. Then, who knows, anything could happen. I know he's not happy about the jilted bride stuff, but what can I do?"

Anna stood up. "I'll go and give him a hand with dinner."

Emily put her glasses on and leaned forward to pick up her passport. She would try to work out where else she'd been, apart from the States for the memorial service for Marcus; what the two small stamps might tell her. Her hand clipped against Anna's mug of coffee, overturning it, the liquid seeping over and into the document. Leaping up she pulled some tissues out of her bag.

Dabbing at the red cover, she opened it with relief, not too much of a mess.

Her relief turned to despair – brown stains seeped through the pages, eliminating any hope of working out where she'd traveled to, and what the two small stamps implied.

Chapter Fifty-Nine

Emily was unusually quiet over dinner. Joe and Anna looked at each other wondering what they could do to lift her mood.

Emily twirled her pasta round and round her plate, then looked at them both across the table. "Sorry, I'm not much company at the moment. It's just I know so much about myself now and, in many ways, it's made everything even more confusing."

Anna nodded with sympathy. Emily pushed her untouched plate away. Joe eyed it beadily.

"I find myself wondering what Marcus looked like."

Anna thought for a moment. "Why don't you go to the American Embassy, Emily, and see if they have anything? They must have details of everyone who died on 9/11, they might well have a picture of Marcus. It's worth a go, I think."

Joe polished off the rest of Emily's dinner, nodding in agreement. "I'll come with you if you like?"

"It's sweet of you, Joe, but I think I'll go on my own. I'll go tomorrow."

Joe leaned back in his chair. "If I were you I'd call first, you'll maybe need to make an appointment for something like this? You're right though, I think this is something you must do alone. Take your passport with you as proof of ID, the Yanks are funny about that sort of thing, bit jumpy after 9/11. I don't think they'll let you in the place without it."

He stood up gathering the plates from the table. "I'll go and make us some coffee."

Harry had arrived from New York earlier that morning, his driver had dropped him off at the Embassy where he walked down a side corridor, letting himself into one of the offices where he waited. They were taking a chance with this, but it would confirm everything if it worked.

An hour later Megan tapped on the door, letting herself in. "The good news is Emily Hunter had no idea who I was. There was no sign of recognition whatsoever."

"What else did she want?" he asked the stout woman standing in front of him.

Megan flicked through the notebook she was holding. "She wanted information on her late husband, wanted to know if we had a pic of him for her to see."

Harry stared at her, his pale blue eyes as hard and unblinking as a porcelain doll.

"Go on."

"I felt it was safe enough to ask her why she didn't have one herself, it would be an obvious question right?

"She explained about her accident, her memory loss. I think we can safely say she has no recollection of him, or what he looked like, none whatsoever. I grilled her thoroughly, showed her a photograph of him, even if her memory returns, and if our experiment was successful, I think she will accept Marcus is dead."

"Did you tell her to wait as I asked, Megan?"

"Yup, she's sitting in my office."

"Okay, let's do the final test then – send her in, tell her some bullshit about me always wanting to meet the relatives of victims of 9/11."

Drumming his fingers on the desk Harry waited for Emily. There was a soft knock on the door and he stood up in anticipation of his visitor, his hand outstretched.

"Mrs Hunter! Good to meet you, come on in."

He saw her hesitate, a slight frown creasing between her eyes. He held his breath as she stared at him intently.

"I'm sorry for your loss. A shocking and terrible day for so many."

He ran his hand through his hair. "Megan mentioned you were involved in an accident last year. I hope you've recovered? Lost your memory I understand?"

Emily was still staring at him. "Yes, I'm well on the way to full recovery. Most of my memory has come back, but there are still things I have no recollection of."

She hesitated, then continued. "Have we ever met before? Your face is sort of familiar?"

Harry shook his head and chuckled. "No, I've just got one of those sorts of faces. We've never met before. I don't live in London, just visit now and again, I live in New York."

Puzzled she felt inexplicable anger building inside of her. "You said you were sorry for my loss? Why would you be? Did you ever meet my husband, did you know him? Is this why you're sorry?"

"It's what people say when they meet someone, or knows someone who's lost a loved one," he said smoothly. "Just an expression we have in the States. No, I can assure you I never met your late husband. He was, I understand, in the world of finance? I'm just a civil servant. I know a lot of people think Manhattan is just a small island, and everyone knows each other," he gave a short laugh, "but I can assure you it's not true."

He held out his hand again. "Well, good to meet you, I wish you well for your future. If you need any more help, or information, please let Megan know, won't you? You may remember something else, maybe have some questions? We're here to help and support you in any way we can."

She took his hand, then walked back to the door where she turned her head, staring at him again, he saw the puzzlement on her face, then she nodded at him and left the room.

Harry strode through to Megan's office. "She doesn't sound as though she's a threat anymore. Let's hope the rest of her memory stays buried. We'll keep an eye on her though."

Megan left her desk, picking up her coat and purse, ready to go home. Then turned around, hesitating. "What if she wants to marry again?"

"Who cares?"

She shrugged. "A new husband might, it wouldn't be legal. Bigamy comes to mind…?"

"And since when did you become a warm and fuzzy person Megan? The man she was going to marry didn't come looking for her, didn't check the hospitals. We were watching. Get over it."

She turned her back on him. "I just can't help feeling a bit sorry for her. Emily's life has been shattered because of Marcus."

"Nothing's fair Megan," he shouted at her. "It wasn't fair over three thousand people were killed on 9/11 either, was it? It's the kind of world we live in now. Marcus is working damn hard to make sure nothing like this ever happens again. There's always a price to pay, and

I'm afraid Emily Hunter was one of many who had to pay. End of story."

Harry returned to his office slamming the door. He didn't fucking like the way things were going in the world either, but he was doing his best to chase down the bad guys.

He didn't even have a private life, the job consumed him, leaving no time for dating, for a chance of love, for a chance to be normal for a few fleeting hours. Christ, he didn't even have a bloody dog for company. Harry had forgotten what happiness was. Joy? He didn't remember what this was either.

Sometimes he hated his job.

But the finger of fate had found Harry, and one day his life would change in a way he could never have imagined possible.

*****

Emily walked aimlessly through the crowds. She was quite certain she knew Harry, it had lasted for just a fraction of a second when she was introduced to him. The impression was as powerful and piercing as an arrow. Why had she felt such anger towards him, such dislike?

But once again her memory refused to help her.

Chapter Sixty

Nick put down the telephone, thinking about the deal he was being offered from London. The publisher of his first book, *Beneath the Shimmering Stars*, wanted him to do another one on unusual English country houses and estates. It would be a month-long assignment, and he would need to travel the length and breadth of Britain to accomplish this.

He gazed out of the window, watching the fat heavy rain pounding and pitting the sand on the beach. It wasn't unusual for it to rain for a solid month in May. The bar would be pretty much deserted; it would be hot and humid, and the mosquitoes would be out in their droves.

May in England could be pleasant and the light, if it didn't rain, would be perfect for his work. His thoughts shied away from Emily. As much as he tried to put a lid on any thoughts of her, he wasn't always successful. If he was busy all day he could do it. But in the evenings, when he sat alone, after closing up the bar, she would thread her way through his thoughts. He would see her face, her big green eyes, feeling his stomach squeeze with longing and regret.

Now over a year later the thought of her didn't drive him mad with outrage. Bitter yes, grief yes. Laughing, opinionated, inquisitive Emily. The sweet smell of her wrapped in his arms the morning after their night of love making in London. The feel of her slim arms around him, the heart-breaking softness of her mouth, the happy wetness of her tears on his cheeks. Emily, standing radiant and breathless in front of him.

Nick picked up the phone again and put a call through to his publisher. He needed to get away.

Chapter Sixty-One

The immigration officer scrutinized his passport, then his face, waving him through.

The man lined up with other travellers, waiting his turn for a taxi to take him to the Ritz hotel where he always stayed when in London.

That afternoon he planned to take a sight-seeing tour of the city on one of the open topped red buses. Get his bearings, gather more information.

After lunch he lined up again to board the bus, his camera held in his hand, like any other tourist. It was a bright sunny afternoon. Just what he needed. For the next four hours he clicked away taking photos of all the iconic buildings. Buckingham Palace (too difficult to get near that one), the Houses of Parliament (a possibility with careful planning), Oxford Street, with its streaming crowds of never ending shoppers, would be easy.

St Paul's Cathedral and Westminster Abbey were high on his list. Where the hated Christians worshipped, it might be possible, again with careful planning, to take out a senior Royal, this would make the world stand to attention.

The London Eye was out, too much planning, not enough return.

The British Museum was a must. Here were stolen treasures from all over the world, including his country. Taken by the hated Christians to decorate their rooms. If his nation could not have their treasures back, then no one else would be allowed to have them.

The National Gallery would be a satisfying target with their disgusting, immodest paintings of half-naked and naked women. He had walked around it on his last trip, appalled at what he saw. An offence to Muhammed, his followers, and to the Almighty Allah.

The Underground and the London buses which plied the streets of London had been an easy target in July 2005, another similar attack was already being planned.

Covent Garden with its restaurants and shops would be hit at Christmas, when the hated Christians were spending obscene amounts of money to celebrate the birth of their heathen God.

They had considered Harrods with its swirling masses of shoppers from all over the world. But he had observed how many Muslim women, dressed with respect, shopped there. They would not risk killing the faithful followers of Muhammed. Or the owner who was himself a Muslim.

A good one in the pipeline was The World Travel Market, held each year here in London, in November. A good target. Thousands of travel professionals from all over the world, meeting with tour operators from around the globe, all under one roof?

Last November he had mingled with casual workers, electricians, stand builders, catering staff, men carrying in furniture, there was no one checking on the credentials of anyone during the frenzied build up to the opening day of the show.

It was unfortunate his particular country, Syria, was not on the list of top destinations to visit, but he would make sure it would be one country, one people, who would be on everyone's lips, in the days after the planned massacre.

People who lived out in the country thought they were safe from the long tentacles of our world of terror. We would, in the future, pick somewhere random, like Cornwall, Dorset or Devon in the south of England, nothing spectacular, but do enough damage so no one would know where they were safe. There were small towns and villages all over the country.

The British are a nation of dog lovers, but we pure Muslims are not. The saliva of a dog is unclean, which makes us impure if touched by this saliva. To get into Battersea Dogs home, looking to adopt a dog, would be simple. A mass slaughter of dogs, with a well-placed bomb, would bring the so called great nation of Britain to their knees with grief. This would be a good thing for them to get to their knees for, instead of worshipping their heathen idol.

After this we would target Europe, where many sites had already been chosen.

We ISIS warriors are inspired and directed by al-Qaeda. A few innovative attacks each month can change a country. Our so-called acts of unspeakable barbarity, are what you deserve. We will go to Paradise if we kill you, but you will go to Hell. Your churches are dirty dens of idolatry. We will change this, we will not stop. You have nowhere to hide. We will win.

We will wipe Christianity off the face of the earth, those Christian infidels. In the Western world women behave like sluts, with no respect for anything, or anyone. They are whores.

Our hatred of the Western world and our attacks on you will only cease to exist when you embrace Islam.

True followers of Muhammad do not fear death as you Christians do. It is your greatest weakness which will lead to your total destruction. Islam will triumph. It is written in the Qur'an. Islam will rule the world as you will see.

The Shadow Dancer, his reconnaissance of the great city of London complete, alighted from the bus and made his way to the Mosque. Here he would be blessed by the Almighty Allah for his great work, in his name, here on earth.

Chapter Sixty-Two

It was week four of the assignment in England. Nick was satisfied with the way things were turning out. He'd more than enough shots for a sizeable book. He would need to spend time on the layout. His mind was as focused as his camera as he worked, until the light began to fade.

He packed his cameras into their bags, hoisting them over his shoulder. He made his way through the sprawling grounds and up to the stately building in front of him. He skirted the lake, stopping to take a shot of a pair of elegant swans their reflections rippling on the surface of the water. In the distant fields he could see sheep, like puffs of cotton wool on a green canvas. He grinned, nothing wild and dangerous over there, nothing to get the adrenalin going – not a predator in sight. No terrorists lurking on the horizon.

He could understand why the British had fought so fiercely for their country during the great wars. He wondered how many veterans looked back at all the lives lost, what it had all been for, given what was happening in the world today, where no one knew who the enemy was, or when they would strike again. Out here in the country it was peaceful and quiet, unlike the city centres. The villages, steeped in history, were chocolate box pretty. The narrow winding country roads unchanged for centuries – like the weather, which kept the countryside so green. A muted world of mists and green fields bound together with ancient low stone walls.

Arthur and Gladys, his godparents, had invited him to use their home as his base for the project. His father and the Duke had been at Eton together, were old friends. When Nick, and Jonathan, had attended boarding school, here in England, they would spend long week-ends, and short school holidays, on the estate. Not having children of their own, Nick and Jonathan were the sons they never had.

He looked at the familiar turrets and crenellations of the vast house, wondering what it might be like to live in one on a permanent basis. Nice in the summer, he recalled with a smile, but in winter it was bone-chilling. Climbing the steps to the entrance he patted the stone lion guarding the house, before letting himself in to the impressive entrance hall. A huge chandelier graced the cavernous ceiling with its ornate gold carvings; large faded tapestries covered the ancient stone walls.

The house had been built in the late 1700's, its green lawns and formal gardens stretching as far as the eye could see. The sumptuous rooms were filled with rare works of art, silver, and china. The French and English furniture formed an agreeable mix in the formal rooms. Beautiful crafted fireplaces graced each room.

He smiled to himself, yes, they needed all those fireplaces going most of the year to keep the place warm. He preferred the sprawl of his family home in Nairobi – with the light and the sunshine.

He let himself into the familiar library. Each shelf from floor to ceiling was packed with rare, collectable books. The handsome leather desk was where he worked at the end of the day. In the corner of the room was a grandfather clock, with its comforting ticking and whirring sounds. He would have to hurry, there was to be a formal dinner in the banqueting hall this evening; he was glad he'd packed his dinner jacket.

*****

Camilla Hamilton-Flanders was studying the man seated opposite her. Men always looked good in evening dress, she mused, no matter what their age, but this one was exceptional. She was sure he could have anyone with a click of his elegant tanned fingers.

As if sensing he was being watched, Nick looked up and smiled at her. She lowered her eyes attempting to look demure. There would be plenty of time to get to know him later.

She checked around the table, seating twenty people for this particular dinner. Not much competition as far as she could see. She knew everyone there, of course, but they were all couples. This left the coast clear for a clean run at him. First, she would find out if he was suitable. No point in having terrific looks if he didn't have terrific pots of money.

At the first opportunity, after dinner, she cornered Gladys. "Who was the divine man sitting opposite me at dinner? I know his name of course, Nick Kennedy, but wherever did you find such a delicious specimen. Is he married?"

"He's the son of an old friend of Arthur's, Hugh Kennedy, Lord Kennedy, he's our godson. He's here taking photographs of old castles and country estates for a book he's going to publish. I have to say he is rather dashing. We've known him, and his late brother, Jonathan since they were babies. When the boys came here to be educated they'd often spend week-ends with us, and short school holidays, it was too far for them to go home, you see. He's not married, no."

Camilla raised a perfectly sculpted eyebrow. Titled, money *and* single? He was getting more interesting by the minute. "I've heard of the family, of course," she said airily, "but I don't think I've ever met them at any social events. I mean I know just about anyone worth knowing. I would have remembered someone like him – without a doubt! Where do they live?"

Gladys turned to her guest. "You wouldn't have met the family at any of these events. They used to have a considerable ranch in East Africa in Kenya, not sure where though. I always had trouble pronouncing the name of the place!"

Camilla stifled a laugh and gave her a brief kiss on the cheek, then went off in hot pursuit of Nicholas Kennedy.

*****

Gladys watched her rush off. Watch out Nick, she thought, Camilla Hamilton-Flanders is famous for hunting down her quarry, then, when she got bored, threw them away like a discarded banana skin.

Knowing Nick was going to be there for the week-end, she'd invited Camilla, hoping they might hit it off. It was time for Nick to get on with his life, get married, and have a family.

She picked up her drink. Nick could handle himself, of this she had no doubt. With all he'd gone through with the woman who never pitched up for her own wedding, Camilla might well have bitten off more than she could chew.

She took a sip of her drink. Not a bad match though.

*****

Camilla had also been invited to stay for the week-end and, after dinner the previous evening, Arthur suggested she and Nick might like to exercise a couple of the horses in the morning.

The Duke was now down at the stables haranguing the grooms over which horses to saddle, his hounds milling around his legs anticipating their daily walk through the ancient maze. He watched Camilla through narrowed eyes as she mounted. Despite his wife's enthusiasm over a possible match, he didn't think she would do at all.

He tossed the reins to her. "Don't go getting any ideas about Nick, my girl, he'll marry someone from his own tribe, someone who doesn't mind the heat and dust of Africa. You would hate it there. The sun would ruin that fine English complexion of yours," he slapped her horse on the rump, and winked at Nick.

"Nice looking woman," he muttered, "but far too flighty for you, son. Enjoy your ride."

Clamping a cigar between his teeth and taking a swipe at a Rhododendron bush with his walking stick, he stomped off towards the maze "Come on you pack of ugly mutts," he bellowed, "let's see how many of you I can lose today!"

*****

Camilla, Nick knew, had set her sights on him the night before, regaling him with funny stories, telling him about herself. With skill he avoided the questions about his personal life without appearing abrupt, but he had to admit, he'd enjoyed her company.

The cool morning air whipped at his face as they galloped across the fields, the horse's manes' streaming. It was exhilarating to be in another country, in the company of an attractive woman, the thought surprised and unsettled him.

*****

They returned to the stables some hours later, the horses snorting and blowing, their sweating flanks quivering with the exertion of the ride. Nick and Camilla handed over the reins to the groom and walked back through the gardens to the castle. She pulled her riding hat off her head, shaking her long blonde hair free. Casually she put her arm through his. For a second she felt him tense, then relax.

As they mounted the steps he disentangled himself from her.

223

"Well, I must get going and work in the library for a few hours. I have a lot to do before I hand everything over to my London publisher. Excuse me."

Camilla frowned with annoyance. She'd never failed to bring a man to heel, but Nick was going to be a hard nut to crack. He'd told her little about his life in Kenya, other than describe the ranch he had been brought up on, his brother, the lodge he had sold and the beach bar he owned in Mombasa, but nothing about any woman in his life.

She spent the rest of the day curled up with a glossy magazine, calculating how she could get Nick Kennedy into her bed - or herself into his. It would be a challenge but she was up for it. She would have him one way or another. Maybe she should try and get him drunk, loosen him up a bit, but he didn't seem to drink at all.

*****

Nick found himself enjoying the dinner and the conversation going on around him. Tonight, they were eating in the kitchen around a long table, its wooden surface pitted with age. There were six of them for dinner. Arthur and Gladys, Nick and Camilla, and another young couple. The discussions flew from one topic to another, the fire crackled in the hearth, despite it being early June. Two Labradors stretched out in front of the hearth, twitching with dreams, snoring in unison.

Camilla didn't miss an opportunity to touch Nick's hand or his arm, to emphasis a point, whether there was one or not. He was surprised at how comforting it felt. He had to admit she was a good-looking woman, a bit heavy on the make-up, but her low cut, off the shoulder, red dress was very attractive indeed.

He felt a pang of envy. This is what life should be about, good friends and good food with the person you love at your side. The security of a big warm family, the comfort of knowing you would never be alone. But the person he loved was not at his side. He was not going to travel down that road again

With some reluctance, he removed Camilla's searching hand from his thigh. The evening was coming to an end, goodnights and goodbyes were murmured.

He lay in bed, thinking about home. He'd enjoyed himself out in the English countryside, but it was time to go back. The rains would be over and he longed for the wide-open spaces, the light and the sun, the

224

familiar sound of the surf making its enduring way towards the soft, sandy shore.

*****

He was dozing off when he sensed someone in the room. "Shhh, Nick, it's me, coming to tuck you in, and kiss you goodnight."

He felt the cover being lifted, the smoothness of her long legs as she slid in beside him – naked. She put her arms around him. He felt himself weaken. It would mean nothing to him, nothing at all, but, oh God, he needed to take some comfort, feel someone warm again in his arms. He would be leaving the country soon, he would never see her again.

With some reluctance, he disentangled her arms from around his neck, propelling her out of his bed. She stood up, stamping her foot in frustration. "What's the matter with you, Nick, don't you find me attractive? No man has ever turned me down before.

"Look, darling, this doesn't have to be a big affair. I want to make love to you – who knows, you might even enjoy it."

He leaned back on the pillows and groaned. "It's not that I don't find you attractive, Camilla, quite the opposite in fact."

Camilla narrowed her eyes, trying to contain her fury. "There's something wrong with you Nick Kennedy. No one is worth giving everything up for, you know…"

His arm snaked out, pulling her back into his bed. "Alright Camilla, you can have what you want but it's not going to lead to anything more, so don't get your hopes up. I don't expect to find you in my bed in the morning either, my godparents wouldn't approve."

With a triumphant smile, she reached down for him. "Once you've tasted what I have to offer I'm sure you'll be back for more. Now, why don't you relax a little?"

Chapter Sixty-Three

With a smooth hiss the train pulled into the station. Nick retrieved his camera bag from the overhead shelf, preparing to disembark. He'd left a note for his godparents apologising for his early departure. He blamed it on his publisher, saying they wanted to move the deadline for the book ahead, and needed to meet with him.

This meant spending more time in London than he wanted, but the thought of looking at Camilla across the breakfast table and knowing things would get complicated, well, it was a good decision. He didn't need complications.

He'd booked a taxi and it was waiting for him when he let himself out of the front door, first thing the next morning. Breathing a sigh of relief at not encountering Camilla en-route, he stowed his cameras and suitcase in the back seat, got in next to the driver, asking to be dropped at the railway station.

Camilla, without doubt, knew her way around a man's body, he smiled at the memory.

Striding towards the exit barrier, he was relieved to be out of the stuffy packed train. He joined the queue for a taxi, waiting his turn.

Giving the driver the address of his publisher, he sat back watching London crawl past the window. How do people live here, he thought, and not for the first time? So many people, the relentless, bumper to bumper traffic, the constant noise. It would drive him crazy to be hemmed in by all this.

Two hours later, after handing over his material and signing a new contract, he was on his way again. He had two days to kill before his flight back to Kenya. He checked into the Savoy, arranging to have his luggage and cameras sent up to his room. He decided to walk around the city and stretch his legs.

He would walk along the Kings Road, explore some galleries, a few of the better shops, then find a decent place for dinner.

Satisfied with his plan for the rest of the day he set off.

Chapter Sixty-Four

Emily was restless. Only half an hour to go before she could leave the gift shop. She was planning to walk to Sloane Square, to buy the shoes she'd seen. They were more than expensive but she loved them and could now afford them. They would cheer her up when she wore them in the coming winter months, they would match the crimson lining of her coat. She stole another look at her watch, by the time she tidied herself up, it would be time to go.

With the discovery of a healthy bank account she neither needed the job, or the money, but it did give her a purpose each day, she enjoyed working there. She'd toyed with the idea of finding a flat of her own but decided against it. She liked Joe's place, she'd been living with him for over six months now and loved having him around.

Strolling along the street, she stopped to admire various shop windows. Dodging a group of shrieking, giggling school girls, she arrived at the shoe shop.

She twirled around in front of the mirror, the shoes were gorgeous, not the most comfortable she'd ever tried on, but she wanted them and was prepared to suffer a bit if she had to. Maybe they would stretch a little with wear.

Emily paid for them on her credit card and picked up the glossy red bag. She paused outside the shop door, undecided what to do or where to go next. She shrugged her coat back on against the sudden cool wind, and greying clouds, longing for summer to keep its promise for a bit longer.

There was a book shop she kept meaning to go into, but never got around to doing it. Now was her chance, then she would find a place for coffee and something to eat. Emily picked her way through the throes of people, until she came to the book shop, called Becoming Books. Pushing open the door she entered, then stopped.

She'd been here before.

Over the last few weeks her determination to find her past had given her courage and confidence, two qualities she thought she lacked. She waited for the woman behind the till to finish talking to a customer. She seemed to be the only staff member around.

"Good Afternoon, I wonder if you could help me?"

The woman sighed and looked at her with a resigned expression.

"I promise I'm not another tourist looking for directions!"

Emily continued. "I lost my memory some time ago, it's coming back, but there are still some blanks. I think I may have worked here and wondered if you recognized me?"

"When did you lose your memory, dear?"

"Over a year ago. In April."

"Well then maybe it's possible you did work here. I bought the shop around about then but didn't open it for two months as we were busy with all the paperwork, so I wouldn't know anyone who worked here. As you can see it's rather small, the previous owner employed just one member of staff."

She smiled at an elderly woman who had entered the shop, before turning back to Emily. "I didn't get to meet her because she left before I took over here. Her lawyer handled everything."

Emily felt her stomach clench. Yes. She'd worked here.

"You wouldn't know where the previous owner lives would you? Or remember her name?" she asked with hope in her voice.

"She left the country. Her name was Rebecca something or other, I can't recall. She lives in France now, but I have no idea where. Sorry dear."

Emily shook her head; the name Rebecca didn't ring any bells. "I'll wander around if it's alright, something may jog a memory or two…"

As she left the shop the heavens opened, the rain seemed to come from nowhere, she shook open her umbrella and headed for home.

Chapter Sixty-Five

Nick had never owned an umbrella in his life. Rain was something they welcomed where he came from. It was an unexpected downpour and he ducked into the first shop he came across.

He stopped, looking around. It was the bookshop where he'd done his book signing, in what seemed years ago now. Becoming Books. He hesitated, his heart ratchetted within his chest, jagged memories of her tumbling back to him. The rain was heavy, he would get drenched if he left now, with some reluctance he moved inside, knowing it was going to hurt.

He nodded at the woman sitting at the desk and strolled over to the section on travel. There was no sign of his book, he made a mental note to speak to his publisher about it.

His eyes lingered on the desk where he had signed his books that night, the place where he had found her again. He closed his eyes – he had to get out of here.

His foot nudged a red bag. He bent down and checked the contents, these days an unattended bag could mean anything. He saw the shoe box and, deciding it was harmless enough, light enough, he took it over to the lady sitting at the desk.

"Someone seems to have left their shopping bag behind?" He held it up with one finger.

"Oh dear! It must have been the woman who came in here ten minutes or so ago. I remember the red bag. I'm sure she'll be back as soon as she realises she's left it behind. She told me she had a bad memory," she said with a short humourless laugh.

He handed it over and left. It was raining harder than ever now. The last thing he wanted was to get soaked. He decided to find the nearest coffee shop and wait until the rain subsided. Spotting one across the road he jogged over to it, weaving his way through the traffic, ignoring the indignant hooting of cars, buses and taxis.

*****

Emily stopped dead in her tracks. Where were her new shoes? Trying not to panic she mentally retraced her footsteps. The last shop she had been into was the bookshop.

Cursing herself, she turned and went back. She'd paid a huge amount for them, what if someone picked them up? She prayed she would find them there – if not then it was her own fault for being so forgetful.

*****

Nick watched the crowds struggling past. He tested the heat of his second cup of coffee with his lips, took a tentative sip and grimaced, pushing it to one side. It didn't taste of anything.

The book shop had brought all the memories back into focus. The moment their eyes met across the room when he arrived for the book signing, how his heart leapt at the sight of her again. How easy it had been to love her wide smile, her deep throaty laugh.

Shaking his head at the memories, he stared out of the window. He imagined the years ahead, alone with his memories of her. The skin of her arms cool and silky under his fingers, the burnished glow of her shoulders reflecting in the sun. His love for her against which everything else had been assessed and measured, in this his un-life.

He pulled himself together, watching the jostling shoppers, heads down and umbrellas up.

Then he saw the girl with the red bag.

She was moving along, through the crowd of shoppers on the opposite side of the road, wearing a light black coat with a crimson lining, a crimson scarf and high black boots. The red bag and lining of her coat, created a searing slash of colour against a sea of black and grey raincoats. Her head was down, an umbrella covered her face.

He watched her struggling through the crowds, then she stopped, glancing left and right, looking undecided about crossing the road. She lifted her head, and he thought his heart would stop.

Emily.

His chest was so tight he had to gulp at the air to breathe.

Pulling the umbrella down, she seemed to hesitate as if she couldn't make the decision to cross the street. He stared at her, willing her to look up again so he could take another look at her, be sure it was her.

Then she turned, disappearing around the corner heading towards Sloane Square.

He threw some notes down to pay for his coffee. He pushed his way through the slow-moving meandering crowds, cursing as they blocked his path. When he got to Sloane Square he saw the traffic jam and red buses, the sea of moving umbrellas hindering any chance he might have had of catching another glimpse of her.

It could have been anyone at all. He must have imagined the whole thing, because he'd been thinking about her minutes before. He'd made a mistake. Okay, so Emily owned a similar coat, he remembered it well, it was striking. He recalled their defining dinner at the Italian restaurant, she had worn it then. This was London for God's sake; hundreds of women were almost sure to be walking around wearing the same coat, or a similar one, to Emily's.

He needed to get out of the bloody rain, the howling traffic, the screeching brakes, the blaring horns. He needed a drink.

A truck lumbered past and he frowned with annoyance. The driver ground the gears revving the engine, black smoke belching into its toxic wake.

Time to get out of London, get back to the blessed peace, the utter sound of silence – time to go home.

Chapter Sixty-Six

J oe? Emily? I have some news for you. I'm going back to Kenya to work in the main hospital in Nairobi.

"I'll be far more useful there, than I am in London." Anna told them. "There are so few nursing sisters to go around. The generous amount of money you gave me, Emily, has paid for a small clinic to be built, out in one of the rural areas, and I want to get more involved with it. My father's anxious for me to go home. He's getting on in years, and my mother tells me they have a string of suitable young men to introduce me to. How can I resist?"

"When are you leaving?" Joe and Emily asked in unison.

"January. It's why spending Christmas with you today is so special, I'm glad we can be together for it. I'll miss you both very much. But it's time for me to go home now."

Emily's eyes filled with tears at the news. "London won't feel the same without you Anna, although I do understand your reasons for wanting to go back to your family. I envy you that."

Joe tried to cheer her up. "Hey! You'll still have me around, not quite the same, I know, but you won't be alone. Let's make a plan to go out to Kenya for a holiday, a safari. I'd love to do that. Come on, cheer up Emily, it's not the end of the world!"

"You're right Joe, just the end of a world I've become so used to." She turned to Anna. "It's wonderful news Anna and I really am happy for you. Joe's idea is great. We'll come and visit you! But I'll miss you."

*****

Anna left London in January. Joe and Emily saw her off at the airport, with tears all round.

A week later Emily wandered into Joe's study and sat down in front of him. "Joe? May I interrupt you for a few minutes? I need to talk to you?"

Joe looked up warily. "Of course you can. You can talk to me about anything, you know this. What's up?"

Emily shifted in her chair and took a deep breath. "Now I know who I am, and I have a fair amount of money in the bank, from the sale of the flat, I've decided to go away. Do something different. I've been thinking about it for the past couple of months."

Joe looked at her with surprise and dismay. "Come on then, don't keep me in suspense. Where are you going? Back to South Africa to see where you born and brought up?"

"No. I've thought about it, but I don't think I will achieve anything by doing that. My parents have gone, there's nothing left for me there. I have enough on my plate at the moment, I think going back to South Africa will make things more complicated. Actually, Joe, I don't want to go back there at all. All my instincts tell me not to go."

Emily took a deep breath. "With all that's happened to me, I feel I'd like to write a book about my experience, it might help other people who have gone through the same thing. I think it could be therapeutic." She fiddled with the silver bracelet on her wrist which Joe had bought her on her birthday, when they found out when it was. He was not looking happy with her news. He took off his glasses, polishing them vigorously.

"I've decided to take some time out and go to the south of France. It looks the ideal place to write. I've done a bit of research on the area, I think Antibes would be a good place to work on the story. By all accounts it's lovely, one of my customers at the shop was telling me about it. I don't think I've ever been to France – well I can't remember if I have."

Noticing Joe's dismayed face, she hurried on. "Of course, I'll continue to pay the rent, Joe. Then when I've finished my book I'll come back."

He nodded. "Of course, you must go write your book Emily, it's a great idea. I want to be the first one to read it when you get back." He said, giving her a smile, which didn't quite reach his eyes. "I'm going to miss you though. I hope it's not going to take years for you to write it. Not going to be a big saga is it?"

234

She raised her eyebrows. "I don't know – maybe. I'm not sure how long I'll be gone, but I promise to come back, and I'll keep in touch."

"You realize you'll need to speak a bit of French?" he said.

"Yes, I've thought about that. I'm going to do one of those online courses, then when I get over there I'm sure I'll pick it up."

Joe stood up and gave her a light kiss on the cheek. "Yes, a good idea. Writing is good for the soul, who knows, it might just be the thing you need to do to bring back those last few elusive memories. Promise me if you ever remember the name of the invisible man, you'll call me straight away?"

Joe polished his glasses again, then put them back on.

"What about your job?"

"I've handed in my notice. I think maybe a different place might jog a few more memories. It feels right."

"Well, here's to your therapeutic book, I'll miss you."

He looked at Emily. "Promise me though? If you remember anything more about your past you'll let me know, even if you think it's unimportant?"

"I promise I will Joe."

*****

Joe stacked the dishes in the dishwasher, then wiped down the counter tops.

He shook his head. This was something he had not anticipated Emily would do. He was going to miss having her around. Miss watching over her, looking out for her, listening to her. Still, she had promised to keep in touch, he would have to settle for this and hope she wouldn't be away too long. He wasn't looking forward to being a bachelor again, living alone again.

No, this was something he had not anticipated Emily might do.

Chapter Sixty-Seven

Nick wiped the sweat from his forehead, heading for the sea. It was unbearably hot again, and he needed a break from the bar.

He jogged down to the water's edge, ploughing through the waves until it was deep enough for him to dive into its cool depths. He did a fast crawl for twenty minutes, his powerful arms slicing through the water with ease, then turned over, floating on his back, thinking about the offer he'd been made.

His publisher wanted him to travel through Australia for his third book. Sales of the second one, on the English country houses, were buoyant. They wanted him to get to work on his next book as early in the New Year as possible. He'd thought long and hard about it.

Australia was a vast country. To get the shots he visualised would mean being away for at least six months, if not longer. Should he sell the bar? There were plenty of keen buyers. Or find a manager to run it for however long his trip to Australia might take? He pondered all this as he turned over, then swam back to the shore. His parents were not going to be happy with his decision to leave the country for a long period of time.

There were many reasons for wanting to take this project. He was bored with the bar, bored with the mindless conversation going back and forth, he missed being out in the bush. Australia had bush, and plenty of it.

He patted himself dry. He would think it over for the next day or so, then make a final decision.

"Hello Nick!"

He turned in the direction of the voice, and his heart sank. There sitting at the bar was Camilla Hamilton-Flanders, with a smug grin on her face, wearing a tiny pink bikini.

He gave her a resigned smile. "Hello Camilla, what are you doing here?"

"I thought I would give you a big surprise. I wanted to get away for some sunshine, September is a social dead end in London, so here I am. I love your bar," she looked around, "although it's a bit rustic to say the least?"

She jumped down from the bar stool, tiptoeing to kiss him on both cheeks.

"You can run, Nick, but you can't hide. I always get what I want! Now I have you cornered. I'm staying at a hotel up the road, I'll be around for a month. Lots of time to get to know each other again. Your godmother gave me the name of your beach bar, and here I am."

She smiled at him. "Naughty you running off without saying goodbye! Now I've found you maybe I should check out of the hotel. It's not quite what I'm used to.

"I know! I could come and stay with you. You told me you have a house here on the beach?"

"I know what you're up to Camilla, but you're wasting your time. I'm not interested in getting involved with anyone. You've wasted your time coming to Kenya, if you thought otherwise. However, the least I can do is buy you a drink. What will it be?"

"A large vodka and tonic would be divine, darling, with lots of ice please."

He winced at the 'darling.' Why did girls like her throw the word around with such abandon?

Camilla took a large mouthful of her drink, looking at him contemplatively, then shrugged her shoulders before checking out the rest of the bar. "Well, darling, what can I say? I shall have to look elsewhere for entertainment and judging by the men in your bar it shouldn't take too long." She wiggled her fingers at a young man seated at the bar, who was showing considerable interest in her.

"Your loss, Nick, you should lighten up a bit. I can't imagine the type of woman who would be brave enough to take you on, even if you were maybe a teeny bit interested. Pity, I fancied being Lady Kennedy one day."

She took another mouthful of her drink. "Never mind, plenty more fish in the sea. Although from what I've seen so far here, most of them will soon be floating on the surface. I think I'll head for Nairobi it sounds like it might be quite good fun, lots of aristocrats lying around from what I can gather. Goodbye darling." She picked up her bag and drink and walked towards the young man who had been watching her across the bar, the bar stool leaving two pink lines on her shapely thighs.

Nick breathed a sigh of relief, with a bit of luck it would be the last he saw of her. Australia was starting to look more than attractive.

Chapter Sixty-Eight

The young African wiped his sweaty brow with his sleeve and leaned on his shovel. His ragged shorts hung from his thin body, his mud caked boots, with no laces, gaped on his feet. This must be an important funeral with all the people and cars. He'd seen many of them with his job as a grave digger.

He looked around the old cemetery at the crooked, leaning, headstones with lichen clinging to the illegible inscriptions. Long forgotten graves, never visited by anyone. Many white people had been buried here over the years, and here was another one. He shrugged his shoulders and carried on with his digging.

*****

Nick stood next to the fresh mound of earth, his arm around his mother. He was still in shock. His main concern now was for his mother who seemed to have aged visibly. He could feel her trembling under his arm, dressed in black. As they lowered the coffin into the grave she wept.

Behind his sunglasses, feeling his own eyes prickle with grief, he lifted his chin. A pair of falcons flew high above, he watched them wheel and turn as he brought his emotions under control.

They buried his father in the country he'd come to love and made his own. Nick watched as the rich red soil was shovelled over the sleek mahogany coffin, until it was smothered.

Hundreds of friends, from all over the country, attended the funeral service in Nairobi. The President sent a senior representative to honour Hugh Kennedy for the hard work, and the enormous contribution, he'd made to the country and its people.

The line of black cars snaked as far as the eye could see, the late September heat shimmering off their roof tops. Following the burial there would be a reception, at his father's old club, to celebrate his life, then he would drive his mother home.

At the club he greeted the many mourners, as they murmured their condolences. He was not surprised to see Anna waiting her turn in the queue. She held him close.

"I'll come and see you soon, Nick. If I can do anything to help, please call me." She gave him a card with her contact details, then moved on, putting her arms around his mother.

Finally, it was over. He drove his mother home, keeping a comforting hand on hers as they drove up the familiar drive, through the canopy of jacaranda trees, their heavy boughs of purple blossom nodded like mourners at their passing.

"It will be empty here without him, Nick," she whispered, as he stopped the car. "Whatever will I do on my own?"

"You're still in a state of shock, Ma. As the days pass you'll come to terms with things. We'll both miss him, but nothing will bring him back. I'll take care of you."

He helped her inside the house, then upstairs to her bedroom. When he was sure she was asleep he left her and went back down to the sitting room. He poured himself a whisky and stood at the window, swirling the liquid around in the glass, the ice cubes clinking in the silent room.

Thunder rumbled ominously overhead, the sky purple and bloated with the promise of heavy rains. His father's Labrador nuzzled his hand.

"Hey, Barney. You miss him too, don't you?" The old dog thumped his tail on the floor, looking mournfully out of the window, before stretching out next to his master's old chair.

Nick looked at his father's favourite chair, feeling overwhelmed. The shocking news had reached him in Mombasa. A massive heart attack right here in this room. His mother was so grief-stricken she was unable to tell him herself. One of her many friends broke the news to him over the phone. He'd flown to Nairobi to be with her, and to arrange the funeral, which he knew would be substantial.

He'd met with the family lawyer. The Nairobi house and his father's money were left to his mother; the beach house to him. There were generous donations to the many charities his father had been involved in, and personal bequests, including his old friend Doctor Kiwathe, Anna's father.

His father's collection of hunting guns was left to the Duke. He'd called them straight away, breaking the news of his father's death to them.

"We'll come over for the funeral Nicholas." Gladys said, her voice thick with emotion. "Arthur, as you know, is not keen on flying, but I'm sure he'll want to be with you at a time like this. Such sad news, my dear, I'm so dreadfully sorry."

"Please don't insist he comes, I know how much he dislikes flying. There'll be hundreds of people at the funeral. Ma is distraught. She won't be able to look after herself let alone entertain. I'll explain things to her."

The heart attack which took his father threw his own plans into chaos. He'd been due to fly to Australia in December, but this he had cancelled. He'd sold the bar, in preparation for the trip to Australia, but his father's death had changed everything. There was no way he could leave his mother alone now. It was unthinkable.

The house was too big for her to live in alone, but he wouldn't discuss this with her now, he would wait until she was stronger, more accepting of her loss.

Sitting in his father's chair, he put his head back, closing his eyes, drained and exhausted. How hard love and life can be. Forty years with one loving partner, then it's snatched away in minutes, in the blink of an eye.

Chapter Sixty-Nine

His mother didn't recover from the death of her husband, or her son Jonathan. Nick stayed with her in Nairobi, helping her through each day, as she became more frail, forgetful, and vulnerable. The two African servants, William and Abel, who had known the boys since they were babies, and worked for his parents for most of their lives, fussed in silence around the house, at a loss as to how to help with the situation.

Then Nick made a difficult decision, one he alone could make, but with his mother's consent. He would sell the house in Nairobi, then take her back with him to Mombasa. He wouldn't leave her now, to cope alone, and Abel and William, were near retirement age anyway. He would make a generous settlement on both of them, enough to see them through the rest of their lives, it was what his father would have wanted – what he wanted.

He tried discussing it with his mother, but she didn't seem to understand what was going on. Most of the furniture, he told her, would have to be sold off. There was no room for it at the house in Mombasa.

"Ma, we have to do something with the house, it's too big for you. Abel and William should be taken care of by their own families now. Remember Pa said they would be leaving at the end of next year anyway?"

His mother's eyes filled with tears. "I want to stay here, I don't want to sell our home. I feel closer to your father here, and Jonathan. I don't have anywhere else to go."

He put his arms around her. "I want you to come and live with me. Pa, and Jonathan, will always be with you, wherever you are. I can't leave you here."

She sighed with resignation. "Alright, darling, whatever you feel is right. I'm too tired to fight, too overwhelmed by everything."

On the day of the auction he dropped his mother off at a friend's house. He didn't want her to see a lifetime of cherished possessions going to complete strangers. She had chosen a few things to take with her, and these were packed up ready for shipment to Mombasa.

He returned to the house. Abel and William worked with determination, bringing all the furniture to be auctioned out onto the lawns at the back of the old house. Boxes of books and records, dinner services, furniture and linen, cutlery and glassware, carpets, curtains and pictures, all labelled, stood on trestle tables. He walked around, touching one object or another, bringing back memories of when he was a boy. Now a lifetime of assets would be dissipated to buyers, who would never know the history behind each piece. He closed his eyes for a moment.

Abel appeared at his elbow. "The man with the loud voice is here Mr Nick, the stranger's cars are parking at the front of the house."

Nick turned at his voice, looking into the rheumy eyes of the old retainer. "Thank you, Abel. This is difficult for me - for all of us. You and William must take whatever you would like from here, tell the man with the loud voice, he'll reserve it for you, keep it for you. My father would have wanted this. After all, everything here must be as familiar to you as it is to me. I'll miss you and William…we've been together for as long as I can remember."

"What of Barney, Mr Nick, and Mr Parrot, what will become of them?"

Nick ran his hand over the head of the old Labrador. "Barney is old Abel, as you are now. I'll take him back to Mombasa with me, and the parrot."

"Let me have Barney, Mr Nick, I will take good care of him, and Mr Parrot, as I have always done. We can spend our last years together. It is fitting. I have known Barney since he was a small boy puppy, it would be an honour for me to own him," he hesitated and looked at the parrot who was crouched on his perch, muttering to himself, his beady eyes watching them, "and the noisy parrot."

Nick hesitated watching the dog nuzzling Abel's hand, looking for the inevitable treat. Barney was generous with his love, considering Abel and William part of his family.

"Alright, I'm sure Barney will be happy to stay with you but only for a short while Abel, I'll send for him when things have settled, but I'll take Mr Parrot, my mother is fond of him, and he'll be company for her until Barney can join us."

"Nick?" He turned away from Abel and Barney at the sound of the auctioneer's voice. "We seem to have quite a crowd here already. I'll get going with the auction if it's alright with you?"

Nick nodded curtly and left.

*****

He left the sale of the house with the estate agent and sold the old Mercedes his father had loved so much. Abel and William said their goodbyes and took their leave. Barney looked back mournfully, as only a Labrador can, then followed Abel with his tail between his legs. Nick felt his throat tighten, feeling a deep sense of loss at the changing of his life.

He walked around the almost empty rooms of his childhood home. Not everything had sold at auction. In the sitting room five forlorn chairs sat on the bare floorboards. Two small tables, lost in a sea of empty space, stood under the window. Pictures leaned against the walls next to a rolled-up carpet, silence permeated throughout the house.

In the kitchen, now eerily quiet without Abel and William bustling around, a clock ticked on its back on the empty table. Oddly matched plates, cups and glasses were spread over the worn solid oak table where Amos and William, over the years, had prepared the hundreds of family meals. Cutlery was piled up in an empty tin bucket. The shelves in the walk-in pantry, now empty. A pair of green wellingtons lying on their sides by the kitchen door, Barney's two dishes now abandoned, his fur covered blanket in a rumpled heap.

All but one of the bedrooms was empty. In his own room, he looked at his stripped bed, the curtains hanging dejectedly at the windows. A picture of a lemon tree, heavy with golden fruit, silhouetted against a brooding dark sky hung at an angle on the faded wallpaper. He straightened it, took a final look around, then shut the door behind him.

In his parent's bathroom, a towel hung forgotten from a peg next to the wash basin where a dry brown stain of water had snaked. A mummified fly lay on a dried and cracked piece of soap, next to the free-standing bath, its gold clawed feet already beginning to tarnish. The sumptuous purple velvet curtains which used to adorn the master bedroom windows, now gone, leaving them empty and exposed, looking blindly out over his mother's treasured rose gardens. The cupboard doors were open, he sucked in his breath at the faint hint of his mother's perfume emanating from their depths.

244

His footsteps echoed around the oak walled dining room. The light fittings already gathering cobwebs, the carpet showing the imprints of the departed legs of the long dining room table. He imagined them all sitting there, the fire crackling and spitting at the far end of the room, the clink of cutlery and crystal glasses, his father at the head of the table, his mother's light laughter. The large ornate mirror no longer reflecting images of them.

The shadows of the once happy boisterous family embedded in the walls. So many memories, all of them gone now.

The hallway table was bereft of the cluster of silver framed photographs. He ran his hand across it, almost hearing his father's hearty deep laugh, his mother's voice calling them for lunch.

He looked out across the lawns, in his mind's eye he could see and hear the laughter of his childhood friends, the clink of glasses, the high excited bark of Barney as he chased across the gardens, tail whirring with excitement, a tennis ball clamped between his jaws, to greet Jonathan when he returned home. The shouts, the laughter, the splashing from the swimming pool, now drained and empty, dried leaves dancing and skittering across the bottom.

The deep covered veranda stretched the length of the house, most of the elegant cane furniture gone. The scarlet bougainvillea climbed the length of the supporting pillars, spilling into the garden. The fireplace at the far end with just the shadow of ash in its depths, either side of it empty sagging baskets which were always piled with wood, now covered in fine cobwebs, a few parrot feathers clinging to the sides. A broken cane chair, its seat sagging. His mother had never quite got around to having it repaired.

He put out his hand to steady himself, then turned, closing up the empty house.

Barney, despite all the love and attention he received from Abel, didn't survive the wrench of losing his own family. He died in his sleep just three weeks later. He never made it back to them in Mombasa.

Chapter Seventy

Nick's mother settled in the guest cottage in the grounds of the house at the coast. She was adamant about not living in the main house. "Too many memories, Nicholas, it's your house now, I'm quite happy to be close to you here in the cottage."

The main house, compared to their home in Nairobi, was simply furnished. Sisal matting covered the floors throughout. Plump cushions in various shades of blue and cream filled sturdy, square, cane chairs and sofas. A large glass bowl holding different types of shells they had collected as children, a piece of driftwood, and some faded magazines, stood on top of a low white table in the centre of the room.

On the walls, prints of the old Mombasa town, seascapes and landscapes. There was a large framed photograph, taken by Nick when he was a young boy. A dhow its single sail white against the sunset, the sea the colour of gold as it lapped onto the sands of the shore.

Curtains throughout the house were of pure white muslin, light and cool against the heat of the day and intense sunlight.

Outside on the long veranda, were more cane chairs with fat yellow cushions, surrounding a long glass table. Two hammocks were strung where they could catch any breeze. Surrounding the house were tall palm trees, whispering and clattering, throwing cooling shadows over the thatched roof.

More white muslin curtains, held back with yellow ties, stretched the length of the veranda. During the heat of the day they were unfurled, floating like released ghosts in the gentle, caressing, wind from the sea.

*****

Each day his mother would amble along the beach, then return to her small cottage to sleep for a few hours.

246

Mr Parrot sat in his cage at the end of the veranda muttering to himself, looking thoroughly fed up with his new surroundings.

Every evening, Nick and his mother ate by candlelight out on the veranda of the main house, fussed over by Tom.

Tom was the eldest son of old William, he'd looked after the house for the past ten years.

Each day Tom would take the family jeep into town to shop for fresh fruit, vegetables and salads, and whatever else he thought they might enjoy for dinner. Mostly they ate fish, prawns and lobster, bought from the local fisherman who called at the house daily with their catch. Watching with concern as the memsahib picked half-heartedly at the food he had prepared with such care.

*****

Towards the end of the year his mother's condition seemed to deteriorate. Worried, Nick called their doctor.

"On the whole, there's nothing physically wrong with your mother Nick," he said after examining her. "Her memory is going, which could be a blessing in many ways, although she'll have moments of clarity. I've seen this many times before.

"When you have a partner for as long as your mother had, and one dies, the other sometimes gives up the will to live. There's little, or nothing, to be done about it. I would suggest you get someone in to look after her, to keep her company for a few hours a day. I'm sorry I can't be more positive."

Nick went down to the cottage and knocked on the door. She was sitting looking out of the window, a blanket wrapped around her even though it was hot and humid.

"Ma," he called softly.

She turned at the sound of his voice, looking confused. He sat down next to her and took her hand in both of his. "Ma, I'm going to find someone to keep you company for a few hours a day. I think you need more than Mr Parrot. Someone who can read to you and walk with you on the beach. I can't give you all the time you need at the moment. There's a mountain of paperwork to be done with Pa's estate, it's taking hours of my time."

She looked at him, her face blank. "Remember Anna, Ma? I spoke to her in Nairobi, a few days ago. She's coming to stay with her family for a month. She said she would pop in each day for a few hours. Would you like that?"

She nodded, then frowned. "Anna? Was she the girl you were going to marry? The one who didn't arrive in Nairobi? I don't want her around me if that's the case. I can never forgive her for what she did to you."

He shook his head at her with resignation. "No Ma, Anna is an old family friend, don't you remember?"

"I don't like the parrot either Nicholas, please take him away. Sometimes I think Hugh is here with me, and Jonathan…and look he's pulling all his feathers out, I don't think he likes being here."

"Don't go getting upset, Ma, of course I'll take Mr Parrot. I'll put him on my veranda under the tree, he'll be quite happy there, maybe his feathers will grow back."

He kissed her on the forehead, then let himself out of the door, taking the muttering parrot with him.

He should have thought about the effect the parrot, who was a brilliant mimic, would have on his mother, bringing back painful memories, with the familiar voices from her past.

248

Chapter Seventy-One

Each day Anna sat with Nick's mother, talking to her about her life in London. Telling her stories about her family and friends, her patients, the girl who lost her memory. She would read to her for an hour before heading back to her father's house.

Anna remembered Nick's mother as a vivacious woman, and the many parties held at their house. Deborah had been one of the most popular hostesses in the city, an invitation to one of her legendary dinner parties had been highly coveted.

Anna had been a guest in the Kennedy house on many occasions, and always loved a particular, silver-framed, photograph, taken long ago, of Deborah sitting at the large white steering wheel of her car, with her pet leopard sitting next to her in the passenger seat.

Now she watched the woman staring out of the window, seeing nothing at all except her own reflection in the glass, lost in a world long gone, not saying more than a word or two.

Anna reached across, stilling Deborah's hands. "Let's go for a walk. It's cool down by the water, it will do you good. Here, let me help you."

After their short walk, Anna settled her back in her room, then went to look for Nick, finding him in his study.

"You should go for a walk or a swim Nick, get some fresh air, and not be cooped up in here."

He shrugged, pointing at the piles of documents and papers heaped and strewn across his desk, and the stack of files balanced precariously at the side of it. "This estate is going to take months to sort out, and I still haven't had any bites on selling the house in Nairobi - but you're right, I should take a break."

"I see you have Mr Parrot up here now? He doesn't look too healthy, he's almost bald, he looks sort of sad. I think he's lonely. He needs some company."

"You're right, he does look sad, and he doesn't say much anymore. He's always loved a lot of family activity around him. I'm not sure what to do with him."

He rubbed his eyes then ran his fingers through his hair. "Not sure what to do about a lot of things at the moment. My main concern is my mother."

Anna went and stood behind his chair, massaging his neck. "Your mother is as well as can be expected, Nick. Maybe it's kinder for her to be in her own world rather than ours? She's loved and taken care of, which is more than can be said for most people in her position.

"We Africans look after, and respect, our old people even though they get a bit muddled sometimes. It's a pity it's not the same in other countries. I've looked after many people at the hospital in London, with similar problems to your mother. Most of them have been abandoned by their children, their loneliness is heart-breaking to see. Some of them end up in some dreadful home with no hope. At least your mother has you, and I'm sure she's aware of your presence, she just gets a bit confused now and again."

"I know you're trying to make me feel better, but I can see how fast Ma has gone downhill. She's lost the will to live. The best I can do is make sure she's comfortable until the end. It's hard to lose someone you love. But it will happen, I know. It'll be hard to be the one surviving member of our family – it doesn't bear thinking about."

Anna bent and kissed him on the cheek. "Come on, I've got my cozzie on under my dress. Let's go and have a swim, then we can go grab a beer at your old bar," she paused. "Now *that's* a good idea! Why don't you take Mr Parrot to the bar – he'd love it there with all the people to swear at."

Nick looked out at the parrot, its cage swinging on its hook. "I remember once seeing something on television filmed in what used to be the Congo. It was a flock of African Grey parrots, just like him, a big flock, flying over the jungle. Just a grey cloud of feathers, interspersed with bright red tail feathers. I never forgot it.

"I hate seeing anything caged. It's an anathema to me." He nodded towards the parrot. "I'd like to set him free, but he would never survive now."

"Where did you get him from?"

"We inherited him from a couple who were leaving Kenya. They had a choice you see, they could go anywhere they wanted, unlike Mr Parrot who never had a choice, he was caged for life. He has no idea what freedom is, no idea what it feels like to stretch his wings and fly away."

He stood up stiffly. "Come on Anna, let's go and have a swim – I'll have a think about finding a new home for Mr Parrot. The bar idea might be a good one."

*****

"I'm worried about Deborah, Daddy," Anna said to her father that evening. "I don't think she'll be with us for much longer. She has this look about her now. I don't seem to be able to make much difference to her state of mind. She spends so much time sleeping, and I know she doesn't have a clue who I am, or Mummy, when she goes to see her, although she sometimes surprises me by mentioning an event at the club, or one of her charities. Then she sounds like the Deborah I remember.

"I've talked to her about both our families, but it doesn't seem to evoke any memories or recollections. Yesterday she forgot to get dressed, she was found wandering along the beach in her nightdress. One of Nick's neighbours brought her back."

Anna's father nodded with sympathy. "Yes, it's difficult to know sometimes. She could well be thinking, and speaking, with clarity then half an hour later becomes quite lost to us. Let's pray it won't be too long now. It would be good to have you around to comfort Nick, he's become such a loner these days. I'm more worried about him than his mother."

Chapter Seventy-Two

Anna let herself into the cottage, Deborah turned her head and smiled, patting the bed. "Come and sit down I need to talk to you about something."

Surprised, Anna sat down, she sounded quite lucid.

"The patient you were talking about – the one involved in the accident in London? It was her, you know, I'm sure of it.

"I can't remember the name of the girl Nick was going to marry, but I do remember the photographs he took of her in a park in London."

Anna looked at her, a blank look on her face. "I sent my old friend in London, Kitty, a copy of Nick's photographs. I'd show them to you but I can't remember what I've done with them.

"Kitty remembered seeing a photo in the newspaper, a woman involved in a car accident.

She looked at Anna. "For goodness sake," she said with impatience, "*say* something! Oh, never mind…

Anna frowned at her patient. *What on earth was she talking about?*

Seeing her so agitated Anna stroked her hair, trying to soothe her. "It's alright, Deborah, try to rest. I'll go and get Nick for you."

Deborah pushed Anna's hand away in frustration.

"Why are you looking at me like that, Anna? You know something about this don't you? I think you've been lying to all of us!"

*****

Nick looked up, startled to see Anna running towards the house. He stood up alarmed.

"What is it Anna? Is Ma alright?"

252

"She's quite agitated and angry, Nick. She's trying to tell me something, but I think she's speaking French. I don't have a clue what she's talking about. Come quick."

Deborah looked up when they both returned, then smiled for a moment, before putting her head back on her pillows and closing her eyes.

Nick sat with his head in his hands. Too late. Anna put her arms around him, offering what comfort she could.

"Your mother didn't say much to me, Nick. But when she did talk, it was always about your father, how much she missed him, and Jonathan. I'm sure she's with them now, and as happy as she was when they were here. She was trying to tell me something. I think it was important. This must have brought on the heart attack. I'm sorry."

He looked at her with tired, blood shot, eyes. "I know she wanted to be buried next to Pa. I'll make the arrangements and fly back to Nairobi with her. Thank you, Anna, for making her last few weeks as easy as possible."

"I'll come with you both, I don't want you to go through this on your own. Let me help. I'll call the hospital now to make the arrangements for an ambulance to collect her.

Chapter Seventy-Three

They sat on the veranda of the now sparsely furnished old house in Nairobi, Nick was staring into the distance, saying nothing.

Anna studied him through her sunglasses as she sipped her wine. He would have made a wonderful husband and, if this had happened, he might well have had children. It could have saved his mother's life, or at least prolonged it. Deborah would have had something else in her life to love, some grandchildren, to take away the pain of losing her beloved husband and son.

Nick had returned to the old family home after his mother's funeral and been there for a month. She visited him as often as her job at the hospital allowed.

Nick didn't socialize at all. He was never at any of the social events or clubs. Maybe it was Jonathan's death, the time taken to wind up his father's estate, and now his mother's death, five months after his father's, which seemed to have made him withdraw even more into himself.

Anna leaned back in her chair trying to coax some kind of conversation out of him. "I wonder what your mother was trying to say to me. It's bothering me. The only bit I caught was something about a kitty – does this mean anything to you Nick? Was it a favourite cat?"

He took a mouthful of beer and frowned. "No, she was one of Ma's oldest friends. Kitty lived here years ago. She was the one who invited Ma here one holiday and introduced her to my father. Her name was Kitty Matthews, she was French, and lived in London. Maybe Ma was rambling a bit, remembering her past."

"No, she wasn't rambling, not at all. She told me she had something important to tell me. She was speaking English then, and was quite lucid. It was when she launched into French that I lost the conversation. Perhaps you should give Kitty a call sometime, see if she can shed any light on what your mother might have been trying to say?"

"Too late I'm afraid. I put a notice in the Times, in London, when Pa died. My godparents wanted to arrange a memorial service for him in London. The Duke, Arthur, received several letters from old friends who were unable to attend. One of them was from Kitty's husband. Kitty died just before Pa, so there won't be any point in calling."

Anna put her hand over his, leaving it there. "Why don't we go to the bush for a couple of days? Let's get away from all these people and the traffic. You need a break from everything, Nick."

He smiled the sad smile she was growing accustomed to now. The one never quite reaching his eyes.

"You're right I need a break. Being back in the wilderness is what I need. I'll see what I can book. Good thinking Anna."

*****

Two weeks later they were at a lodge in the Mara. Nick breathed in the familiar dry smell of the bush, and the animals, feeling his spirits lift. This was the life he was born to. He wanted, and needed, another lodge to own and run. He would make enquiries when they got back to Nairobi. There was nothing to keep him in Mombasa now. He could close up the beach house, leaving Tom in charge, then return to the bush where he belonged. He would take the Nairobi house off the market – it was his last tenuous link with his family – he wanted to keep that link.

On their last evening, Anna and Nick sat around the crackling fire, all the other guests having retired for the night.

Nick looked up at the eerily bright moon illuminating the bush, transforming all colour into silvery hues of blue and white, for as far as the eye could see. He knew on the last few occasions when he was with Anna, he hadn't been good company. He'd been too wrapped up in his own problems, not listening to what she said most of the time. He would make more of an effort, and what better time than now?

"Tell me about your life in London, what you did there, apart from your nursing?"She raised her eyebrow at him. "Now why should I repeat it all again to you Nick?"

He gave her a lopsided grin. "Sorry."

"I didn't share a flat at first, well not at all really. A friend, who needed some help, stayed there when I came over here for my five-month break – she was the girl I nursed, the girl who got hit by a car."

Nick nudged the fire with his boot sending up a shower of sparks. "Oh yes, I sort of remember you talking about her. What happened to her?"

"When I got back she moved into another flat, with a nice guy, a researcher called Joe. Then she began to remember her past, she'd lost her memory you see.

"The police were able to give her a lot of information, it's all in a data base these days, where she was born, who her parents were, her husband's name, her old address etc.

"Anyway, she went back to the flat she lived in before the accident."

He grinned at her. "So was her husband sitting in the chair waiting for his dinner, having not noticed she'd been gone for months on end." He stood up and threw another log on the fire, red hot embers shooting up into the dark sky before falling to earth in the darkness.

Anna laughed, stifling a yawn with the back of her hand. "I'm bushed Nick, it must be all this fresh air. Time for me to go to bed, I can't keep my eyes open. I'll see you in the morning. I'll tell you the rest of the story on the flight back to town.

"It's good to be out here in the bush. It puts things back into perspective somehow, doesn't it? Animals don't give a hoot about what's going on in the big bad world, they don't need anything more than each other, a mate."

"Yes, that's true. God, I must have been mad to sell Honey Badger, I wish I hadn't now. But too late I guess. I'll see you to your room Anna, come on."

He walked her back then returned to the fire, looking up at the swarming stars, counting out three now.

Nick stamped the fire out and walked back to his suite.

Chapter Seventy-Four

The sun rose up over the acacia trees as Nick sat sipping his coffee out on the deck of the lodge. It would be another scorcher of a day. He watched the vultures circling high up in the sky, wheeling and dipping then catching the thermals as they searched for the remains of a predator's kill.

The call of a fish eagle sent a shiver up his spine; the cry haunting and distinctive. He watched a herd of impala, their short white tails twitching, nibbling the juicy young grass, lifting their heads at intervals to check for danger. A herd of elephant drank deeply from the waterhole, before ambling off into the distance, foraging as they made their silent ponderous way along ancient worn paths, where their ancestors had walked before them.

He checked his watch and saw Anna walking towards him carrying her small safari bag. He stood up. "Here let me take that."

"Thanks. Haven't you packed? The Land Rover will be here in ten minutes to take us out to the airstrip."

"I'm going to stay on here for a few more days, Anna. Then I'm going to spend some time in Nairobi, see what's up for sale in the way of game lodges. I want to change my life, start anew.

"I'll need to fly out to see any lodges on the market. I didn't sell the Cessna when I sold the lodge, it's been gathering dust in a hangar at Wilson Airport, it's time I gave her a work out. I'll call you before I leave town, let's have dinner."

Anna hugged him. "Great idea. As you said last night, there's nothing to rush back to Mombasa for. Good luck hunting for a lodge then, I'll look forward to having dinner with you. I'll be the talk of the town! You realize you're even more eligible now, especially with your posh title, the women will be beating a path to your door, hurling their daughters over your garden wall."

He threw back his head, laughing for the first time in weeks. "It's not going to happen, I can assure you. Here comes your ride to the air strip. I'll come with you, see you off."

They sat in the vehicle waiting for the arrival of the aircraft. Nick saw it long before he heard it, a tiny blip in a peerless sky. The pilot lined up ready to land, coming in low to chase a lingering group of impala on the airstrip. The impala scattered, leaping like ballet dancers in all directions, before regrouping, looking indignant, in the distance. The pilot turned the plane around and made a bumpy landing, bringing the aircraft to a halt, before turning off the engines.

Nick stowed Anna's bag and kissed her goodbye. He stepped back, watching the pilot do her pre-flight check, ready for take-off. The propellers began to turn, churning up the red dust. He started to walk back to the vehicle, then turned around.

"The woman you were telling me about last night," he shouted to Anna. "When she found out her real name, what was it?"

Anna cupped her ear so she could hear his question. "What…?" but her voice was drowned out by the roar of the engines. She shook her head, lifting her shoulders and hands at him. With a cheerful wave, she watched him through the small window of the aircraft. As the plane gained height he got smaller and smaller, then they turned towards Nairobi, leaving him standing there alone, the dust settling around him, the silence broken by the forlorn cry of a small flock of guinea fowl. *"come back, come back, come back."*

Nick turned and walked back to the waiting vehicle.

Chapter Seventy-Five

For the next month, Nick flew to and from Nairobi, to inspect the lodges up for sale, staying overnight in each one, as a guest of the sellers. He knew most of them, and their owners, from his time at Honey Badger, and being in the same business. It was an opportunity to catch up on how the tourism business was doing - who was doing well, or not so well.

He visited his old lodge but didn't stay overnight there, much to the disappointment of the English owner he'd sold it to. As he flew back up into the clouds he realized the place held too many memories for him. The many childhood holidays with his parents, and his brief time there with Emily. No, it wasn't a good idea to go back. He wanted to keep moving forward. Away from the people he had loved and lost.

Nick checked the last lodge on his short list. Fish Eagle Lodge. He flew low over the bush scattering herds of buffalo and other game. He whistled tunelessly through his teeth as he looked down for the landing strip. The game was abundant; the lodge was built close to a shimmering lake, which meant the bird life would be prolific, spectacular.

He came into land on a well-maintained strip, keeping a wary eye out for any wandering animals. Robert Grayson, the owner, was there to meet him.

As they drove to the lodge, Nick took a look at his surroundings. So far so good. He heard the familiar cry of a Fish Eagle, watching it drop like a rock down to the lake, and without effort snatched a plump unsuspecting fish from its watery home, then flying off with his slippery dripping meal clutched in its talons, landing on the top of a tree with the grace of a dancer. A good omen.

A short platform was built out over the lake leading to a seating area with a generous, but sagging, thatched roof offering protection from the sun.

It would be a superb place for bird watching; Nick's mind was already visualizing ways to improve it. The platform could be extended, chairs and tables could be put there, with binoculars and bird books for the guests. Monkeys might be a problem, but he'd figure this out later. Guests would enjoy having sun-downers there, looking out over the tranquil lake, watching the birds heading home to roost, as the sun sank in a blood shot red sky.

After a light lunch, Robert took him on a tour of the property. The lodge was well maintained but looking tired and a little unkempt. The main lodge huddled beneath ancient trees, the fifteen guest rooms were built amidst the bush, blending into the landscape, he hadn't even spotted them from the air.

It was what he was looking for. The lodge met all his exacting criteria.

Later, as they sat drinking their coffee, Nick and Robert discussed the terms and conditions of the sale, the time frame for the handover, and the confirmed bookings for the following year. With his generous inheritance, Nick could well afford the asking price and the additional cost of the renovations he envisaged.

The tented suites and main areas needed a complete refurbish, and the safari vehicles were showing their age. He made a mental note to contact his old manager, Mike Connelly, to see if he would work for him again.

Robert, like Nick, had been born and brought up in Kenya. Now well into his sixties he'd decided it was time to sell up, move back to Nairobi, and spend more time with his daughter and the grandchildren.

"Sorry to hear about your parents, Nick, always a shock when they follow each other so quickly. They'll be a great loss to this country."

Nick nodded in agreement as Robert continued. "Much as I love my lodge, and I've owned it for thirty years now, I feel it's time to hand over to a younger man. My wife has been hinting about me moving back to town, she doesn't want to commute back and forth anymore. I would stay here 'til I dropped dead, but the family has always supported me with my venture, now it's time to give something back."

Robert looked around his lodge with an air of nostalgia. "I can't think of a finer man to sell it to. It'll be in good hands with you. Let's turn in now, tomorrow we can start the paperwork."

"Thanks Robert. I'll endeavour to keep your legacy alive. Anytime you fancy a break from town, feel free to come and spend a few days here, and your family of course."

They shook hands and turned in for the night.

Nick lay awake listening to the nocturnal sounds, in the distance he could hear the unmistakable, intermittent, throaty roar of a male lion. He turned over closing his eyes. God, it was good to be back in the bush.

*****

Two months later Nick was the proud owner of Fish Eagle Lodge. Six weeks later he took up residence. The owner's cottage was set back from the main lodge and guest accommodation, giving him privacy when he needed it.

Feeling happier than he'd been for a long time, he threw himself into renovating and upgrading the lodge. He kept on all the staff, hiring more where necessary. Mike Connelly had leapt at the chance of managing Nick's new lodge.

Nick bought a sleek blue and white boat, big enough to accommodate all his guests when he was full, planning to use it for sundowner cruises across the lake. At one end of the boat was a full bar, seats and cushions were spread invitingly throughout. He built a structure over the main body of the boat to hang filmy white muslin curtains, which would protect guests from the harsh sun, these were held back by heavy gold tassels completing the unusual look he'd envisaged.

During the day, the more adventurous guests would be able to go out with one of the rangers and fish to their hearts content. In the late afternoon they could sit, or lie back, on the cushions, watching the sizzling sun sink down beneath the lake.

There was a large pod of resident hippo who lived in and around, the lake. The guests would be able to get close to them in the water, but not too close. He knew hippo killed more people in Africa than any other animal. He watched one now as it silently broke the surface of the water, twitched its ears, gave a cavernous yawn, displaying huge yellow incisors, then sank without a sound back into the depths of the lake, barely rippling the surface of the water.

A troop of monkeys clambered through the trees and he smiled at their antics as they somersaulted through the branches.

If he was honest with himself, this was as close as he was going to come to being happy. He would focus on making his lodge one of the best in East Africa, just as Honey Badger had been.

Chapter Seventy-Six

Harry

Harry looked up irritated at the hammering on his office door. "Come! No need for all the bloody noise. Another of his top agents, Josh, entered, his face drained of colour, a single bead of sweat traversing down the left of his face. Harry's fingers paused their habitual drumming on the desk.

"What?"

"You need to see this Harry." He handed three sheets of paper across the desk, "There's a fox in the hen house…"

Harry scanned the document with disbelief. Then stood abruptly and crossed to the window, staring unseeingly at the relentless New York traffic, the blue and white NYPD patrol cars, interspersed with thousands of yellow cabs, steam, like dragon's breath, rising from the manholes, crowds of meandering or hurrying pedestrians clogging the sidewalks.

He turned around and walked back to his desk, leaning his knuckles on the leather top he looked at the man across the room. "How did this happen, Josh?" he muttered, almost speechless with shock.

"How the fuck did we miss this?"

Chapter Seventy-Seven

The taxi sped away from Nice airport en-route to Antibes. Emily, on impulse, asked the driver to give her a quick tour of the town. Now she looked at the yachts bobbing around in the azure sea, the incredible blue sky, and the last of the winter snow on the tips of the mountains. The taxi slowed down as it made its way along the Promenade des Anglais. Palm trees and royal blue benches dotted the promenade, and the pebble beach was attracting quite a crowd, despite the fact it was still only the beginning of April.

Couples strolled along with their dogs and children, avoiding the skateboarders' and cyclists. On the opposite side of the beach she marvelled at the architecture of the Negresco Hotel, the Belle Époque buildings, the sleek lines of the more modern apartment blocks and hotels.

Waiters, in long black aprons, moved with speed, and expertise, between the tables of restaurants and cafés, serving coffee and croissants.

All too soon the taxi was inching its way through the old town of Antibes, pulling up at the side of a hotel overlooking the square.

She checked in, then went to her room, on the first floor. Throwing open the pale blue shutters she leaned out. The French flag fluttered over some sort of parapet. Down below a big square surrounded by old plane trees. Tables were set with white tablecloths, anchored at the corners with metal clips, the menu scrawled in white chalk on blackboards. To her right were more restaurants, the tables already filling up for lunch. To her left pedestrians were meandering along the sidewalk, stopping to admire the stylish cakes and pastries in the window of the Patisserie. Leading off the square was a warren of cobbled streets.

It was just as she had imagined. She couldn't wait to unpack, then explore the old town. She had an appointment with an estate agent the following afternoon.

Her plan was to stay in the hotel until she found an apartment to rent. She opened her suitcase and hung up her clothes. The room was not luxurious, but it was large and clean, the bathroom more than adequate, although she winced at the vivid pink tiles on the walls.

Half an hour later she was ready to go. She would head towards the market she'd heard so much about from the receptionist. She wandered along the Rue de la Republique, circled the ancient fountain surrounded by noisy tourists and locals, eating at the pavement cafés, then made her way up the narrow street to the market.

She studied an old photograph at the top of the stone steps leading to a side entrance. It must have been taken over a hundred years ago, nothing much had changed. It was still the bustling place it had always been.

Trestle tables groaned with fresh produce, vegetables, fruit, cheeses, meat and fresh cut flowers. Bulging salamis hung from iron hooks, the stall holders shouted good-naturedly, across to each other, whilst serving their customers. Plump purple and green olives nestled in their juices, herbs and spices were displayed in such a way as to attract the attention of buyers, the smell of tied bunches of lavender hung heavily in the air.

Her mouth watered at the sight of all the food and she realized she was hungry. She plunged into the crowds and shuffled her way through to a café she spotted, at the other end of the covered market. Cheese mongers urged her to try a piece of their cheese, or a slice of salami, smiling she obliged, chatting to them in French.

What a bonus it had been! She spoke French! As soon as she began to listen to her tutorial she realized the language was familiar to her, she marvelled at how her brain had forgotten so much but could remember a foreign language with such fluency.

Emily found an empty table at the café, sitting down she ordered a coffee from the smiling waiter. With all the things sampled on her way through the market stalls, she was no longer hungry. She took off her now too warm coat and sipped her coffee, unaware of the admiring looks she was getting.

When she found somewhere to live she would get stuck into her writing. Antibes had attracted many famous writers and artists over the years, including Hemingway, Scott Fitzgerald and Graham Greene, she

264

could understand why the south of France inspired such passion in their writing. Not that she had any ambitions of being a best-selling author. Her writing would be more therapeutic as she tried to explore her mind, write down her thoughts and feelings.

The estate agent showed her apartments the following afternoon. After the fourth one Emily's heart was beginning to sink. They were so gloomy, none of them seemed to get any sun. The entrance halls and common areas were not too clean. She'd seen an old banana skin and cigarette butts in the stairwell of one of the buildings. The estate agent lifted her shoulders, with a typical Gallic shrug, explaining it was one of the downsides of living in the old town, but if Emily could increase her budget by two or three hundred more Euros, she might prefer some of the other properties she had on her books.

"I can go a little higher. I must have a place which is light and airy."

Emily walked into the apartment knowing straight away it was the place she was looking for. The sitting room was filled with afternoon sunshine, heavy wooden shutters painted pale blue framed the tall windows. She leaned out of the window, looking over the burnt orange rooftops to the sea beyond. She could see the occupants of the apartment opposite, who waved cheerily at her, and she waved back. Well, as the agent told her, smiling, if you live in the old town you get to know your neighbours sooner rather than later.

The cobbled street beneath her was lined with shops selling jewellery, clothes, and bric-a-brac, clothes displayed on hangers hung outside some of them, the material fluttering in the languid breeze.

The bedroom was adequate, although cupboard space was limited, the bathroom was acceptable. The kitchen was open plan and part of the sitting room.

"When can I move in?" she asked eagerly.

The agent shuffled through her papers on the table, telling her she could move in on Monday, in three days' time. Emily signed the lease, paid the deposit, and the first month's rent, arranging to collect the keys first thing on Monday morning. Satisfied, she returned to the hotel on the square.

Lying in bed that night she thought about the events of the day. She knew she'd made the right move, coming to France, even though Joe had teased her.

265

"Why on earth would you want to go and live somewhere where you don't know anyone. Didn't you have enough of that after your accident?"

She smiled in the dark. It was a perceptive remark given the circumstances, a remark she'd had no answer for.

She spent the week-end exploring Antibes. Twice she got lost in the maze of narrow streets, all looking the same to her, but soon she began to get her bearings, learning to watch out for noisy mopeds, which seemed to come from nowhere, driving dangerously fast. Getting knocked over was something to be avoided.

She loved the narrow cobbled streets with colourful window boxes, and quaint shops, old men sitting half in the shadows drinking coffee, smoking and gossiping. The boulangeries with the smell of fresh baguettes, light as air pastries, and the decorated flans and tarts were exquisite. A feast for the eyes she thought, buying a fresh baguette. She tore off pieces of bread, nibbling as she walked along the ramparts, looking at the expensive yachts glinting in the sunshine, some of them resembling small cruise liners.

Emily sat on one of the benches. It was a pretty town and the people were friendly. She'd been told the French didn't have much time for the English. But she found them courteous, speaking French was a distinct advantage.

She walked along Boulevard Albert towards Place de Gaulle, another large square with cafés on two corners. She found a table at the nearest one and sat in the sun with her coffee, surprised by how many people were smoking. Idly she wondered if she ever smoked. Well if she had it would have been a good thing to have come out of being in the coma, she would have got past any cravings for a cigarette.

A couple walked past hand in hand, with eyes only for each other. They stopped to cross the road, exchanging a lingering kiss whilst they waited for the traffic lights to change, oblivious to everyone navigating around them.

Emily stared at them with envy. She must have been in love with someone once. Had they too walked along hand in hand, kissed each other, oblivious to everyone else?

What had he looked like, sounded like, where was he born, what country was he from?

She was being ridiculous. Whoever he was he'd disappeared. Thinking like this was not going to get her anywhere. Meanwhile there was the book to write.

266

Feeling herself being observed, she turned around. Four young Arab men were sitting at the table watching her, with unconcealed admiration, as they drank their coffee. She turned away, putting up her hand to catch the eye of the waiter. He bustled over, his smile filling his eyes, and she felt herself blushing.

She'd watched this particular waiter flirting with an older woman earlier on. A woman in her late sixties, with a flawless skin made up with care. She had been wearing beige linen trousers and a white shirt, the pale lemon leather belt matching her high heeled shoes, draped across her shoulders a cream suede jacket. Her hair piled on her head, secured with a tortoiseshell clip.

Emily thought she looked more than elegant, finding her own eyes, along with many others, following the woman as she left the café, wondering how she negotiated the cobbled streets in such high heeled shoes?

French men, she had decided were more daring, more overt, with their flirting, checking out the women over their coffee cup, checking their figure, clothes, accessories. Twice she had been followed back to her apartment, an ardent suitor begging to take her for a drink, pleading, joking and quite charming. Something which didn't happen to her in London.

She paid her bill, left a tip, then headed back to the hotel.

On her left was a monument of some kind, she stopped peering at the inscription, fumbling in her bag for her glasses.

It was dedicated to members of the Resistance who had died for their country. Even in this small town heroes were not forgotten. Unlike in today's world, she thought cynically, where people were forgotten, and discarded with such ease.

What had it all been for anyway? They had died for nothing. Just as thousands of others had died at the hands of The Shadow Dancer, Bin Laden and their fanatical followers. There were threats of terror everywhere now, there was no hiding place for the innocent, no justification for the violence in the world today. No one knew who the enemy was, where he was, or when there would be another terrifying attack. It was disturbing, frightening.

They had been responsible for the Madrid bombing of a train in 2004. Emily was quite sure they had their eyes on Europe now.

Chapter Seventy-Eight

Emily stepped back, almost losing her balance. The young man on the moped was driving too fast. She swore at him, in French, under her breath, whilst realising she hadn't looked where she was stepping. Another down side to Antibes; a lot of the owners of the many dogs around town didn't clean up after their pets. Most of the time, instead of looking around at the historic medieval buildings, she was glancing down to make sure she didn't step in anything unpleasant. She scraped her shoe on a brick and carried on towards the old town centre.

The sun beat down on the cobbled streets. She pulled the brim of her hat down, anxious to get to the café on the square. The August heat was intolerable and had been for weeks now. The town was crowded with boisterous tourists, hot babies squealing in prams and harassed waiters hurrying back and forth with their trays of cold drinks, sweat dripping off their faces, their shirts sticking to their backs in dark patches.

Crossing the square, she fought her way through the crowds, exhausted. She spied an empty table and sank into a chair, fanning her face with her hat.

She'd settled into a routine here. She rose early and took a shower. Once dressed, she would watch the news, then have breakfast. At nine on the dot, she would be in front of her lap top, trying to put her thoughts down. When she stopped writing for the day she would take a walk along the ramparts, finishing up in one of the many cafés for a glass of chilled wine.

The days flew past and November arrived with breath-taking speed. Tomorrow she would take the bus into Cannes and have lunch there. A few hours away from her lap top would give her eyes a break, not that she was making much progress.

Thoughts of what she would do when she returned to England were pushed to the back of her mind. This could be dealt with later. As for a job, she would deal with this too, she would have to do something to keep herself occupied. She thought of Joe, as she often did, wishing he was sitting opposite her now, polishing his glasses.

Chapter Seventy-Nine

Rebecca ran her tongue around the rim of her cappuccino watching the crowds in the square. Her life had changed since the sale of Becoming Books in London, a change she was happy with. Ben still travelled back and forth, to Paris and New York, whilst she stayed in the south of France. The progress on the book she wanted to write had stalled. Then Ben suggested opening an English book shop in Cannes.

"There are hundreds of English speaking people in this neck of the woods, Becks, just as there are hundreds of yachts. Most of the crews are from New Zealand, Australia or South Africa, they love to stock up on books before their next trip. I think it's worth thinking about."

Rebecca had warmed to the idea straight away. She knew getting a book published was akin to winning the lottery. Selling books was far easier than writing them, and more lucrative.

She sipped her coffee. The book shop was a success, and a wonderful way of meeting people. There were a number of famous writers living on the *Cote du Azur* and she'd roped them in for book signings and promotions.

Rebecca checked her watch then reached for her bag and coat. It was time to get back to the shop and let her assistant take her lunch break.

She waited with the rest of the pedestrians for the traffic lights to change then crossed the road. A girl coming from the opposite direction bumped into her, they exchanged brief apologies and carried on.

Rebecca stopped and looked back. Oy, that girl had an uncanny resemblance to Emily even though she'd been wearing dark glasses.

No, she must have been mistaken. Emily would be married now, living in Kenya. They'd promised to keep in touch, Emily was going to send her contact details, via Ben in Paris, once she had settled in Kenya but, to her disappointment, Rebecca had heard nothing from her. She had no idea how to get in touch with her old friend with no contact details.

*****

"I saw a woman in town today who looked like Emily," she said to Ben over dinner. "We collided crossing the road with all the crowds."

Ben looked up surprised. "She wouldn't be here in Cannes surely? Maybe someone who looked similar to her as you said."

"That's why I hesitated and decided not to chase after her. Emily and Nick would have been married a couple of years by now. It's possible, they could be here on holiday, although I doubt this is Nick's kind of place…he's only happy when he's sitting in the bush surrounded by wild grunting and growling beasts. It's odd she never kept in touch though."

Ben filled her glass. "Why don't you see if you can find her then? I know this possible sighting is going to niggle you. Look Nick Kennedy up on the internet, see if you can find his publishers. Maybe they have an address for him, or at least some sort of contact numbers?"

"I've got a copy of his book *Beneath the Shimmering Stars* back at the apartment, which will tell me who the publishers are, or were," she shook her head thinking back. "Two years ago, I would have been able to give the name of the publisher of any book in my shop, now I can't remember any of them, it must be all this decadent living," she put her hand over his. "Not that I would change our lifestyle for anything, I love being decadent!"

*****

Rebecca called Ben at his office. "I hit a brick wall with Nick Kennedy, I'm afraid. The publisher was more than helpful though. It seems Nick produced another book on country houses and estates in England. They signed him up for a further book on Australia, but he broke the contract for personal reasons, then disappeared off the radar.

"I trawled through the internet but, apart from reviews on his two books, there's nothing about him. Not even a mention of the wedding or anything. All a bit odd…"

"Maybe they're doing what a few other couples do," Ben replied. "He's a first-class photographer – maybe they're spending a couple of years out in the bush somewhere, making a documentary on wild life, camping out under the stars, living rough. The sort of thing I imagine Nick would relish. It's a possibility, it would explain why you haven't heard from them?"

Rebecca doodled on the notebook in front of her. "I hope the 'personal reasons' for breaking his contract had nothing to do with Emily. Maybe, Ben, it didn't work out. Maybe they got a divorce already?

"I hope you're right, though, and they're making magnificent documentaries. I'll see you tonight, darlin'."

Chapter Eighty

A sharp crack of thunder woke Emily. She lay in bed listening to the hissing rain. She'd remembered nothing more of her past, but she was happy with what she did remember. The thing making her anxious now was the recurring dream, the dream where the tall man calls her name – *Emily*. Sometimes as she came out of it she would try and sink back into the dream, so desperate was she to find out who he was.

Dawn crept over the old town, the sun washing over the buildings turning them to gold and then pink. She fell into a light sleep, praying her dreams would offer up their elusive secrets.

*****

Emily buttoned up her coat, turning up the collar. The sky was the colour of cigar ash, and the Mistral was blowing with force through the town, dislodging old tiles and rattling window boxes. Shutters banged against their walls and the cafés were deserted, their chairs and tables stacked up against the canvas side awnings. What a contrast to summer, she thought, when it was almost too hot to go out. Now it was cold and rather unpleasant.

She strolled through the market, greeting the now familiar, cheerful, stall holders. Her shopping done she ducked into a café and ordered a hot chocolate.

Her writing wasn't going well; she felt restless. With winter closing in, she wanted to see Joe. They stayed in contact with emails but it wasn't the same as being with him. She missed him.

Moodily she took a gulp of her hot chocolate. Maybe she should go back to England, instead of staying here for the duration of her lease.

She paid for her drink, collected her basket of food from the chair next to her, and headed out the door. It banged behind her as the wind caught it, trapping her coat. She wrenched it free, turning up the collar against the cold December wind.

When she got back to her apartment she took off her coat and scarf and hung them up, noticing the slight tear in the lining from when she'd tugged it from the closed door.

Emily stifled her laughter. Could she sew? She ran her fingers over the rest of the lining to see if there was any more damage, feeling something lodged in the hemline. With care, she nudged it up to the split in the lining. A tight ball of paper which must have slipped through the hole in the torn pocket of her coat after the accident..

Spreading it out on the table, she stared at it.

It looked as though it might be the remnants of an old email, the edges thin and tattered, the words illegible as though they had become damp at some point. Emily picked it up, moving to the window to get a better light. Frowning and half closing her eyes she tried to pick out the faint letters. Giving up she reached for her glasses.

I'll be waiting for you, my darling, it seems so long since we were together, I'm not sure I'll recognise you after all this time...the rains have been...the ring is...waiting is so hard...love you so much. Hurry up and come to me, don't want to lose you again!

The rest was illegible. Emily sat down again. It was from him. But just how long had they been apart? Was it months or years? *Where was he? Who was he? What did he mean by lose you again?*

*****

Emily stirred the large bowl of soup simmering on the old gas ring, giving it a tentative sniff. It smelled good, her tummy growled in anticipation. A fresh baguette and three different cheeses were set on the table; the glow of a single candle softened the walls. She poured the soup into a bowl and sat down.

The church bells began to ring, she looked at them up in their tower, as thousands of people down the ages had done, as they swung back and forth, back and forth, like fish gulping air. She sipped her soup listening. Then as the last peals rang out, she watched them slow down and stop, then there was silence except for the hissing of the rain and the sputtering candle.

For no reason, she felt tears burning her eyes. What did the note mean?

274

Emily cleared the table, opening up her laptop, she searched for the British Airways website.

It was time to go home.

Chapter Eighty-One

Nick put down the telephone at the lodge, glad to hear the old guns, bequeathed to the Duke by his father, had been delivered. Arthur called him straight away.

"Wonderful dear boy! They arrived three days ago. I've been trying to call you every hour on the hour since then. Why don't you live in a civilized place where they have proper working telephones?"

Nick grinned into the phone. People never understood how difficult it was, deep in the bush, to have access to a telephone twenty-four hours a day, seven days a week. Sometimes the lines went down for days.

"I'm glad you like the guns, they'll complement all the others in your rather impressive collection. Pa knew you would appreciate them.

"Why not think about coming to Fish Eagle lodge some time, as my guests? The fishing is excellent, I think you'd enjoy it and it'll get you past winter your end."

Arthur interrupted him. "My dear boy, if you think I am going to queue up with thousands of people for hours on end, then have to take off my shoes, socks, belt and just about everything else, then be body searched by someone I've never been introduced to, then you are sadly mistaken. That damn Shadow Dancer and his bloody murdering friends have a lot to answer for. I personally won't be happy until they string them all up. He's made travelling a nightmare. Impossible!

"Good Heavens, even if you fly First Class you still have to go through all that, like a herd of cattle. No definitely not."

Nick could hear him puffing on his cigar "But we will be escaping the winter. We're taking the Euro star to Paris, then another train to Nice, we're going to be guests on an acceptable yacht. Our own suite, Nicolas, complete with sumptuous surroundings. Now *that's* what we call traveling. Not herded into a tube with a lot of sneezing, coughing strangers, with bulging rucksacks.

"Why not think about joining us," he continued, "you know our host and hostess – the Beltons? We're going to cruise the Med for a month; Antibes, Cannes, Monaco, all my favourite watering holes. We'd enjoy your company and it'll do *you* good to have some first-class comfort, instead of sitting in the middle of nowhere swatting elephants off your telegraph poles and using drums to communicate."

Despite himself Nick laughed. "I'll think about it. It does have a certain appeal. As long as bloody Camilla Hamilton-Flanders, isn't on board."

Arthur cut in. "The parents married her off to a family who have even more money than they have. Excellent match we thought. No, she won't be around. Be clinging to her new husband for all she's worth, or rather, for all he's worth. Give it some thought and let us know."

Nick replaced the receiver. He collected his fishing rod, then headed for the jetty. The invitation to join them on the yacht was tempting. Winter in the Med could be pleasant after the harsh heat of an African summer. Mike, his now lodge manager, could run the place without him. He cast the line into the sparkling water, waiting for the first bite. Why not?

Chapter Eighty-Two

Joe had been ecstatic with the news she was coming home, he was waiting at the airport to meet her with a bunch of yellow roses in his arms.

With the scrum of people milling around the arrivals area she didn't register the pretty young girl standing next to him.

"Good to have you home again Emily, it seems like years!" He hugged her then turned to the girl standing next to him. "Emily, this is Julia, or Jules as I call her. Jules this is my flat mate Emily."

Emily shook her hand. "Hi Jules, nice to meet you."

Joe grabbed her case, hauling it along behind him, firing questions about her trip, asking about her book, the progress made.

In the taxi, she answered his questions, hiding her dismay when she noticed he was holding Jules' hand.

Joe unlocked the door to the flat ushering them both in, before taking her suitcase up to her room.

In seconds he was back. "How about some coffee? Yes? I'll go put the kettle on."

"I'll do it Joe." Jules said casually. "I know where everything is."

Emily sat down, listening to Jules clattering the cups and saucers in the kitchen. She knew her way around.

She raised an eyebrow at Joe. "You never mentioned Jules in your emails. Is there something I should know?"

He took off his glasses, rubbing them vigorously before putting them back on. "I wasn't sure how to tell you, to be honest. I met her in the wine bar a couple of months ago. I was lonely – I needed company." He smiled at her, somewhat defensively, she thought.

"Is it serious Joe?"

"Dunno. She seems to be quite fond of me and I like her a lot. She's fun to be with, easy going."

278

Unlike me, Emily thought to herself, with all my problems and questions. No wonder Joe had found someone a little more light hearted – someone more normal. Who could blame him? After all she'd never given him any reason to hope there could be a relationship between them. Like any sensible person, he'd made a decision, and found someone else.

It must have been difficult for him, living with the ghost of the man who had disappeared out of her life. Hard for him having to sit and listen to all her speculating as to what might have happened in her past. Hard for him to ignore she had been in love with someone else.

"I'm happy for you Joe, a bit surprised, but happy."

Jules came back balancing the tray of steaming coffee. Emily couldn't bear to watch another moment.

"I'll take my coffee up to my room. I'm going to take a shower, unpack, and have a nap. Nice to meet you Jules. See you later Joe?"

"Um, not sure. We're going to the movies later, then having dinner. It's Jules' birthday."

"Oh, Happy Birthday Jules. You will be coming back later won't you, Joe?"

He gave her a wide smile. "Maybe not – remember the house rules?"

Her heart sank – this was serious if he was spending nights at her place. No doubt Jules had spent many nights here as well.

Well, this was not what she had expected for a happy homecoming. Spending her first night back alone. She'd been too presumptuous.

Half an hour later she heard the front door close, then there was silence. She reached for her laptop, deleting everything she had worked on in France, not that there was much to delete.

*****

Emily took a sleeping pill which threw her into a shallow sleep, fraught with anxious dreams. She awoke some hours later, the sheets twisted around her body. Groggily she looked at her watch, surprised it was the middle of a gloomy January afternoon.

Wrapping her gown around her she went down to the kitchen, seeing the empty unwashed coffee cups on the draining board. The image of Joe and Jules. Jules with the perfect eyebrows and long golden hair, holding hands, had almost floored her.

She was hungry. Opening the fridge, she checked out the contents, dismissing one choice after another – her appetite flat lining.

She took a half empty bottle of wine out and filled a glass. Wandering through the flat, she sipped from her drink, trailing her hands over the familiar furniture. What would happen now? Would he ask her to move out? They'd never got around to signing the lease agreement. He could ask her to go anytime, if he wanted to.

Then what?

Going back to her room she lay down on the bed again, the silence of the place running like acid through her veins.

She should have taken more care with Joe, but she hadn't. Loading all her problems onto his shoulders, oblivious to what he was thinking and feeling. Yes, she should have taken more care of him and his emotions. No doubt Jules was making a good job of it, with her perfect memory.

Dragging herself to the bathroom she reached into the cupboard for her anti-depressants. During her stay in Antibes she had depended on them, as she had the sleeping pills. Her brain would not leave her alone, so many questions with no answers, her nights, without taking a pill, one long nightmare, leaving her feeling tired and helpless when dawn crept through the shutters.

So, Joe had given up on her, something she'd not anticipated. He'd found someone else to love. He'd let her go. As the other man had.

Stifling a sob, she lay back on the bed. Was there any point to anything anymore?

She knew she would have to make some decisions about the future. She had enough money to buy a place of her own, start her own business if she wanted to. She would need to do something to fill up her days, with no job to go to.

She had tried with her writing but found it hard to concentrate, eventually giving up. How could she write a story about her life when she didn't even know what it was about herself? Instead of it being cathartic, the opposite had happened.

She put her hands to her ears, trying to block all the thoughts swirling around her head, trying not to unravel, trying not to let go.

More sleep was what she needed. She fumbled for the sleeping pills, swallowing two. She had to get out of her head for a few blessed hours.

She was so tired of trying to work out who she was – and now, what was the point? She seemed to have lost everything. Her parents, her husband, the man she was going to marry who hadn't loved her enough to come and find her. Anna was gone to another life far away, and now Joe. She'd lost him too.

With this turn of events it could be she would soon have no home, along with having no job.

She could find somewhere else to live, this wasn't the problem. The problem was, she was terrified of being on her own, fighting all her ghosts without the support of Anna and Joe, especially Joe.

Returning to the kitchen she filled her glass again, emptying the bottle of wine, putting her hand on the table to steady herself, feeling the pills kicking in.

Outside it was almost dark, the trees stark without their leaves. Rain slithered down the windows, in the distance, she could hear the mournful bark of someone's dog. She hated January.

Feeling the darkness starting to devour her she turned on the side light. It was going to be a long week-end, maybe he would come home in the morning, maybe without Jules. They could sit down, discuss the whole situation – she would need to find out what his plans were.

Feeling cold she made her way back to her room, burrowing back under the duvet. Reaching for her book she tried to concentrate, tamping down her negative thoughts.

An hour later she was staring at the same page. Reaching out her hand she felt for her sleeping pills. She squinted at the recommended dosage on the side, she needed her glasses but felt too weary to go and search for them. What had Doctor Harrington said? Take them when needed? But how many? She couldn't remember. Well, a few more wouldn't do any harm, she would get a solid night's sleep – everything would look different in the morning. She turned off the bedside light.

All she wanted to do was escape, disappear, be no more trouble to the people who had wanted to help her, knowing now, they couldn't. Then she was falling, falling – then nothing.

Chapter Eighty-Three

Joe tried to concentrate on the movie he and Jules had come to see, but his mind kept drifting back to Emily. He should have spent a bit more time with her, but she had taken off to her room for a nap as soon as Jules had made the coffee. He would give her a ring and see how she was settling back.

He leaned over to Jules. "Just going to make a quick phone call – be back in a minute," he whispered to her.

Standing in the foyer he stabbed in Emily's number, waiting for her to pick up, tapping his foot and pushing his glasses up with his finger. It went to voicemail. "Hey, Emily, pick up will you. Just checking to see if you're okay."

He tried again, the same thing happened. Frowning he put his phone in his pocket. That was one hell of a long nap she was taking. He found his way back to Jules and tried once again to concentrate on the film.

Emily's face had lit up when she saw him waiting for her at the airport, then, when he'd introduced Jules, it had turned to slight puzzlement, then in the taxi, complete bewilderment. He should have at least spent her first night back with her, but Jules had only told him that morning it was her birthday. It had been a tough choice, but he had wanted to see her reaction.

Emily had been away for ten months, giving no indication when she might come back, although she paid her rent, without fail, at the end of every month.

Before she left she'd announced to him, that she wanted to change her routine life in London, needed a break. Time out somewhere different Thinking about it afterwards, he wasn't sure if the break included him, if she would even come back. He had asked her a couple of times, by email, but she hadn't committed to a date for her return but promised she would come back.

The flat had felt empty without her, he missed her creamy husky laugh, her chatter whilst they cooked dinner, the walks in the park, watching television together.

He'd missed the constant digging into her past; not growing weary with the endless questions, the possibilities, the speculation as to where, and who, the mystery man might be. He had taken it on as a sort of project right from the beginning, committing himself to listening to all her questions, prodding her memory when he could.

He'd wanted her all to himself, for reasons she would never know about, but every time she remembered something else about her past, he felt the gap widening in their relationship. He knew one day she would remember everything, then there would be no room in her life for him. Emily. The girl he wanted to know more about, but who didn't even know herself, or who she was... yet.

In comparison to Emily, Jules she was easy to have a relationship with, no baggage, no secrets. He was fond of her, not in love with her, but fond of her.

He pulled himself back to the present. The credits were rolling and they stood up to leave.

Outside Jules put her arm through his as they walked towards the restaurant they had booked for dinner. "I'm not going to ask you what you thought of the movie, Joe, I don't think you were concentrating on it at all. Is everything alright? Who did you go outside to call – was it Emily?"

"Yeah. I feel a bit bad about leaving her alone on her first night back at my place. She doesn't know many people in London, and her best friend Anna has left the country."

Jules interrupted him. "Look Joe, she's a big girl, she'll be fine. Come on, here we are. I'm hungry and I know you are!"

Halfway through dinner Jules put her knife and fork down on her plate, reaching across the table for his hand. "Hey, you're miles away! It's not much fun celebrating my birthday with someone who's not saying a word."

She narrowed her eyes. "You're worried about her aren't you Joe? Maybe a bit in love with her I think."

He nodded. "I'm sorry Jules. Just seeing her again...now I'm worried about her. I keep seeing the look on her face before she took off for her room. She looked bewildered - scared."

Jules stood up, shrugged on her coat, emptying her wine glass in one gulp. "Go home Joe. Go to Emily." Turning on her heel she left the restaurant, slamming the door behind her.

With haste, Joe paid the bill and ran outside, looking for a taxi. The waiter came jogging after him with his coat.

Fumbling for his keys, he looked up at the flat – it was in complete darkness. Throwing open the door he reached for the light switch. "Emily? Emily, are you alright?

There was silence.

Taking the stairs two at a time he knocked on her door. "It's me Joe. May I come in?"

Getting no response, he pushed the door open. "Emily, it's time to wake up, you've been sleeping for hours. I tried to call you."

By the light of the streetlamp he could see her. One arm outstretched, her knees drawn under her. He shook her lightly. "Hey, wake up."

He reached over, turning on the bedside light. "Emily?"

He sucked in his breath. Pills were scattered over the night stand and on the carpet. Her lips were tinged with blue.

"Emily! Oh God, Emily! Nooo!"

Chapter Eighty-Four

Joe sat next to her bed, holding her hand. His terror at thinking he had lost her, now replaced with anger and concern. It was selfish of her to try to take her own life after so many people, particularly him and Anna, had worked hard to get her back on her feet again.

He had contacted Anna straight away, and she'd booked her flight to London, not listening to Joe's protestations that Emily was going to be fine. She'd landed this morning and was on her way to the hospital.

Doctor Harrington entered the room, and nodded at Joe, introducing himself. He checked Emily's pulse. Satisfied, he turned to Joe.

"She's doing fine. Your quick action saved her life. She's going to be a bit sore when she wakes up – not a pleasant thing to have your stomach pumped out. You're a friend of hers I take it?"

Joe stifled a yawn, he hadn't slept since he found her last night "Yes, we share a flat. She's been away in France for ten months. Came back yesterday."

Doctor Harrington nodded. "I wondered why she hadn't been to see me for her regular check-ups. Emily was my patient. Any idea what may have caused her to try and do this?"

Joe bit his lip. "I have an idea it might have something to do with me."

He explained Emily's arrival back in London and what had happened. "I should have taken better care of her, Doc, I know I should." He picked up her hand again, stroking it, concern washing over his face.

Doctor Harrington patted his shoulder. "Don't blame yourself son. Emily will pull through. She should wake in the next hour or so, then you can ask her why she did this…Well, hello Anna! Good to see you again."

Anna nodded at him, dropping her suitcase she hurried to Emily's side. "*Eish*! Oh Emily, what on earth were you thinking? Why did you do this?" Tears glinted in her eyes as she looked at her friend. She put out her hand for Joe's.

"Joe, it's good to see you, but I wish it had been under happier circumstances. What happened here?" Doctor Harrington left the room, closing the door behind him.

Joe rubbed his eyes with his knuckles, then put his glasses back on. "It was me Anna…" his voice trembled.

Anna folded him in her arms stroking his back, comforting him. "Tell me everything Joe."

*****

Anna persuaded Joe to go home, get some sleep, she would stay with Emily. Stifling a yawn herself, she found herself dozing in the chair. It had been a long flight.

"Anna," Emily said groggily, looking around the unfamiliar room. "What are you doing here – what am I doing here? Am I in hospital again?"

Anna woke with a start, rubbing the sleep out of her eyes. "Joe called me. I was worried about you, now I'm so cross with you. What were you thinking Emily? How could you do such a thing to us?"

"Do what…what am I doing in hospital?"

"You took an overdose of sleeping pills – that's why you're here, they had to pump your stomach out. But why did you do this. Did something happen in France – tell me?"

"Oh, no Anna. I didn't try to kill myself, I just wanted to sleep. I thought the pills would help. I would never do that to you, or to Joe."

Anna passed her a glass of water. "So, what happened Emily, what went wrong?"

Emily lay back against the pillows, taking a deep breath. "Things didn't go as I planned in Antibes. I came back earlier than I expected to, I wanted to see Joe."

She picked at the edge of the blanket. "I loved my first few months, it was all so different, it was what I'd planned – a new start.

"I wanted to make friends but I found it difficult. When you meet new people, they want to know all about you, which meant talking about myself and what had happened to me. People reacted in different ways, it's true, but most of them seemed to find it hard to deal with."

286

Emily wiped an escaping tear away as it gathered speed down her cheek. "It was like I was some kind of freak or something. So, I ended up pretty much on my own. I didn't have the energy for anything. I missed Joe, being able to talk to him all the time, follow my thoughts through with him. I missed you."

Anna stilled Emily's plucking fingers. "Go on."

"It left me thrashing around in my own head, with no one to talk to. I couldn't sleep at night, couldn't write. I thought the pills would help – and they did for a while; then they didn't so I upped the dose, then became dependent on them.

"I didn't try to kill myself, I promise you! I was so looking forward to coming home, seeing Joe. When he introduced me to Jules I realised he had a new life, and it didn't include me. Well, not the way it had before."

"Here have some more water and rest for a moment."

Emily closed her eyes for a few moments, then continued. "All of a sudden my future was as uncertain as my past. I panicked. When we got home I could see Jules was familiar with it, knew her way around. Then Joe said they were going out and he wouldn't be back that night. I fell apart. I just wanted to get out of my head and sleep. I'm sorry. It was stupid and selfish of me. It was an accident.

"Where's Joe, Anna?"

"He went home to get some sleep, you scared the hell out of him. I would imagine he's throwing all your pills down the loo as well."

A ghost of a smile flickered across Emily's face. "I ruined his date, right?"

"Worse. It was the end of the affair. Jules left him sitting in the restaurant on his own."

Emily's hand flew to her mouth. "Oh God, no."

"Yup. It was never going to work according to Joe. When he saw you again, well, he was certain. Although I'm not sure I'm going to forgive him for leaving you alone on your first night home."

"Anna, I can't promise Joe anything. I need him, yes, and I love him, but not in the way I think he wants me to. I still need to remember some things…

"I'm sorry you came all this way, but I love you for caring so much. I want you to let me pay for your ticket, it's the least I can do?"

Anna smiled at her. "No way. I was planning a trip to London anyway, I just brought the date forward a month. I need to do some serious shopping. I need a dress."

"A dress? Don't they have any dress shops in Nairobi?"

"Of course they do! It's just, um, this is a special dress."

Emily leaned over the side of the bed, wincing with sudden pain, then clutched her friend's hands. "Harrods's bridal department, right?"

"Yes!"

"Well, I can help you there," Emily said smiling. "I know my way around that particular department. Now, tell me about this man you're going to marry?"

Anna told her about David. They had met at the hospital, he was a doctor, much to the delight of her parents.

"Are we invited to the wedding?"

Anna put her hand on Emily's shoulders looking at her sternly. "Joe is invited; but there's a proviso attached to your invitation now, Emily.

"I'm getting married in September. This gives you eight months.

"Eight months of counselling before you get the invitation – okay? I want you to do some voluntary work as well. Sitting at home with nothing to do won't be good for you.

"You need to get some balance in your life – get outside your head. Meet people with bigger problems than you think you have. I'm concerned you might be taking steps backwards with this business of sleeping pills. You need some focus, my friend.

"Joe will help you, he'll give you all the support you need. We've talked about this, whilst you were sleeping, and both agree it's the right thing for you – okay?"

Emily nodded meekly, leaning back into the pillow on the bed. "I promise I'll do something Anna. I wouldn't miss your wedding for the world!

"After the wedding perhaps, Joe and I could go on one of those fancy safaris, maybe spot some lions and tigers. At least I won't have to shop for anything, I've already got the right clothes for the bush."

"Just lions, my friend, we don't have tigers in Africa!

"My friend Nick Kennedy will be coming to our wedding, so you'll get to meet him. If you're thinking about going on safari you should think about going to his lodge, Emily, it's stunning. I've been up there a few times and loved it."

Chapter Eighty-Five

The agency's brilliant young scientist, Brett, or the Bloodhound as he was referred to, had made the discovery. He had a nose for digging deep, an instinct for finding things others might have missed.

The agency, and the Bloodhound, had unlimited access to domestic and international agencies. A couple had died in a fiery car accident in Idaho, identification unknown. The police had been unable to trace the car. As a matter of course, the DNA of the couple had been entered into the unidentified DNA data base.

The DNA of the Bali bomber had also been entered, and it pinged against a match with the two bodies in the burnt-out car.

The Bloodhound set about eliminating outstanding and yet unidentified profiles, when there was a further ping, as another match was made. He double checked, unable to believe what he was looking at.

He did another check, to be absolutely sure.

There was a link between two brothers and their parents – irrefutable evidence connecting them all.

He grinned. Harry was going to go ballistic.

The bloodhound sniffed. He loved his job, full of secrets and surprises.

Chapter Eighty-Six

Marcus

I did work undercover, making forays into the desert and mountains of East Africa and through the teeming streets of Pakistan and Iraq gathering information on the Shadow Dancer.

But I wasn't always out in the field. I spent time in London. I knew, through my contacts, a hit was being planned for London. The consequences would be as catastrophic, if not worse than 9/11.

There were things in the old apartment I needed. Emily had secured the place and buttoned it up like Fort Knox. There was no way I could get inside with my old set of keys, and to try any other way would have attracted unwanted attention.

So, I'd waited, alerted to any calls she, or the man in the hoodie made.

I knew she was getting married again and moving to Kenya, even though her marriage would be illegal as she was still married to me.

My phone alerted me to a call being made by Emily to Harry, asking him about the passports she had found in the apartment – mine.

Shortly after Harry made a call to the man in the hoodie.

The game was on. I followed him and watched him push Emily headlong into the traffic, hearing the thud as her body hit the car. I followed the man in the hoodie through the crowds and down a dark alley. A quick kill and I had Emily's purse, his cell phone, and my four passports.

Using the hoodie's phone, and the voice distorter, I called Harry on it and brought him up to date on the accident, promising to send the FedEx parcel off.

Harry had no idea it was me on the end of the phone.

He never got his FedEx parcel. There was no way I wanted Harry to see those four passports.

Emily had done nothing wrong except discover my hiding place in the apartment. Those passports would have caused untold damage to our operation.

She didn't die, of course, I hung around for a while, then when the threat had passed I headed back out into the field.

Besides Harry had another plan for Emily – much better than mine. If he was successful we would use this information as well.

*****

The couple who adopted me and emigrated to America were anything but going to contribute to their adopted country. They were hard line radicals called to do the work of Allah.

I wasn't adopted by them. They were my real parents – I also had a brother, he was brought up, and trained, in Syria. He was responsible for the attack on the Bali nightclub, he died a martyr. A job well done. Allah was happy and welcomed him to Paradise.

My parents were instructed to groom me for the great task ahead. I was to be brought up as an all-American boy. They also knew when their task was finished, when I had joined the mighty US military intelligence, they would be expected to do the right thing.

I knew the face of the Shadow Dancer as well as my own, I knew where he was at any given time.

Working with Harry I was privy to all the intelligence in the world of terrorism. I had all the information on who was being looked for, and in which country.

The exchange of information on terrorists was being given without exception between the great powers of the world, everyone sharing everything, since 9/11, in their bid to stop more attacks.

Harry thought I worked for him, but what he didn't know was he had been working for me.

Allah would forgive me for not using a prayer mat and facing Mecca five times a day as required, and for eating pork and drinking alcohol. He had chosen me to do his work and I had served him well – and I wasn't finished yet. The world is full of great capitals, seething with millions of inhabitants.

I would take out many more thousands before my work was done.

Finding a photograph of Aaquib Salim Ahad, the so-called Shadow Dancer, had been easy, because he didn't exist, well, not any more. I bought the photograph from one of my fellow jihadists.

It was a photograph of his cousin who had no links with our movement. He had been disfigured by the enemy in an attack on Afghanistan and had been rendered deaf and dumb.

I killed him. He was no use to anyone, not even himself. I took his name.

Aaquib Salim Ahad.

I am the Shadow Dancer.

Chapter Eighty-Seven

Harry

Despite the second tragedy in his life *Oupa* Pieter was relentless in his gathering of information for the agency. I had never met him, but now I was on my way to South Africa to rectify this. I needed him to do something for me.

He was thirsty for revenge. When I asked him for his help he didn't hesitate. He met me at the airport and flew me back to his ranch.

He was a man of few words, but I didn't know if this was how he always was, or because he was still grief-stricken over losing his sole child, Janine, in such terrible circumstances.

After dinner we moved outside onto the wide veranda surrounding the front of the ranch house.

Oupa Pieter drank deeply from his balloon of brandy, smoking in silence, looking at the thousands of dazzling stars above us.

Then he turned to look at me. "So, you think you will find this Shadow Dancer, this murdering bastard who killed my Janine?"

I took a sip of my wine and looked him straight in the eyes. "I know who he is. He is one of our own. He betrayed us. You met him. He was the one who enlisted you for the agency."

Oupa Pieter smashed his glass on the table in front of him, bowing his head. Then he looked up at the stars again, as if to steady himself. I waited for the spasm of impotent fury to pass.

"That murdering bastard slept here under my roof, enjoyed my hospitality, tainted my home with his evil. I will find it hard to live with this, Harry." The old man's naked emotion was shocking to behold.

"I'm sorry, my friend, it will be difficult for you, I understand this. But what is done, is done. There will be no trial, no publicity, he will be killed, and save the taxpayers money. I don't want some smart New

293

York lawyer dragging out his case for years and years. He doesn't deserve to live that long. I'm going to kill him myself."

The old man nodded again, as I continued. "I want to dispose of his body, put it somewhere where no one will ever find it. I don't want him to become a martyr. I need your help?"

Oupa Pieter scratched the stubble on his chin, staring into the distance. "This place," he threw his arm wide, "this place is remote. The coastline is rugged and dangerous. A good place, I think, for making a body disappear?"

I thought about it for a moment – he was right.

He interrupted my thoughts. "This evil man, may God have no mercy on his soul when you kill him. This man he is married?"

"Yes, *Oupa* Pieter, he is."

"His wife – she is a radical too? A jihadist?"

I took another sip of my wine. I could trust this man. "No, she is a South African girl. Born here in the Eastern Cape."

Oupa Pieter raised his eyebrows in surprise. "*Here*? In the Eastern Cape, this cannot be! It is rare to see a Muslim woman hereabouts."

"She wasn't a Muslim girl. She met Marcus in London. You see he was brought up in America, looked more Italian than Arab, as you may recall. She had no idea of his true identity. He used her, well, we used her too, if the truth be told.

"Marcus moved to London, he needed to marry a British girl, to add another layer to his secret undercover life. He found one, she fell in love with him and they married. With my consent unfortunately.

"His wife was just part of his cover. I almost had her killed."

"We are a small community here Harry. What is the name of this wife?"

"Emily Hunter, or Emily Brandmore, as she was before she married him."

The colour drained from the Afrikaner's face. I thought he was going to have a heart attack.

"Emily," he whispered almost to himself, "my little Emily."

He stood up his body shaking, the tears streaming down his face. When a big man is in pain he sounds like a wild animal. He stumbled into the house and I sat there stunned, hearing the great grunts, the bellowing of grief from within the walls of the house.

He knew her?

Twenty minutes later he came out again. His eyes red and swollen. He sat down heavily, putting his head in his shaking hands.

"Emily's father was a good friend. We hunted together, worked together on some projects. Many times, Emily stayed here on the ranch. Her best friend was my Janine, Emily was like a second daughter to me. We lost touch with her some years ago when she left South Africa."

He took a deep breath, sitting back in his chair. Then turned his head and looked at me, his piercing blue eyes as hard and as cold as pieces of stone, his body stiff with unconcealed anger and rage.

"I am a God-fearing man, Harry, I know my bible. Mark Six, verses fourteen to twenty-nine. John the Baptist.

"Bring me *his* head on a platter, Harry. I will make sure no one ever finds his body. You will do this for me?"

I left the next day, already planning Marcus's last journey. Marcus had said he wanted to go back to South Africa, travel around the country a bit, he liked it. I was going to make his wish come true.

He would be coming back. But not in the condition he had anticipated.

Chapter Eighty-Eight

Harry set up the appointment. They would have lunch at Rules, the oldest restaurant in London. It was quiet, discreet, and served the very best of traditional British food. He was looking forward to seeing his old colleague again.

Both men studied the menu, settling on the roast pork. Harry managed to hide a smile, behind his boiling rage at being betrayed. His whole agency had been betrayed, by the monster, the traitor, sitting in front of him.

After a meal accompanied by light conversation, nothing serious with the crowded tables and hovering waiters. This could wait. Harry suggested they take a stroll through the park. The serious business with the Shadow Dancer would be dealt with there.

Pleasantly full with a bottle of red wine under their belts, they strolled towards Green Park. Dark bloated clouds, their under bellies heavy with rain, hovered overhead. The park was gloomy, almost deserted.

Harry sat down on a damp bench, gesturing for his companion to join him, and looked around. It was as good a place he could manage at such short notice. Two men, one in a wheelchair with his head slumped forward, walked past. Harry gave them a courteous nod.

Balancing his umbrella along the back of the park bench, he withdrew a small pistol from its folds.

His luncheon guest had no inclination his last day was here. The muffled rumble of far off thunder masked the sound of the upward shot to the back of Marcus' neck, killing him instantly.

Harry took off his scarf wrapping it around the body's neck. Picking up his umbrella he shook it out and raised it, squinting up into the rain filled skies.

The wheelchair and the two agents sped back towards them. The agents bundled the body into the chair. Without a word being said they set off towards the gates of the darkening park, and the waiting car, which would take them to the airport where a private jet stood on standby.

En-route the car would stop at a funeral parlour. Here the body would be transferred to a coffin. The funeral director would provide the necessary paperwork, including a death certificate, embalming certificate and proof of identification, thus ensuring all legal requirements were met for the transfer of the body out of the country. Working with another funeral company in Johannesburg, the required documentation for entry of the body to South Africa had been FedExed through, ready for the pilot, who was himself an agent working with Harry.

From the international airport in Johannesburg, and with the correct documentation, the private aircraft would continue on its way to East London. Finally landing on the more than adequate air strip of the remote ranch on the Wild Coast.

The towering Afrikaner farmer, *Oupa* Pieter would be waiting. The body, the wheelchair and the car would disappear over the side of a renowned and dangerous part of the coast.

The old fisherman, Jakub, would have to be eliminated. There could be no witnesses. He had served his purpose although he had been invaluable. He was their man on the ground, listening and watching.

Oupa Pieter Harry could trust. The farmer, in turn, trusted the old fisherman, and respected him. Perhaps he should be spared. If there was even a sniff of ISIS rearing its head in South Africa, the fisherman would hear about it, and pass it on to the Afrikaner. No, he would spare Jakub, he still had his uses.

$$*****$$

Oupa Pieter had refused to dispose of the body himself, his hatred so embedded in his soul, he would have no part in even touching it. The pilot had driven the body in the old car to the chosen spot, with the farmer following in his 4x4.

Jakub was waiting for them.

The Shadow dancer would be denied the dignity, and the respect of a Muslim burial. There would be no washing, or shaving, of the body, no white sheets to wrap around him and his head would not be facing Mecca – unless the wild thrashing sea chose otherwise, if it did, then it would be brief, before he was swept out with the tide.

Harry had ordered the body to be dressed in a priests' frock, a Christian cross taut and tight around his wretched neck, the final and most offensive thing Harry could think of inflicting on him. The pilot had followed his orders and this was done.

There would be no shrine, no place of worship for sympathisers. Marcus was a terrorist who had lost all his rights to any respect or dignity.

Should the car and the wheelchair be found at some point, which was most unlikely in Harry's and Jakub's opinion. It would be assumed some unfortunate person, with no more reason to live, had committed suicide there.

The old fisherman, Jakub, had advised against the car and wheelchair being pushed over the cliff at the same time as the body.

"It might be," he had said, "this dead man will get stuck with the car and chair with wheels. *Eish!* This body will be found. No, the sea is hungry for this body, it must go alone. I myself will come tomorrow and push this chair with wheels, and this old car, into the sea. It is better this way with the tides. The body will be much gone by then."

The thing Harry had been determined to achieve was that Marcus would disappear without a trace. There was no way he wanted any DNA to be taken, this would lead back to his highly skilled, dedicated team of agents, "the fox in the hen house" would be revealed to the world as Marcus Hunter.

Harry's department would not be able to take the heat from the powers that be, from the White House. His whole operation would be closed down, their years of work, their large secret network of agents and spies worldwide, would be discredited, it would all have been for nothing.

It was something Harry would not allow to happen. He would put out a story, in due course, about the reported death of the Shadow Dancer, come up with a body in the desert somewhere, and the world would rest easy in their beds until the next monster raised his ugly head above the parapets.

The Bloodhound would eliminate the sample he had from Marcus, along with his parents and brother's connection, out of the system. The tip of Marcus' finger would be removed from the Bloodhound's deep freezer.

Whistling through his teeth, Harry felt in his pocket for the two phones he had taken from Marcus's pocket, along with the four passports; passports he had been unaware of. A veritable trove of priceless information.

Harry had never had any qualms about the things which had become necessary in his life, the things which needed to be done to keep the world a safer place.

But he did have one regret.

Emily.

She had been innocent. He had almost had her killed, and scuppered her chances of marrying Nick Kennedy.

It would take one phone call from him to Emily. He could give her the name of Nick Kennedy and all his details.

Or he could call Nick Kennedy, tell him where Emily was now living.

He had the power to bring the two of them back together again. She was free to marry Kennedy now.

He hailed a taxi. No, it was too complicated, he himself would be implicated. He could never be in touch with her again, without revealing how the accident happened. It wasn't his job to get involved in other people's love affairs. His job was to hunt down the bad guys and eliminate them.

But there was one other thing Harry was going to do for Emily. After all she had been through, and for what he had put her through. The media would never find out Emily had been married to the world's most wanted terrorist. Her life would once more be wrecked, and this time, he knew, she would not be able to put it back together again. The media would be out baying for her blood, pursuing her twenty-four hours a day – the wife of the Shadow Dancer.

Harry didn't think Emily would cope with that kind of persecution, she had been through enough, her mind had fought to remember who she was, and he wasn't sure, despite all his experience in the field, and the experiments which had been carried out, just how much the human mind could handle.

It was enough that "the fox in the hen house" – the Shadow Dancer, her husband, Marcus Hunter, was now indeed dead.

When *Oupa* Pieter had suddenly picked up a large rock and smashed Marcus's face into a bloody pulp even the most hardened amongst them had been shocked by the savagery of his final act of revenge for his beloved daughter.

But no-one had stepped forward to stop him.

Chapter Eighty-Nine

Harry

Two weeks after we'd got rid of Marcus, *Oupa* Pieter put a pistol between his lips and blew his brains out. He left a letter addressed to me. His lawyer found it amongst his papers.

I love this land, my homeland, Harry. I have embraced all the changes here and welcomed them. Yes, there are problems with this fledgling new country, but I believe they can be overcome. So many South Africans have left this country for England, Europe, Australia and Canada. Perceiving it to be better than here in their homeland, thinking they will be safer in their brave new world – but the ugly face of terrorism makes nowhere safe.

I have lost my wife to illness, my beloved daughter blown apart in New York. Emily, little Emily, embroiled in something she had no idea about. If this can happen to me, to the people I have loved, then I have no wish to be part of this changing world. It will not get better, this hatred against Christianity, this murderous attitude towards innocent men, women, and children, old and young, killed for some cause which I do not understand, nor wish to.

The man responsible for my daughter's death was married to her childhood friend. It is more than I can accept. It is a fact I cannot change. I met him and he stayed here in my house.

I am tired. I am tired of trying to understand man's inhumanity to his brothers. There are good, decent, people, in this world, and here in my country. But they are overshadowed by the evil I see. The media will not be interested in the good things being done - they want gruesome bloody images to show on their screens.

I do not wish to start my day in this beautiful place, with images of such graphic and appalling violence.

I will not.

300

South Africa is seen the world over as a crime-ridden country. I believe it is one of the safest. We do not have people driving into crowds to kill them, we do not have suicide bombers blowing up innocent people at night clubs and musical concerts. I fear things will not improve. The world is on a dangerous course fuelled by fanatics who care little for life, not even their own.

God bless you Harry for what you are doing, but you will never win this war. I have one wish now. To be with my beloved wife and daughter. I leave you the responsibility of keeping Emily safe.

I know the world you live in Harry, and I fear for Jakub. He has been a witness to what happened, I beg you not to take his life. He is a good man, a simple fisherman, but spare him Harry.

I have forty good men working on the ranch, and a manager. They all live in the staff quarters and have done so for thirty years. They are good, hard-working, people and I would like them to be looked after. I want them to remain on the farm and continue the work I started with the animals. I have made provision for this in my will.

With gratitude for killing the man who murdered my daughter, and shattered little Emily's life, I wish to leave you my house and its contents. This too I have made clear in my will.

It may be, Harry, in years to come you, will tire of the world, as I have done, and wish to find somewhere more peaceful to live than New York?

It shames me to say I never want to see Emily again, even though you tell me she was innocent. She married the beast who killed my Janine. I can never feel the same way about her again. There it is.

May the Shadow Dancer burn in hell for eternity.

Nice gesture from the old man, but what the fuck was I going to do with a property stuck in the middle of nowhere?

I'm a New Yorker, always have been, born and bred there. No way would I ever come and live in bloody Africa.

Chapter Ninety

Emily slipped back into her old life with Joe with familiar ease and considerable relief. At first, he watched her like a hawk, then began to relax again when he saw how serious she was about her voluntary work at the local shelter, how determined she was to make things up to him, and Anna. But he only relaxed slightly, he still watched over her, monitoring her mind and her memory.

Anna, back in Nairobi, checked in with Joe every week, following her progress.

With two months to go before they left for the wedding, Emily shopped around looking for a wedding gift, settling for an exquisite antique silver tea service.

She carried the shiny green bag back to the flat and showed Joe what she'd bought.

He rubbed his hands together, pleased. "Well done Emily, you know how much I hate shopping at the best of times - I'll give you the cash for my half. Don't gift wrap it though, customs might want to see it. I'm beyond excited about this trip!"

Pleased he approved of her purchase Emily wrapped the tea service up again. "So, how did you get on at the travel agency?"

"Well I booked the tickets to Nairobi, so that's sorted. I picked up loads of brochures on various lodges but couldn't decide which one we should go to…I thought we should decide together?"

Emily interrupted him. "Anna suggested we try her photographer friend's lodge, she said it's stunning. Go and get the brochures, I'll try and remember the name of it. Anna told me about it when I was looking after her flat."

He returned to the sitting room, almost bouncing off the walls with excitement, waving the brochures at her. "Did you remember the name of the lodge?"

"Yes, something about Badgers."

Joe shuffled the brochures. "The agent suggested a place called Honey Badger Lodge, his second choice was a place called Fish Eagle Lodge. I've got both brochures here, and a few others to look at."

Emily studied the brochure on Honey Badger Lodge, looking at the superb animal shots first, before reading up on the lodge itself. She flicked through the pages and caught her breath. A tree decorated with lanterns, a table set for two beneath it. Something shifted in her memory. Either she'd seen this lodge on some documentary, or she'd been there. Then another memory threaded its way back to her.

She had met him there.

The man who tormented her dreams. He must have been one of the guests there. At some point, she'd travelled to Kenya. Maybe the two small stamps in her damaged passport had been the entry and exit stamps? They had to be.

Flustered, but determined, she turned to Joe. "Yes, let's book this one then, Honey Badger, it looks great." She wouldn't say anything, not until she'd had time to think things through. Joe was so looking forward to this trip. She didn't want to spoil anything with her endless speculations and risk the chance of losing him again.

He looked up at her. "Cheer up. We'll be winging our way to Africa in two months' time, flying into the sunshine. It'll be great to see Anna again and meet her husband to be. I'll ring the agent now and book the lodge. I don't know what I'm looking forward to most, the wedding or the safari. It's going to be fantastic!"

Chapter Ninety-One

The Kenya Airways flight came to a drawn out wheezing halt at the terminal in Nairobi, the runway shimmering like liquid in the heat haze. Joe and Emily stood up and stretched. It had been a long flight, they were eager to get off and get some fresh air.

They went through passport control, paid for their visas, and collected their luggage from the carousel, relieved the wedding present had also arrived in its well packed box.

Anna jumped up and down waving to them, excitement all over her face. "Emily! Joe! Over here, I'm over here. It's so good to see you again. I thought this day would never come." Emily flew into her friend's open arms.

Joe kissed and hugged Anna then pushed the wobbly-wheeled trolley, squeaking like a trapped mouse, with their luggage through the bustling airport, and out to the car park. He loaded the luggage into the car boot then sat in the back, leaving the two girls to chatter about the wedding plans, and who was coming on the big day. He looked at the chaos of traffic outside as they entered the city of Nairobi. Vehicles struggled for position on the road, colourful hand painted trucks, loaded with people edging the smaller cars out of the way, it was a real scrum, but a happy good natured one, no road rage here, he thought to himself, grinning with excitement.

Anna, with some skill, negotiated the seething mass of traffic and deposited them at the Norfolk Hotel.

"I won't come in, still heaps to do. The restaurant is excellent here, and the Lord Delamere terrace bar is a great place to people watch. Guests from all over the world, including the rich and famous, stay here before they set off on safari. You never know who you might see, maybe a celebrity or two. Oh, and by the way, don't forget to take your malaria pills okay?"

Joe rolled his eyes. "As if we would Anna! Not going to let those pesky buggers have a go at me!"

*****

They checked into the hotel and walked through the lush gardens to their rooms. Passing an arrogant peacock who flared his glorious tail and gave a cat like wail, before strutting off indignantly.

After lunch they were going to take a tour of the city, although Joe doubted they would get through the traffic, let alone around the city. The following day they would visit the other places of interest in and around Nairobi.

"I'll meet you in the hotel shop Emily. I need to get a map and see where we're heading after the wedding," he was almost levitating with excitement.

*****

They browsed through the wood carvings, safari clothes and books. "Hey Joe," Emily called over to him. "Here's the book by Nick Kennedy, the one Anna had in her flat."

He came over to her, resting his chin on her shoulder as she flipped through the pages.

"Remember the flattened flower I found in my passport? Well this is what it looks like. It's called a frangipani, he's used it to indicate the end of a chapter. I think it's the most beautiful flower in the world." She turned to the inside front cover. "This is what he looks like. Quite dishy, and we get to meet him at Anna's wedding..." She paused as a ghost of a memory flickered, then dissipated like vapour. "Look here's a shot of his lodge – and I was right, it's called Honey Badger." She shivered, putting the book back on the shelf.

"Come on, you've got your map, let's go see what Nairobi is all about. I think this is where they filmed the movie 'Out of Africa' and I'd love to see the Karen Blixen museum."

Joe put his arm around her. "You're such a romantic Ms Hunter. Let's go and do that, then come back here and people watch from the Delamere terrace. I can understand why so many famous people came here, and still do, to go on safari, there's a magic about the place!"

*****

Anna glanced at her watch. It was time to check with Nick. He'd promised he would be at her wedding, nothing would stop him coming, he'd said.

Relatives bustled around her, carrying in wedding presents, extra chairs and tables to feed her large family. Cousins, aunts, and uncles, were arriving from all over the country, some of whom she'd never even heard of. She glanced through the kitchen door of her Aunt's house, watching all the activity going on in there, as she waited for her call to connect.

"Nick! I thought you'd never answer the phone, God this line is terrible. I'm just checking," she shouted. "You are coming to see me get married on Saturday? Promise me you won't let me down? I have so many people I want you to meet. My friends have arrived from London. I've just dropped them off at the Norfolk."

"Wild horses wouldn't keep me away on your special day, Anna, I'm looking forward to meeting your friends."

Anna cursed as the phone went dead in her hand, cutting off her reply. One thing she could never quite get used to was the erratic behaviour of the phone system in her country.

Chapter Ninety-Two

A nna's wedding day dawned, clear and warm. Joe and Emily met for breakfast on the terrace of the hotel. The church service would start at eleven, the reception would take place in the grounds of an old country club, just out of town. The hotel car was booked to deliver them to the church.

"You're quiet this morning, Emily. Are you alright?"

She put her menu down and looked at all the tourists congregating on the pavement outside of the hotel. Cameras and binoculars slung around their necks, as they waited with their safari bags for the various lodge vehicles, all lining up on the road, to take them away on safari.

"I didn't sleep much. I had so many dreams and flashbacks. I've been here before, Joe, I'm sure of it. Remember we talked about the dream I had of a strange tree and the man in a uniform of some kind? You thought it might be somewhere in India or the Far East? Well, it wasn't. It was right here in Africa."

She reached down, pulling the Honey Badger brochure from her bag. She pointed to the photograph. "This is the tree I remember. Game rangers wear khaki, so it's a sort of uniform. I've been to this lodge, I know I have. It's where I met the man I must have fallen in love with. I think he might have been a guest or maybe a game ranger."

Joe reached for a piece of toast and frowned. "That's a bit of a stretch, isn't it? Maybe lots of game lodges decorate their trees with lanterns to create a romantic atmosphere. It could be any lodge Emily. I looked at a few lodge brochures at the travel agency, they all look similar."

He took a mouthful of toast, brushing crumbs of his khaki shirt but missing a blob of marmalade. "I mean the landscapes and settings were different, but lots of the lodges were tented, it could have been any one of them. I'm not convinced about you having been to Kenya before either.

"You were born in South Africa, the police told you that. You might have gone on safari there, or in a neighbouring country, um," he frowned as he tried to remember his geography. "Botswana maybe?" They have loads of safari camps and lodges there. I think you're reading too much into this."

Joe's eyes darted around looking for a waiter. "Come on, let's order breakfast, I'm starving, and I've already finished all the toast!" He lifted his arm to attract the waiter, then turned back to her.

"Sorry, maybe I was a bit harsh with you. Look, if you did meet the man here in Kenya, and you think it was at this lodge, then maybe you're right. When we get there, it might all come back to you. Let's wait and see, shall we?

Chapter Ninety-Three

Anna's father walked her down the aisle of the packed church. The bride looked fabulous, her dazzling white gown shown off to perfection against her ebony skin, a triple pearl choker around her slender neck. Her husband-to-be, David, looked nervous, but striking in his tuxedo, as he waited for her to join him at the altar.

An African choir sang the final hymn in Swahili, Emily shivered, reaching for Joe's hand.

"Such a haunting sound," she whispered, "and not an instrument in sight, it's so emotional."

He passed her his handkerchief, surreptitiously wiping his own eyes before taking her hand in his.

Now the guests moved back out of the church, making their way to the reception being held at the famous Muthaiga Club.

There Emily and Joe made their way across the lawns, through the celebrating crowds, until spotting Anna and David, surrounded by friends and relatives.

"What a wonderful service Anna, and so many people here, it looks as though you invited the entire population of Nairobi!" Emily took her friend's hands in hers, the sun glinted off her wedding ring.

"You look so beautiful Anna. I'm so happy for you both. David?" She hugged him. "It's good to meet you, at last. Take care of my best friend, won't you? Just as she took such good care of me?"

David nodded, putting his arm around his new wife. "I most certainly will. It's good to meet you at last Emily, you too Joe, I've heard so much about you both."

"I'll be in touch as soon as we get back from our honeymoon." Anna reached for her husband's hand and turned to go.

"Hey, wait Anna! Where's the photographer you wanted us to meet? Is he here?"

Anna scanned the grounds of the club looking for Nick, being so tall he wouldn't be difficult to spot amongst the crowds, but she couldn't see him.

She turned back to Emily. "Maybe something happened at the lodge and he couldn't get away. If this isn't the reason I'll give him a roasting when I see him again! Enjoy your safari, oh, by the way which lodge are you staying at…"

Emily's reply was swept away with the crowds of well-wishers surrounding the bride and groom, eager to congratulate the pair.

*****

The telephone lines at the lodge were still down. There was no way Nick could get word to Anna. His agent, in Nairobi, was away for the week-end so even a message via the two-way radio would not be delivered. He shrugged his shoulders with resignation.

Mike had come down with a bad bout of malaria and been flown to Nairobi for treatment. Without him Nick had no choice but to stay at the lodge and look after his guests. He would make it up to Anna, but there was no way he could attend her wedding now. She would be as mad as a snake when he didn't pitch up.

He hoped his generous cheque, his wedding present to them both, would go some way to mollify her, but he wasn't too sure.

Chapter Ninety-Four

The messenger knocked at the door, the note lying on a silver tray. Getting no response, he pushed the note under the door and returned to reception.

The receptionist looked up. "Delivered the message?"

"I tried Mr Challis's room first, but no reply. I left it under the door in Mrs Hunter's."

The receptionist turned back to her computer. An e-mail had come through from the travel agent in England. Honey Badger Lodge was overbooked. The couple would have to be moved to another lodge.

In his haste to find somewhere at short notice, the travel agent failed to notice two rooms were required. He sent a short e-mail through to Fish Eagle Lodge to see if they had availability.

The lodge, with the power now back on, confirmed with the agent, yes, there were rooms available. He'd asked the hotel to let his clients know about the change of plan.

That evening, exhausted by their emotional day, Emily and Joe dined in the hotel's restaurant, then retired to bed early. Emily found the note and knocked on Joe's door to let him know.

"There's been a bit of a muddle with the booking. So, we won't be going to Honey Badger after all, we're now going to Fish Eagle Lodge instead."

"That was the other one we thought of booking. I'm sure it'll be fine."

"Yes, I'm sure it will be. But what won't be fine is they've booked us into a double room under your name. Mr and Mrs Challis."

Joe grinned at her.

"Joe, I'm more than fond of you, as you know, but your timing's all wrong. I need a little more time to sort myself, and my memory, out. I'm almost there. Don't give up on me, will you?"

Joe rubbed his hands together. "Of course I'm not going to give up on you! Look we can sort this muddle with the rooms when we get there. We'll ask for another room. Go and get some sleep."

*****

Emily stared out into the night trying to work out her feelings at this unexpected turn of events with the lodges. A desperate part of her wanted to go to Honey Badger Lodge, because if this was where she'd met him, then maybe something would click into place, like his name.

She chided herself. What was the point of thinking about this? Whoever he was he had not cared enough for her, unlike Joe, who would have searched high and low for her. She crawled under the mosquito net and tried to get some sleep.

Joe would make someone a wonderful husband.

Chapter Ninety-Five

They flew low over the bush, the pilot pointing out the various animals to them. Joe was like a child on Christmas morning, but his excitement was infectious and she felt her apprehensive mood lift.

Over a wide lake, she saw a small herd of elephants enjoying a splash in the water. The game was fantastic. Herds of buffalo and impala dotted the landscape as it passed beneath their wings. A crocodile sunbathing on the banks of a river. She nudged Joe, mouthing above the noise of the engines, pointing to the elephants.

The Cessna began its descent and the pilot pointed out a pride of lion lying in the shade, then they were rumbling over the dirt air strip. The lodge vehicle was parked under a tree, waiting for them.

"Wow! That was the best flight I've ever been on," said Joe, his eyes shining. He shook the pilot's hand, pumping it with enthusiasm, then gathered up their soft bags, and practically ran to the waiting vehicle.

*****

Nick watched the aircraft as it flew over the lodge, knowing it would be bringing his last two guests, Mr and Mrs Challis. They would either be retired, or on their honeymoon, that was usually how it worked out.

He walked back to his cottage. One of the rangers would show them to their room.

*****

Emily unpacked her safari bag, ran a brush through her long hair and put some cream on her face and arms. On the twenty-minute drive to the lodge, she'd felt a prickling sensation on her skin, putting it down to the strong sun. Nothing more.

*****

Joe tapped on the table outside her tented suite. Hearing no response, he let himself in. She lay there in a deep sleep, dust motes dancing in their own galaxy through the shafts of sunlight from the window.

He hesitated. Should he leave her to sleep or wake her? He decided to leave her. He left a note, next to her bed, telling her he would see her later, and crept back outside. They would be here for four days, so one missed game drive, wouldn't make much difference. He jogged his way to the main lodge and the much-anticipated game drive.

*****

Nick saw the vehicles with his guests heading out to find the animals. He loved the place when it was empty. A lot of the guests didn't realize there was plenty of game around the lodge, often the animals wandered in, as if they knew humans had gone out to look for them. Helping themselves to a drink from the pool.

He adjusted one of the lanterns on the tree, then went back to his cottage to shower and change for the evening ahead. He would introduce himself to his guests over drinks before dinner, as he always did.

Chapter Ninety-Six

Emily woke with a start and for a moment wondered where on earth she was. The sky was shot with orange and pink, she checked her watch. She read the note Joe had left for her, then showered and dressed in a long pale-yellow dress. She applied a few light brushes of mascara, a little blusher and some lip gloss. Throwing a shawl around her shoulders she stepped off the deck, heading for the main lodge.

Finding it deserted except for the staff, setting up for dinner, she decided to check out the library in the sitting room. One of the waiters glided up to her.

"Perhaps you would prefer to have a drink, down at the jetty? The sunset should be spectacular this evening. It's quite safe there. I'll bring you some *bitings*."

Seeing her puzzled look, he laughed. "It's what we call snacks here in Kenya."

He pointed to the short path which would take her down to the jetty and the lake.

The sky was extraordinary. Emily looked right and left watching out for any animals. Then came to a dead stop.

He was standing there with his back to her, unaware of her. She felt the blood drumming in her head as her heartbeat flickered, then thundered in her chest. There he was, just as he had always been in her dream.

She took a deep breath but failed to stop her legs from shaking. The man seemed to scnsc something behind him and turned. She saw the incredulous look on his face as she looked into the eyes of Nick Kennedy.

He stared at her, disbelief on his face. She stared back rigid with shock. Neither of them said a word, they stood like stone statues, the silence holding its breath around them.

"Emily," he whispered, "it's you." He took a step towards her.

She turned, dropping her shawl as she did so, and fled up the path and back to her suite. She sat down on the edge of the bed, her legs collapsing under her.

Nick Kennedy.

Now it all came back to her with overwhelming clarity.

She'd met him at Honey Badger Lodge, they had fallen in love. There was a misunderstanding. She searched her mind until she remembered. Yes, she'd been angry with him and left the lodge. Then he'd been the guest author for the book signing, in London. It all came tumbling back. He'd asked her to marry him and she had accepted. Then she'd had the accident. Why had he not come to look for her, to find her?

*****

Nick resisted the temptation to run after her, his own thoughts in uproar. He'd recognized her at once but been too shocked to say anything except her name.

He knew the names of all the guests in the lodge, but there was a late booking which had come in yesterday, giving their expected time of arrival. Mr and Mrs Challis. He shied away from the one thought hammering through his mind as he remembered her last words on the phone to him. *If I don't pitch up it will mean I've met a man who's even more fabulous than you – which would be impossible because I love you too much."*

Emily Challis.

He felt the anger building up in him. So, this is why she had not come to Kenya. She'd met someone else and dumped him. It had nothing to do with her dead husband re-surfacing, as he had thought, at one point, might have been the case.

He thought quickly. All he could do was distance himself from her and her husband. He'd have a quiet word with the waiter, making sure Mr and Mrs Challis sat as far away from him as possible.

316

Chapter Ninety-Seven

Emily heard the knock on the table outside her suite and froze. Please God don't let it be Nick Kennedy she prayed. She wasn't ready for any kind of confrontation with the man she'd been in love with, the man who had let her down, turned his back on her, just like in her dreams. She breathed a sigh of relief when she saw Joe's familiar tousled head come around the tented door.

"You missed some fantastic sightings…" his voice trailed off.

"Are you alright? You look as though you've seen a ghost or something. Your face is as white as your knuckles. If you hang onto that bedhead much longer you'll bend it. What the hell happened?"

"Well in a way I have seen a ghost, Joe." Without pausing for breath, she told him what happened. "He must be a guest here at Fish Eagle. Honey Badger Lodge was where I met him, I know this now. He owned it. Nick Kennedy is the mystery man – the man I was going to marry."

He interrupted her, pushing his glasses up. "No, he isn't a guest. I asked one of the rangers who owned Fish Eagle, and he told me – Nick Kennedy."

She shook her head with impatience. "Well maybe he owns both of them then, I don't know, I can't think straight."

"What are you going to do now?"

"The muddle with the booking might turn out to be in my favour after all," she said thinking on her feet. "He'll have seen the reservation for Mr and Mrs Challis. He'll assume we're married. It's important he continues to think this way, Joe. Otherwise I'll never be able to get through this. Will you help me?"

He looked at her a dubious expression on his face. "Don't forget we asked for separate rooms on arrival. He's not stupid enough to think we're married and have separate rooms. It's not going to fly Emily. You'll have to think of something else."

She held up her hand. "It will fly. I would imagine owners don't go around checking which rooms their guests are in, he would leave it to his manager who is apparently sick. That's why we were checked in by the ranger, remember? He was going on leave and catching the flight back to Nairobi which brought us here. With a bit of luck, he wouldn't have had time to mention to anyone we're in two rooms. We'll have to hope for the best."

"How do you feel about this Nick now?"

She shook her head, saying nothing.

"Look why don't you just confront him, ask him why he didn't try and find you after the accident?"

"No. I'm not going to do that, I just can't. I'm too shocked at the moment." She rubbed her arms feeling cold. "He didn't bother to come and look for me, did he? It maybe worked out for the best in the end." She shuddered, glancing at her watch. "Come on, they'll be expecting us for dinner. Let's go and pretend we're a happily married couple."

With a shaky laugh, she took his hand, steering him back down the path towards the main dining area.

*****

Nick watched the couple walking hand in hand through the trees and lanterns. He felt a jolt of pure undiluted anger shoot through him. He fought it down and walked towards them.

"Good evening Mr and Mrs Challis, welcome to Fish Eagle Lodge, I'm Nick Kennedy." He shook Joe's hand and turned to Emily.

"Mrs Challis," he said coldly, "you left this down at the jetty." He handed her the shawl she'd dropped.

Emily stared at some point over his shoulder, saying nothing, her face rigid.

Joe fell into his required role of being her husband. He put his arm around her. "Good to meet you Nick, nice place you have here. Come on, my darling, I'm starving."

Emily pushed the food around her plate, as Joe told her about the game he'd seen on the drive. "Then we came across a kill," he told her with excitement, "a whole bunch of lions gorging on some poor buck. It didn't smell too good, I have to tell you. Everyone on the vehicle was thrilled to sit and watch as they sipped on their drinks, the ranger passing around snacks.

318

"There we were, civilized people, enjoying the whole thing. I mean you wouldn't sit around a road accident with drinks and snacks, would you? It made me wonder just how civilized we are."

Joe looked at her and sighed, she was somewhere else in her mind, not listening to a word he was saying. He reached across the table, taking her hand.

"We're supposed to be married," he hissed like a goose at her, "the least you can do is smile at me and look the part! Come on he keeps glancing over here."

Joe watched her make a supreme effort as she played her part in the charade, laughing and touching his hand across the table. At last the meal was over and the guests gathered around the camp fire for their nightcap. Joe and Emily excused themselves, Joe grabbed her hand as they left the main dining area.

"Great looking couple," one of the guests commented. "Oh, to be young and in love again, nothing like it is there?"

*****

Nick felt the stem of the glass snap between his fingers. Emily would have been the wrong choice for him after all. He was good at working out a person's character. But he'd got it wrong with Emily Hunter, or Challis as she was now. Completely and utterly wrong.

Tomorrow more guests would be arriving. He would go back to Nairobi with the return flight, putting as much distance between him and the Challis couple as he could. Four days of her at the lodge would be more than he could handle. She was still as beautiful as he remembered – and she still didn't seem to have much of an appetite.

He dabbed at the blood on his finger with his sleeve.

No wedding ring either, but this meant nothing these days.

Chapter Ninety-Eight

Emily lay in her bed, hot tears of regret coursing down her cheeks. She tossed and turned until she was exhausted. Joe was right, she had to confront Nick Kennedy at some point. When she eventually fell asleep she saw his face with clarity as she drifted away, and the hand holding hers was not Joe's.

*****

Joe and Emily had breakfast together the next morning, the only noise above the birdsong was the faint whine of an engine. A plane buzzed over the lodge, then disappeared. Joe raised his head when he heard one of the vehicles start up.

He nudged Emily. "There goes Kennedy with an overnight bag in his hand." He pointed with his fork at Nick's receding back.

"It looks as though the boss is leaving, which will be a huge relief to you. Now we can get on with enjoying this safari."

She bent her head, but not before he saw the wetness of her eyes. Then her head snapped up. "Oh, dear God, Joe – he's Anna's friend, remember? They grew up together. Anna must have known all along. She must have worked it all out and not said anything. But why?"

"Emily get a grip on yourself, you look as though you're going to pass out. Why would Anna know everything? Take a deep breath and tell me what you're thinking."

"She loves to tell the story about me, she tells everyone as you know…"

Once again, he interrupted her. "Yes, yes, I know she tells your story but don't forget when you stayed at her flat, when she came here for her holiday, she only knew you as Diana. So, if she told this Kennedy guy the story it would have been the name she used."

"Joe, Anna's been back here for over a year, and I know she's been to his lodge several times. She wanted us to meet Nick at the wedding. He *must* know my real name now, Anna would have told him. He didn't pitch up for her wedding because he couldn't face me. I was going to confront him, as you suggested, but now it's too late, he's gone again."

Joe put his fork down. "But hang on. Why would she want you to meet him, if she knows you already have? What possible motive could Anna have to keep the truth from you? I think it's far more likely when you didn't pitch up in Kenya, he married someone else. It's why he didn't bother coming to look for you. Maybe Anna did tell him about you, but by then it was too late.

"He must be married, or something happened. Otherwise he would have dropped everything as soon as he found out the truth and come to get you. You're well out of it as far as I'm concerned. He never loved you enough, you were another affair that's all - you have to accept it. He must feel guilty otherwise he would have stayed here, instead of flying away, look there he goes."

The aircraft whined overhead.

"Joe, nothing makes any sense to me. Even if he did marry someone else Anna would have known. They're close friends for heaven's sake. She must have known all along I was engaged to him, so why didn't she tell me, why say nothing at all? It sounds so out of character.

"Anna was the one determined to find out the real story. She was as keen to know the name of the man who was going to marry me, as I was. No, she would have told me the truth as soon as she put two and two together. I know she would, so, why didn't she?"

"Listen Emily, I've lived with this story for over three years now, I don't have any answers for you. Maybe Anna has misguided loyalties. After all she's known this Kennedy character longer than she's known you. From what I can gather, the expats are a small community here in Kenya, and the Kennedy's are a well-known family. There could be any number of reasons why she didn't tell you what you think she should have.

"Look, I'm fed up with talking about Kennedy." He stabbed at his poached egg. "I'd like to get on with this safari and enjoy it. I don't want to sit and thrash this whole bloody business out over and over again. I've reached the end of my tether I'm afraid."

Emily looked at him, she had never heard him raise his voice or be angry with her. "I'm sorry Joe…"

He pushed his half-eaten breakfast to one side and stood up. "We can continue this whole saga when we get back to London. Yes, that's it. When Anna gets back from her honeymoon, I suggest you call her and confront her with all your questions, but right now I fancy doing a bit of fishing. You can come with me, or maybe you just want to sit on the deck and feel sorry for yourself?"

She shook her head. "I'll stay here I think."

Joe polished his glasses distractedly. "Kennedy might be a big part of your life right now, but he isn't part of mine, I'm fed up with hearing his name. This is an expensive trip Emily and I'm going to enjoy myself. All my life I've wanting to go on a safari, and I'm not going to let you spoil it with this bloody Kennedy guy. If you're still in love with him, which I think you are, then do something about it – sort yourself out."

He began to walk away then stopped, turning back. "You have to face the facts Emily, he's not interested in you. Sorry but it's how it's coming across to me. I'll see you later."

"Joe wait…"

"No, I think I've waited long enough. I can't do this anymore Emily."

*****

Mike Connelly watched Emily sitting on the lodge deck. Nick had told him she was staying at the lodge, with her husband – that's all he'd said.

Wisely he decided to avoid meeting her. He was still recovering from his bout of malaria. He would lie low until Mr and Mrs Challis left. He wasn't going to get caught up in this little drama if he could help it. He had noticed at breakfast that Mr Challis looked frustrated, and more than a little angry, about something. He'd made her cry.

Although he would have been flattered if Emily remembered him, even though he'd shaved his beard off. He didn't want to have to deal with any awkward questions, or risk upsetting her husband in any way, although her husband had certainly upset her by the looks of things.

Chapter Ninety-Nine

After a month on honeymoon in Italy, Anna and David returned to Nairobi. As soon as she'd settled into her new home, in the leafy suburb of Karen, she set about writing her thank you letters for the wedding presents.

On Emily and Joe's note she thanked them for coming all the way to Kenya for her wedding, and for their gift, and hoped they'd enjoyed their safari.

The telephone rang, startling her. Reaching over she answered it using her new name.

"Sounds pretty good to me," she recognized his voice straight away, and launched into her attack.

"How *could* you let me down by not coming to my wedding Nick Kennedy! No excuses please unless your manager dropped dead," she scolded him.

"Pretty close Anna. He came down with a bad bout of malaria, I had to stay on and look after the guests, we had a full lodge, so I had no choice. The lines were down again and I couldn't get a message through to you, then you took off to Italy. I'm sorry.

"Look, I'll be in Nairobi for a couple of days next week. I'd love to make it up to you by taking you both out for dinner."

"I haven't forgiven you yet Nick, but why not come here for dinner? On our honeymoon, we ate out almost every night. I'll cook for you. Besides I want to bore you to death by showing you our wedding presents."

They agreed on a day and time and rang off. Anna shook her head and smiled, then carried on with her letters and notes. She made a mental note to give Emily and Joe a ring in London. She hadn't spoken to either of them since the wedding reception. And with all the excitement of the day and the lead up to the wedding, she had forgotten to ask them where they were going on safari, which lodge they had chosen, when she finally got to asking Emily at the reception her reply had been swept away by all the crowds.

Clearly it wasn't Fish Eagle Lodge or Nick would have mentioned he had finally met her London friends. Emily would certainly have recognized his name and introduced herself.

*****

Anna opened the door as soon as she heard the bell ring. "Bad luck Nick, my darling husband has been called out on an emergency, so it's just the two of us for dinner. I'll pour your usual, then you have to look at the presents."

She chatted away to him about their honeymoon in Italy, as she pointed out the gifts and who they were from. The antique silver tea service sat in the centre of the long table. She lifted it up for him to see.

"Isn't this gorgeous! It's from my friends in London. The ones I wanted you to meet," she said pointedly. She placed the silver tray back on the table and playfully punched his arm.

"I think you would have liked her. Your loss though, serves you right for not coming to my wedding. Although I have to forgive you because of your wonderful gift. I can do so much good work with it – at least another three clinics. Thank you, Nick."

"Liked who?" he said sounding vague.

"Honestly Nick, I'm going to hit you over the head with this damn tray if you don't start paying attention – Emily, my friend Emily Hunter, the mystery woman. The one I nursed for all those months!"

She turned back to the table. "I told you about her. I never did get to tell you the whole story, when we spent those few days in the Mara, because you stayed on and I flew back. Then you bought your lodge and we were both so busy I didn't see you at all." She reached for another wedding gift and carried on chatting.

Nick didn't say anything.

She turned back to him, seeing the colour had drained from his face, as he stared at her. She put her hand out to steady him. "Hey, are you alright – you don't look too good."

He collapsed on the nearest sofa, pulling her down beside him.

She could feel his hands shaking in hers. "Tell me the story again, every single detail of it. Don't leave anything out."

"Nick, I've told you the story twice, why bother a third time." She looked at him concerned, seeing how stricken he was looking.

324

"Alright," she relented, "let's go and sit outside, it's cooler there. I wouldn't do this for anyone else, but I can see it's important, although why it should be now is beyond me. I'll pour you another stiff drink. You look as though you need one, I'll make it a double."

For the next hour, he sat and listened, not interrupting. When Anna finished, he pushed his hand through his hair, leaning back in the chair, he pinched the bridge of his nose.

"So that's what happened to her," he murmured, almost to himself. "I got it so wrong."

"Got what wrong Nick, tell me?"

So, he did. Anna couldn't believe her ears. All this time she'd been in the middle of a thwarted relationship between her two best friends. All the clues had been right in front of her, but none had come together in her mind. But then why should they have? And here he was in front of her, the invisible man, the man she, Emily, and Joe had speculated over for so long.

"So, you met her at your old lodge, the woman you told me about, the woman you fell in love with, and all the time I was nursing her, trying to find out who she was. But when she failed to turn up at the airport, why didn't you go to London and try to find her?"

"I was in a state of shock, Anna. I hung around the airport for days, waiting for her, thinking she might arrive on another flight. Then my brother was killed. I flew to Singapore via London, I had a few hours there. When I discovered she hadn't collected her wedding dress, well, I was shattered, couldn't believe it.

"I even wondered if her husband had maybe risen from the dead. I heard from one of her neighbours that an American had been hanging around anxious to see her – I thought maybe it was him, and, of course, if it was, there was no way she could marry me, if she was already married."

He rubbed his face, bringing some colour back into it, then pressed his temples with his fingers. "After my trip to Singapore, I went back to the bush, closed up the lodge and took off for a couple of weeks. I didn't know what clse to do, I thought she'd changed her mind. Maybe gone back to her husband."

Anna sat, saying nothing, as she listened to his side of the story. "My mother suggested Emily might have been taken ill or been in an accident. But if that had been the case then someone would've contacted me. Emily had all my contact details on her because I knew she would need all the information to complete her entry requirements into Kenya.

Of course, if she was in a coma, and when she came around she'd lost her memory…"

Anna interrupted him, her mind racing. "Your contact details would have been in her handbag, which was never found."

She stood and paced up and down the veranda. "You remember the last conversation I had with your mother? When she was speaking French?"

He nodded. "I think she worked it out for herself," Anna continued, "she had a lot of friends in London and it's conceivable she would have tried to find out the truth herself. She had all the resources at her fingertips. I think she knew she was dying that's why she was so agitated, and I failed her. I think she asked that friend of hers, Kitty Matthews, to help her find Emily. But now we'll never know for sure – oh dear, what a glorious mess this all is."

Anna sat down next to him again and took his hands in hers. "You still love her don't you Nick?"

"I loved her from the moment I saw her. Even when it all went wrong at the lodge, I couldn't get her out of my mind. I was given a second chance when we met up again in London. I didn't think it was possible to love someone as much as I loved her. I never forgot her. I tried dating other women but not one of them evoked the kind of passion, the love in me, as she did. I was devastated when I lost her for the second time."

He rubbed his eyes with his knuckles and turned to her. "I need to think all this through, Anna. I want you to promise you won't get in touch with her. Give me a couple of days. I'll call you and let you know what decision I've come to."

She shook her head not understanding. Here was a man who was so obviously in love, yet he still needed more time? She wondered how Emily would take the news, how much of a shock it would be to her to know the truth about the man she thought had deserted her, but hadn't, and still loved her.

"I'm going to give you three days, Nick, then I am going to call her, in London," she said firmly. "Emily has a right to know about her past life, the part you played in it, just like anyone else. When her memory started to return it was the thing which bothered and tormented her the most. Who was the man she had fallen in love with, and why hadn't he come to find her? You owe her that much Nick, you have to tell her!"

326

*****

For some reason, he couldn't explain to himself, he hadn't mentioned Emily and her husband were guests at his lodge after Anna's wedding. There was so much information still to sift through. He understood everything now, and it hurt like hell.

He was surprised Anna hadn't mentioned Emily had married, and why shouldn't she have married someone else? He felt his stomach clench. He hadn't lost her to her dead husband. He'd lost her to Joe Challis.

Chapter One-Hundred

The next day Nick flew back to the lodge. At the back of the drawer he pulled out the black velvet box and opened it. The brilliant cut diamond ring flashed in the light of the lamp. As beautiful as the girl who was supposed to wear it, he thought bitterly. He closed the lid, throwing it back in the drawer.

He made the promised phone call to Anna, three days later.

"I won't be calling Emily. I feel it's too late now, and I don't want to cause her any more pain. What happened, happened. Nothing I can do now will change it."

Anna exploded at the end of the telephone. "What on earth are you talking about? What do you mean about causing her any more pain? You're not making any sense at all, which is unlike you. *Eish*! What's the matter with you! Here you have a wonderful opportunity to get back together with Emily, but you're dragging your heels. I don't understand you at all."

He heard the anger and frustration in her voice and knew he would have to tell her.

"I know you didn't want to tell me Emily was married, but you see she and her husband were guests here at my lodge, after your wedding. They were booked into another lodge but ended up at mine. I don't want to be responsible for damaging her marriage. What we had is all in the past, she deserves to be happy with Joe. It's all I can hope for her."

Anna was speechless. Then she began to laugh. "Joe? Oh no, Nick, you've got this so wrong. They share a flat together in London that's all, and I can assure you they're not married. He's sweet on her, but I promise they're just close friends. Oh, this is fabulous news!"

"I think they're more than close friends, they were booked in as a Mr. and Mrs. They shared a room."

He heard the hesitation in her voice. "Are you quite sure? It doesn't sound like them at all. Did you check them in yourself?"

"No. It was all a bit chaotic. They arrived late, my manager, as you know, was recovering from Malaria. I'm not sure who checked them in, to be honest."

"Well before you make any more hasty and impulsive decisions, you should check this out. There's probably a simple explanation to it all. Hurry up Nick, I'm itching to call Emily. I've been in the middle of this from the word go, maybe I should set up a place for you both to meet, it will be easier than trying to explain things over the phone, what do you think? I can't imagine what it must have been like to see her again at the lodge. What happened, how did she react?"

"Shock and horror would be how I would describe it. I couldn't believe she was standing there in front of me. I left the next morning. I couldn't bear to see her there with who I presumed to be her husband."

"Well Nick, I can assure you, Emily is *not* married to Joe."

*****

He felt his heart lighten feeling a little more hopeful. Perhaps there would be another chance for them. All he had to do was find out who slept where on the night in question. Despite Anna's protestations about Emily and Joe's relationship, they could still be involved in one, if they'd shared a room.

Joe had put his arm around her and called her 'darling' and they'd seemed happy and affectionate when he'd watched them having dinner together, watched them walk back, hand in hand, to their suite.

He had to find out. Whistling softly, he headed for his office, looking for the ranger who had booked them into the lodge.

Ten minutes later he had the answer he was looking for. Separate rooms. He prayed the telephones were working, he needed to speak to Anna. Then he would be on the first flight to London.

Chapter One Hundred and One

Anna put the telephone down after Nick's call and danced around the room. He was on his way to London to see Emily! She picked up the telephone again and called Joe's number in London. He answered on the third ring.

"Sorry to be a bit abrupt, Joe, but I need to speak to Emily, it's urgent. Is she around? She isn't answering her phone."

"No, she isn't here," Joe replied, rather coldly Anna thought. "But of course, you wouldn't know. She decided not to come back to London with me. She wanted to sort her muddled thoughts out. I couldn't handle it anymore, so I came back and left her there – it's what she wanted. It's what I wanted.

"She's rented a house somewhere on the coast, I'm not sure where though. She was in a state I have to tell you." He told her what happened at the lodge.

"You should have told her Anna. We worked it all out. Kennedy married someone else, didn't he? It's why you didn't tell her, but you should have you know. I don't believe you played a part in any of this, but I'm afraid Emily does."

Anna closed her eyes, what a fabulous mess it all was. She interrupted him. "Look Joe, nothing is as it seems, I promise you. Yes, yes, I know all about what happened at the lodge, Nick told me. He thought you were married to Emily.

"I'm going to do everything in my power to get those two together. It was all a terrible misunderstanding, too complicated to explain over the phone. Now I have Nick's side of the story, I need to get hold of Emily as a matter of urgency and explain things."

There was silence at the end of the phone. "Look Joe, I know how you feel about her, I know this is hard for you. Emily and Nick love each other, nothing will change that now. Please help me."

"I know she didn't want to rent anything other than on the coast somewhere in Mombasa, Anna. It would be somewhere quiet, but I don't know the country. I'm sure you'll think of something."

Anna was already working out ways to track her down. "When you do find her," he said, "please give her my love and tell her...tell her, I'm rooting for her."

"I will, of course I will. I know you're fond of her... but this was meant to be, you have to trust me. I'm so sorry, Joe."

Joe put his phone down and smiled. His assignment was over; one that he had enjoyed this time, and it had been more than successful.

He picked up his phone and called Harry in New York.

Chapter One Hundred and Two

After the call to Joe, Anna called the lodge. Unable to contain her excitement she tapped her foot impatiently.

"Don't book your flight to England, Nick. She's still here!"

"*What?*"

"Emily didn't go back with Joe. She decided to stay on for another two months. You must find her and explain everything. She's somewhere on the coast, that's all I know. Get cracking with your huge network of friends, Nick, and don't call me until you find her!"

*****

She was still here! He would track her down. He would find her. He wouldn't give up until he did. He thanked Anna with an enthusiasm he didn't think he had anymore and rang off. He hurried back to his cottage, packed his bag, then briefed his manager.

"I don't know how long I'll be away, a few days at least, Mike. I'm going to find someone I lost. I need to put a great wrong right."

"Where are you going boss?"

"Mombasa."

"Wouldn't have anything to do with a woman called Emily, would it?" Mike said grinning. "I wouldn't recommend getting involved with a married woman boss, nothing but trouble will come of it."

Nick laughed. "You're right Mike, but the thing is Emily isn't married! I'm going to get her."

Nick picked up his overnight bag and headed for the vehicle; he turned around and jogged back to his cottage. He pulled open the drawer, feeling for the velvet box, he dropped it in his pocket. One last chance - he wouldn't let her get away this time. She was on his turf now – he would track her down and find her.

*****

Anna's mind was racing. How on earth had she not put two and two together? She remembered bumping into Nick at the grocery store, then having coffee with him. He had told her a little about the woman he'd fallen in love with, but not mentioned her name, and at that point Emily had been called Diana. She knew she'd told him more than once about the girl in a coma, she had talked about her when they spent those few days in the Mara, after the death of his mother.

The wedding dress, the suitcase and passport should have given her some clues, but they hadn't. Nick had only told her he'd met someone but it hadn't worked out.

Nick would find her, of this she was quite certain.

Chapter One Hundred and Three

Joe

It's quite true that I work in the field of research, but not for a pharmaceutical company. I'm part of Harry's team, a scientist. My specialty is mind enhancing, mind changing drugs. Substances which can be used to act as an effective chemical screen to block out a subject's memory. It used to be called "brainwashing" in the old days.

By chance we found a guinea pig. A terrorist who was on Marcus's list of people we wanted to talk to. He had been responsible for the bombing of a restaurant in Paris. With a little pressure from Marcus, the terrorist had agreed to change sides, as it were.

For the first time we were inside a terrorist cell. Terrorists have just one strength – secrecy. They strike whenever they want to, and wherever they want to. There's only one way to stop them. You have to infiltrate their network, infiltrate their brains.

The idea was simple. Turn around people close to terrorist networks, inject them with artificial memories, for example a motive for revenge – so as to convince them to co-operate and hand over their fellow brothers in arms. We were going to change the mind set of these terrorists, modify their personalities and their cerebral make-up.

There's only one way to round up fanatics. Turn one of them against the others. Get one of them converted, with this particular drug I've been working on, and we'd be able to read the depths of their madness. It's called Twilight Twice.

When Emily was released from hospital with her empty mind, she stayed with Anna. When she started work at the shop, Harry saw a golden opportunity present itself.

Another drug we were working on was to wipe out a terrorist's memory completely. Render him, or her, completely harmless, by taking away their murderous thoughts and plans, their obsession for

334

revenge. My particular research was to see if it could also be used to wipe out partial sections of memory. Let me explain.

There are pills for everything. Pills for headaches, backache, toothache etc. Take a pill for a headache and, boom, headache gone. Same with the pills I was working on, except they would take partial sections of the memory for good. The tricky part was engineering and evoking a particular memory in order to wipe it out.

Emily was, Harry suggested, perfect for the experiment.

My assignment was to build up a relationship with her, become her friend, her confidant, and whatever else it might take. Meanwhile I would be able to continue with my research but stay close to Emily, my on-site guinea pig.

I would be able to measure just how much she remembered, if her memory ever came back completely. I would be able to study her brain, and reactions, which would enhance my studies of the human brain. I could prod and poke at her memory, even use some drugs on her if I thought it would accelerate the greater cause we were all working towards.

And, of course, I knew everything about Emily, after the intensive briefing I'd had with Harry. I knew who her husband was and what he did. I knew what particular part of her memory Harry wanted blocked out.

It wasn't difficult to win her trust, she was lonely, frightened and confused. She was also rather attractive so the assignment was, for a change, going to be a pleasure. When she agreed to move into my flat it was the cherry on top. I could watch her all the time, and report back to Harry if she remembered anything about the bloody passports she had discovered. I was waiting for this one to rise to the top of memory pile. It was crucial to the whole experiment, crucial to the future of the Agency.

I played my role as required, and she learned to trust me implicitly, keeping me updated on things she remembered, things she couldn't remember, and for once in my life I could lead a near normal life, living with a more than nice girl. I could carry on my research within a normal environment and not dwell too much on the ugly world of terrorism.

I was now ready to try out the, yet untested, drug, Twilight Twice, which had the enormous potential. Deep down in Emily's mind was the memory of finding the passports, and this we needed to block out. If she remembered that part of her past she would, we knew, pursue all possibilities to find out who her husband really was, where he was.

Harry approved the use of the drug, even if the FDA hadn't. We don't have the time for such niceties. I watched and waited to see when the opportunity would present itself.

There was another memory he wanted monitored. Her deep suspicions about the circumstances of her husband's supposed death on 9/11.

I had tried various situations to stimulate Emily's memory. Making sure she watched the documentary on 9/11 for instance (I had recorded it). When I went rooting around for the pills she needed, when she had her nightmare, I slipped my yet untested one in her glass of water. It was the perfect opportunity to see if this drug, with so much potential, would work.

I watched her closely when she found her old passport in her lost suitcase, to see if that would evoke memories of other passports. But nothing happened.

When Emily decided to move to France to write her experiences with her memory down on paper, I knew I wouldn't be able to go with her but made her promise she would let me know if she remembered anything at all, no matter how small.

Jules, my so-called girlfriend, was another test. I wanted to see Emily's reactions to a situation when I was not going to be around her anymore, to see if it evoked anything, triggered anything relating to losing someone. My assignment would, after all, have to end at some point.

The night she took all those pills was a bleak one. I was supposed to be guarding her, monitoring her, but I screwed up. Neither Harry nor I wanted Emily dead, after all she was part of our vital experiment, and we were the cause of everything she had been through so far.

Anna was someone I had to be careful with. Being in the world of medicine she knew all about drugs. But not the ones we were working on. She'd asked me what I was researching, I told her about the new Malaria vaccine we were working on, which was of great interest to her, coming from Africa. Believe me mosquitoes are a hell of a lot easier to deal with than fanatical terrorists. I had to swot for hours through the night to have some credible answers to whatever Anna might ask about my so-called research, when I knew Emily was going to introduce me to her.

336

Spending so much time with them both, before Anna went back to Kenya for good, and living a normal life, dinner parties, drinks at the wine bar down the road, brought me close to both of them which was dangerous. It would all have to end somewhere at some point.

Harry would pull the plug on the operation and it would all be over. I had become fond of Emily and Anna.

So, when Anna invited us both to her wedding in Kenya she made a dream of mine come true. I had always yearned to go on safari – and there it was, about to happen. Harry gave me the go-ahead, this could be a true test of Emily's memory, now tumbling back, Harry wanted me to stay close to see if the drug had been successful.

When Emily and I joined the long snaking queue of passengers at Heathrow, all clutching their passports, it was the ultimate test, I even asked her to hold mine. There was no reaction from her, no memory tumbling back about holding four other passports in her hand.

The drug had worked.

I think those two weeks on safari in Kenya will stay in my memory forever.

Being in the bush was a million miles away from the world of terrorism and all the dangerous things we were doing with as yet untested drugs to use against the perpetrators of the war on terror.

Then Emily finally recovered her memory, when she met up with Nick Kennedy again. I prodded and poked at her memories but still she remembered nothing about the passports. The other memory I had wiped out of her brain was the relationship she had had, as a young child, with the Afrikaner farmer called *Oupa* Pieter. He was like a second father to her, according to Harry.

The old farmer's daughter had died at the hands of the Shadow Dancer, and *Oupa* Pieter now knowing the bastard had been married to Emily, topped himself. Harry didn't want Emily to know the truth about her marriage – it was the first time I had ever seen a slightly softer side to him. So, I fixed that part of her memory as well.

Harry was now ready to move on and use this drug, as well as the others, on the bad guys.

I played the final curtain as best as I could, becoming angry, that morning at breakfast in the bush, when she so clearly knew she was still in love with Kennedy. Telling her I'd had enough of the whole thing. I knew I was going to miss her company after all the time we had spent living together. But I did want her to be happy. I had to break off the relationship and end that particular chapter in her life she had spent with me.

I went back to London and left her there. The flat was cold and empty without her, but it was something I soon became used to, after her months in France.

I often think back to that time in the bush in Kenya, it was another world, the high wide blue sky, the endless sunshine, the animals – and Emily. Something I will never forget.

Harry and the Agency had a lot to thank Emily for, but, of course, they never did.

Chapter One Hundred and Four

Emily parked the jeep in her driveway, hauling her shopping out of the back, she let herself into the cool house. Surrounded by softly clattering palm trees, and perched on the beach, it was the perfect hideaway.

She unpacked the shopping, turning on the ceiling fan in the sitting room. The room was furnished with white cane chairs and two sofas, bright blue flowered cushions adding colour. The glass doors opened out onto the pool area. She opened them, stepping out onto the patio, squinting at the glare from the sun and sand. She picked up her hat and sunglasses from the table and walked out onto the beach.

Families and couples dotted the wide stretch of beach making her feel even more alone. Her thoughts returned again and again to Nick and his behaviour, and the part Anna must have played in it.

Her stomach squeezed when she thought about Joe, how upset and hurt he was, he had been kind and good to her, helping her along the long road to recovery. And this was how she had rewarded him – she had no idea how she could sort the situation out but knew living with him again in London, would now be out of the question.

Seeing Nick again had been a monumental shock, putting her thoughts and emotions into overdrive. She couldn't get him out of her mind. She woke in the morning with his name on her lips, he was the last thought on her mind before she fell asleep at night.

Joe had come up with the only feasible answer. He must have given up on her and married someone else. Anna *should* have told her. Why hadn't she? What on earth had been her motive? Even now, wanting to know the answers, she couldn't bring herself to call Anna for an explanation. She didn't want to talk to her at all.

She paddled through the water until the sun and the heat drove her back to the coolness of the cottage, cursing the day she got her memory back. She felt distraught with the turn of events, wishing she hadn't remembered the part about Nick. Wishing he had stayed in a bubble somewhere, and never been retrieved. Wishing Joe hadn't been so angry with her and ended their special relationship.

Even remembering her failed marriage, and Marcus's death, was not as painful as her memories of the man she'd fallen so hopelessly in love with. If there hadn't been the muddle with Honey Badger Lodge, and they'd stayed there instead of being bumped to Fish Eagle Lodge, she would never have seen him again.

It would have been better that way.

Chapter One Hundred and Five

The scheduled flight touched down in Mombasa. Nick drummed his fingers on the arm of the seat, anxious to get out and be on his way. He picked up a hired car and headed up the coast. He would open up his house, have a quick shower, then begin his search for Emily.

The first thing he would do was make a few telephone calls to the local holiday letting agents. He knew a lot of people in the area.

In his mind, he began to formulate what he would say to her. Like Anna he was overwhelmed with the facts he now had. Emily didn't change her mind about coming to Kenya, she was pretty much on her way when the accident happened. None of it was her fault, he had jumped to the wrong conclusions. Just as she had done with the American woman she thought he had slept with.

He parked outside his house, the front door keys slippery in his hands, then he raced for the telephone and rang one of his childhood friends. "Hey Monica. Nick Kennedy here, I need your help with something, it's important - urgent. I'm trying to find someone called Emily Hunter, she rented a place down here, or maybe Lamu, for two or three months I think. I have to find her."

"I can phone around some of the other agents for you, Nick, I don't have her on my books. If she rented a place for a couple of months, then she would have booked it through one of them, I only do short term lets. Give me a couple of hours, I'll see what I can come up. Not in love, are we?" Without waiting for an answer, she continued. "Is this the elusive woman who never turned up for her own wedding? Sorry, Nick, we all heard about it. Must all our hopes be dashed now?"

He could hear her tapping on her keyboard. "What's her surname again? Hunter, did you say? It sounds to me you might be the hunter in this particular case!" She laughed at her own joke. "Any chance of meeting up for dinner whilst you're here?" she asked hopefully.

"I'm in enough trouble as it is, Monica, but thanks for the help. I'll wait for your call. If you find her for me, I'll take you out for dinner. I'll bring Emily with me!"

Monica sighed over the phone. "Not quite what I had in mind, Nick," she said dryly.

"Sorry, but I have to find her and I don't care if the whole of Kenya knows. I love that woman and I'm going to find her."

He showered then paced the room waiting for Monica to call back. He wasn't sure what he would say to Emily when he saw her, but he wasn't going to worry about it. He would find her.

The phone rang startling him. He knocked over a chair as he lunged forward to answer it. He listened intently. Minutes later he was striding to his car, the small velvet box tucked into his trouser pocket.

*****

Emily changed into a long loose pink dress and studied herself in the mirror. Despite her unhappiness, the gnawing feeling in her stomach, she thought she looked alright. Feeling restless she decided to take another walk on the beach. The sun would be setting soon, turning the sea golden red, it would be cooler by the water.

The young African cook who came with the rented house was busy preparing a simple supper for her. "I'll be back in an hour Simon," she called out to him. He gave her a broad smile before turning back to his cooking.

Emily would have been lost without his cheerful company in the early evening. She would perch on the kitchen chair, listening to his stories about the country, the politics and other people who had stayed at the house. Then, when he left, she would feel the silence and loneliness biting into her.

Emily walked along the edge of the sea, her dress fluttering around her ankles, skimming the warm water, as it hissed and sucked at the sand beneath her feet. She bent down and picked up a smooth stone, rolling it back and forth in her palm.

I have to get over him, she thought to herself, *and I will, it will just take time.* She knew she had enough money to sit here for months. But the day would come when she had to go home, to a world without Joe. At least here she was closer to Nick, which seemed to hurt rather than help. One thought she skittered away from now was whether he was married.

342

She scooped up a shell. Even if he was married it wouldn't change the fact she loved him.

*****

The frantic hammering on the front door surprised Simon, as he hurried to see who it was.

"*Jambo*," Nick said, greeting the young Kenyan in his own language. Is Miss Hunter here?"

"She is walking on the beach. She will be back soon. Perhaps you would care to wait for her?"

"No, this can't wait. I'll go and look for her. Thank you. *Asanta sani.*"

He looked left and then right, spotting the lone figure in pink, at the end of the now deserted beach. Throwing off his shoes he set off, the soft sand impeding his progress, anxious to close the gap between them.

*****

Emily turned around and began to walk back to the house. She saw the tall figure heading towards her and her mouth went dry.

He was running towards her, tripping and stumbling in the soft sand, and she quickened her pace. She flew into his arms, laughing and crying at the same time, any thoughts of him being married overriding her need to hold him again, to touch him.

"Oh, God Emily, I'm so, so sorry. Anything that could go wrong did. Anna has explained everything to me. I thought you changed your mind about marrying me. I tried to find out what happened to you, but you'd disappeared. If I'd known you were lying in a London hospital don't you think I would have scoured each and every one, until I found you?"

She sank down onto the sand, crossing her arms across her chest defensively. Shielding herself from the final, inevitable, blow.

"You're married now Nick– how can this ever work?"

"No, my darling, I'm not married…not yet. But believe me I plan to be now!

Chapter One Hundred and Six

They sat on the beach and talked for hours, neither of them believing, despite everything, they were finally together again. She leaned back into his familiar arms.

He felt for the box in his pocket, opening it with one hand. "I think this belongs to you. I want to marry you more than anything in the world, having you back is beyond my wildest dreams, I won't take no for an answer!"

She turned in his arms and looked at the familiar ring sparkling in the moonlight. "Yes, Nick, of course I'll marry you. This is the third time you've asked me and the third time I've said yes," she was laughing, crying again. "Shall we get on and do it - before something else happens!"

He slid the ring on her finger, closing his eyes, thanking God for second and third chances. "I don't want to wait to marry you, my love, let's do it right now, something small I think. I don't want a big wedding with half of Kenya turning up. We can get a special licence in Nairobi – we can fly there tomorrow, even though you hate flying."

She looked at him incredulously. "Do I?"

He laughed. "Yes, it terrifies you – how did you manage on the flight out here?"

"Um, I just did, I didn't feel frightened at all, but the best thing, the very best thing was finding you again."

She buried her face in his neck. "Let's get married right here – in the place where you found me. I think you promised me a beach wedding? Yes, that's one thing I do remember!"

Chapter One Hundred and Seven

Anna perched on the end of Emily's bed, shaking her head. "I still can't get over all of this. To think I was right in the middle of all this drama, and I had absolutely no idea. It's a story I shall dine out on for years and years to come."

Emily hugged her knees. "Imagine if another nurse had been caring for me after the accident – I would never have found Nick again."

"He watches you like a hawk, he thinks you might disappear in a puff of smoke. I can't help but feel sorry for all the women, countrywide, weeping into their cocktails, cloaked in black, lamenting the fact Nick Kennedy is about to get married."

She glanced at her watch and stood up. "I'm off to bed now and you must get some sleep – tomorrow is the day we've all been waiting for."

*****

Joe had shipped Emily's wedding dress to her but declined to attend the wedding itself. She phoned to thank him and he'd wished her well.

"We both want you to come out to Kenya again Joe, you must come, please? You can stay at Fish Eagle Lodge as our guest for as long as you want. You loved it there, didn't you? Anyway…you never know it might turn out to be a life changing moment, after all look what happened to me!"

"Hmm. I don't think I want as much drama in my life as you've had in yours. Give my love to Anna," he paused, and cleared his throat, "and my congratulations to Nick, he's a lucky man."

Emily could almost see him polishing his glasses vigorously, she swallowed the lump in her throat.

She knew he wouldn't come. Knew she wouldn't see him again.

"All set?" Anna whispered as she fussed with the back of Emily's wedding dress. "You look stunning, absolutely gorgeous – and so does Nick who is now waiting for you. I feel a bit tearful, no, I feel very tearful. I'm not sure I'm going to be able to hold myself together."

Emily hugged her bridesmaid. "God, what a journey it's been! And you've been there all the way – what would I have done without you?"

"Well you wouldn't be marrying my childhood friend today, for a start. But the best thing is you'll be living in Kenya, and we'll be able to see each other when you come into town.

"Now come on, Nick's godfather, that scary Arthur, is waiting to give you away. I hope he puts out his cigar before he sets off with you."

*****

They stood together on the beach. An arch of frangipani covering a simple wooden frame above their heads. Emily whispered her vows, then Nick took his. He slipped the wedding ring on her finger, lifted her veil and kissed her. Emily looked spectacular, she had worn her hair up, and the curls cascaded around her head, tiny white flowers decorated her veil and her hair.

She looked at her husband. "Why, Nick Kennedy, I do believe you have tears in your eyes," she whispered as she kissed him again.

The small crowd of friends assembled on the beach whistled and clapped their approval. Anna smiled through her tears as she watched her best friends finally marry.

The Duke hadn't stopped grumbling about the flight since he arrived. After the wedding service, he managed a few moments alone with Nick.

"Damn shame your parents, and Jonathan, couldn't be around to see you get married. Emily is a fine girl, it was an honour to give her away. Always did enjoy a cracking good story, and you certainly gave us one. You'll always be welcome to stay with us in the ancestral heap. Now let's toast your health, where's that wife of mine. "Gladys!" he bellowed over the sea of guests' hats. "Where the blazes are you?"

Nick shook his head ruefully at the Duke's retreating back, hoping he wouldn't cause too much chaos at Fish Eagle Lodge. He had warned

Mike, in advance, to watch out for the Duke's walking stick after a few glasses of port, when he was inclined to take a swipe at things which annoyed him, animal or human.

Emily moved amongst the guests, accepting their good wishes and congratulations. She spotted Rebecca and Ben and headed towards them. It had been easy enough to find Ben through his business contacts and the internet, and from there she had contacted Rebecca at her book shop in Cannes.

"I'm glad you were able to come Becks. So much happened after you left London to be with Ben…but then you know all about it now. I have to keep pinching myself when I look at Nick, it seems years ago when we had the book signing. I swear I will never travel anywhere unless he is glued to my side!"

"Yes, quite a story, my girl. It'll be a huge change from London, living in the bush, but having said this there are hundreds of women out there who would give up a kidney, maybe even a limb, to be married to Nick," she looked at him as he chatted to Ben. "He's quite something."

Rebecca took a sip of her champagne. "Just think if I hadn't chosen his book for the signing none of this would have happened. Be happy Emily, the wedding was beautiful, so much so I think the next time Ben asks me to marry him I might say yes and be done with it. I'll become a good Jewish girl and make my parents happy!"

Emily grinned at her. "Why not Becks, you'll make Ben very happy and I'm sure you'll get stuck into the Shabbat stuff, you also have roots you know, they're good things to have, they ground you."

Emily looked around at all the guests, sipping drinks as the sun began to set on her perfect day. "I love it here, Becks. Africa is where I belong, where *my* roots are. I might miss going shopping now and again, but my wardrobe will be somewhat different to the one in London! Joe is packing up my belongings and sending them out here. I must remember to tell him not to bother with the high heeled shoes, I won't have much call for them in the bush!" she giggled her eyes following her husband.

"Look, I have to mingle a bit more, have a wonderful time at the lodge, you'll be flying up in Nick's plane with the Duke and Duchess. They're a dear old couple, a little eccentric though. They'll probably terrify all the staff. Let's hope some of them will still be there when we get back from our honeymoon in Lamu."

"Hello Emily." She turned at the sound of her name. "I'm Natalie, I've been looking forward to meeting you. Congratulations on capturing the most eligible bachelor in East Africa!"

A tousled haired young boy was clinging to her legs. "Now, of course, we have all heard the story about how you both met, how it all went wrong – twice! I hope we'll become friends?"

Emily smiled at Nick's childhood friend, then hugged her. "I hope we'll become friends too Natalie. I remember seeing the engagement photographs of you both in some glossy magazine - I thought I'd lost him forever."

Nick headed towards them and put his arm around his wife. "Ah, so you two have met. Good to see you Natalie! How is this young godson of mine?" He ruffled the little boy's hair.

"Growing up wild and free, like we did. Congratulations. So, you found your girl, and every single woman in the country has gone into deep mourning. Nairobi will be awash with ladies in black, their faces covered with veils."

Nick looked down at Emily and grinned. "Yes, she wasn't easy to capture, but everything worked out in the end; she's got a bad habit of disappearing!" He kissed the top of her head. "I'm not letting her out of my sight for the rest of my life."

He hugged Natalie. "We'll call you when we get back from our honeymoon – come for dinner at the house?"

"We'd love to. I'm glad you decided not to sell the old house, Nick, I practically grew up there, it holds some great memories. I'm sure your parents would be happy to know the Kennedy's live on there. By the way what happened to that bad-tempered old parrot of yours?"

Nick laughed. "He's entertaining the guests at the beach bar I sold. He loves the company, he's picked up some pretty bad language I have to tell you. They love him."

*****

The last guests had left. Anna could see them beneath the shimmering skies. Emily still in her wedding dress, Nick minus his jacket and tie, both barefoot. She watched him turn towards his bride releasing her hair from its clip. Hand in hand they were oblivious to everything.

348

Anna sighed; they seemed to be floating across the sand, Emily's dress sparkling in the moonlight, the train of it swirling like a cloud through the soft warms waters of the sea.

Silhouetted by the moon, and with the soft whisper of the waves, she left them there together.

Chapter One Hundred and Eight

Harry also fell in love.

At the age of fifty, after a mild stroke, he looked for somewhere far away from the brutal unpredictable world he had inhabited with the Agency in New York City.

He wanted a place where he could live a clean and normal life.

Under the African sun he acquired a deep tan, his hair, now white, reached his shoulders, his white beard hugged his chin.

He continued to breed animals for auction, keeping on the old man's staff, and manager, who taught him all he needed to know.

In the evenings he would sit in *Oupa* Pieter's old chair on the veranda, the silence, music to his ears, after living in noisy, overcrowded, New York City. The velvet black skies above and the glorious canopy of stars were heart-breaking in their beauty.

Jakub, the old fisherman, would visit once or twice a month, and they would sit outside in comfortable silence, listening to the night sounds of insects, and the grunts of the animals, Jakub puffing away on his pipe.

Jakub, he learned, had no particular religion. He had no God he worshipped. His people worshipped and had great respect for the desert, the mountains, the sea and nature. It was to Jakub a more natural, touchable, and enduring faith, with no name, no anger, hatred, or thirst for revenge. Harry learned a lot from the simple fisherman.

How only the land endured, impassive, unmoved by the blood of generations spilled over it in the greedy search for power, land and money. The whispering wind, the shifting dust and sands, the dark, brooding, immovable rocks, the grasses the colour of a lion's mane, and the seething sun remained immune to the greed of man.

The incident with the wheelchair was never mentioned. Jakub sometimes passed Harry some information which would, at one time, have been useful. But Harry declined to act on any of it. It was a world far removed from the one he lived in now. He didn't have the stomach for it anymore.

Yes, Harry had fallen in love. With Africa. As so many had before him. He knew South Africa had her problems, but they paled into insignificance compared to what the world was now facing, and what he had seen and experienced with all the years at the Agency.

Harry felt safe. Harry was happy. He finally had a dog of his own.

Harry was in Paradise.

If you enjoyed reading this book and would like to share that enjoyment with others, then please take the time to visit the place where you made your purchase and write a review.

Reviews are a great way to spread the word about worthy authors and will help them be rewarded for their hard work.

You can also visit Samantha's Author Page on Amazon to find out more about her life and passions.

Also by Samantha Ford:

The Zanzibar Affair

A letter found in an old chest on the island of Zanzibar finally reveals the secret of Kate Hope's glamorous, but anguished past, and the reason for her sudden and unexplained disappearance.

Ten year's previously Kate's lover and business partner, Adam Hamilton, tormented by a terrifying secret he is willing to risk everything for, brutally ends his relationship with Kate.

A woman is found murdered in a remote part of Kenya bringing Tom Fletcher back to East Africa to unravel the web of mystery and intrigue surrounding Kate, the woman he loves but has not seen for over twenty years.

In Zanzibar, Tom meets Kate's daughter Molly. With her help he pieces together the last years of her mother's life and his extraordinary connection to it.

A page turning novel of love, passion, betrayal and death, with an unforgettable cast of characters, set against the spectacular backdrop of East and Southern Africa, New York and France.

*****

The House Called Mbabati

The Mother Superior crossed herself quickly. "May God have mercy on you, and forgive you both," she murmured as she locked the diary and faded letters in the drawer.

Deep in the heart of the East African bush stands a deserted mansion. Boarded up, on the top floor, is a magnificent Steinway Concert Grand, shrouded in decades of dust.

In an antique shop in London, an elderly nun recognises an old photograph of the mansion; she knows it well.

Seven thousand miles away, in Cape Town, a woman lies dying; she whispers one word to journalist Alex Patterson – Mbabati.

Sensing a good story, and intrigued with what he has discovered, Alex heads for East Africa in search of the old abandoned house. He is unprepared for what he discovers there; the hidden home of a once famous classical pianist whose career came to a shattering end; a grave with a blank headstone and an old retainer called Luke - the only one left alive who knows the true story about two sisters who disappeared without trace over twenty years ago.

Alex unravels a story which has fascinated the media and the police for decades. A twisting tale of love, passion, betrayal and murder; and the unbreakable bond between two extraordinary sisters who were prepared to sacrifice everything to hide the truth.

Mbabati is set against the magnificent and enduring landscape of the African bush - where nothing is ever quite as it seems.

"A cracking good story with a totally unexpected twist at the end!"

John Gordon Davis

"Anyone who has read any of the John Gordon Davis novels, in particular Hold My Hand I'm Dying, will understand this author is in the same league."

Mike Preston

"Having read all Wilbur Smith's books, this author ranks up there with the best of them. Best read I've had for years!"

Peter C. Morgan

Made in the USA
Middletown, DE
21 May 2021

40196091R10215